Destiny's Tide

J. D. Davies is the prolific author of historical naval adventures. He is also one of the foremost authorities on the seventeenth-century navy, which brings a high level of historical detail to his fiction, namely his Matthew Quinton series. He has written widely on the subject, most recently *Kings of the Sea: Charles II, James II and the Royal Navy*, and won the Samuel Pepys Award in 2009 with *Pepys's Navy: Ships, Men and Warfare, 1649-1689.*

Also by J. D. Davies

The Matthew Quinton Journals

Gentleman Captain
The Mountain of Gold
The Blast that Tears the Skies
The Lion of Midnight
The Battle of All The Ages
The Rage of Fortune
Death's Bright Angel
The Devil Upon the Wave
Ensign Royal

Jack Stannard of the Navy Royal

Destiny's Tide
Battle's Flood
Armada's Wake

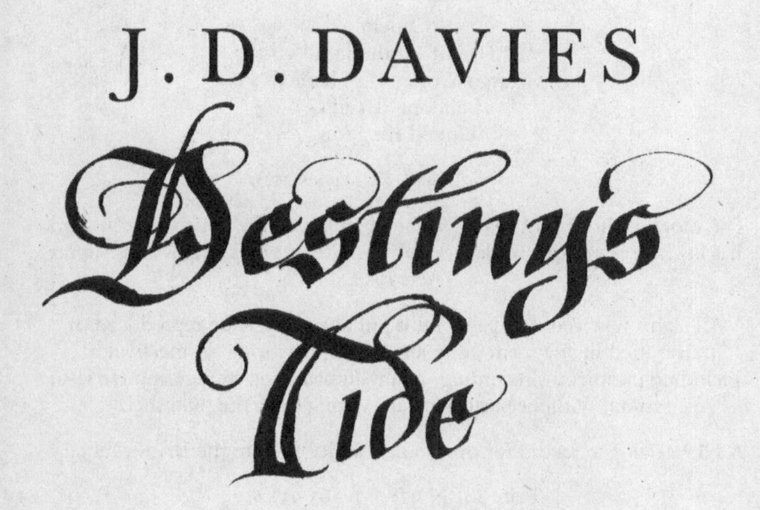

CANELO

First published in the United Kingdom in 2019 by Canelo

This edition published in the United Kingdom in 2021 by

Canelo
Unit 9, 5th Floor
Cargo Works, 1-2 Hatfields
London, SE1 9PG
United Kingdom

A CIP catalogue record for this book is available from the British Library.

Print ISBN 978 1 78863 937 8
Ebook ISBN 978 1 78863 230 0

Printed and bound in Great Britain by Clays Ltd, Elcograf S.p.A.

1

For Felix

Prologue

October 1537

Off the coast of Suffolk, a three-masted ship of some eighty tons cuts the waves of a heavy sea as she approaches the coast. The land is home, the far distant lights and fires of the little town just in sight. But the stiff wind, very nearly a gale despite the bright sunrise astern, is easterly, turning the familiar, beloved coastline into a lee shore, the dread of all mariners. The ship's helmsman, though, is determined to bring his hull home, on the flood tide, despite the huge risk he is taking.

The helmsman is a pale, skinny youth of middling height. His hair, unruly at the best of times, flies in the wind like a ragged reed-bed. By rights, his hands should not be on the whipstaff at all. Although he has taken a helm many times, it has always been in easy waters and fair winds. But of the vessel's far more capable shiphandlers, one lies in a grave in Emden, dead of a sudden bloody flux while they were lading. Another sits on a barrel just behind the youth, his hands raw, his face lined with exhaustion, his eyes closed more than they are open. As for the other—

'Can you see it yet, Jack?' says the old man on the barrel.

John Stannard, known universally as Jack, squints his eyes, and stares into the distance. The shore is familiar to him, but so are its dangers. He can see the cliff, at the foot of which many brave ships have met their ends, and the tower of All Saints high upon it. He can see the waves breaking upon the Kingsholme, the vast bar of shingle that stands like a castle wall between him and the safe haven behind it. He scans further to starboard, to where he knows the seamark to be, trying to keep his focus even as the hull bucks under his feet.

'Not yet, Master Nolloth! No, wait – yes! Yes, I have it!'

As the ship crests a wave, Jack catches another glimpse of the tall pole that marks the end of the Kingsholme, and the narrow entrance to Dunwich harbour to starboard, north of it. The youth has learned from the first day he drew breath that Dunwich harbour was once so open, so commodious, that it was the finest haven in the entire east of England, and the port a rival even to London. But that was before the great and terrible storms of years long past; before the shingle swept across and sealed the entrance, like the bolting of a gate; before the sea swept away so much of the town itself, the town that had once been a great and mighty city, if legend spoke true.

It is said that the ancient Greeks and Romans spoke of Atlantis, but Englishmen speak of Dunwich.

'Very good,' says Jed Nolloth, rising from his makeshift seat. 'I'll take her now, and bring her in.'

The timbers of the *Matthew of Dunwich* groan as the forces of wind and tide work upon the hull. She is heavily laden, her hold full from a successful voyage, and although this makes her slower, it also makes her steadier, less prone to being blown off course by the breeze. But with such a full cargo, the *Matthew* will also be the very devil to get back on course if her helmsman makes an error and deviates from it by the merest fraction. And this particular helmsman has never steered this course before. He has only ever observed others, much older and more experienced than him, con ships through the eye of a needle that is the entrance to Dunwich harbour.

'Let me, Master Nolloth! You stood watch for ten hours – Christ's nails, you can barely stand, Jed. And look at the state of your hands, man!'

Nolloth glances over his shoulder, and nods toward the stern cabin, below decks.

'He'll want me to do it, Jack. He won't trust you to. You know that as well as I. Recall, lad, how he bellowed at you when you merely suggested coasting down to Thorpe Ness and lying over there until the wind changed.'

'He won't know, Jed,' said Jack Stannard, impatiently. 'He's too drunk. Too ill. He'll sleep for hours yet, mayhap until long after we berth. He may never even know that it was I who conned us into harbour. You know I can do it, Jed, even if he doesn't. You taught me more than he ever did. If you stay at my side and help me with the commands for the sails, I can handle the helm.'

The old man's expression is a battlefield of conflicting thoughts. But in his heart, he knows that young Jack Stannard is right. After his efforts in the latter part of their voyage home, Nolloth no longer has the strength or the grip to handle the whipstaff in such a sea, and with such a tight course to steer. Besides, Jed Nolloth has experienced the wrath of the man below decks many times before, and has less fear of it than most.

'Aye, well then, Master Jack, let's be about it, and pray to *Maria maris stella* we don't come to grief on Kingsholme or Southwold shore.'

The young man smiles, sets his eyes upon the distant seamark, then hums a note. Quietly at first, then louder upon each line, his tone a warm tenor, he sings a song that Jed Nolloth has never heard before, a song that is certainly not one of the staples of the Dunwich alehouses. Nor is it a prayer to Mary, star of the sea, the light and hope of all mariners.

Benedicite, what dreamed I this night
Methought the world was turned upside down…

It is a difficult tune – as difficult, in its own way, as steering a ship – but Jack voices it easily, even adding his own little inflections and improvisations. It reminds him of another time, when his life seemed to be set on a very different path. The song earns him curious glances from the half-dozen nervous seamen huddled on deck, in the waist of the ship, awaiting the next commands from the helm. But they are Dunwich men who know the Stannards as well as their own kin, so they well know Master Jack's singular talent. They also know that he has never been responsible for bringing a ship into the haven.

The sun, the moon, had lost their force and light,
The sea also drowned both tower and town…

Jack Stannard sings on, holding every note as he keeps his eyes on the seamark and the rapidly approaching shore, his hands gripping the whipstaff firmly despite the growing pain in his forearms. From time to time, he breaks off from his song to order an adjustment to the sails, none of which Jed Nolloth sees fit to contradict. With every yard that the *Matthew* takes, though, a little more of Jack's confidence in his ability to steer her into harbour vanishes, like spray off the cutwater. He thinks instead of dear Alice, his young wife, of her warm, flawless body, and of her cutting wit. Perhaps she is watching from a window ashore, praying to the Virgin and all the saints that the next hour will not make her a young widow. He thinks of Meg, his little daughter, by far the most precocious two-year-old in Dunwich. He thinks of the good days he once knew at school, of his singular sister, of the solace found in song, of the happiness he implored God to bestow upon his family, friends and himself.

He thinks of everything but these two things: of the possibility that he will fail to bring the ship safe into harbour, and of the creature of nightmares below decks.

His father.

–

Never again would the Grey Friars of Dunwich sing the office of *Terce*, or any other. Even as rays of morning sun streamed through the stained glass in the east window of their church, they were stopped, in the middle of the second verse of *Nunc sancte nobis spiritus*, by the abrupt entry into the chancel of their church of a gross, sweating pig of a man, wearing a rich black gown over a grubby blue jerkin. At his back stood four ill-attired brutes in buff-jerkins, all of them the size of heifers. All had daggers at their belts.

'I am Fane Rudsby,' bellowed the pig, his voice suggesting the east of London, 'commissioner acting with authority from the Lord Cromwell, tasked with the dissolution of this place!' Rudsby looked about imperiously. 'This travesty of a service is ended. Done. Finished! The whore of Babylon is brought low, I say!'

Another strong gust of wind rattled the glass in the windows, as if providing an affirmatory chorus to the commissioner's words. In the misericords, friars looked at each other in confusion, and at their prior, Gilbert, a stooped, quiet and godly man, who seemed as bewildered as any of them. A little apart from the others, in the second row of choir stalls, a short, wiry fellow, his face unusually tanned and scarred in that company, held his emotions in check. Friar Thomas's own shock at the unexpected proceedings was no more than momentary; he had experienced many worse calamities. Indeed, there was a time when he had inflicted them. But he saw tears streaming down the ancient, cracked cheeks of Friar Anselm, the eldest of their community. The voices of the others faltered and broke as they tried to resume the singing of the familiar words of the hymn.

'Cease your caterwauling, you papist shits!' bellowed the commissioner.

'Pray, sir,' said the prior, with a calm that astonished Friar Thomas, 'for God's sake, let us complete our last office—'

The commissioner's face turned puce.

'By no means! The king's order, Master Prior! Signed by the Lord Cromwell himself!' The fellow waved the paper before him as though it were a dagger. 'This place, this abomination of corruption and bestial sin, is done! It is finished! You will all be gone, I say, all of you foul boy-fuckers, you simonists, you whoremongers! *Now*, sirrahs!'

With one exception, the friars moved out into the body of the church, where most milled around, looking at each other in bafflement. Friar Anselm, though, remained where he was, and attempted to sing the remaining verses of the hymn in his cracked and quiet voice. The commissioner's men piled into the misericords and manhandled the old friar out of his place. Friar Thomas made a step forward, intending to intervene, but was pulled back by the firm grip of the prior.

'They are too many, my friend,' said the senior man, too quietly for Commissioner Rudsby to hear, 'and what would it serve? See, Anselm complies.'

Comply he might, but the ancient man still cast one defiant look back toward the image of the Virgin above the altar, crossing himself as he did so. He, of all of them, had been the one least willing to face the truth of what was about to happen, seemingly unable to comprehend that the life he had known for half a century was about to end. In those last few weeks of the community's existence, Thomas had often asked Anselm what he would do when the commissioners finally came.

'*Deus providebit*,' was all the old man would say, with a beatific smile.

But God had not provided.

Friar Thomas did not take one final, lingering look at the colours and images adorning the priory church, as the prior and Anselm did. Instead he turned, went up the day stairs, and joined the half-dozen brethren who were hurriedly taking up their few worldly goods and packing them in sackcloth. He nodded to young Martin, barely a month short of the completion of his novitiate, who would now never embark upon the vocation for which he was so obviously and ideally suited. Better suited than

Thomas, for certain, no matter how fiercely the older man had once believed the flame of the Holy Spirit to burn in his unworthy breast. Martin was wrapping a well-thumbed prayer book, a gift from his mother, and his string of paternoster beads. He, like old Anselm, was in tears.

For his part, Friar Thomas reached under his trestle bed, and drew out the bag containing his worldly goods. There was nothing to pack: he had undertaken the task weeks before, unlike those who had retained false hopes until this, the very end. But his bag was substantially larger than any other in the room, and as he lifted it onto the bed, a glint of metal caught his eye. It was almost as though his old sword, once the alpha and omega of his life, was tempting him, as it had so often in his old existence. The king's vile commissioner might be alone in the church, he thought, and it would be the easiest thing in the world to run him through, especially for Thomas, to whom wielding such a blade had once been as much second nature as singing the words of *Terce* now was. He looked at the metal, then wrapped the sackcloth more tightly around it. Rudsby might, indeed, be alone, but his men were all over the Greyfriars, they were armed to the teeth, and in any case, no one man's death could prevent the fate that had been decreed far away, by King Henry and his fateful agent, Thomas Cromwell. He thought of a nun of his acquaintance at Campsey Priory, killed like a worthless dog while trying to protect a beloved statue of the Virgin when the convent was dissolved the year before. Futile beyond all measure.

Friar Thomas crossed himself, took up his bags, then turned to say a final farewell to his fellows.

The thousand-year existence of monasteries, of holy and devout communities of good men and women, was over in England. Blythburgh priory had not long surrendered to the king's commissioners, even proud, mighty, Sibton and Leiston abbeys were gone, and now the conventual houses of Dunwich were brought low, too. None would now chant the monastic hours, none would ever again take God's word out into Dunwich town and the Sandlings beyond. What the town – what the kingdom – would do for schools, hospitals, and simple Christian charity, remained to be seen. For Friar Thomas, the last ten years of his life had just become a closed book, and no matter what some of the younger and angrier friars said, that book would never be reopened. The young men placed their faith in the disquieting talk from Lincolnshire, where thousands were said to have risen in Louth and other towns. There was even a fresh, wild rumour that a great army of them had marched on Lincoln itself, occupied the cathedral, and demanded the return of the monasteries and the other old ways of faith.

Friar Thomas gave little credit to such talk. Even if there was truth in it, he knew what a royal army would do to a peasant mob, no matter how large.

He walked out into the monastic precinct, passing two of the commissioner's men. They were tearing pages from books ransacked from the library, then casting them onto a fire. Many pages, though, were caught by the strong wind, and fluttered in the air like dying birds. Friar Thomas caught one, and recognised it as a page from the *Consolations of Boethius*. The friary's copy had been very fine, and a favourite of his, so he thrust the page into his bag. The commissioner's men laughed at him. Friar Thomas had wielded the sword in his bag to kill men for much, much less, and knew that if he wished, he could easily despatch the two sneering louts faster than they could cast another book upon the fire. But he was older and wiser now, and ten years in the Greyfriars had taught him to call to mind his Saviour's words.

> *Father, forgive them, for they know not what they do.*

Friar Thomas made his way to the splendid gate in the west wall, and stepped out into the world, not stopping to look behind him. Curious, he thought: the bells of Dunwich's three remaining churches were ringing, as if in celebration. Thomas wondered for a moment whether they were rejoicing at the fall of Greyfriars, but he dismissed the notion. The Franciscans were loved in Dunwich – no, *they had been loved*. It was all in the past tense for the monasteries now. As the bells rang Thomas realised that he was no longer a Franciscan, no longer a friar, no longer bound by the Rule. But there were other lives to live, as he had told himself many times in recent weeks, since the prospect of the surrender of Greyfriars was known. Above all, there was the other life that he had once known, and to which, in some form or other, he would now return.

The life of the sword.

–

The shore was very close now. Jack Stannard and Jed Nolloth could see and hear the waves breaking on the Kingsholme. The seamark, the tall post, was obscured behind the skeletal ribs of the *Nicholas of Walberswick*, wrecked on the bar in the previous year after her helmsman failed to hold his course. Jack kept his eyes trained firmly upon where he believed the post to be. He was sweating, an unaccustomed condition for him. But then he was aware of a noise under the deck beneath his feet, heard what sounded like a scream of pain, and cast a horrified glance toward Nolloth, whose expression was equally fearful. Jack felt his heart beat faster, and his mouth turned dry.

'Saint Mary's cunny!' bawled Peter Stannard, emerging onto the deck, swaying drunkenly, and rubbing the terrible lesions on the back of his hand so fiercely that blood dripped upon the deck. 'What are you – *you!* – doing with your hands on the whipstaff, boy?'

What are you singing for, boy? Why are you playing at Robin Hood, boy? Where's your sister, boy? You dare to be happy, boy? You're never going to be a bishop, boy, nor a lawyer, now the fucking Cardinal's fallen and his school with it, so let's see if you're cut out for a seaman, boy.

No, you don't steer for a lee shore like that, boy. Fuck and blood, boy, I'll strike you if I want, boy, and as for that sister of yours—

You're not your brother, boy. You'll never be your brother.

The litany of assaults, verbal and otherwise, flooded into Jack's mind, stretching back into his very earliest memories. Oh, his father could charm, and be generous, even devout, but only rarely, those occasions being as unpredictable as the wind. Without warning, the mood would change, as though he was being possessed by Satan himself. The mysterious illness meant that, for most of the last two years, the dread side of Peter Stannard was the only one he presented to the world, making the ugly, broad-nosed countenance he bore at the best of times into a fearsome mask. Unaccountably, the one exception, the one matter in which Jack had steeled himself to expect a terrible confrontation with his father, was his determination to marry Alice, to which his father had assented with barely a word. The reason had become apparent in short order, but Alice was a creature of infinite resource and intelligence, who deflected the attentions of Peter Stannard with an easy laugh.

Deflected them for the brief interlude until there was no longer any need to do so.

That day, upon the deck of the *Matthew* off Dunwich shore, was evidently not to be one of Peter Stannard's more tolerable interludes.

'Nolloth, have you turned Bedlam-man, to allow this? Can ye not see Kingsholme, yonder? We need to be more northerly by a good point! Get off your arse and take the helm, you lubbering slug!'

The crewmen forward of their position glanced knowingly at each other, then turned once again to stare apprehensively at the fast approaching shingle bank.

'No, Father,' said Jack, summoning all the courage within his young frame and shouting to be heard above the wind. 'Jed is spent, and you're not well. I can do this. I will do this.'

Jack did not know where the word came from. Three times before, to the best of his memory, he had mouthed a 'no' to his father. Twice, when he was a boy, he had been leathered until his arse was raw. The third time, barely eight months before, Peter Stannard had pummelled his son so fiercely that he cracked ribs and nearly took out his right eye. But his father could no longer use his hands so readily. Even so, Peter took an angry step toward his son, his bloated and strangely scarred face contorting with fury. But, contrary to Jack's expectation, his father did not reach out to try and take hold of the whipstaff himself, nor to strike him. Nor did he bark another order at the slumped, spent figure of Jed Nolloth. Instead, he stood stock still, staring at the makeshift, bloodied bandages on his hands, then out toward Dunwich shore. A minute, perhaps two, passed with Peter Stannard looking from one man to the other, then at the shore again, as all the while the Kingsholme drew ever nearer. Jack kept his hands on the whipstaff and his eyes on the seamark, finally visible again behind the wreck, only glancing briefly at his father out of the corner of his eye. Then, at last, Peter Stannard did something that Jack had never witnessed before, not even at his mother's funeral.

He wept.

At first, Jack was aware only of a dampness on his father's cheeks, easily attributed to the salt spray. Then the old man shuddered, his head and shoulders fell forward, and he sobbed loudly and piteously. Jed Nolloth looked up in astonishment, and exchanged a lengthy stare with Jack.

Peter Stannard collected himself, turned as if to go below again, but then turned back to his son.

'All right then, boy,' he said, his voice at once drunken and strangely hesitant, 'sing us home, if you think you can. Sing us into Dunwich haven, or kill us all on her cliff or Kingsholme, for I no longer care. Kill me above all, for all the saints in heaven know I deserve it. Seventh son of a seventh son, thus blessed, but look upon me now. Look upon my fortune. Look upon my sins.' He looked at the bloody cankers on his hands. 'The Devil of the Doom is coming for me. I see it in my dreams, boy, I hear its wings beating. May your mother forgive me, God bless her sainted soul and speed her from Purgatory. *Ave Maria, gratia plena…*'

With that, Peter Stannard went below, still muttering the Hail Mary. Jack and Nolloth said not a word to each other, for both had heard the litany often enough. *Seventh son of a seventh son*, and thus feared by many in case he possessed the supernatural powers often associated with such a condition. Two of his brothers dead of plague, one washed overboard off Iceland, one killed in a fight in Southwold, one fallen at Flodden Field, and the last, so both whispered rumour in Dunwich's alehouses and the opinion of Jack's sister Agatha had it, an other-worldly simpleton murdered by his youngest brother so that Peter could inherit unchallenged.

Jack and Nolloth concentrated once again on the spectacle before them. Driven by wind and tide, the *Matthew* was approaching the narrow mouth of estuary at what seemed an impossible speed. Jack could feel the strength of the sea working upon the whipstaff, trying to force him from his chosen course. A fraction to the south would cast them upon the Kingsholme to share the fate of the wrecked *Nicholas*, while a fraction to the north would run them aground upon Southwold's shore, a fate akin to being wrecked on the wrong side of the River Styx. The Kingsholme was coming up ever more swiftly, the spray from the waves crashing upon it all too visible from the *Matthew*. Jed Nolloth fingered his paternoster, repeating the *Ave Maria* to himself, but Jack dared not take even a finger from the whipstaff. He had no feeling in his hands, and the pain in his arms and shoulders was worse than any he had ever known, but still he did not alter his grip. Any prayers from him would be superfluous, he believed; but there was one thing that Jack Stannard could do to bring divine assistance to the voyage of the *Matthew*. One thing that nobody else on the ship could do.

He hummed a note, then, loudly and confidently, began to sing the tenor line of *Non nobis*, the great hymn of humility and thanksgiving, in the setting by the Frenchman, Mouton, which he had learned at school.

'*Non nobis domine, non nobis, sed nomini tuo da gloriam…*'

Not unto us, oh Lord, not unto us, but unto your name be the glory.

A quarter mile, no more.

A furlong.

Eight chains.

Six.

Four.

He could see the seabirds, perched upon the jagged ribs of the *Nicholas of Walberswick*, and sang louder still.

Three chains.

Two, if that – no more than forty feet…

During his third rendition of *Non nobis*, the *Matthew* just cleared the seamark at the northern point of the Kingsholme, the post only a few feet, a chain or less, from her larboard beam. Without waiting for a command from Jed Nolloth, Jack put the whipstaff hard over, bringing the ship's head around into the mouth of Dunwich river.

'Well done, lad,' said Nolloth, taking the whipstaff.

Jack released his grip, staggered backward, and fell to his knees upon the deck.

They were home.

-

The *Matthew* finally came alongside the Dain Quay of Dunwich haven, the cables making her fast. Jack Stannard could see his Alice, standing upon the quayside and smiling, little Meg alongside her, waving happily and jumping up and down. Alice's belly was even larger than when it was when the *Matthew* had sailed for Emden, so the new child was evidently prospering. Jack longed for nothing more than to take her in his arms, but there was business of securing the ship to attend to first. There was no sign of his father, who was still below decks, no doubt drinking yet more to alleviate his terrible pain. Jack knew his father was terrified by the prospect of what his illness might be; of course, he would never admit that before his son, but Jack had heard some of the prayers he muttered under his breath, and knew, for Dunwich had no secrets, that he had consulted infirmarians at the Blackfriars and Maison Dieu more than once. Jed Nolloth, who had voyaged more than once to the coast of Castile, believed he had an inkling of what Peter Stannard's condition might be, and had spoken to Jack in hushed tones one night, as they drank together in a quiet corner of the Pelican in its Piety. Jack would speak to Alice of it that night, after Meg had been put to bed.

Just then, the bells of Dunwich began to ring, followed almost at once by those of Walberswick and Southwold, her neighbours to the north and perpetual foes. Saint Peter's rang out, and All Saints high upon the cliff, and Saint John's upon the market square, the greatest of the three remaining churches of the town, its peal seemingly louder than the other two combined.

'Alice!' cried Jack. 'Why the bells?'

She laughed.

'What, be Jack Stannard the last man in England to know?' she shouted back. 'A prince! Queen Jane be safely delivered of a son! God be praised, Jack, the king has an heir at last!'

Jack Stannard smiled and clapped. A son, the prize the king had sought so desperately all the years of Jack's life – aye, and long before he was born, too. Perhaps now all the changes would cease, the killings too, and the Pope and the monasteries would be restored. Perhaps, Jack thought, Englishmen would now be united at long last, and the land would have contentment again.

But it was not to be.

Part One

Rough Wooing

April to May 1544

> *The principal cause of sending the army into Scotland is to devastate the country... burn Edinburgh town, and so deface it as to leave a memory for ever of the vengeance of God upon their falsehood and disloyalty. Sack Holyrood House, and sack, burn and subvert Leith and all the towns and villages round, putting man, woman and child to fire and sword where resistance is made...*

Henry the Eighth, King of England; orders to his erstwhile brother-in-law, Edward Seymour, Earl of Hertford, for the invasion of Scotland, 10 April 1544

One

The war fleet lay in the Horse Reach, a south-westerly breeze set fair for it to move out into the Blyth haven and then the open sea beyond, the flood tide nearly spent.

Jack Stannard could see the topmasts of the four ships, all at single anchor in the nor'easterly lee of Hen Hill, the Kingsholme beyond, the distant church towers of Walberswick and Southwold beyond that. Men were busy in the shrouds and on the yards. His men, aboard what were now his ships, about to sail for King Harry's war against Scotland. A rough wooing, some called it, to force the treacherous Scots to marry their infant queen Mary to the king's son, Edward, Prince of Wales, as they had promised to do, only to later renege on their word and promise her hand instead to the heir of France.

The waves of the last of the incoming tide were breaking on the beach and the Kingsholme, singing the eternal song of the relentless sea, and Jack should be setting sail upon the ebb. But he would bury Alice first, laying his lost wife to rest in the soil of All Saints' churchyard, high on Dunwich cliff, on the April day that would have been her twenty-seventh birthday.

'*Et ne nos inducas in tentationem...*'

Old Overfield, the priest of All Saints, sprinkled Holy Water over the corpse as he sang the plainchant litany for the commitment of the body. His acolytes swung their censers vigorously, wafting a great cloud of incense over the large congregation at the graveside: a cloud so dense that it briefly suppressed Dunwich's perennial stink of fish. Several of those nearest the censers coughed violently, even as they uttered the familiar, ancient response.

'*Sed libera nos a malo.*'

Jack had filled out in the course of the previous six years. Now he was sturdy, but in no way inclined to fat. To his still untameable hair, he had added a short beard, which made his face seem even more angular than it already was. Six more years of voyaging had further weathered a visage that only his late wife had considered handsome. Two years younger than Alice, most people who met the couple together considered the husband to be by far the older of the two. Others considered Jack's appearance striking, or even unsettling. This was on account of the marked resemblance to his father Peter, who had unsettled many folk in his day, his son among them, and still did, albeit for very different reasons. Otherwise, though, the younger Stannard seemed a picture of mournful respectability, clad in his guildsman's black mourning gown, with the hood drawn up over his head.

Jack knew his thoughts should have been full only of prayers for Alice, whose body, wrapped merely in a winding-sheet, lay on the ground before him, or else for his two motherless children.

But they were not. In part, this was because he knew such thoughts as those would have overwhelmed him, and had him sinking to his knees in dire misery. Had he grieved as good Christians were told to grieve, and as the pain in his heart ached so very much to do, he feared he might hurl himself into the ground alongside his lost love, and cry out for the gravediggers to shovel the sods onto his living body.

'*A porta inferi*,' said Overfield, somewhere seemingly far away.

Nor was Jack more than dimly aware of the crowd around the grave, the throng of family, friends, fellow members of Saint Catherine's Guild, more humble mourners, and even old foes like Mark Cuddon and his brothers, many of them also clad in hooded black gowns. A dozen perfectly still figures, also gowned and hooded, paid for from the Stannard monies, stood on either side of the grave, bearing lighted torches.

Instead, Jack Stannard thought the thoughts that drove out those of feelings, and grief beyond all measure, and of a heart that seemed to be weighted down by a great anchor. Instead, he concentrated on other thoughts, the ones that distracted him from the void caused by the absence of a living, vibrant, laughing Alice. The Alice he longed for and always would, not that stiff, shrouded shape, the merest husk of his wife, lying at the graveside to await its committal. What he would give to see her smile one more time, to hear her laugh one more time.

If Overfield did not make haste, Jack mused, the fleet might miss the tide, and the opportunity to wage war against Scotland. A war that might bring blessings untold to Jack Stannard, and to Dunwich. Blessings that might provide a certain future for Tom and Meg, and pay for countless masses for Alice's soul.

True, Nolloth and Eagle would have the two Dunwich ships, the ships owned by the Stannards, in good order, but he could not be so sure of Maddox from Walberswick, and as for Raker of Southwold—

'*Requiem aeternam dona ei, Domine.*'

From the moment the royal summons was received, and it was decreed that young Stannard of Dunwich should command the contingent, Raker had been—

He recalled the words Alice had used. *That Raker, he be a blowbroth jakey, right enough.* A meddling toad. Alice always had the knack of saying the right thing.

'*Et lux perpetua luceat ei.*'

Jack heard himself murmur the response, and crossed himself, but to his eternal shame, he was thinking of Martin Raker of Southwold, and of the smell of candle-tallow within the greatest castle in the whole of Suffolk. Yet even within that thought, he held an image of Alice, as if she were a shadow there, in the corner of the ancient baronial hall, those very few weeks past. She was smiling, as she always was when she chided him in jest.

'Ever thinking of your ships and your cargoes, Jack Stannard, not of your wife and children. Thank God you have me for a wife, for no other woman in Suffolk would put up with you. No other woman in England, come to that.'

'*Grant her eternal rest, Lord. Let light perpetual shine upon her.*'

–

'Honoured sirs, I have nought but the greatest respect for the family of Stannard and the town of Dunwich,' Martin Raker had lied on that cold evening early in March, in the cavernous, tapestry-lined, candle-lit great hall of Framlingham Castle. He was a small man with an unruly grey beard, and hands that seemed to be in perpetual motion. 'But it would be remiss of me – nay, good sirs, failing in my loyal duty to the king – not to say that Master

John Stannard, there, is too young to command over us. He has been on many voyages, as he says, but almost none have been outside the German Ocean. Whereas I, sirs, have sailed to Bordeaux many a time. Aye, and to Danzig, Lisbon, even Madeira. I have fought the sea-robbers of Scotland, Galicia and Morocco. I have seen the sea serpent. All this and much more, as sworn to in my deposition. So, sirs, I implore you – set aside ancient precedence in this case, and appoint an admiral fit for the mission.'

Jack shifted uncomfortably on his feet, and pulled his best gown a little more tightly around him. For all his belief in his own cause, he knew that what Martin Raker said was only the truth. Of course, there was more to Raker's objection than that, and every man in the room knew it. But it was clever of the Southwold man not to found his argument upon his town's ancient quarrel with Dunwich, nor his own bitter history with Jack's father, a history that, in Jack's estimation, had never been fully explained to him. Instead, Raker emphasised the youth of his rival, the one charge that Jack Stannard simply could not deny.

The two judges in the case, seated upon stools upon the dais, were impassive. One, Sir William Drury, sheriff of Norfolk and Suffolk, was clearly neutral, as his few cursory interventions to that point had indicated. He was a Norfolk man, and a landsman, and gave off the air of someone who wanted the whole trivial business over and done with, so he could get on with more pleasurable pursuits. Thus Drury was evidently content to let the decision rest with his companion, an old, white-bearded man who seemed nearly asleep for half the time, and utterly distracted for the other half, his eyes roving wildly around the hall. William Gonson was the vice-admiral of Norfolk and Suffolk: in truth, largely an honorific title, but it gave him a certain jurisdiction over the men and ships being sent to the war by the two counties. That alone would have given Gonson the authority to judge in the case between Raker of Southwold and Stannard of Dunwich. But the two rivals knew well enough that Gonson's decision would be given even greater weight by the fact that he was also the treasurer and storekeeper of the king's Navy Royal. Many men, including the very tall, very young man at Gonson's shoulder, said that even with due respect to the new and unusually active Lord High Admiral, this old man effectively *was* the king's Navy Royal.

Gonson mumbled something, and the young man stooped down to whisper in his ear.

Gonson nodded, raised his head, and looked directly at John Stannard.

'Stannard of Dunwich,' he said, very slowly, as though turning over each word to see if something lay beneath. 'There was a Stannard of Dunwich with the fleet when we sailed against the French in the year thirteen. An old one-armed man.'

'My grandfather, sir.'

Gonson smiled, as though sharing a private joke with himself.

'That I have lived so long,' he mumbled, 'that I now appoint the grandsons of men I once knew.'

Gonson shook his head, lowered his eyes, and fell silent. Drury looked sideways at him. The tall young man moved forward again, but before he could act, Gonson looked up.

'Dunwich has undoubted and incontrovertible precedence,' he said, his voice suddenly stronger, and very nearly that of a man twenty years younger, 'as is proven by letters and charters of the ninth year of King Henry the Fourth, the ninth year of King Henry the Fifth, the second year of King Henry the Sixth, the sixth year of King Edward the Fourth, and many other preceding monarchs of this realm. That precedence cannot, and will not, be overridden, in this case at any rate. Thus, by the powers vested in me by the king's most excellent highness, and by the Lord High Admiral of England, I declare John Stannard to be admiral and commander of the ships set out from the havens of the Blyth and Dunwich rivers for the war in Scotland.'

Jack cast a sideways glance at Raker, whose mouth was set in a grim rictus, his cheeks rapidly reddening. Then he turned back to formally thank the old man, and saw the tall youngster at Gonson's back wink at him.

-

Later, in a corner of the low principal room of the Crown Inn, across the way from Framlingham's huge church, Jack and Gonson's attendant raised pewter tankards of ale to each other.

'Might Gonson have decided the other way?' Jack Stannard asked.

William Halliday smiled.

'Unlikely, Jack, even if I hadn't k-k-kept emphasising your m-many and undoubted m-m-merits, and laying before him copies of every charter your t-t-town has ever obtained. However he may appear, Gonson still has a sharp m-mind, and he knows the law of both sea and land better than any man I've ever m-m-met.' Halliday took a sip of his ale; Jack knew from long experience that after a pot or two more of it, his friend's stutter would vanish entirely. 'Besides, he knew His Grace of Suffolk's opinion in the m-m-matter, and as he said, he knew of your grandfather, too, thanks be to God. Hard to believe, be it not, that the old man was a bold fighting c-c-captain all those years ago, in the k-k-k-king's first war, let alone a gentleman usher to great Harry himself. But he were both, once. And now, my friend, the success of the k-k-k-king's wars rests heavily upon that old man's shoulders. God grant him the strength to bear the responsibility.'

Jack and Will Halliday had first met at school, and whenever a Stannard ship went into Ipswich, which was often, Jack made a point of seeking out his old friend. Will was still very much a grown version of the boy he had once been, his face much younger than his years and his habitual expression still inclined to child-like eagerness. This impression was reinforced by the stutter that had caused him to be bullied mercilessly at school, and that he had never shaken off in adulthood. Jack, though, who first met Will when coming to his aid against a gaggle of the more relentless bullies, was already threatening to look old long before his time. In the fullness of years, when Will sought a clerkship under the newly-minted vice-admiral of the coast, Jack Stannard used his family's influence, such as it was, to help procure it. Now Will, who had swiftly risen in Gonson's estimation, had repaid the debt, but Jack was profoundly aware that having a friend so close to the effective organiser of the Navy Royal was a connection well worth maintaining, even if Alice did not emphasise the point every time Will's name came up in conversation. Indeed, Jack had already told his old schoolmate that, if he ever needed to call on Stannard influence again – or, if it came to it, Stannard money – then he had only to write.

Jack cradled his tankard in his hands, thinking hard upon Will's words about Gonson.

'Such a burden for one man,' said Jack, 'and such an old man, at that.'

Will nodded.

'It overwhelms him at times, and now the k-k-k-king has decided upon such an ungain as two wars at once... It were too much for one m-man before, but now, Jack, he sits hunched over his desk, sometimes even until dawn or beyond. He tried to retire, y'know, back in C-C-C-Cromwell's time, but that arch-devil threw him the bone of the vice-admiralty of Norfolk and Suffolk. Gives him a large share of the p-proceeds of all wrecks on the shores of the two counties, it does. And you'll know better than I how many of those there are on this coast.' Will Halliday raised his tankard. 'But Master Gonson should sleep well in his bed tonight, knowing he's appointed the best admiral for the ships from the Blyth. As well as he ever sleeps, at any rate, since...' Will's voice trailed off, an unspoken secret left hanging in the air. Then Will brightened, and raised his drink. 'So here's to you, my friend.'

Jack nodded in acknowledgement.

'I doubt if Martin Raker is toasting me tonight,' he said.

'Raker! I don't think you n-need worry about Raker, Jack. If I were you, my friend, I'd worry about the Scots instead.'

But when he returned to Dunwich from Framlingham, relieved and proud to have been confirmed in his command, John Stannard found that he had an even more pressing worry to concern him: the sudden illness of his sweet, beloved wife.

Two

High upon Dunwich cliff, in the corner of All Saints churchyard, Overfield moved on to the final committal of Alice Stannard, the words in English now.

'We commend to Almighty God our sister Alice. We commit her body to the ground, earth to earth, ashes to ashes, dust to dust…'

Alice Stannard's body went into the soil of Dunwich Cliff. It should have been a solemn, silent moment, but the priest's final benediction and Jack's conflicted thoughts were interrupted by the sudden sound of distant hammering. Men were at work on the sea wall down by the Old Quay, repairing the last spring tide's breach.

Hammering was ever a part of Dunwich's music. That's what Alice always said, and she was right, as she was about so much else.

Jack felt a tug on his left hand, and looked down at his son, a healthy six-year-old already sporting a fine mop of characteristically untameable brown Stannard hair. The lad was newly breeched, and infinitely proud of it.

'Father, do we sail for the war now?'

'I sail for the war, son. Remember what your mother, there, always told you, Thomas Stannard. Eat, grow, learn to sail, learn to hold a sword, then you'll be ready for a war. Not this one, but the next one, or the one after that.

There'll always be wars, Tom, so there's no need at all to be rushing for this one.'

'But I can hold a sword now, Father.'

'A dirk, Tom.' Jack kneeled down, and took both his son's hands. 'You can hold a dirk, which is a good weapon, it's true, but you've got a few years yet before you'll be able to wield a sword. No, son, I sail for this war, but your turn will come, my lad. As the sun rises and sets, your turn will come. But if I'm to catch the tide, you need to go to your aunt now, Thomas Stannard. God be with you, my son.'

The boy looked up at him uncertainly, the eyes wide and nearly welling, the mouth trying to form a protest, or else a scream of pain for his lost mother. But, in the end, the child knew his duty. No matter how young, a Stannard of Dunwich always knew his duty. Two glances across to Jack's sister Agatha, already holding the hand of Tom's own sister, Meg, tall and impossibly determined in only her ninth year. One long stare back at his father. Then he was gone, walking reluctantly but purposefully across the greensward to take his aunt's other hand, while his sister stared at him disdainfully. It was the same way Agatha had often looked at the younger Jack, and was doing so again, now. To her, the war was a far distant affair that could be fought by other men, whereas, as she had told him often in the days since Alice's death, Tom and Meg had but one father, and what if he were to perish on the end of a Scotsman's blade? Women, Jack told her, did not understand such things; but Alice, God rest her soul, had understood them well enough.

Jack looked away from his sister's critical gaze, which, these days, seemed to be the fixed expression upon her smallpox-ravaged face, especially when in the company of her brother. He stood up, crossed himself, whispered a prayer for his wife, crossed himself again, offered up a prayer to *Maria maris stella* to watch over him on this voyage, and crossed himself a final time. He took a final look down at Alice's corpse, so small, so still, barely hearing the platitudes Overfield was murmuring to him. He wished, once again, that she had been laid to rest in their own parish of Saint John's, not here in the alien soil of All Saints, the poorest parish in Dunwich, and that she had been laid in a coffin, which the Stannards could easily afford. But even in her final agony, Alice's good sense triumphed over all.

'No point laying me in John's churchyard, Jack Stannard,' she said between gasps of pain, 'only for the fish to be feasting on me within a year. And no point laying me in a coffin, either, wasting good wood you could use to repair the *Blessing*. No, Jack, lay me in All Saints, like my mother before me, in a winding-sheet. Then the first thing I'll see when I rise on the Day of Judgement is dawn coming up over the cliff. There's nothing on this earth like a Dunwich dawn, Jack. Remember it well. Remember me with every dawn, my love.'

Jack Stannard paid Overfield his groat for conducting the series of funeral rites, the *Placebo* on the previous evening, then the *Dirige*, then the Requiem, then the interment, all exactly as Alice had specified. Alms for the poor had also been distributed according to her wishes, and no fewer than fifteen shillings spent on a drinking at the Pelican in its Piety, to which it seemed the entire town was invited. But if he was to catch the tide, Stannard had no time left him to attend. Instead, he turned away at last from the grave, toward the vast, empty bulk of Greyfriars, which nearly abutted the west wall of All Saints churchyard, making for the road down to the harbour.

He pulled back his hood and cursed the hint of sea spray afflicting his own eyes, although he knew full well that All Saints was too high on the cliff for the spray to reach it, and the day's sea too gentle in any case.

That was when he saw the old man in the corner of the churchyard, leaning upon the wall, staring intently at him. For an ancient well past his fiftieth year, the fellow still had the strong, wiry frame he had possessed for as long as Jack had known him, albeit now slightly stooped. His face was the colour and texture of aged leather, his grey hair cropped very close to his skull, his clothes of broadcloth rather better than they should have been.

Jack walked over to him, and the men exchanged the slightest of bows.

'Master Thomas,' said Jack.

Despite the vast gap in age, they had been friends for ten years, but Jack still adhered stubbornly to the title he had always accorded to Thomas Ryman.

'Master John Stannard. I hear you sail for Scotland.'

'Your hearing's improved, if you heard that from Kenninghall.'

Ryman nodded.

'Kenninghall hears everything before Dunwich. Christ's wounds, Dunwich men are the last to know what occurs in Orford or Aldeburgh, let alone in the king's wars. Ever thus, ever will be, world without end.'

The old man's voice was an oddity: purest Suffolk, yet overlain with traces of stranger accents, and faraway tongues.

'You're a Dunwich man, Master Ryman.'

'True enough, Master Stannard. Ah, true enough. No matter how I try, I can't ever remove that stain on my name.'

Thomas Ryman maintained his fixed, serious stare for a moment longer, then broke into a broad grin, strode forward, and embraced John Stannard. The younger man held him close.

'I've missed you, Jack.'

'And I you, old man.'

Thomas Ryman nodded toward the grave, where Agatha and the young Stannard siblings still stood, all three now weeping copiously.

'My condolences. She was a good woman, your Alice, taken too soon. I've paid the duke's chaplain to say a mass of *Scala Coeli* to speed her soul from Purgatory.'

They broke apart, and Jack nodded. He had a reply half formed, but the sea spray was still stinging too harshly. Jack turned his head, and noticed the sack that Thomas had laid down by the wall. A sword hilt protruded from it.

Thomas looked in the same direction, and smiled.

'I thought you might have use of me on this voyage,' he said.

'The duke's given you leave?'

'The duke… ah well, His Grace of Norfolk has more urgent concerns at the moment,' said Thomas. 'Notably, invading France. But if any at Kenninghall notice my absence, I doubt they'll make much of it. And my charge would be the last child on earth to tell his grandfather that his teacher has forsaken him. Or his father and mother, come to that, if they cared a jot, or ever asked him a few proper questions. But to do that, Jack, they'd have to cease warring with each other. Maybe live under the same roof every once in a while.' The ancient shook his head. 'The young Lord Howard is a born conspirator, adept at lying to his grandfather, his parents, his other tutors, the stableboys, the world. Alas, though, Jack, in every other respect, he's but a very poor pupil. Not like some of the others I've taught in the past.'

Despite the pain in his heart, Jack grinned.

'When I was your pupil, Thomas Ryman, you told me many times that you'd had your fill of wars.'

Thomas nodded. His face was lined with age, but two of the longer lines on his right cheek were deep, long-healed scars, souvenirs of battles past.

'Ah, but I was still a friar then, Jack Stannard. It's the sort of thing friars who were once soldiers are meant to say, when they're asked whether they prefer the contemplation of God's grace to the bloody slaughter of their fellow men. But then, of course, the king, whom God preserve, closed the friary, there.'

They both glanced to the west, toward the great, grey, empty buildings behind the high wall that nearly abutted All Saints churchyard. Thomas Ryman had not been within the precinct in all the years since the day when the royal commissioner came and abruptly ended its existence. Jack observed only that more tiles had gone from the roofs of the chapter house and infirmary during the last storm, but Ryman was thinking of his old brothers in Christ: of poor Anselm, dead in poverty and squalor barely weeks after Greyfriars went down, and young Martin, gone north to join those who called themselves the Pilgrims of Grace, and, in consequence, summarily hanged from a tree as a rebel and traitor.

'Aye, well,' said Ryman, turning away from the sight of the empty monastery, ''twas a song whose last note was sung long ago. And so, Jack, if the best the world can offer old Tom Ryman in this new dispensation is teaching the lumpen little dolt who'll one day be Duke of Norfolk how to hold a sword he'll never have to wield in anger – well, then, I'll take a return to the wars any time and say my *Ave Marias* if I get back.'

Jack knew well that at least part of this was bravado, the speech that a former teacher would make to a former pupil. But he knew enough of Thomas Ryman's past life to sense that there was more than a grain of truth in it, too. 'Besides, John Stannard, you've never fought the Scots. I have, remember? Flodden Field, where we slaughtered their king and ten thousand of their men. Several of whom were killed by the sword in the bag, there. And I was on campaign with the duke in that sodden realm no more than eighteen months past. Surely that alone earns me a free passage northward?'

Jack smiled.

'Perhaps it does, old man. Yes, I think it does.'

–

The Dain Quay was empty but for old Wychingham's ship, the *John Evangelist*, newly returned from Newcastle with coals for the Cuddons' account, and the longboat that was to take John Stannard and Ryman out to their vessel, far down river, beyond Cuckolds Point.

Like her consorts in the Horse Reach, the *Blessing* of Dunwich rode high in the water: she would only receive her warlike cargo at her first port-of-call. Of a hundred tons, and four-masted, she was large for the town – indeed, one of the largest ships that still regularly made their way up to Dunwich's quays – and larger than the other three ships at anchor around her, all of them three-masters. The *Grace* of Southwold, Raker's ship, was the next largest at eighty tons, while the *Virgin* of Ipswich, under Maddox of Walberswick, was no more than sixty, as was Dunwich's second ship, the *Peter*, Christopher Eagle's vessel. All of them had been taken up for the king's royal service, and were being paid tonnage money, wages, and expenses, all upon generous terms, to go to the Scottish war.

Fore- and sterncastles stood proud from the hull of the *Blessing*, the only one of the four ships equipped with them. These were new features, intended to make her seem more like a true man-of-war, and had been fitted over the winter by the thin, grey old man who awaited Jack and Thomas Ryman as they stepped up onto the waist of the ship.

'Master Stannard,' said Jed Nolloth, with apparent deference. 'And Master Ryman, as I recall. Welcome aboard the *Blessing*.'

There was no reprimand for very nearly missing the tide, and no words of condolence either. But there did not need to be, for each knew what was in the other's mind. Jack had known Nolloth almost all his life, from the first time his childish steps ran along the quay to greet his father as he returned from a voyage. Nolloth's vast nose and high forehead had fascinated the young Jack, and he often sat on the knee of the stoop-shouldered shipwright, trying to learn the mysteries of his impenetrable art. Nolloth soon had the boy cutting and carrying timber, hammering planking into place, caulking, and God knew what else; and when the young John stood upon his dignity and complained that this was no business for a merchant's son, his father leathered him. For all his black moods, distempers, and all the rest, Peter Stannard knew what his son came, in time, to learn too. All the long hours spent in the shipyard and then in taking Stannard ships to sea, so very different to the course he thought he was set upon, gave the boy a fair grasp of the nature of ships, made him healthy and strong, and above all, earned him the respect of the men of Dunwich, even if not that of his own father.

–

Jed Nolloth was originally a Walberswick man, born and raised in the rival village across the Horse Reach, but Jack's father had noted his talents and bought his services for Dunwich. Nolloth was not content merely to build ships, as so many shipwrights were. He loved to sail them, too, and often acted as helmsman, or even as master, on Stannard voyages, always seeking ways to make his ships sail better, and to learn lessons for the next hull he built. He had very nearly given up going to sea after the voyage of the *Matthew* in the year 'thirty-seven, chiding himself for months on end both for his weakness in being too human to stand watch for longer than half a day, but also for not being able to persuade Peter Stannard to carry another competent helmsman. But Jack, his fortunes unexpectedly altered in ways that both men still found difficult to comprehend, managed to tempt the old man back. On this voyage to the war, Jed Nolloth would serve as master's mate under Jack himself.

'Let us be brisk, then,' said Jack Stannard to the old shipwright. 'Fetch home the anchor, Master Nolloth! Stand by to stretch halliards, fore and aft! Stand by to loose the courses! Stand by the spanker on the bonaventure!'

The men were already at the capstan, awaiting the order, and the *Blessing*'s single anchor rose through the hawse from the bottom. When it was clear of the water, the main courses were loosed and made fast, all to cries of 'well, well'. On the other three ships of the little fleet, the same scene was repeated. Sails unfurled, and were sheeted home. The ships began to move down Horse Reach, past Walberswick Quay, making for the mouth of the Blyth. Jack could see Dunwich folk standing on the great dunes called Cock and Hen Hills, some waving, some on their knees in prayer. He could just make out a familiar woman's form standing before Saint Francis Chapel, between the two hills, and thought for one impossible, soaring moment that it was Alice. But it was his sister Agatha, and Jack knew that the two small shapes by her could only be Tom and Meg, the last precious parts of Alice left to him now. He waved toward them, they seemed to wave back, and he returned to the business of the ship.

'Ease main shrouds, there! Well!'

Jack was too busy barking orders to the men upon the yards and sheets to hear Raker's shout across the water to his ally Maddox of Walberswick. But Ryman, alone at the stern rail, heard it well enough.

'Behold, friend Anthony, our great admiral has deigned to join us! The Scots will be shitting themselves now!'

Maddox laughed, and Raker made the gesture of an evil eye toward the *Blessing*.

Ryman frowned, but put the insolence of the two shipmasters out of his mind. Southwold might be a den of lagarags and rogues, Walberswick little better, but they were all, at bottom, Englishmen, setting out to fight Scots, and when the time came, that would surely trump the old hatreds between Dunwich and her neighbours.

And so the four ships emerged from the mouth of the Dunwich river, then passed out of the Blyth, put on sail, and turned their helms northward, toward the war.

The summer previous, the Scots had made a solemn treaty with King Henry, promising to marry their Queen Mary, aged some eighteen months or so, to England's heir and hope, Prince Edward, aged six. A few months later, with what Thomas Ryman called all the perfidy of their breed, they tore up the treaty, and were now seeking to promise her tiny hand to the French king's newborn grandson instead, the principal mover in all this being the Scottish Beelzebub who went by the name of Cardinal David Beaton. This was his and their newest affront, as the Scots unaccountably refused to recognise the rightful, God-given overlordship of the King of England, daring instead to count themselves a fully independent nation. Worse yet, the French king, Francis, with whom Harry the Eighth had alternately warred and caroused for thirty years, stirred the pot by sending aid to the obnoxious Scots. This was only the latest, and by no means the greatest, of the perverse stratagems of the Valois monarch. No: that was the cursed, unnatural alliance between, on the one hand, the man who termed himself the Most Christian King, and on the other, the arch-enemy of Christendom, the Ottoman Sultan Suleiman, in order to make war upon their mutual enemy, the Holy Roman Emperor Charles the Fifth. King Henry was no lover of the emperor, whose aunt he had acrimoniously divorced, but he was, when all was said and done, Defender of the Faith, even if he had broken with the Pope, the man who had granted him the title. So now, in the spring of that year of grace, 1544, Henry, King of England, was intent, in God's righteous cause, upon war against both Scotland and France at the same time: an invasion first of the one, then of the other.

Like most Englishmen, Jack was confident of victory. God and Saint George would fight for England, as they always did. The Scots would be driven down, as they had been at Flodden, and the French crushed, as they had been at Crécy and Agincourt. But Ryman, who had actually fought against both the Scots and the French, seemed strangely reticent about the prospects of victory. Then there was old Spatchell, a fixture in the corner of the Pelican in its Piety, who was the only man in the town to be both so old and so singular that he was unafraid of denouncing the king when in his cups. War against two enemies at once is madness, Spatchell said, and Jack suspected that in his heart, Ryman shared this opinion. All well and good if the king wins, Spatchell said, but what if he loses? Scotland might be lesser than England, but France was greater. Much greater. Worse, both were Catholic kingdoms, still loyal to the Pope, whereas King Henry had broken with Rome and declared himself head of the Church in England. To the rulers of France and Scotland, war with England would be a holy crusade against a heretic kingdom, a realm of apostates from the true faith, the very mirror image of the English king's reason for fighting them. And what if they were joined by the greatest Catholic ruler of all, the Holy Roman Emperor Charles V? Charles was friendly for the moment, Spatchell reminded whatever audience would listen to him, but he, the French king and Great Harry himself had all changed sides in the blinking of an eye over thirty and more years. What if all of Europe came against England, Spatchell demanded?

He was often challenged by young pothouse hotheads, all beer and bluster, who called him a coward and a traitor. Jack thought him so, too, but kept his counsel.

There were two reasons for this. First, Spatchell was Alice's uncle, and she often spoke of what an educated man he had been in his younger days, of how well he knew the affairs of kings and kingdoms. Second, Spatchell's grandfather – Alice's great-grandfather – had been killed at the Battle of Castillon, ninety years before. Englishmen, including, it seemed, King Henry, remembered only Agincourt, his namesake's great and God-given victory against terrible odds, the triumph about which hymns were still sung and poems written. They conveniently forgot Castillon, nearly forty years later, when the French destroyed England's army, drove the English out of France, and decisively won what some men called the Hundred Years War.

What, then, if these new wars culminated, not in an Agincourt, but in a Castillon, or even a Hastings?

Jack Stannard watched the last glimpse of Dunwich's shore fall away astern, and shut out such thoughts.

No: England had God and destiny on its side. It could only be so.

Revenge and glory for the old king, then, and blood on the blade for Jack. Perhaps the killing of Scots and Frenchmen would go some little way toward assuaging his grief for Alice. And if the ships sailing out of the Blyth haven really did venture forth in God's righteous cause, and if England brought the Scots and French to heel, then perhaps the king would be content to cease his interminable tinkering with matters of religion, so folk could know harmony again. Perhaps, too, the Heavenly Father would then finally look kindly upon Dunwich once more, especially if Jack and his little squadron distinguished themselves in the war to come. Perhaps He would subdue the relentless waters that threatened every day to overwhelm the ancient town, as they had so often before, and restore it to its ancient glory.

Perhaps.

Three

The fleet from the Blyth made its way north. This was a familiar passage for Jack: the very first time he had gone to sea, in his eleventh year, was on a voyage to Newcastle in one of his father's ships. As he fixed his backstaff on each seamark, and pricked his card to make his dead reckonings, he could still recall a little of the awe and dread his young self felt at that time.

'Cromer, boy,' his father had said, taking a bearing and checking his meridian compass. 'When the church tower, yonder, bears *thus*, bring her round to starboard, no more than four points, your course set for the Spurn. Are you listening to me, boy? You'd best not have a tune in your head – pay heed to me, and me alone, or I'll have you lashed to the mast and flogged, son of mine or not, you hear me, boy? Good. Now, I'll tell you this for free, the fainthearts coast further west, and don't turn to the north until they see Blakeney or even Scolt Head, then run for the Lincolnshire shore. But Stannards aren't fainthearts, boy.'

Jack had nodded as gravely as he could, but he still clearly remembered the shock of it all: the pitching deck, the smells, the noises, the countless ropes whose names had to be learned, the mysteries of courses and bearings, the strange shouts and words of the seamen, the eternal tyranny of the four hour watches, the back-breaking voyages to the Iceland fishery before his sixteenth year, the vicious beatings from his father when he made the slightest mistake, the infinity of the grey sea. Only a few months before, his life had been set on a very different course. He was singing *Kyrie Eleisons* in the choir of Cardinal College at Ipswich, alongside Will Halliday, when word came that his elder brother, Adam, was dead, killed on a voyage from Dunwich to Dokkum by a loose clewgarnet block that drove in the side of his skull. Within weeks, the college itself was gone, dissolved in the wake of its founder, the opulent Cardinal Wolsey, fallen because he had failed to find a legal way for the king to marry Mistress Anne Boleyn; and that meant his glorious vision, of a school in his home town of Ipswich which would enable poor boys of the town and district to rise from lowly origins, just as he had, came crashing down. John Stannard of Dunwich was no longer a second son and no longer a scholar, bound for the law or the Church, the careers which his father had seen as vehicles certain to enhance the family's status and connections, and which he had seen as high roads by which he could escape the tyranny of Peter Stannard. In his own dreams, though, Jack wished for nothing more than to write a Western Wynde mass exceeding that of Taverner, and for that briefest of moments, the choir school of Cardinal College seemed to offer him the opportunity to follow his dream. Instead, his brother's death meant that one day, and no matter how often or how loudly his father raged against the injustice of it, all the Stannard ships, ship-shares, warehouses, monies and interests would come to him, and him alone.

That day had dawned much sooner than he expected, in a way he could hardly have envisaged. Looking back, he thought of the voyage home from Emden in the old

Matthew, especially his steering her safely into harbour, as the moment when everything changed; the moment when both Peter and Jack Stannard realised their new destinies.

You'll never be your brother, boy.

True: but not in a sense that Peter Stannard could ever have imagined when he uttered those words.

From the Spurn, the four ships made their way along the Yorkshire coast, both the *Grace* and the *Virgin* constantly falling off to leeward. Neither Raker nor Maddox were such bad shipmasters, nor their ships so foul; Jack knew they were doing it deliberately, giving too much bunt to the sails and a dozen other sly tricks, all to make the squadron's commander look a dolt. But he could never prove it, so he shortened sail repeatedly to wait for the sluggards. The squadron spent two days and nights sheltering from a northerly gale in Bridlington Bay, whence they sent letters back to Suffolk, then weathered Flamborough Head and continued their voyage northward. Despite running repairs at Bridlington, the *Blessing*'s leaks multiplied by the hour. She was an old ship, there had been insufficient time to caulk her anew after her return from a voyage to Antwerp, and Jack prayed that she made it through the campaign. Then, God willing, she could be replaced by the new ship that he was having built: a ship that would be finer than any other set out from the east country of England.

All the while during their passage northward, Jack and Thomas Ryman talked of much, both on deck and over pots of ale in the tiny, stinking space that did duty as Jack's cabin. They talked of Jack Stannard's father, and of what he had become. They reminisced about Alice, of her good humour and her many kindnesses, with

Ryman reminding Jack to hold fast to Revelation Twenty-One. They talked of the many Dunwich people they both knew. They talked of the war, of Ryman's part in the Duke of Norfolk's ruthless campaign in the Scottish borders after the Solway Moss fight, of the erstwhile friar's dismay and anger at the duke's inexplicable decision not to take him on his much greater campaign in France. Above all, they talked of the duke's household at Kenninghall, which was, it seemed, a hotbed of intrigue, where the very latest rumours from court were discussed, mulled over, and argued about into the early hours. But even there, no man or woman was certain whether their lord and his conservative allies, the likes of Lady Mary, the king's elder daughter, and Bishop Gardiner, were rising or falling, winning or losing, in the endless battle for the old king's ear. The new queen, the sixth of the reign – the former Lady Latimer, once mere Mistress Parr – was said to be a reformer, and a friend of Cranmer, the archbishop, who favoured many of the radical ideas coming out of Germany, where the old firebrand Luther still spouted his bile. The last monasteries had gone four years before – they stared in silence from the larboard rail at the great shell of Whitby Abbey, gaunt and empty upon its headland – and none knew what might be next. There was talk, Ryman said, of an end to chantries; and the old friar shook his head, as he had always done over wayward pupils. But the king kept his own counsel, and none truly knew His Majesty's mind. Yet of one thing, every man in England was certain. At that moment, Henry the Eighth, whom God preserve, wanted one thing more than any other, and that was to crush the perfidious Scots.

The precise means by which King Henry intended to achieve that aim became apparent as the four ships from the Blyth edged north-west at dawn, their course set for a light burning high in a great, dark building upon a headland. As the sun rose, and Jack offered up his daily silent prayer in memory of Alice's last words, he and Ryman could see the location of the light: the corner tower of a huge sandstone priory church, empty like all the rest, but a church that stood within the bounds of a fortified enclosure encompassing the entire headland. From the ramparts flew a host of banners of Saint George, while on the level ground before the large gatehouse, campfires, flags, and hundreds of colourful tents, betrayed the presence of a mighty army. The roadstead inshore of the headland contained five or six dozen ships of varying sizes, most at anchor, a few moving into or out of the Tyne. Like the *Blessing*, they were drawn from the ports of the kingdom, as had been the way of forming a navy in England since time immemorial. A war against Scotland placed the burden firmly upon the east coast, so in addition to the Dunwich contingent, there were ships from the likes of Yarmouth, Lynn, Lowestoft, Scarborough and Hull. Over toward the north shore lay a dozen or so of the king's own ships, pennants streaming from their mastheads. Their vast hulls towered above everything else in the anchorage, the high, colourfully painted sides of the carracks surmounted by elaborate wooden castles fore and aft.

'Good thinking, this,' said Ryman, 'whoever conceived of it – be it the king or Lord Hertford. The latter, I'd reckon. Avoid any prospect of another Flodden, come what may.'

'You won at Flodden, Master Thomas.'

'Aye, but should have lost. The Scots outnumbered us. They had the higher ground. The bigger and better army.

The better weapons. Only their king's stupidity saved us that day, Jack, and I doubt if Lord Arran, or whoever they've got in command, will make the same mistakes again. Besides, you can beat the Scots all you like in the borderland, but you'll have taken heavy losses of your own, and there's still three days' march to Edinburgh, with them harassing you every inch of the way. No, this I like. This I like very much.'

It was, indeed, a simple scheme. If the Scots had an army at the border, then let its men kick their heels. The host of England would simply take ship and sail round them, directly for the Forth. The Scots, bankrupt and beset by feuding between Cardinal Beaton and his opponents led by Arran, could not send a navy to sea; but King Henry, his treasury awash with the proceeds from all the dissolved monasteries, certainly could.

The *Blessing* and her consorts came to an anchor in the Narrows at the mouth of the Tyne, in the midst of a number of Yarmouth ships. Skiffs, longboats, and pinnaces, thronged the river, taking men and provisions from shore to fleet, and between the ships.

Jack Stannard went below to change out of his sea-gown into his best doublet and hose. After all, Dunwich's commander could not pay his compliments to his squadron's admiral in what was little better than a tar-stained smock; and Jack could imagine Alice fussing and fretting over his appearance, trying to give some semblance of a shape to his hair—

He was aware of heavy boots upon the deck above his head, and of raised voices. Thomas Ryman's raised voice, above all. He went back up on deck to see the old man remonstrating with a junior officer, no more than seventeen or eighteen by the look of him, clad in a gown of black fustian bearing a coat-of-arms that Stannard did not recognise. Gathered around their officer like a phalanx were four billmen, the blades of their weapons gleaming in the sunlight.

'What's to do?' said Jack.

'You're John Stannard of Dunwich?' said the officer.

A youth he might have been, his voice still touched by the reediness of childhood, but he spoke with certainty, and an arrogant authority.

'I am.'

'Then, John Stannard, I arrest you in the name of the Lord Admiral of England.'

Jack looked across to Ryman, but the old man could only shrug.

-

Throughout the crossing to the shore, Jack demanded to know the cause of his arrest, and of any charges laid against him. But the young officer was determinedly silent, and remained so during the forced march along the rough street that led through a narrow village of fishermen's cottages, huddled beneath a cliff. A few local women glanced their way, but displayed little curiosity. As they walked up toward the headland, through the encamped army, none paid any attention at all. Soldiers were sharpening blades, polishing breastplates, drinking ale and eating bread or pies. The prisoner being marched toward the castle might have been invisible, or no more than an ant upon a dungheap.

Through all the journey, Jack racked his brain to think of any cause for his arrest. The Stannards paid their taxes; or, at least, as great a proportion of their taxes as any other merchants in Suffolk. Their ships engaged in no piracy, or at any rate, none that had ever come to attention of the Lord Admiral of England. They paid their customs duties in full.

Pater noster, que es in caelis—

Jack stopped himself, and changed the prayer in his mind to English, to 'Our Father, which art in Heaven'. He and his entire family adhered to the letter of every new law in matters of religion that the king and his Parliament decreed. But what if the king had somehow recently changed a central article of faith, and he knew nothing of it? What if all of Dunwich had unwittingly committed a gross offence against some newly adopted orthodoxy? Perhaps even as he trudged toward his fate, royal officers were going through the town, hammering on doors and starting to build the pyres. His sister Agatha, mixing her potions in her remote cottage across Dunwich Heath, would surely be a prime candidate for the stake – perhaps she had somehow incriminated him—

Oh Jesu, forgive us our sins, save us from the fires of Hell.

They came to the great gatehouse of Tynemouth Castle. Built of sandstone, like the towering empty priory behind it, the gatehouse was a mighty square, with a barbican before it and a deep earth ditch stretching away on either side, cutting off the headland completely. Jack walked through the gate passage, staring up at the ancient walls. It was all a mistake, he told himself over and over again. It had to be a mistake. But even now, a part of him wondered if he would ever walk out of this passage as a free man.

Across the open ground of the headland, a party of nobles and gentry, along with several armed, breastplated and evidently very senior soldiers were making their way from the priory toward the gatehouse. Jack recognised none of them, but one in the centre of the group, a man of forty summers or thereabouts, was especially lavishly dressed in black velvet, and sported a finely groomed red beard. Several of those nearby seemed to be competing for a word with him. Even in his confusion and despair, Jack realised that this could be only one man, easily identifiable by the Seymour hair he shared with his nephew, the Prince of Wales: the Lord General himself, Edward, Earl of Hertford.

The party around the great lord ignored the prisoner entirely. John Stannard was marched across the headland. At one side of the west front of the priory church, less grand than it must have been when statues of the saints stood in what were now empty niches, was a thin detached tower, which could only be a belfry. He was taken inside, and marched up three floors of a narrow spiral staircase. Groans, shouts and the stink of shit came from each room that he passed. So this was the gaol of Tynemouth Castle, and at the top of it was a tiny, empty room which might once have accommodated the monk who tended to the bells. Jack was thrust into it, the door slammed behind him, and a key turned in a heavy lock. He thought of Alice, and for the first time since her passing, he thanked God she was dead. At least she could not know his shame, and would not witness what it seemed to presage: the downfall of the Stannards of Dunwich.

Four

Ryman watched the boat carry young Jack away. The men of the *Blessing* crowded at the wale, murmuring to themselves, fearing aloud for their own futures. Jed Nolloth's face was ashen. Thomas Ryman, though, had no time for emotion, or for worry. He prayed, then he thought, hard and long. Then he got Nolloth to bring the ship's boat alongside, and to provide a crew to row him ashore.

Ryman had three names in mind. It took him four alehouses and nine coins to establish that one of the three had been killed at the Solway Moss fight, one of only seven Englishmen to perish in a victory so great and so humiliating for the enemy that the Scots king promptly turned his face to the wall and died of shame; but then, the man Ryman had known of old was always notoriously unfortunate. In the same breath, he learned that the second of the three was in the Pale of Calais, making the lives of the garrison of Guines an utter misery, as he had once made Ryman's.

That left the third man, who sat alone in the fifth alehouse, staring deeply into a wooden tankard.

'Petty Captain Vaughan,' said Ryman. 'You're a difficult man to find.'

Vaughan looked up, screwing his eyes to try and make out the man who addressed him from the doorway. Slowly, recognition came to him.

'Thomas Ryman,' he said, his accent still bearing the unmistakeable stamp of his native Wales. '*Y mae dafad ddu ym mhob praidd*, indeed it does. Every flock has its black sheep, and here you are to become ours. Last I heard, you'd adopted a tonsure.'

'Tonsures have fallen out of fashion, Gwynfor Vaughan, in case you hadn't heard. Swords, though – ah well, they seem to have fallen into fashion once again.'

'They never fall out of it. So which lord do you serve now, Sergeant Ryman? And what brings you to share my table?'

Ryman took that as an invitation, and seated himself on a stool opposite Vaughan.

'No lord, in this matter. In others, the Duke of Norfolk.' Vaughan raised an eyebrow. 'As for sharing your table… let's say a remembrance of times past. Of debts owed.'

'I owe you no debts, Thomas Ryman.'

'We could argue that into the small hours, perchance. But no, your debts don't concern me, Welshman. But the debts of another who's known to us… that's quite another matter.'

–

Jack was in the prison for three days. For much of the first day, he spent every waking hour continuing to convince himself that this could only be some sort of mistake, that he would be released before the next hourly tolling of the priory's tenor bell, directly above his cell, his innocence fully established. He tried to shut out the cries of the three men in the room below his own: soldiers, blaming each other for the insolence to an officer that had brought them to this pass.

During the second day, he tried to remember every aspect of his life in the last two or three years, thinking to identify anything that might have been reported as a crime. He had been very drunk at Martinmas, the year before, having been persuaded by his bibulous cousin Simon Bulbrooke to celebrate the success of the herring season; had he then spoken against the king while in his cups? But he had confessed the sin of drunkenness to Reverend Seaward at Saint John's, and surely any arrest for treason would have come sooner, and at Dunwich. He had been faithful to Alice, even after her death, so surely he could not be charged with fornication, certainly not with fathering a bastard. He said his prayers by morning and evening, and paid amply for masses for the soul of his dead mother, as he would also do for his dead wife upon his return from this campaign. Surely he was a good man?

But his father was not. Had the sins of the father been visited, after all, upon the son?

By the third day, Jack was sunk in despair, offering up the same prayers over and over again, begging Alice for forgiveness, praying to her to intercede with the Virgin and all the saints on his behalf. He did not know who accused him. He did not know what he was accused of. He had been forgotten, and would languish in this prison until he died of the sickness consuming one of the men in the room below, whose coughing and spewing kept him awake half the night. He would never see Dunwich again, never weep at Alice's grave, never see Tom and Meg grow up.

Salve, Regina, mater misericordiae…

Hail, Holy Queen, the mother of misery.

The gaoler came a little after three in the afternoon of the third day, unlocking the door and crying 'Stannard! You John Stannard?'

He rose, and nodded his head. The gaoler beckoned for him to come forward, and placed him in the custody of two guards. They took him up out into the open ground of the headland, to the light and the air. Jack breathed deeply, felt the sun on his face, and thanked God that he still lived.

The guards led him across to the gatehouse, up two flights of broad stairs, into a large room directly above the gate passage, filling what seemed like nearly the whole width of the building. Tapestries with scenes of Roman emperors hung on three sides. Through the windows of the fourth, the west wall, John could see the fleet at anchor in the estuary of the Tyne. The sun glinted on the helmets and breastplates of soldiers, many hundreds of them, aboard row-barges going out to the ships. The army was embarking, so the expedition was under way. The *Blessing* would be out there somewhere, Nolloth making her ready to sail and working to stop her leaks.

'Stannard of Dunwich', said a man of forty or thereabouts, sitting behind a large oak table at the end of the room.

His clothes, an elaborate confection of velvet, sable and cloth-of-gold that must have been far too hot for the season, indicated a man of very high rank. His beard and hair were a very dark brown, the former small and neatly pointed; but the most remarkable things about him were his eyebrows, high, dark and arching, which gave him a look of permanent amusement.

'My Lord,' said Jack, certain that the man could only be a lord, and having a shrewd suspicion of exactly which lord he was.

'You are accused of many things, John Stannard,' he said gravely. 'Endangering the squadron from the Blyth by incompetent seamanship, for one.'

'My Lord—'

The proud figure seated before him ignored the interruption, continuing to fix his eyes on the paper in his hands.

'Bribery of customs officers, for another. Then, it seems, misappropriation of royal stores. False musters, too.'

Jack saw his entire future unravel before him. It was as he had feared during the long hours in the cell at the top of the bell tower: charges that were both inherently plausible and exceedingly difficult for him to disprove.

'And here, I see, you are charged with heresy.'

The word struck like a gale against Dunwich cliff. Heresy was, perhaps, the most dreaded charge that could be brought against any man or woman. Heresy, if proved, meant burning at the stake, the flesh literally roasting to a crisp even as the accused still lived.

'My Lord, I beg you – I am true to the Church—'

The lord raised a hand.

'Heresy, I say.' The lord paused, and looked again at the paper in his hand. He shook his head. 'But not just heresy, it appears. There is a charge here of manslaughter.' He frowned. 'Another of affray.'

'My Lord—'

But the hand rose again, and the lord returned to the paper, taking a draught of ale from his pewter tankard as he did so.

'Sodomy. Witchcraft. Even High Treason. That is quite a catalogue of crimes, Master Stannard. Indeed, I think I can safely say that no single man in England has probably ever been charged with quite so many heinous offences. So many capital ones, at that. Certainly not in the reign of the king's present highness.'

The lord leaned back, the eyebrows seeming to laugh, and steepled his hands. For his part, Jack looked around in bewilderment. Several men were over against the far wall, beneath a tapestry of a triumphal procession. Some seemed amused at his predicament, others were entirely impassive – and then there were two others, who seemed to shrink back into the shadows thrown by the afternoon sun—

Raker and Maddox.

Everything was clear now. Oh, so very, very clear.

'Now,' said the lord, 'of this vast sheet of charges that has been brought against you, Master Stannard, many do not fall under my remit as His Majesty's Lord Admiral of England.'

John turned back to face the man he now knew for certain to be John Dudley, Viscount Lisle, privy councillor and Knight of the Garter, one of the great men of Henry the Eighth's kingdom.

'My Lord,' he said, his faith and confidence flowing back into him like a flood, 'I will make answer to each and every charge that my accusers have brought before me. Ample answer, indeed, with witnesses aplenty. But, My Lord, if I may beseech you most humbly – how was it that these charges came before you?'

The Lord Admiral looked at him steadily, assessingly.

'By letter, Master Stannard. From your little fleet, when it lay in Bridlington Bay.'

Jack nodded, then turned to face his accusers.

'Not brave enow to challenge me back in Suffolk, eh, boys? A sawny game even for Southwold and Walberswick men, to sarnick along like a bargain of dauzy hodmadods.' Jack saw Lord Lisle raise an eyebrow, but the Suffolk invective, comparing Raker and Maddox to a gaggle of demented snails, was aimed at a different audience. 'Wait 'til we were at sea, then hope that martial law would do your business for you? Poor, boys, poor. And you'll pay, on the word of John Stannard.'

Raker and Maddox exchanged glances. The former took a step forward.

'You're unfit to command, Stannard. Too young. Only put over us by old Gonson because of who your father and grandfather were, and what Dunwich was. That's all your dungy little town has left now. History. Hopeless dreams.'

'Jealousy of a young commander, sirrahs?' said Lord Lisle. 'Then what of the charges you have brought? Of treason? Of heresy? Of all these other great crimes?'

'We've witnesses to them all,' said Raker.

'These witnesses,' said Jack. 'Might they all be men of Southwold and Walberswick, perchance?'

Raker opened his mouth, but no words came.

'Speak, Captain Raker,' said the Lord Admiral. 'Whence do your witnesses hail?'

'One of them is an Ipswich man,' said Raker, his voice now much less certain. 'Another of Blythburgh.'

'And the rest as Captain Stannard charges?'

Raker nodded, his eyes cast to the floor.

'Well, then,' said Lisle. 'Even when I was a young boy, growing up in Kent, I knew the tale of Dunwich and its rivals. The ancient, decayed city with all the privileges, the newer ports round about that had none. The vicious little pups snapping at the heels of the ancient lion. Would that be the sum of it?'

'Southwold and Walberswick have long sought to bring Dunwich low, My Lord,' said Jack. 'And my father had bad blood with Raker, there.'

Bad blood indeed: cargoes destined for Southwold that somehow berthed at Dunwich instead; harbour duties owed to Southwold that were paid, instead, to Dunwich; and, yes, a woman once betrothed to Martin Raker, who somehow spent twenty years in the marital bed of Peter Stannard.

'Aye, that he did, right enough,' cried Raker, with a sudden burst of passion, 'but look how bad your father's own blood became!'

He stepped forward angrily, making for Jack. Lisle waved a finger, and Jack heard the sound of a sword being drawn from a scabbard, behind him. He turned, and saw Thomas Ryman, his blade in his hand. Two of Lisle's guards stood behind him, levelling their halberds toward Raker.

The Lord Admiral rose to his feet.

'Great God, enough of this mime, this play-acting! We have hard business ahead of us – the beating of the Scots. And you men trouble me with *this*? I need every ship, every man, and I will waste not another minute on trumped-up charges and the petty jealousies of one pitiful little Suffolk port for another. The ancient grievances of one man against another's father? I should have you flogged, Master Raker, or else hanged, both for your false witness and for assuming that I, a Dudley, could be so easily gulled.' The Southwold man blanched. 'But as I say, I need your ship, and as we need to sail at the first opportunity, that means, alas, that I need you, too. So be obedient to Master Stannard, here. He is well spoken of, whatever his age, and he commands your squadron with my authority, in addition to that with which you originally sailed. I will have no more of this foolery. Should there be more of it, bodies will swing. Necks will break. You have my promise upon it.'

With that, Lord Lisle turned and strode from the room, the entire gathering bowing to him as he left. Raker gestured angrily to Maddox, who followed in his wake. They seemed to make to leave, but then paused before Jack and Ryman.

'This is not done with, Stannard,' hissed Raker. 'Lisle will see. They will all see, when we get to Scotland, that ye're nought but a worthless hobbledehoy, the son of a murderer and a whore.' Jack stepped forward, his hand raised in a fist. Ryman gripped his arm urgently, and nodded toward the nearest guard, who was grasping his halberd. 'Oh, we'll make them all see through you, John Stannard,' said Raker, jabbing a finger, 'I swear it upon the holy blood of Saint Edmund, king and martyr.'

He turned, Maddox with him. They brushed past Ryman on their way to the other door, Jack still straining to go after them.

'Steady, lad, steady,' said the older man.

'No man speaks so of my father and mother—'

Jack stared hard at Ryman, his eyes wide with anger.

'Aye, true, a good son should always say so. But a thinking son will wait for his moment.'

Jack nodded slowly, and even managed a slight smile.

'When you were in the friary, Thomas Ryman, you would have told me to turn the other cheek. You often did – that time with Mark Cuddon, for one—'

The sometime friar laughed.

'And did it serve? I recall you beat Cuddon senseless anyway.' He slapped the younger man on the shoulder. 'Come, Jack Stannard, let's find an altar where we can sing Alleluias, then an alehouse where we can raise a mug or three to God's good grace for freeing you. When we're drunk enough, we can call down damnation on Southwold and Walberswick, and thank Saint Felix that our friends Raker and Maddox overplayed their hand by throwing every charge they could conjure into the pot. Idiots. Whatever other faults could be laid at the door of our Lord Admiral, the lack of a brain is not one of them.'

'So is my freedom due only to God's grace, then, Thomas?'

The old man shrugged.

'In truth, Jack, the Almighty could have done a little more to expedite my interview with the Lord Admiral – I feared you would be left behind when the fleet sailed, left to rot in prison even without Raker bringing his charges against you. It was only this morning that My Lord agreed to see me, and that only because one of his old corporals served with me in Picardy in 'twenty-three. But once I had the admiral's ear, it was a children's game.'

'A children's game, Thomas Ryman? With My Lord Lisle? The Lord Admiral himself? One of the greatest men of the kingdom?'

'Just so, lad, just so. You see, Jack, I reminded him of three facts. One, that he was knighted by the Duke of Suffolk, to whom he owed his early advancement. Two, that this same Duke of Suffolk has always been the patron of Dunwich, had a regard for your father, and approved your command of our expedition. Thus, His Grace would certainly not look kindly upon the hanging of a Stannard of Dunwich upon such patently trumped-up charges.

My Lord Lisle is said to be mightily ambitious, having risen so far in such a short time, so methinks offending His Grace, the king's closest friend and erstwhile good-brother, would be unlikely to further those ambitions.'

'You said all this to him? I had not thought you such a Machiavel of statecraft, Master Ryman.'

'Oh, not in so many words, Jack, and not before I had reminded him of my third fact.'

'Which was?'

'Remembrance of a day in the Pale of Calais in the winter of 'twenty-three, on the border between Guines and Ardres, when the ground was frozen hard. A sudden French ambush, and a very young, very new knight being thrown from his horse in the snow. A young knight whose life was saved by a certain sergeant.'

'Lisle? You saved Lisle's life? Sweet Jesu, Thomas Ryman, is there no end to your secrets?'

'Sir John Dudley, as he then was. It was my Christian duty to save him from a Calvary that day, and my duty as a soldier, too. But until I had the saving of your life as reason to appeal to him, I wondered whether I did the right thing, that day in the snow.'

'You spared the life of the future Lord Admiral of England, Master Thomas – a great favourite of the king, they say. How could that not be the right thing?'

Ryman looked around to ensure no others in the room were listening to their conversation.

'My Lord Lisle, Jack, is one of the most vigorous of the reformers around the king. It's said he favours the catechism being in English, and denies the Real Presence during the Mass. God alone knows what other heresies may lurk in his bosom.'

'Do men not say the same of the queen? And the archbishop?'

Ryman glanced behind him once again, then took Jack's elbow and began to lead him away. In a very low voice, he said, 'Talk for another place and another time, Jack. You've just become a free man again. Don't, then, tempt a reversal of your fate, or still worse – whatever faith he may hold in his heart, Lisle is a hard man, and a man of his word, so when he speaks of the noose if you, Raker or Maddox offend him again, he means it. So let's find that alehouse, my young friend, and toast your liberty.'

Five

From the sterncastle of the *Blessing* of Dunwich, Thomas Ryman looked out over the dreadful scene. The sea-legion of England was edging into the Firth of Forth upon the flood and a favourable breeze, the great royal men-of-war to the north, covering the slow advance of the transports, like the hull in which Ryman sailed, and the wafters, the smaller warships, mainly single-masted ballingers, detailed to escort the others. The banners and swallow-tail pennants of Saint George streamed out from the staffs and topmasts of the *Swallow*, the *Great Galley*, the *Minion*, and the rest of the king's ships. Their guns were run out in case of resistance, the early May sun gleaming on the polished brass barrels of cannon perriers, demi-culverins, sakers and fawcons. There was the vanward, under Lord Lisle; there, the rearward, under the Earl of Shrewsbury. There, over toward one of the islands and at the heart of the middleward, lay the flagship, the carrack *Rose Lion*, adorned with more flags than any other ship in the fleet. One of them was the red and gold banner of the Seymours, signifying the presence of their general, the Earl of Hertford, Great Chamberlain of England; another, the royal standard of the kingdom, signifying that although the king himself was not present, his authority as supreme commander of England's forces most surely was, in the form of the man who had been his brother-in-law.

Of their enemies, the Scots, there was no sign. The *Blessing* was one of the vessels closest inshore, and also one of the most westerly, but no ship was stirring out of any of the creeks or bays. There was no sign of any troops massing on the nearer shore, nor on that of Fife, to the north. Scotland might have been a desert, a land entirely devoid of people, but for the dark mass in the shadow of a great hill, away to the south-west of the approaching English fleet. Ryman could see the wisps of smoke from the city's chimneys, and the black outline of a castle upon a high, dark cliff.

Edinburgh, then.

Thomas Ryman drew his sword and inspected it. Fifteen years before, when he entered the Dunwich Greyfriars, convinced that this was God's chosen course for him, he had sheathed it for what he thought was the last time. Then, England was still a part of the Universal Church, still happy under the eternal truths, its people content and prosperous. Fifteen years before, though, the newly-minted Friar Thomas had known nothing of the king's lust for the Boleyn harpy, nor that Cardinal Wolsey would soon topple, nor that there could be such a thing as a Supreme Head of the Church who was not the Pope, nor that the friary, with its little burying ground where he expected to be laid to rest, would die long before him. So England, lashed by the waves of discord and the gales of war, now faced a future as uncertain as Dunwich. Young Jack and his father both dreamed of it being great again, one of the few matters upon which they agreed, but Ryman knew better. He had fought in Italy, and seen the huge ruins left by the old Romans. Greatness, once lost, never returned; but he could never say that to any man by the name of Stannard.

As he studied the blade, still scrupulously sharpened and polished through all the years between, it also sang to him of their times together. It sang of Flodden, of Marignano, of Pavia, of the half-forgotten skirmishes in the snow-shrouded foothills of the Pyrenees and the scorched plains of Lombardy: fighting alongside Germans and Frenchmen, Spaniards and Italians, all of whom now shunned Englishmen as though they were Satan's spawn. It sang of the snows in the Pale of Calais, where he had saved the life of the man who was now Lord Admiral of England. It sang, too, of the men it had killed, of the times it had saved his life. And it sang of the basilica in a small town lost in the Umbrian foothills, of the screams and the blood of nuns, women and children, and of the vision of the Blessed Virgin he had experienced that day, which caused him to abandon the wars and return home to the Greyfriars, seeking redemption and absolution. It was strange how, with the sword in his hand, the memories and terrors of war seemed like yesterday, while his more recent time in the monastery seemed like a far-distant, almost lost, recollection of an age long since vanished into the mists.

Thomas Ryman raised the sword and contemplated it. He swung it right and left, swept it up and down, slowly at first, then faster, ever faster.

No, he had not forgotten how to use it.

'You and me, my angel,' he murmured. A sailor within earshot turned, and looked at him as though he were a Bedlam-man. 'You and me, once again.'

-

The old man's screams woke Will Halliday once more, as they had done every night that week. The clerk slept on a trestle bed at the far end of the room which William Gonson used as his office in his work as treasurer and storekeeper of the navy, so, abandoning his own, infinitely pleasant, dream of Mistress Marion Bartleby, Will was at his master's side in a moment. None of the others in the house in Tower Street Ward stirred: the servants had learned long ago to ignore Gonson's nightmares, while the old man's wife was as deaf as a statue. His other sons had their own households, partly because they could afford them, partly – as Benjamin, the son who worked alongside Will, had told him – so they did not have to listen to their father's screams.

'Sir!' cried Will, shaking Gonson's shoulders. 'Sir!'

'Mm? Mm? No – *no*! David! God spare him – David, my boy—'

'Sir! Master Gonson! Wake, sir, for God's sake! It's but a dream, Master. A dream again, sir.'

Gonson's breathing was very rapid, his words urgent and terrified.

'I see the knife tearing him open – I see his entrails held up to the crowd – I see it, I see it, I see it still—'

As Gonson's head turned violently from side to side, Will Halliday continued to shake him. At last, the old man's eyes opened, and stared at him blankly. Then, finally, a word:

'Will.'

'Just a d-dream, sir.'

'No, Will, not just a dream. Would that it were. Not a dream, but a memory.' Gonson sighed, rubbed his eyes, and made to rise from his bed. 'Ah, well, let's make the best of it, then. Bring my wine, lad, and my pen. Time to prepare the orders for Erith yard.'

'But Saint Dunstan's has yet to chime three, sir!'

'As good a time as any. I'll not hope to sleep now until the afternoon – you know that, Will, you've been with me long enough. Oh, and open a shutter. Let me breathe some London air, and clear my head.'

Will nodded, and went to the window. With the shutter open, the bright moonlight enabled him to see over the rooftops of Thames Street, down to the river, west to London Bridge, east to the black bulk of the Tower, the flaming torches and braziers of the guards upon the wallwalks just visible. Even at that time of night, there was noise everywhere: the sounds of arguments, and fornication, and drunks singing as they rolled their ways homeward, and of the night soil men, laughing and talking as they scooped up Londoners' dung. Once, Will Halliday had thought Ipswich mighty and the centre of his world, but now, he could not imagine being anywhere other than London. He took a deep breath before turning back to the table, which held a jug of claret.

Yes, he'd been with William Gonson long enough to know his habits: how night could be made day if business was urgent enough, as it always was these days. He'd been with him long enough to know that his master got nothing like enough sleep for a man of his age. He'd been with him long enough to know that in Gonson's mind, one inventory forgotten, one order not sent, one bill not paid, might be sufficient to destroy the navy of England, perhaps even to bring down the throne of King Henry. And he'd been with him long enough to know that when those waking thoughts gave way to sleep, their place was taken by the even more terrible offspring of the imagination, the recurring nightmare that plagued the old man every night.

Except he was right, of course.

It was not a nightmare: it was a memory.

Three years earlier, David Gonson, knight of the Order of Saint John of Jerusalem, the bravest, finest, and most beloved of William's six sons, was hanged, drawn and quartered for high treason. He had not plotted against the king's life, he had not fought for the return of papal authority, and he had not spoken derogatory words against King Henry, whatever the solitary witness against him, a perjured renegade knight named Sir Philip Babington, might have said. David Gonson died both because of the malice of that one inveterate enemy, and because he belonged to an Order respected the length and breadth of Christendom: the Order whose men-of-war, sailing from their invincible base at Malta, David had commanded with skill and success against the Ottoman foe, the common enemy of all Christians, Catholic or Protestant alike. But then, King Henry the Eighth suddenly took against the Knights of Saint John. First, he sent out a new turcopolier, the title given to the lieutenant of each *langue*, or nationality, of the Order. This fellow, Sir Clement West by name, Gonson had told Will, was an arrogant, charmless puppet of the king, who marked his arrival in Malta by placing the lion of England above the arms of the Order, as well as having an officer march before him, bearing a mace with the English royal crest. After insulting virtually every English knight and belittling the Grand Master, he was arrested and deposed, only to be reinstated at the king's insistence. Sir David Gonson had been one of the turcopolier's many opponents in the English *langue*, his nemesis, Sir Philip Babington, one of West's very few supporters. In the end, though, the king decided that the Order, which swore loyalty to the Pope, represented a threat to his headship of the Church of England, and outlawed it from his kingdom. But in the taverns and alehouses that Will Halliday frequented, there were a few bold enough to whisper that the true reason for the Order's downfall was because Henry had set his relentlessly avaricious eyes upon its substantial English properties, notably its great palace at Clerkenwell.

Regardless of the cause, the upshot was that the English knights who remained loyal to the Order, like Sir David Gonson, suddenly found themselves condemned as traitors. By the time-honoured convention of English law, a charge of treason had to have two witnesses to support it. But David Gonson was tried, condemned and executed by a new legal process, attainder, which did not rely on such wearisome and inconvenient matters as witnesses and evidence, judges and juries. Justice was so much more efficient in Great Harry's new imperial island.

So William Gonson's son was judicially murdered, and his father had watched; but King Henry, in his infinite mercy, judged that otherwise, the sins of the son should not be visited upon the father. All of this happened before Will Halliday joined William Gonson's service, but he heard of it soon enough from Benjamin, the penultimate son, who was of an age with Will, and who was the only one of the master's boys to show an aptitude for naval administration.

Will placed the glass of wine on the one small patch of uncovered wood upon Gonson's desk. The old man got out of bed, stiffly and slowly, donned an overgown, crossed to the desk, lifted the glass to his lips, supped, and then looked up at his young clerk.

'How stands the wind, Will?'

'North-westerly, Master.'

No matter if you never set foot on a ship, William Halliday, Gonson told him, on Will's first day in his service, *always know where stands the wind. It is the alpha and omega of the navy. Besides the wind, all else is but frippery.*

'Nor'-westerly, the seamen would say. Not ideal, not ideal.' Gonson was fully awake now, alert, and not distracted by wild thoughts and memories, as he so often was. 'But sufficient. If Lord Lisle and the fleet have the same wind, they will be going into the Forth, perhaps today, perhaps tomorrow. Perhaps they are there already. So we have done all we can for them, Will. Now is the time for the warriors.'

Six

'All hands, make the ship predy! Waller, yonder clewline is flapping like a widow's tit – make it fast, man!'

As he gave his commands, Jack Stannard's eyes scanned the shore, east to west, then back, searching for any sign of movement, any sign of an attack. Christopher Eagle, that good and consummate seaman, was keeping the *Eagle* on station on the *Blessing*'s starboard quarter, two cables or so away, but Raker and Maddox, who had avoided their commander's company since Tynemouth, were thankfully away in the midst of the fleet. Like all the ships close inshore, the *Blessing* was struggling to maintain leeway. The conjunction of north-westerly breeze and a fresh flood tide pushed her inexorably toward the shore, and Jack was having to relieve his helmsmen every half-glass before they dropped with exhaustion. Not only were the elements challenging: the ship was deep in the water, laden down with her passengers and cargo, her leaks only making matters worse. Many of the passengers in question were on the upper deck, getting in the way of Jack's men, tripping over ropes, slipping or puking or pointing excitedly at the shore. The eighty soldiers entrusted to the *Blessing* were dressed simply, in shirts alone or gambesons also. Their breastplates, helmets, bills, halberds and pikes were in the hold until they were ready to disembark, or until an attack developed. But of the latter, there was no sign.

'An easy victory,' said the very young man at Jack's side, the only soldier on the ship already clad in part armour. 'Truly, the easiest. These Scots are cowards with no stomach for a fight. We'll burn Edinburgh by nightfall.'

'Perhaps you will, Captain Daubeney,' said Ryman, patiently. 'England has burned it before, and will burn it again, many times, I expect. But it signifies nothing.'

'How nothing, Sergeant Ryman?' said Daubeney, insisting on the rank that Thomas had not borne in nearly twenty years. 'Burning their principal city can hardly be a nothing. If the French burned London, it would not be a nothing.'

'A city is quite one thing. Houses can be rebuilt, warehouses refilled. But burning Edinburgh means nothing if you don't take the castle, up there on its rock. Many an English army has tried to do that, and precious few have succeeded. And even if you do take it, Captain, you've still got all of Scotland north of the Forth, here – hundreds of miles of empty land, thousands of wild heathen warriors who like nothing better than stirring the bloody guts of Englishmen with their blades.'

Daubeney shook his head very slightly. He was a tall, thin youth from Dorset, with a few wisps of hair, which he deigned to name a beard, protruding from his chin. He wore a splendid red doublet and carried what was evidently a new sword, with which, he proclaimed proudly, he intended to revive the martial reputation of his family, which had provided many great soldiers during the endless French wars of previous centuries. Daubeneys had been at Crécy, and Poitiers, and Agincourt, he said, and he fully intended to honour their memory by adding new glory to his name.

Daubeney had the eagerness of most very young warriors, and that urgency to spill blood characteristic of so many young men who were not long past crying at the sight of their own, seeping from childhood grazes. Since he came aboard at Tynemouth, Daubeney had listened dutifully to Ryman's tales of the old wars, nodding in the right places, expressing admiration when it was required. But Jack Stannard could see the blankness in Daubeney's eyes, and those tell-tale little shakes of the head which proclaimed that *yes, perhaps that was how you oldsters waged war, but we, the young, with our new weapons, our new tactics, and our new minds, know better.*

'Ho, Master! Yonder!'

The lookout's cry was shrill, and heard at once on the *Eagle* and several of the other ships in closest company to the *Blessing*. Jack ran to the little fo'c's'le, erected hastily when it was first known that two Dunwich ships were going to the war.

'What ho, George?'

George Copping, the lookout, a skinny lad of fifteen from Saint Peter parish who possessed the keenest sight in the town, pointed to the south-west, to the tight assemblage of masts, cranes and warehouses that stood on the shore, a mile or two distant from Edinburgh town.

'Yonder, Master Stannard. Two hulls, being towed out of the harbour.'

Jack screwed up his eyes. Yes, two hulls. Large ones, three hundred tons or so, but lower and narrower than many of the tall English ships. Galleasses, then, almost certainly. Cut for many gunports, even if they were presently closed. Longboats full of men, towing them out into the Forth. Hard work against the flood, but once they were in the stream, much easier.

Ryman and Daubeney joined him.

'What's afoot?' demanded the young captain.

'The Scots are moving two men-of-war,' said Jack. 'Big ones, the biggest in Leith haven, there. Intending to tow them upstream beyond our reach, I'll venture.'

'I recall the French king gave the Scots two great ships,' said Ryman, 'before their King James died.'

'The *Salamander* and *Unicorn*,' said Daubeney. He straightened himself and put on what he must have thought of as a stern expression. 'That's what they'll be, then. Our duty is clear, Master Stannard. We must stop them getting those ships away. We must attack. I can order you to attack by virtue of my commission. But I know it is your ship and you take it where you will, so I don't doubt you could somehow obstruct me if you wished it. But I say to you that it is your God-given duty, your duty to your king, to obey me, John Stannard.'

Jack bridled at the younger man's tone, but caught the amused look on Ryman's face, and said nothing. Instead, the master of the *Blessing* looked around, north and then east. The great royal men-of-war were too far offshore, covering what they expected to be an unopposed invasion, and would have to tack several times to try even to approach the fleeing Scots. But if they attempted to do so, their own transport fleet would obstruct their most direct course. The Scots were known to have formidable blockhouses upstream, where the Firth narrowed, and if they could get their two great ships beyond those, they would be safe.

Jack looked for a command flag, for some senior officer who could overrule Daubeney, but he could see none.

The lumbering London ships lay between him and the nearest royal vessel, and every other ship round about was taken up from the ports of the kingdom, just as his was, and had one order alone, which was to take the army into Leith haven and disembark it there. Lord Admiral Lisle had not anticipated that the Scots might try to save their largest men-of-war, and Jack knew that most shipmasters would not, of their own initiative, risk their precious hulls to attack without order. Every instinct he possessed told him to hold his course, to obey the letter of his orders and nothing more.

Not quite every instinct. There was one more, and it was encapsulated in the faces of Daubeney and Ryman, who were both looking at him intently. It was encapsulated in his remembrance of Alice. *Blood on the blade.* He turned and leaned on the starboard rail, closed his eyes, and offered up silent prayers to *Maria maris stella*, his name-saint John the Baptist, and Saint Florian, whose day it was. When he opened his eyes again, his mind was clear.

He turned back to the two soldiers, the old and the young.

'Very well, Captain Daubeney,' he said, 'you have your way. We attack.'

-

Christopher Eagle and the *Peter* followed the shouted order from the *Blessing*, as did the five ships nearest to her. The shout did not come from John Stannard, as no ship, other than his own and Eagle's, would follow the order of a mere Dunwich merchant, and such a young one at that. But although Daubeney was even younger than Jack, he was a soldier, and he was of high birth. Thus, in war, he commanded by natural right, and none of those within earshot would have dared challenge the order of their very temporary, very local general.

Thomas Ryman smiled to himself. Daubeney sounded the part, that much was certain, but whether he would be quite as convincing with a sword in his hand would soon be tested. *Oh, I have seen you before*, Ryman thought. *I have seen scores of you, veritable hundreds. The Lord Viscount Lisle, he was you, twenty years ago. And I have seen so many scores of you cut down, as was he, very nearly.*

Ahead, the Scots almost had the first of their ships out into open water. There were six large longboats ahead of her, the towropes taut as the men heaving on the oars struggled against the rushing tide, and another two at the stern to keep it from swinging. But each longboat had a score of men in it who were not at the oars, and even from a distance, Ryman could see that they carried a formidable array of weapons. Then there were the men on the upper deck and in the castles of the huge ship. He could count the best part of a hundred, but there were probably others below. Even with the numbers embarked in their own little fleet of seven ships, the odds would be close, and that was without counting the similar numbers of Scots who were bringing out the second ship. Daubeney was convinced that they would not come to the aid of their consort, once the English had fallen on it; surely, the young captain stated with confidence, the enemy's only concern would be to use the attack on the first ship as a diversion, enabling them to escape upriver. Indeed, Ryman had to admit that it was the most sensible course by far, the one that he himself would have taken. If the Scots committed their second ship in defence of their first, there would surely be ample time for the English royal ships to come up and overwhelm them both. But Ryman had fought with them and against them, and he had never once known any Scot to be sensible in war. They were the first to charge, the first to the breach, the first to propose attacking against the most impossible odds. If they had followed the sensible course at Flodden, King Jamie the Fourth would probably be reigning in Whitehall to that very day, rather than his corpse mouldering in a woodshed and his head being employed as a football.

'Sergeant Ryman,' said Daubeney, rudely tugging Tom away from his thoughts. 'We have no priest, but we have need of prayer. A friar surely knows all the words, even if he is not consecrated.'

'Not consecrated, and no longer a friar, Captain. There are no friars in England now.'

'I could order you.'

'Nowadays, I serve no army other than my own.' Thomas held the young man's hostile gaze for a moment, then smiled. 'But if I am the closest we have to a man of God – aye, well, then so be it, although I fear the chaplain of Kenninghall would be greatly amused by the notion.'

He went to the rail of the forward castle, and looked out over the expectant soldiers and sailors in the waist of the ship. Ryman raised his hand in the air, made the sign of the cross, and uttered the timeless words, '*In nomine patris, et filii, et spiritus sancti, amen.*' The men below crossed themselves and echoed the amen.

Ryman closed his eyes, and for a moment he thought himself back in the church of the Greyfriars in Dunwich, about to sing the hours of compline or nones with his fellow friars. He could see the faces of Anselm, Martin and the others as plain as if they stood before him. All gone now, scattered to the four corners of the kingdom or buried in some alien soil, the dream of a godly community scattered and buried with them. Then he heard the first faint sounds of defiant screams from the distant Scots, opened his eyes, and spoke loudly the words of the eighteenth psalm.

'*Diligam te Domine fortitudo mea. Domine petra mea et robur meum et salvator meus Deus meus fortis meus sperabo in eo scutum meum et cornu salutis meae susceptor meus...*'

Aboard the *Blessing*, all was silent, but for the whistling from the sails, the water breaking at the bow, the creak of the hull, the shrieks of the seabirds, and the mumbles of the few men who knew the words. John Stannard was not one of them, his schooling in theology having ended abruptly when he was torn from the embrace of Cardinal College. Despite Nolloth's misgivings, Jack had taken the *Blessing*'s helm himself, guiding the ship inexorably on a course toward the first Scots man-of-war. But as he listened to Ryman's recitation of the psalm, he prayed for Alice, for Tom and Meg, for all those he loved, even for his father, and for Dunwich. He prayed, above all, for victory.

And thus the *Blessing* sailed into battle.

Seven

'Set a course for the man-of-war, shipmaster,' said Daubeney, the excitement palpable in his young voice.

Jack bridled at being addressed thus aboard a Stannard ship, but he complied nonetheless. It was his own inclination too: let the ships following in their wake deal with the longboats, he and Eagle's *Peter* would make directly for the great prize that lay before them. There lay the glory, there the honour, there the reward.

As they closed, they heard ever more clearly the Scots' howls, screams and obscenities. Then, suddenly, there was a new sound, that of several loud cracks. Little spouts of water rose from the waves ahead of the *Blessing*. The enemy was firing on them.

'Not many guns,' said Ryman, who had concluded the psalm and returned to the poop. 'And they should have held fire until we were within range. Now, those who've fired won't be able to reload in time. Give thanks that they don't have any guns behind those gunports, otherwise they'd have shattered us long before now.'

The shots were joined within moments by arrows loosed by bowmen in the castles of the Scots' vessel. The bowmen were pitifully few, but they knew their business. There was a scream from the waist of the *Blessing*, and Jack saw one of Daubeney's soldiers turn sharply, an arrow having unluckily struck hard into his neck, only just above the protection of the gambeson. The man's fellows tried to hold him up, and one pulled the arrow from the flesh, only to unleash a fountain of blood that spattered a dozen men or more.

Now the Dunwich ships replied in kind. Daubeney had no archers or handgunners among his men on the *Blessing*, but his sergeant had two dozen of each aboard the *Peter*. As Jack brought the helm over to larboard, Eagle held his course, directly for the bows of the Scotsman, and the men on the poop of the *Blessing* heard the sergeant's successive commands – 'shoot!' 'give fire!'

A shot shattered part of the midships rail, and four Scots, who had been pressing hard against it, fell flailing into the sea, one of them minus the right leg that had been torn off by the ball fired from the *Peter*.

Aboard the *Blessing*, Daubeney's men were screaming defiance and readying their weapons. Their young captain moved among them, giving encouragement. Jack had most of his own men in the foreword castle, holding grappling irons. With a nod, Jack handed the helm to Nolloth, and went forward with Thomas Ryman.

'Your first battle,' said the old man.

'Not so,' said Jack. 'Was once in a fight with pirates off the North Foreland, and with a Scotsman off the Lemon and Oar in the last war.'

'Those were fights, Jack. Mere skirmishes. Yonder, a hundred or two Scotsmen. Some of them will have served as long as me. Mostly fighting each other, true, but there are few battles as ugly as Scot against Scot. They'll have as many scars, I'll wager. Beating off a few pirates is one thing, my boy. Today, you fight an army. Today, John Stannard, you discover what battle is truly like.'

The *Blessing* came in alongside, midships to the Scots' man-of-war. Jack's men tried to affix their grappling hooks to gunports, to wales or cables, to whatever might give them a hold. But all the while, enemy soldiers from the deck and castles above sent down arrows, ballast stones and pitchers of caulkers' tar, screaming obscenities as they did so. Daubeney's soldiers responded as well as they could, both with missiles and with choice oaths of their own, but the defenders held the advantage.

Jack looked astern. Eagle was up with the nearest of the longboats, and two Blakeney ships were tacking round to gain the advantage of the wind before attacking from the west. There, the odds were reversed, the longboats much lower in the water than the English ships, and unable to manoeuvre while their towlines remained secured to the man-of-war.

'God for King Harry! God for Saint George!' cried Daubeney, evidently fancying himself quite the Achilles.

Jack turned back, and saw that two hooks were securely fastened, one to the footings of the aftercastle, the other to one of the gunports. Two soldiers were trying to lever this open with halberds, and at last, it gave way. It was the last thing the men saw: seeing the danger, the Scots had massed men behind the port, and pikes impaled the two Englishmen. Daubeney ordered more men forward, while three of Jack's own men hauled themselves up the cable toward the aftercastle.

The Scots ship shuddered. Jack looked astern, and saw the reason at once: the longboats had cut their lines, the crews knowing it was the only chance they had to save themselves. The headway came off the great ship, and that served to pull forward the *Blessing*, which was still under sail and answering her helm. That, in turn, would swiftly bring the sterncastle of Jack's ship level with the waist of the Scotsman.

Ryman saw the danger and the opportunity at once.

'Captain Daubeney!' he shouted. 'Give me the rearmost score of your men!'

Daubeney, who was pushing forward to lead the assault on the open gunport, may have been young and raw, but he seemed to grasp Ryman's meaning at once.

'God go with you, Sergeant Ryman!' he cried.

Jack did not need to be told where his own duty lay.

'Blessings, with me!'

The seven or eight of his men who were nearest to him, armed with a rough seamen's arsenal of knives and clubs, formed a phalanx behind him. Together with Ryman's soldiers, they hurried to the aftercastle.

Slowly, the distance between the after part of the *Blessing* and the midships part of the Scotsman closed. It was easy range for bowmen now, and a Scot in the waist of the great ship loosed a quarrel that struck Oliver Chever, one of Jack's Dunwich men, hard in the chest. Jack Stannard had known him since childhood, and gasped as Chever took two short steps backward, rolled his eyes toward heaven, and fell dead to the deck.

In the blinking of an eye, the gap closed further, and now the soldiers on the two ships were at pike and bill range, then halberd, then sword. Ryman pressed forward, ducked under a Scots pike with the agility of a much younger man, drove his sword into the man's unarmoured groin, then pushed himself off the *Blessing*'s wale and onto the deck of the great ship. Five or six of Daubeney's men came with him at once, along with Jack and a couple of the Dunwich seamen.

'*Saint George*,' prayed Ryman, '*guard and keep young Jack this day. I would not want to have to report his death to his father, and face his rage at me.*'

With that, he traded blows with a Scotsman, evidently an officer of some sort, who wore a tabard bearing unfamiliar arms. The man was a good swordsman, controlled, cautious, but he fought with a Scots weapon, a basket-hilted broadsword, and in a Scots way, cutting for the flanks.

'*You have not been beyond the bounds of this kingdom, friend*,' thought Ryman, '*and that will be your undoing. Learn how the Italians wield a sword, and how they kill.*'

Ryman parried, feinted left, thrust right, then retreated, tempting his adversary into an advance. Despite his age, he was still nimble on his feet, and still able to recall the skills he had learned from Brambilla, the Milanese sword-master he fought with in the Pavia campaign. *Balance. Feint. Advance. Thrust. Advance again.*

The Scot drew back his right arm, thrusting forward the buckler on his left wrist to defend against any attack by the old soldier before him. A less experienced warrior would have moved right to avoid the inevitable cutting stroke from the broadsword. Ryman duly feinted right, but then shifted all his weight to his left side. Rather than thrusting again, he made a backhanded cut of his own, directly under his opponent's swordarm. The man wore no chain mail and only a flimsy gambeson, and Ryman's stroke sliced deeply into his flesh, bringing forth a tide of blood. The Scot looked down, horrified, and forgot to keep a tight grip on his buckler, which dropped. It was all the time Thomas Ryman needed to thrust upwards, into the neck and onward into the skull. The man fell dead at his feet.

'*Dona eis requiem, domine*,' said Ryman, and then, to his bloodied sword, 'Brave work, my angel'.

He glanced up quickly at the bulkheads of the steerage and fo'c's'le. No murderers, as far as he could see – the evil little swivel guns that could scour a deck and slaughter a score of men with one shot. Mayhap, in their haste to get the great ship to safety, the Scots had simply not enough time to fit them, Ryman thought, and thanked God if that were so.

A few feet away, John Stannard had one eye on potential Scots opponents, all of whom seemed to be engaged with Daubeney's men, and one on the movement of the ship beneath his feet. No towropes now secured the great ship – the *Unicorn*, it seemed, from the desperate shouts of some of the Scots defending her. The two longboats astern were very nearly back at the shore, while of the four ahead, one was losing a bitter battle with Eagle's *Peter*, while the other three were rowing west up the Firth as though pursued by the hounds of hell. One of the Blakeney ships was manoeuvring toward the starboard bow of the *Unicorn*, a contingent of fresh soldiers upon her upper deck, all eager to join the fray. If the battle was won quickly enough, it should be possible to take the great ship as a prize. But with every moment that passed, her bow was swinging a little further round with the tide, her head pointing for the shallow channel between a small island and the shore. And whereas the shore further east had been empty, this certainly was not. A large army of horsemen, perhaps five or six thousand strong, was massed along the coast, the saltire standards of Saint Andrew seemingly legion. By Jack's reckoning, there was less than an hour until the tide turned. Even if they secured the *Unicorn* within the next few minutes, it might already be too late to stop her drifting into the shallows, where she would run aground; and if they, the English, were not off her before that happened, they would certainly be cut to pieces by the vast army that awaited them. He had to tell this to Daubeney…

He saw the young captain emerge onto the upper deck by the foot of the aftercastle, he and his men having presumably fought their way through the main deck below. He saw the look of triumph on the face of a youth who knew he was about to taste his first victory. And he saw that expression turn in a moment to shock and impossible pain as a hackbutt ball struck him square in the chest from no more than two yards' range, close enough for it to punch through the breastplate. As blood began to flow through the hole and down over the polished metal, Daubeney mouthed what could only have been an *Ave Maria*, slumped to his knees, and fell dead upon the deck.

Ryman was close enough to the hackbutter to be able to turn against him and run his sword into his chest before the fellow could draw his dirk. Then he drew breath, and did what he knew he had to do: what he had done before, at the Sesia and Pavia fights.

'Daubeney's troop!' he cried. 'Rally to me!'

The authority of an old sergeant was unmistakeable, and sufficient. The remaining Scots were falling back toward the aftercastle, intent on a last stand. The English formed up behind Ryman, bracing themselves for the final assault.

Jack Stannard saw all this, but he had concerns of his own.

'Jed Nolloth!' he called to the helmsman of the *Blessing*.

The old man looked up and waved.

'All well, Master Stannard?'

'Not well, Jed. We're set fair to lose our prize. *Blessing*, too, if you don't unmoor from us and gain sea room.'

'I see that, the way the tide's running.'

'Well, then, Jed, here's what we need to do.'

–

In the minutes that followed, Thomas Ryman was only vaguely aware of the movements of the *Unicorn*, the *Blessing*, and the Blakeney ship. He was intent only on what lay ahead of him: a sterncastle full of armed Scotsmen, seemingly with no thought of surrender in their minds. But they seemed to have no thought of aggression either, beyond the usual curses and insults to their enemies' parentage and genitalia. They were loosing no arrows, firing no hackbutts, waiting to see what their enemies would do, waiting for the tide to carry them to their friends ashore. Daubeney, whose corpse had been taken into the shelter of the fo'c's'le, would undoubtedly have insisted on a frontal assault, a glorious and honourable attack, fighting to the last man if necessary. But Ryman saw no reason why more men should die that day on the deck of the *Unicorn*. No more Englishmen, at any rate.

'Corporal Payne,' he said.

Daubeney's corporal presented himself. He was a stolid man, near to thirty, who seemingly considered it a great mercy from the Lord that a man of Thomas Ryman's experience had miraculously appeared on their voyage, thereby sparing Payne, who had never seen battle before, the agonies of command following his captain's death.

'Sergeant?'

'Take two men below, Corporal. I want an inventory of what lies between decks.'

'An inventory?'

'Specifically, of barrels. Any containing water or beer, you can ignore. Inform me of any others, Corporal.'

'As you say, Sergeant Ryman.'

While Payne and his men were below, Ryman watched the *Blessing* part from the *Unicorn*, move a little way downwind, and then begin to turn north-east. He glanced to the forward castle, saw young Stannard watching her movements intently, and decided that whatever sea-business the lad was about was best left to him.

Payne returned, saluted, and reported. Ryman gave his orders, and as they were executed below deck, he watched the *Blessing* tack back toward the *Unicorn*, while off to larboard, the Blakeney ship had also moved away, and was turning to the north-east.

Payne returned and reported once again. Ryman nodded, and then took a step forward.

'Scotsmen!' he shouted.

At first, there was no pause in the cacophony of abuse coming from the aftercastle. Ryman raised his arms.

'Valiant Scots, who have fought well this day!'

One fellow, a gentleman and an officer by his garb, pushed his way through the throng and raised a hand for silence.

'I am Sir John Haliburton of Glenmalloch,' he said, in heavily accented but clear English. 'What say you, Englishman?'

'I am Thomas Ryman of Dunwich. A mere sergeant, the brave Captain Daubeney being slain.'

'Aye, he fought well, that laddie. I'll pray for his swifter passage through Purgatory.'

'As I shall pray for yours, Sir John.'

'I've no intention of entering Purgatory this day, Sergeant Ryman.'

'Oh, you will, Sir John. You'll either surrender this very instant, or you'll be in Purgatory long before the noonday bell.'

'Surrender, y'say? And why should we do that, sergeant? Ye've yet to storm this castle, our numbers are equal, and ye have no man of honour in command. Rather, I think ye should surrender to *me*, before we run onto Cramond shore and a braw welcome from Cardinal Beaton's army. A welcome that won't extend to you and your men, sergeant, ye ken.'

The Scots around him laughed heartily at that.

Ryman stared long and hard at Sir John Haliburton. A veteran warrior, by the look of him. A foe of honour, a man worthy of respect. A shame, then, to defeat him by dishonourable means. But such was the way of war, and always had been.

Ryman lifted his hand in a beckoning gesture. The two men who had gone below decks with Corporal Payne emerged from beneath the aftercastle, pouring a trail of powder from a small barrel. Some of the Scots made to loose arrows or fire hackbutts, for the men were barely feet from them and certain targets. But Haliburton raised his hand to prevent any attack, and the two men reached their own ranks safely.

'Perhaps now, Sir John, you'll reconsider your opinion of surrender? There are a half-dozen barrels of powder directly beneath where you stand. I have only to light the powder trail, and you and your men will see the face of Saint Peter. Or else the fallen archangel below, perchance.'

There was alarmed murmuring among those Scots who understood English, and triumphant jeering from the men behind Ryman.

'Ye're a madman!' cried Haliburton. 'Blow us up, and ye'll kill yerselves, or else fire the ship, by all that's holy!'

'Well, now, Sir John, by my reckoning, the amount of powder should be right to blow up the castle on which you stand, and no more. But, you see, my problem is this, Sir John, and it's a rare one… I don't know the sort of powder you Scots employ. If it's weaker than I think, it should still bring down the deck beneath your feet, leaving us to fall on you. If it's stronger… I'll leave that to God, Sir John.'

Ryman gestured to Payne, who went below decks beneath the forward castle. Moments later, the corporal reappeared, carrying a lighted brand. He passed it to Ryman, who held it above the powder trail.

'Fire,' he said. 'Unpredictable business, fire. Why, Sir John, even if I don't apply this light to the fuse, who's to say that a spark won't fall from it by accident?'

'Ye're bluffing, Englishman!'

'Bluffing, you say, Sir John? Am I indeed? Daubeney's troop, take cover below decks!'

The soldiers behind Ryman jostled and shoved to get to safety, as far forward and as far below decks as they could manage. That left the old sergeant of Dunwich alone in the waist of the ship. He glanced behind to check that all the men were secure, and saw Jack Stannard and his seamen, looking down on him in horror from the fo'c's'le. Ryman understood enough of sailors to know that not one of them would have treated fire so irreverently, nor deliberately set off powder in the belief that it would wreck only one part of a ship, not sink the whole.

Perhaps Sir John Haliburton of Glenmalloch was right: perhaps Thomas Ryman really was a madman. That would explain the nightmares he suffered nearly every night, and why, six years after he left the dissolved Greyfriars, he still woke unfailingly just before three, ready to perform the office of Lauds.

On the sterncastle, the Scotsman was in urgent conference with his officers and sergeants. Finally, he stepped down into the waist of the ship, inclined his head toward Ryman, and without a word, drew his sword, presenting it hilt first.

Ryman took it with his left hand, and with his right, threw the burning brand into the sea.

On the fo'c's'le, Jack and his men broke out into cheers, joined within moments by Daubeney's soldiers as they emerged from below.

The *Unicorn*, greatest of Scotland's royal warships, was theirs.

Eight

The *Blessing*, the *Peter*, and one of the Blakeney ships, had the *Unicorn* under tow, and were moving her north-east, toward Lord Lisle's squadron of royal men-of-war. The wind had come slightly more westerly, and the fresh ebb tide further aided their passage. Truly, thought Jack Stannard as he looked out from the sterncastle of the *Unicorn*, God was with them this day.

To the south, the army was starting to disembark along the coast between Leith and what he now knew to be Cramond Island. The mounted Scots army that had been drawn up on the shore when they attacked the *Unicorn* was nowhere to be seen; either moving east to position itself between the English and Edinburgh, said Ryman, or retreating west toward Stirling, awed by the sheer size of the host under Lord Hertford's command.

Only one concern marred Jack's contentment in the scene. Among the most laggardly of the entire English fleet, very nearly the most seaward of the host of ships making for the shore, were the other two vessels that he had taken out of the Blyth, Maddox's *Grace* and Raker's *Virgin*.

'The saints know what they're about,' said Jack to Ryman. 'If I were in their position, I'd want to show myself forward in all business, to redeem myself in the eyes of the Lord Admiral. If they still think to play the sluggards, then they're at a fool's game. Who will note or care that they hang back so far? How can they undermine what we've done in taking this ship? How does this diminish me before Lisle, as Raker threatened to do? Damn them, *what are they about*?'

The old man shrugged.

'The ways of Southwold have always been a mystery,' he said. 'A seething throng of rogues, whores, malcontents and jobanowls. Walberswick, little better.' Ryman chuckled. 'And no, John Stannard, I know those words should never be uttered by a man who once took the cowl. The penances I would have had to suffer in the Greyfriars... But as you say, Jack, it matters nothing against the possession of this hull. A pretty prize to lay before King Harry.'

Jack smiled in his turn. A pretty prize indeed. And after the war was done.

He pointed away to the north, toward the rocky island that his father's chart identified as Inchcolm. A group of buildings was coming into view: a small abbey, by the looks of it, lying on a low spit of land between two headlands. The Scots still had monasteries, and there were clear signs of life in this one.

Too many signs of life. A half-dozen longboats were pulling away from the beach below the abbey, the same number emerging from the lee of the westerly headland. Each was crowded with two or three dozen warriors. And all of them were setting course for Christopher Eagle's *Peter*.

'Madness,' said Ryman. 'Even if they take the *Peter*, what can they hope to do? They'll never retake this hull before our own ships can come up!'

Jack was barely listening.

'Smith, there!' he shouted. 'Ned Smith! Hoist red at the main!'

The seaman, a stout, dependable fellow from All Saints parish, ran to comply. Already, a red flag was breaking out from the main of the *Blessing*: the signal agreed in Lord Lisle's orders for all ships who saw the colour to rally to the defence of those flying it. The towline came away from the *Blessing*'s stern. Nolloth would do his best, but he would have to tack back to close the *Peter*, and the *Blessing* was no greyhound. As for Ryman and Jack, they were powerless. The *Unicorn* had no momentum of her own, and unless help came swiftly, the Scots were bound to take the *Peter*, then turn their attention to recapturing their former flagship.

But help should come swiftly. The royal ships were still well to the north-east, toward the Fife shore; perhaps so far away that they would not be able to see the distress flags on the English ships. But the nearest vessels of the landing fleet could use the wind which so impeded Nolloth and the *Blessing*. Above all, Raker and Maddox could not fail to see the red flag, and were bound to be up with the Dunwich ship before the worst of the Scots strength could come against her.

'Put your helms over,' murmured Jack. 'For God and Suffolk!'

'No God in Southwold, Jack,' said Tom Ryman, 'only devils.'

With that, he went down into the waist of the *Unicorn* to give orders to Daubeney's men ahead of the anticipated onslaught of the enemy. On the sterncastle, Jack prayed to every suitable saint he could think of, to the shade of Alice, to the Archangel Michael, and to *Maria stella maris*,

Mary, Star of the Sea. But still Raker and Maddox did not move. Some of the ships inshore of them were responding now, including a couple of the Blakeney vessels that had supported them so valiantly in the previous fight, but they could not possibly reach the *Peter* in time.

Jack watched as the inevitable unfolded. The first Scots boats came in under the stern of the *Peter*, while others secured to her bows. Only a dozen soldiers had been left aboard her, to assist Eagle's men with the heavy work of towing; after all, no attack was anticipated. Those men, and the seamen of Dunwich, resisted valiantly. Across the water, Jack could hear the shouts, the clashes of metal on metal, the screams of the wounded and dying. But with every minute that passed, there were more and more Scots on the deck of the *Peter*, and fewer and fewer Englishmen. He could not see when the last man fell, nor whether that man was Christopher Eagle, his father's friend. But fall Eagle must have, shortly before the flames began to spit out of the hold of the *Peter* and set light to the shrouds and canvas. The last Scots were back in their boats well before the *Peter* was fully alight. Now their longboats were setting course for the immobile *Unicorn*. Nolloth was struggling to bring the *Blessing* as close to the wind as he dared, but the Dunwich ship was far too many cables away. And still Raker and Maddox did not move.

Jack looked down into the waist, and saw that Ryman had the soldiers ready at the wales. The Scots would find a stiffer reception on their erstwhile flagship than they had met aboard the *Peter*, but they were able to move independently, whereas the *Unicorn* could not. No matter how well the defenders fought, there would be only one conclusion, especially if the Scots decided simply to fire the great ship, burning alive every man aboard. A part of

Jack wished for such a fate, for then he would be with Alice again, to run and laugh with her for all eternity. But a larger part of him, a much larger part, wanted to live.

The first Scottish arrows struck the timber of the sides or deck. One soldier, a fellow of no more than eighteen or nineteen, fell dead, killed by a lucky shot from a hackbutt. Ryman murmured encouragement to the men, walking slowly up and down their ranks. On land, he would have taken these odds, would have been confident of the victory. But the sea was a cursed, strange world, where no man of sense had any right to be. He could see the first of the Scots boats pulling round to the stern of the *Unicorn*, hoping to repeat the tactic that had overwhelmed the *Peter*.

But something was not right. The outermost Scots boats were not pressing home their attack on the *Unicorn*. Far from it; they were turning away, making either for Inchcolm or the Fife shore.

'There, Sergeant Ryman!' cried Jack from the sterncastle. 'There, by God!'

He was pointing off to the east. Ryman pulled himself up onto the fo'c's'le, looked out, and muttered a prayer of thanks to the Virgin. There, approaching rapidly, the water spilling from their slender bows, came two of Lord Lisle's galleys, the Saint George pennants streaming in the westerly breeze. The larger he recognised as the *Galley Subtile*, the most elegant of all the king's men-of-war. The oars cut the water easily, in time with the now audible beat of the drums, driving the galley against wind and tide in a way that would have been impossible for any ship. These were good crews, Ryman told himself, trained crews, for the young John Dudley whose life he once saved had grown into a man who took pains over all sorts of business, not least the business of war and the office of Lord High Admiral of England. A cloud of smoke billowed from the bow of the more southerly galley, followed a moment later by the blast of the chaser cannon. A waterspout rose half a cable from one of the Scots longboats. The galley had fired from beyond her effective range, but Ryman knew the gun captain would not have expected a hit. The point of the shot was to announce the galleys' arrival and terrify the enemy, and in that, it was succeeding. The longboat crews that, only moments before, had been competing with each other to secure to the *Unicorn*, were now equally enthusiastic to free themselves and row as though the devil himself pursued them.

The most easterly of the Scots longboats was making for Inchcolm, directly across the path of the *Galley Subtile*. The latter's captain eschewed expending powder as his companion had done. Instead, Ryman heard the drumbeat increase its rhythm, and the English oarsmen responded. A few of the Scots, realising their imminent fate, stood and jumped over the side of their craft. A few others raised their hands, as though they could somehow push back the instrument of death that closed upon them with terrifying speed. The bow of the galley struck the longboat, briefly pushing it forward like a stone being swept by a brush. Then the galley drove clean through the hull, throwing the Scots into the water. Those who could swim were picked off by archers from the galley's deck. Those who could not splashed, screamed, and then sank, the waters of the Firth closing over them as they perished. The remaining Scots boats were redoubling their efforts to flee the scene as swiftly as they possibly could. Thomas Ryman crossed himself, murmured an

Ave Maria, commended the lost souls to God, and then offered up a prayer of thanks. The great prize, the *Unicorn*, remained England's, and he and John Stannard lived to return to Dunwich.

Thomas Ryman smiled, and then began to sing the old, familiar hymn of thanksgiving, as he had so often on battlefields and in the church of the Greyfriars.

'*Te deum laudamus! Te dominum confitemur...*'

We praise thee, oh Lord.

There was another voice, joining his, the flawless tenor voice of a much more proficient singer.

'*Tibi omnes angeli; tibi caeli et universae potestates...*'

Thomas Ryman, the erstwhile friar, and John Stannard, the erstwhile choirboy, sang their song of victory.

-

Edinburgh burned.

From the deck of the *Blessing*, sailing slowly back out into the Forth with a score of the other ships, John Stannard and Thomas Ryman could see the flames rising from the houses, all the way down the great hill to the old royal abbey of Holyrood, at the foot, which burned too. The wind was south-westerly, and that carried the smells of a city ablaze, the sounds of collapsing houses. But there were also other sounds: the unmistakeable blasts that signified exchanges of artillery fire.

'You wish you were up there,' said Jack to his old mentor.

'If I were thirty years younger, perhaps,' said Ryman. 'But it'll be a hard business now, Jack. I've been in Edinburgh. High, narrow houses, with alleys snaking between them. A killing ground every yard or two. They'll be fighting from house to house, Daubeney's lads and all the rest of them, never knowing if there's a man with a blade round the next corner or at the top of each stair, or someone about to drop a cannonball on you from three storeys up. And then there's a steep hill up to the castle gate, with the enemy able to fire down on you all the time. Burning houses just makes assaulting it more difficult – gives the Scots gunners clearer fields of fire. Lord Hertford and his generals should know that.'

'But we'll win?'

Ryman pointed away toward the city, to the wisps of smoke beginning to rise from the crowded mass of buildings upon the hill.

'There are different kinds of winning, Jack. Flodden was one kind, this another. The city is ours already, but if we don't take the castle, the Scots will claim a victory of their own.'

At first, the Scots had put up barely any defence of Edinburgh. Cardinal Beaton's army made a show at the stream called the Water of Leith, but after a cursory exchange of a few shots, it melted away. The Scots regent, the Earl of Arran, also abandoned his city to its fate, and the English secured the port of Leith, enabling them to land their remaining men, supplies and heavy guns with impunity. Jack had brought the *Blessing* alongside there, having handed the *Unicorn* over to a crew appointed by the Lord Admiral, and disembarked Daubeney's troop, who awaited a new captain. He and Ryman took mass in a chapel that the soldiers chose not to burn, and offered prayers for the eternal souls of Christopher Eagle and the good men of Dunwich who had fallen with him. Jack also paid the priest to say further prayers for Alice. After all, if God ultimately gave the victory to the Scots' ally, the Most Christian King of France, then perhaps Scottish prayers would be more efficacious at speeding her soul from Purgatory than English ones.

By the time the English army assaulted the city itself, the Scots were ready to put up a stiffer resistance, and that was what Jack and Ryman could see from the *Blessing*. Above all, there was the castle, perched formidably on its dark rock, inviolate above the smoke and flames rising from the town below.

'Perhaps it will be enough to bring them to terms,' said Jack.

'Perhaps,' said the old soldier.

The *Blessing* moved out into the fullness of the great Firth, Jack setting course for the squadron of royal men-of-war, which lay at anchor off the shore of Fife. There was no need for the Dunwich vessel to sail so close to the great ships, but Jack had two reasons for so doing. He told himself it was not vanity, but he wished to look once more at the *Unicorn*, the prize that he had been so instrumental in taking. There she lay, shipwrights swarming over her, erecting topmasts and taking down the Scots royal arms at the stern, ready for their replacement by the emblems of Henry of England.

The second reason became apparent as Jack helmed the *Blessing* close to Lord Lisle's flagship, the *Rose Lion*.

He thought back to the summary trial in the great cabin of the flagship. To his evidence, so damning. To the testimonies of the other witnesses, notably those who could be considered neutrals – Blakeney men, Corporal Payne, masters of other ships in the invasion fleet. To the supine, mumbled defence put up by the accused. To the wrath of the Lord Admiral against them, and, by contrast, Lord Lisle's very public and undoubtedly genuine praise for Jack's skill and courage, echoing his earlier remarks in private, in his own cabin, when he had even raised a glass to toast John Stannard of Dunwich.

To the chilling finality of the sentence.

The *Blessing* took in her topsails and lowered her flag in salute to the royal flagship. A few of the men on her deck looked down curiously at the Dunwich ship, so small and plainly adorned among such proud men-of-war. The *Rose Lion* did not respond to John Stannard's gesture of honour. But then, it did not need to: the best salute that Jack could possibly receive dangled upon ropes from the main yard of the flagship, swaying to and fro in the breeze.

The corpses of Maddox of Walberswick and Raker of Southwold.

Part Two

The Doom Of Dunwich

May to June 1544

Oft gazing on thy craggy brow
We muse on glories o'er.
Fair Dunwich! Thou art lowly now,
Renown'd and sought no more...
How proudly rose thy crested seat
Above the ocean wave;
Yet doom'd beneath that sea to meet
One wide and sweeping grave! ...
Those through each forgotten age
With patient care will look,
Will find her fate in many a page
Of time's extended book.

Agnes Strickland (1796-1874)

Nine

The Doom painting displayed above the Rood screen of Saint John's church in Dunwich, on the tympanum at the top of the chancel arch, was renowned far beyond the Palesdyke. Men and women came to look upon it from all over Blything Hundred and the distant parts of High Suffolk, even from as far afield as Norfolk or Essex. Such strangers barely noticed the usual, expected features of a Rood: the Cross itself, and the wooden figures of Christ, John the Baptist and the Virgin Mary. Instead, they were always struck first and foremost by the great devil, its fiery wings outstretched, so huge, so lifelike, so malignant, its brilliant red eyes burning into the souls of the sinners below it in the nave. Women in the congregation had been known to faint, men to fall to their knees, trembling and frantically thumbing their paternosters in fear of the hellfire. To that very day, there was still talk of a Frisian helmsman, stormbound in Dunwich harbour in the old King Henry's time, who gazed into the eyes of the Doom's Lucifer for a little too long and was struck blind upon the spot. But for the parishioners of Saint John's, who looked upon it every week, the devil was familiar, reassuring, very nearly an old friend. The devil of the Doom had always been there. No: what terrified the folk of Dunwich was the scene behind him, the hell playing out beneath Beelzebub's long, black wings. The long-dead artist had conjured up the image of a great blue wave, rearing up to Satan's very shoulders. A vast blue wave breaking on the shore before it, sweeping all away. There were the church towers falling as the inexorable waters struck them, there the ships overwhelmed and sunk, there the tiny bodies of honest citizens drowning in the wall of water, there the souls of the already dead awaiting judgement. It seemed as if the relentless ocean conjured up by the devil was even about to consume Christ, the Baptist and the Virgin, a paradox that had caused many vicars of Saint John's endless difficulty in their sermons. This was the image that gave the children of the town nightmares, at least until they grew old enough to make their peace with the ancient daubing above their heads.

With the Doom of Dunwich.

–

Jack Stannard thought upon the Doom as he stepped out of his house, the home he had formerly shared with Alice. Joan Cowper, the thickly-built, square-faced housekeeper to the Stannards, warned him of the folly of going out on such a day, but he had been ignoring Joan's advice for as long as he could remember. Even so, she was right in one thing: the rain was parney, as Suffolk goodwives like Joan termed a torrential downpour, the rapidly growing puddles possibly concealing God knew what treacherous holes in the road, but that was not the only reason why Jack dared not look round. He knew Meg would be at the window, squinting through the broken shutter slat, staring after him accusingly even as she stroked Tiberius, the large, shapeless and pungent Stannard dog. Unlike her brother, Meg had no fear of their grandfather, saw no reason why she should not accompany her father to visit him, and saw through Jack's feeble lie, parroting Joan Cowper, about the conditions underfoot and the risk of catching a cold from the deluge.

Instead, all Meg Stannard's fears were for the Doom.

'Miriam Day says the Doom is ungodly,' she had said that morning, as they left Saint John's after Mass, wrapping stoles around them against the rain. 'Miriam Day says they're taking down Roods in Kent, and burning them. Miriam Day says Candlemas and creeping to the cross on Good Friday are sinful, too. Miriam Day says—'

'Miriam Day listens too much to her brother,' said John. 'And whatever they do in Kent, or whatever Jack Day hears in London, doesn't mean it'll happen in Dunwich.'

'But Miriam Day says—'

There was a time when Jack Stannard had hung on every word John Day said, too, even though his friend was younger than him. When they were children, the two Jacks spent many hours at the Dain Quay or the East Quay, playing hide-and-seek amid the bales and in the warehouses, watching the ships as they loaded and unloaded. They approached sailors, eager to pick up words of their many languages, to beg for scraps of stockfish or swigs of ale and wine, and to question them for news from the lands beyond the sea. But whereas Jack Stannard always sought news of the wars, and the doings of the Emperor and the King of France, John Day craved only word of Luther's latest protestations. The day when a Bremen cog berthed at the East Quay, and a sailor from her gave John a copy of the rogue monk's *Small Catechism*, was the happiest Jack Stannard had ever seen his friend. At ten, John Day could hold forth on the falsehoods of transubstantiation with the ferocity of a hell-fire Lollard.

Now, years later, he printed those ideas upon a press in Saint Sepulchre-without-Newgate in the city of London, always somehow staying just on the right side of the law. But from time to time he came back to Dunwich to visit his widowed mother, to infect his much younger siblings with his heresies, and to rail against the great Doom painting in Saint John's church.

Jack Stannard's house lay just behind Cock Hill, half way along the road that ran from the market place, in the very middle of the little town, to the Dain, the harbour at the northern end of it. This day, though, he took neither familiar direction. Instead, he walked west, along Maison Dieu Lane, in the shadow of the low hill of the same name. The house that adjoined his own was but newly ruined, the Woodthorpes having removed themselves to Lowestoft no more than five years past. Gulls now sat in its empty windows, watching him malevolently as he passed. Beyond that, the house that had once belonged to Alice's family, the Easeys, was no more than its bare walls, and on the other side of the lane, on the lower slope of the hill, the only traces of the houses that once stood there were overgrown mounds and the forlorn fruit trees that were once the pride of several gardens. As a child, when the Iceland fishery was its height and Dunwich seemed reborn, he could remember this street full of houses, and crowded from end to end with carts and wagons. Shop-fronts stretched almost down to the Bridge Gate, their gaily painted signs swinging noisily in the breeze, their smells by turns intriguing and disgusting to a young child. But there were no shops here now. Even the Maison Dieu itself, the ancient half-timbered hospital that stood beneath the hill named after it, under the northern slope of Dunwich Cliff, was decayed, with great holes in its thatch from the last storm sealed only by thin canvas, and its small chapel all but a ruin.

Jack turned right and made his way out of the town proper, onto Saint James Street, the last vestige of the Roman road that ran due west from the fort those mighty legends of old established at Dunwich. There were many more buildings here, the homes and businesses of those who thought that this far inland, at least, would be safe from the sea until Doomsday. The rain was easing, and folk were appearing from their doors, resuming their normal trades and activities. He doffed his woollen hat to Goodwife Vicary, who was preparing to beat a sodden mat upon the step of the Pelican in its Piety. Her early customers, old Spatchell included, would already be quaffing their wooden pots of ale, no doubt having made excuse of the need to shelter from the rain. Jack stopped and exchanged a few words with Valkenburg, the Brabanter who brewed Dunwich's beer, a jolly and well-liked fellow whose English was better than many of those who were Dunwich born and bred.

Jack realised he was slowing his pace, pausing to look at stalls from which he had never bought and never would. He knew why. Every step nearer to his father was a little purgatory, a very little way closer to discovering which Peter Stannard awaited him this day. But no matter what mood the old man was in, one thing above all was certain: they would disagree about something. Jack sighed loudly enough to attract a curious stare from the cobbler whose wares he had been examining for a fraction too long, and moved on.

A little further down the street, and despite the sodden ground, Venison sat in his usual place, on the step by the water-trough, emitting his familiar stench.

'God's blessing upon you, Master Stannard,' said Venison.

This little miracle always intrigued Jack; no matter how silently he approached, or how recently he had washed, the ancient blind beggar always knew it was him.

'And upon you, Venison.'

'So you're set for the war with France, then, your uncle Spatchell says.'

Dunwich had no secrets, not even from its beggars.

'That's why I go to my father.'

'They say, though, that the Scots haven't been defeated. They say we may have burned Edinburgh and half their borderlands, but our army has withdrawn, their regent still rules, their queen is still set fair to marry the little French prince, yet our king is still determined to invade France instead. Would that be the weight of it, Master Stannard?'

Jack stifled a laugh.

'You should be at Greenwich Palace, Venison, counselling the king. You're wasted upon Dunwich.'

'I ponder upon the injustice of that in every waking hour, good sir. But would you bestow your bounty upon me this day, Master Stannard, just as your late wife was good enough to bestow alms on me in her will?'

Jack smiled at the memory of Alice's kind-heartedness. There were fewer beggars now than in the Dunwich of his childhood, when the short-lived prosperity of the Iceland fishery brought a steady stream of them into the town. But then the king closed the monasteries, far and away the best market for Friday fish, and both the beggars and most of the peterboats vanished almost overnight. Venison was the only one who still remained in Dunwich all year round, never chancing to the greater fortunes of Yarmouth, Lowestoft or Ipswich. Alice had always shown a particular kindness to him; as she said, the saint after whom she was named was the patron of the blind, so it was only proper for her to regard Venison as her charge.

Jack reached into his purse, pulled out a farthing, and bent down to give it to the old man, who turned the coin over and over in his hand.

'Not clipped,' said the beggar. 'Bounty indeed, then. Bless you, John Stannard, and my respects to your father.'

Jack nodded, even though he knew the blind man could not see the gesture.

He walked on, struggling through a flock of sheep being driven down from the edge of Westwood to the market square. But that was not the only reason why his pace slowed as he neared his destination, nor why his heart seemed to weigh heavier with every step he took. One thought was in his mind; or rather, one question. A question he had asked himself countless times, from the time of his very first memories. A question that had gained a new and terrifying currency since the onset of the most dreadful and Biblical of afflictions.

What was his father's temper today?

Ten

Jack Stannard went through the doorway of the place that had been his father's home for six years. It was a large building, shaped like a church with an apse at the east end, but it was no longer what it had been. The western range was in ruins, and the only figure in sight was that of the porter, Franklin, a corpulent creature with the look of a stuck pig. He said not a word to Jack, merely nodding his head toward the door into the infirmary hall, at the east end of the church building.

The old man sat upon his bed, placed in one of the alcoves lining the old wall. The upper part of the alcove contained a picture of Saint John Schorne, surrounded by candles; Peter Stannard had convinced himself that the saint's considerable reputation for curing gout might somehow extend to his own case, although Jack found it difficult to comprehend either the notion or the efficacy of a saint who hailed from, of all places, Buckinghamshire, who had never been formally canonised, and who, moreover, was said to have cast the devil into a boot. The thought of the vast black demon which adorned the Doom of Dunwich being crabbed and confined within a single clog stretched Jack's credulity, but it was Alice who had given voice to his doubts, some months earlier. Even if John Schorne really had brought off such a miracle, she said, surely the Devil must have escaped thereafter, else why was there still so much evil in the world? That being so, Schorne could hardly rank with the most successful or powerful of the saints, and was not worth having a single candle lit in his honour. Peter Stannard, though, begged to differ, as he did on so very many matters.

Even though there was no need for such a garment indoors, the old man still wore the threadbare broadcloth gown in which he had swaggered when it was new, and he was in his pomp. He was reading the copy of Livy that had engrossed him for months. He turned a page, albeit with great difficulty.

'Thought you'd have come yesterday, boy,' said Peter Stannard, without looking up.

The old man's voice was still strong, even if his ancient body, long past its fiftieth year, was not.

'Too much work on the top timbers of the new ship, Father. Hard, slow work, too, with all the rain this last week. But needs be done.'

Jack pulled up a stool and sat in front of his father.

'Ah, the new ship. Always the new ship.' Peter Stannard put down his book and looked at his son. His voice was a strangled rasp, a mere remnant of the strident bark he had once possessed. 'As it should be. As I'd have it, too, if she was mine in more than name. Nolloth will have her ready by the autumn, or for when the summons comes?'

The same question as always, which John would grace with the same answer as always. Thus far, his father's temper seemed equable enough, a fair and gentle breeze. But, as at sea, a sudden storm could blow up at any moment.

'She'll be ready, Father, whether the summons comes or not. You sent the letters?'

Peter Stannard nodded.

'I did. And the summons will come, boy. As Saint Peter's my judge, it'll come, after the number of letters I've dictated to Franklin since you were last here. He says it's beyond his duty, not his place, and more such nonsense, but a few gleaming groats change his tune. So aye, the letters were sent. To Girdler and Clampe, to bestir themselves if they want another term as bailiffs. Even from this place, I can still make or break them as that, and they know it. To Browne and Coppyn, for there'll be another Parliament soon, that's certain according to George Barne, and they'll be our members, no question of it. Add your new favour from the Lord Admiral, and, God willing, Ryman's efforts with the Howards when he returns to Kenninghall, and there'll be no doubt of the issue. We'll deliver a ship for the king's campaign in France this summer, as long as your sot of a cousin brings *Osprey* home in time. Then we'll have the new ship ready for next year, so that if and when the king calls for it – and it'll be when, for certain – Dunwich can deliver him a true man-of-war. Sailing agin the French. A proper enemy for you, eh, boy?'

His father raised his right hand, and jabbed it decisively at his son, just as he had done so often when Jack was young. But in those days, his father's hands had ended in fingers.

Peter Stannard was the last leper of Dunwich.

Jack knew that his father spent many waking hours searching his memory for any clue as to when and how he might have caught his terrible condition, which seemed to have all but gone from England. Although he had no evidence at all to support his supposition, Peter Stannard had ultimately settled upon a passing encounter with a Moorish merchant at Antwerp, twelve or thirteen years earlier, about the time when the king put aside Queen Catherine in favour of the Boleyn woman. It was no more or less plausible than the opinion held by Jack's sister Agatha, namely that the illness was God's righteous judgement upon their father for his manifold sins: for the various kinds of abuses he had inflicted upon the two of them, for the murder (if popular rumour was to be believed) of his simpleton brother, and for countless other crimes, any one of which would be sufficient to condemn him to eternal hellfire.

'As you say, Father,' said Jack, neutrally. 'God willing.'

Jack nodded, and prayed that the old man was right. But it all hinged upon Dunwich being able to supply a ship that summer of the year 'forty-four, to the second great campaign upon which the king had embarked. And with the *Blessing* too leaky and worn out for immediate service, that meant everything depended upon Jack's cousin, Simon Bulbrooke, and his ability to bring the *Osprey* back from a curtailed voyage to Oslo.

'What's the talk in Dunwich town, then, boy? When I ask him, Franklin does no more than grunt.'

Jack felt the tightness in his muscles ease a little. The tattle of the streets should be safe ground.

'Of the war, mainly – the usual variance between those who shout that the king will conquer France in a week, and those who fear the French army wading ashore on Kingsholme on the next flood tide. Otherwise, Goody Cowper says it's common talk in the market square that Southwold conspires against us again,' said Jack. 'It seems Raker's son is to be made bailiff this year coming, despite his age, solely to spite us—'

Peter Stannard frowned at the mention of Southwold and the Raker family, a frown which heralded a flash of his old temper.

'Christ's blood, boy, Southwold has conspired agin Dunwich since the first day of God's creation! My father told me how they crowed when Harry Seventh gave them a borough charter and our rightful rank as a royal harbour, saying they were now equal to Dunwich and would soon be greater. A turd in their teeth for that, as good old Christopher Eagle would have said. And Martin Raker should have hanged years ago… as for the runt Stephen, also…'

The old man's voice faltered, and he looked into the flames of the feeble fire in the opposite wall.

Jack moved the stool to be more in front of him, but his father's eyes were blank. Just then, though, one of the other patients, a consumptive from Peter's parish called Mulsford, came into the infirmary and made his way toward the chapel, behind the decayed wooden screen that divided the building in two. The former lazar hospital of Saint James had to take all sorts and conditions now, thus putting it in direct competition with the Maison Dieu; many, though, preferred the latter, simply because they would not be in the company of Peter Stannard.

Leprosy, and the Stannards, cast long shadows.

Mulsford nodded to Jack, then went into the chapel. Through the door, Jack could see him kneel at an altar on the far side of the chapel and begin his private devotions, fingering his paternoster as he whispered and coughed out his prayers.

The sound seemed to bring back Peter Stannard from wherever his mind had gone.

‘The children,’ he said, amiably enough. ‘They continue well? Young Tom grows strong?’

‘They do, and he does. Meg sends you her love.’

‘A good girl, is Meg. Proud. Questioning. Make a decent match for her, in the fullness of time. Although I think she’ll lead any husband a merry dance – if you can even find one who won’t be frit shitless by a girl who can read.’

This had been at Peter Stannard’s insistence: if it was good enough for the Princess Elizabeth, he said, it was good enough for Margaret Stannard of Dunwich, too. As much as he could, he helped her with her learning, to the horror and disgust of Jack’s sister, Agatha.

‘And,’ said the old man, ‘good girl as she is, she comes to visit her old grandfather. Dutiful, she is. But I don’t see enow of your Tom, and may Satan take the black heart of that ungrateful sister of yours—’

The distant but ever-present storm was threatening to break. Jack needed to steer a steady course now.

‘Agatha is—’

‘Ungrateful, I say. Unforgiving. Oh, I sinned agin her mightily. Agin you, too. You know that. Our Lord knows it, and see how God has punished me. I’ve no need to go into John’s church ever again, boy, for the Doom of Dunwich has come upon me, and enveloped me in its wings.’ Peter Stannard’s voice was even more strained. ‘But your sainted sister – I tell you, boy, she can’t see what I am now, only what I was then. She don’t hear the prayers I offer up, imploring God’s forgiveness for my sins agin her. A heart as hard and immovable as the Kingsholme, that one.’

Jack had no response. He had lost count of the number of times he had heard the same litany from his father, and strangely similar sentiments from the lips of his sister. It was very true that Agatha could only see what Peter Stannard had once been. Jack believed that his father was genuinely repentant, and posed no threat to Meg. In this, Alice, who always saw the best in everyone, had seconded him, saying that her father-in-law would dare not do anything to offend her, the namesake of the saint upon whose intercession he depended. (Her confidence on this point had led to many terrible arguments between the sisters-in-law.) The message had been reinforced by successive priests of Saint John's, who reminded Jack in the confessional of Matthew Six and Nineteen, Luke Seventeen, the Lord's Prayer itself, and all the other texts urging good Christians to forgive those who sinned against them. Besides, the Stannard business still depended greatly upon Peter Stannard's name, reputation and contacts; Jack could afford no breach between himself and his father. All of this was why Jack continued to resist his sister's dire warnings that their father's true nature would burst through again one day, and that Jack's children would suffer for it.

The threatened storm passed even before it began. The old man began to stare into the flames once more, and Jack thought he had tired him enough. Mulsford coughed again, and this time his father made no response. Jack stood, but Peter Stannard suddenly turned and looked up at him, his eyes seeming as sharp as they were when he first took his son to sea.

'That idea you had of sending one of our ships to the Greek islands when the war ends, boy. Candia, Chios, the rest of them. Explain it to me again.'

Jack blinked. He was accustomed to his father's strange and rapid changes of subject: Thomas Ryman was of the opinion that the decay and immobility of Peter Stannard's body had somehow made his mind even more active, but also more impatient, forever flitting from one thought to another, like a songbird hopping from branch to branch.

'There's a good trade to be had there, Father. Will Halliday's Master Gonson sends his own ships out there. He's not an impetuous man.'

Peter Stannard emitted a sound that might have been a neutral grunt.

'Distant trades, present risks, boy,' said Jack's father, 'and I'll wager this Master Gonson has more capital to his credit than we do. Told you that enow times. We make safe money, good money, from the North Sea trades—'

'Yes, safe money, good money. But not enough to restore Dunwich to what it was, Father.' Jack felt his heart sink; this was an old quarrel between them, the arguments long rehearsed and almost as long exhausted. 'You told me many times that when my grandfather led the way into the Iceland fishery, it was thought a great risk. You said there were plenty in this town, the Cuddons above all, who mocked and sneered. But he proved them all wrong, Father, didn't he? The town was rising again thanks to the fishery, and would be still, were it not for the monasteries going down.'

Peter Stannard jabbed the stump of his right hand at his son.

'What? What, boy? You dare use my own father agin me, boy?' The shout had an echo of the old force, the old rage. 'Aye, Iceland nearly saved the town, but it was a certainty – a near part of the world, and Dunwich men have always known how to fish. It was no risk at all, but the Cuddons and the like were too stupid to see it. But these places that men talk of now... Greece and the Levant, these Americas... folly, all of them. Too far, too strange, no trade worth having in any case.' Jack thought of the gold and silver the Spanish were mining in the Americas, but remembered his father's furious reaction when he had last contradicted him with that point. 'No, I'll tell you what'll happen, boy. The king'll make his peace with the Pope, just like King John and others did before him. The monasteries will come back, mark my words on that, and the Iceland fishery will revive with them. Once there's a proper peace with King Francis, all the French trades will revive, and Flanders too. They'll want High Suffolk's wool again, just as they've always done.'

Jack had heard it all before, just as had heard all his counter-arguments shouted down before: that the king enjoyed holding power over the Church without the interference of the Pope, that he had made far too much money out of the monasteries ever to contemplate restoring them, that the fashions of Europe no longer depended upon English wool. Peter Stannard had no time for such uncomfortable truths, just as he closed his ears to evidence of the wealth of the Americas. Had he been less weary, Jack might have been prepared to argue one or all of those cases yet again, but as it was, he felt none of it was worth the candle.

'We should talk more of this matter of distant trades when the war is over, Father.'

The stump jabbed at Jack once more.

'Aye, I see what you're doing, boy. Humour the old leper, put him off – mayhap he'll be dead before the war comes to an end.' Peter Stannard's voice was rising. Mulsford shot an angry glare in his direction. 'But I know what I'm talking about, boy. Your brother did, too.'

You're not your brother, boy.

Jack had learned patience, and, unlike his sister, he had learned forgiveness of their father, up to a point. But in all these years, the one thing he had not learned was to dismiss the ghost of his dead brother, whenever his father chose to summon it forth as a weapon against him.

'Adam died, Father!' Jack yelled, an outburst that caused Mulsford finally to abandon his prayers and leave the building. 'He lies in John's churchyard, next to our mother. And his shade in Purgatory doesn't hold power of attorney over your affairs.'

The storm had broken; but Jack's was the gale and the tumultuous sea hammering against the cliffs, not his father's, whose response was cold but quiet.

'As you remind me, every chance you get, boy. Aye, you've got power of attorney, all right, though the saints know what state our balance sheets are in. But I'm still head of this family, and that gives me rights which no lawyer's screed can take away.'

Jack expected his father to respond to rage with rage, as he invariably did. The mildness of the response nonplussed him. Peter Stannard even smiled, and Jack was utterly bewildered.

'You've been widowed eleven weeks, boy,' said Jack's father. 'More than enow time for any man to grieve. For any man to be alone. And Jennet Barne is a fine woman.' Peter Stannard pushed himself further back on his bed. 'Stop gawping, boy, you look as you did when you were Tom's age. Yes, though, I wrote to George Barne in London, and about more than your taking another ship off to the war. A sound man, George, even though, God knows, he has ideas of his own for embarking on some of these strange new trades – Muscovy, and the like. Bound to fail and cost him a fortune, I'd say. But he has a host of connections in London, and he's sure to rise there. London's the font of all power now, boy. The font of all money, at any rate, which is the same thing these days.'

Jack Stannard stared at the ground, an abashed schoolboy once again. He knew his father had rehearsed this; that whatever else they might have spoken of this day, Peter Stannard would have ensured that he brought the conversation round to say precisely this, and would have compelled himself to keep his temper, no matter what other disagreements they might have. Moreover, Jack knew that when it came to the question of remarriage, his father was right. Somehow, though, Jack had begun to think that he would meet another as he had met his Alice. Neighbours. Young. Playmates. Friends. Until friendship became something more, and flesh encountered flesh. Fortunately, the Easeys were folk of good substance, and to his son's astonishment and relief, Peter Stannard had seen nothing amiss in the match of his only surviving son and their daughter, even at such a young age.

Agatha, as was her wont, had been scathingly direct about their father's granting of consent: 'New young flesh for him,' she said. At first, it seemed to be so. But then, within a year or two, Peter Stannard learned the true name of his sickness, and began to look very differently on his good-daughter. Saint Alice was the patron of the blind, but she, who was a leper herself, was also the patron of the paralysed. The old man convinced himself that an earthly Alice coming into his life was a providence, that her intercession on his behalf might cure him. And the higher Peter Stannard placed Alice upon a pedestal, the less he raged at his son. So the love match prospered, and Jack had been thankful for it.

But now, it was different. His father's sickness was no longer just a whisper on the stairs, he no longer the young heir but the effective head of the Dunwich Stannards. And as responsibility came in by that door, the chance for careless love left by another.

'Jennet Barne is a fine woman indeed, Father,' said Jack, as calmly and slowly as he could. 'So reputation has it, at any rate – I've met her, what, twice only, since she came back from London? A fine woman, all concur. But she is not Alice, and it is yet too soon.'

The heavy, disfigured lids of Peter Stannard's eyes blinked twice.

'True, boy. No other woman could be your Alice, bless her soul, who said so many prayers for mine. Likewise, no other woman could be my Anne, your mother. So mourn Alice still, recite *De Profundis* for her every dinnertime if it's still permitted, as I do for your mother, pay for more masses to speed her soul from Purgatory, and then, son, find another who is utterly unlike her. One like Jennet Barne.' The old man was tiring, and was struggling to get out these, the words he had to speak. 'And it isn't too soon, for if you don't take her, the Barnes will make another match for her, that's for sure. This could be Dunwich's chance, boy. It has to be. It must be. Marry her. That'll get us a foothold in London – God knows what fortune could spring from that. Then keep in with Lord Lisle. And in the campaigns to come, if God wills it, distinguish yourself before Lord Hertford, too. After all, he's the young prince's uncle, the king is very old, and who else will rule England when Great Harry is gone?'

Jack glanced around in alarm, for even mentioning the possibility of the king's death could readily be construed as treason. But Mulsford had gone, and there was no sign of any of the other patients, or of Franklin the porter.

'Father, please—'

Peter Stannard seemed oblivious to the interruption.

'But keep Ryman close, too, so you keep a foot in Duke Norfolk's camp, in case it yet goes the other way.' The old leper shook his head. 'Thomas Ryman, of all men… when I think how he was as a child, in that hovel in old Nicholas parish, before it went into the sea… that he became what he did, that he almost became…' A pause, then another shake of the head, and his eyes focused on Jack again. 'God willing, boy, you may rise with the favour of one or other of Hertford or Lisle or Norfolk, and if you do, then Dunwich will surely prosper once more. It can be the place it once was, in the times of the Stannards who came before us.' Peter Stannard reached out, and rested the stump of his right hand on John's. 'All my life I've known that one man could save this town. Aye, could make it great again, even. I thought I was that man, but my sins have been too great, boy. See how God has punished me by having my flesh, the flesh I loved too much, betray me. So make it you, boy. It has to be you. You be the man I could not be. You be the man to make Dunwich great again, Adam Stannard.'

Jack gasped. His father was still staring at him intently and with recognition, but he had called him by the name of his long-dead brother. The old leper's dreadful face showed that he knew what he had done, but there was no correction, no apology.

You're not your brother, boy. You'll never be your brother.

But perhaps, at last, Jack was.

Eleven

The Pool of London was a very hell.

Horses whinnied their protests as they were pushed onto hoys. The soldiers were little better, companies of Irish kerns jostling at the waterside with northerners from the wilds of Tynedale and Redesdale. Officers and men shouted in a dozen accents or more, trying to make themselves heard above the horses and the barking of dogs. Small boys ran excitedly through the throng, some playing at soldiers, some hoping to steal a coin or two from poorly guarded purses. At the waterfront, men hauled on ropes, blocks and pullies strained, and great cannon were swung from the quay onto the lighters lying alongside. Out in the tideway, ships were getting under sail on the favourable south-westerly, beginning their voyage to France, or else coming to an anchor in mid-stream, awaiting their cargoes. Barges collided with each other, and watermen bawled a seemingly inexhaustible range of colourful oaths.

The dark walls and turrets of the Tower brooded over all. From within came the sound of hammers striking metal as new armour and swords were forged, and the deep rumble of cartwheels upon cobbles as guns and barrels of powder were moved from the ordnance stores toward the river. Incongruously, a gaily decorated skiff lay just downstream of London Bridge. This was filled with expensively attired ladies of the court, whose interest, Will

Halliday speculated, was probably less in the detail of the martial preparations, and more in the physical attributes of many of the soldiers in the process of embarking. For a moment, he wondered whether Marion Bartleby, the current object of his affections, might be among them; but even from such a great distance, it was clear that the fashions sported by these women were well beyond the purse of a master pewterer's daughter, even if she might be inclined to flout the sumptuary laws as blatantly as she dared.

In the midst of it all, upon one of the wharves just west of the Tower, stood William Gonson, seemingly convinced, despite all the evidence to the contrary, that only he could bring order to the apparent chaos around him. Will thought that his white beard and faded gown gave him the look of an Old Testament prophet, alone and defiant amidst the countless hostile worshippers of Baal.

'The hackbutters must take precedence!' cried a red-faced, gaudily dressed, proud-voiced young captain, pushing his way through the throng around Gonson and Will Halliday. 'Get us a ship, I say! A ship, now!'

'The hackbutters,' said Gonson tiredly, 'should not be here at all. They should have embarked at Ipswich, as ordered by your Lord General.'

The young man blustered.

'There was no such order.'

Will Halliday shuffled the papers in his hand, and passed one to Gonson.

'From Whitehall, the first day of May, with the additional authority of king and council,' said the old man. 'So you can account to the Lord General for your disobedience to his orders, or you can wait your turn.'

The young man looked around wildly, saw he had no support whatever from his fellow soldiers in other companies, glowered at Will, and then turned on his heel.

'Let us hope he is just as b-b-bold and impatient against the French,' said Will.

'Amen,' said Gonson. His voice was tired, his eyelids heavy. 'Thirty thousand men, Will. And I have found ships for all of them, praise be to God. The king will have his war with France.'

The king will have his war with France because of you, thought Will. But he could see the cost of the colossal effort in Gonson's grey cheeks, and could hear it by night, as dreams brought together the countless orders to countless ships with the gross injustice that had destroyed his son. Sometimes Will heard the old man speak as he slept, and when he did, it was often just the one word: Babington. Will was certain that if William Gonson ever encountered the false, perjured Knight of Saint John in the flesh, the years would fall away, and he would slaughter the rogue with his bare hands.

Another company of men, archers this time, was pushing its way down toward the Thames, oblivious to the protests of the Irishmen in their way.

'Christ's nails, boys,' cried their grizzled old sergeant in a broad country accent, 'this causey's snided with naught but strangers!'

This brought laughter from the men behind him, and prompted a strange response in Gonson. The old man looked up, smiled, and stepped forward with a sudden speed that surprised Will.

'Hold, boys!' he cried. 'Thisens hail from whereabouts?'

The sergeant studied him curiously, noting the dress of a man of high rank, but clearly perplexed by his words, spoken in an accent Will had rarely heard his master employ.

'Company of Captain Hastings of Kirby Muxloe, my lord. An' thee? One of ussens?'

'That I am, sergeant. William Gonson, of Melton Mowbray born and bred. Good to see the men of Leicestershire sally forth for God, king and old England!'

The sergeant broke into a broad grin.

'Amen to that, Master Gonson! And y'usen? D'you go to the war, sir?'

Gonson did not answer, but swayed on his feet. Will stepped forward and addressed the sergeant.

'Master Gonson, here, is the treasurer and storekeeper of the Navy Royal. But he captained at sea in the wars at the start of the k-k-king's reign.'

The sergeant looked at his men, who whispered among themselves. Some inclined their heads with deference and respect, but others looked at Gonson as though he had two heads.

'One of ussens, going to the seas,' said the sergeant, shaking his head. 'Never thought I'd hear the likes. Mesen, I've naught been on the sea. Ne'er e'en seen it afore. Be that it?'

He pointed to the crowded Thames.

'The s-s-start of it,' said Will. 'It widens and widens, until you can no longer see the shore.'

The sergeant frowned. He consulted with two of the men behind him, then turned back to Will and Gonson.

'Well now, sir,' he said, 'what be this "shore" ye speak of?'

Will barely heard him: he could see tears streaming down Gonson's cheeks, and moved to his master's side. But the old man took a deep breath and recovered himself. Perhaps, after all, they were tears of suppressed laughter, not of ancient memories of better, simpler times.

'God go with you, boys!' he cried to the archers, then turned away.

'You were of this Melton Mowbray, sir?' asked Will. Gonson nodded. 'And where would that be?'

Gonson took a moment to compose his reply.

'As far from the sea as it is possible to be in England,' said the treasurer and storekeeper of the Navy Royal. 'My brother Bartholomew stayed there all his days, he is the vicar there now. You should see his church, Will – our church, our parents' church – a glorious celestory all around, filling it with light. We laid a brass to our parents there, only last year. Our father was a merchant in the wool staple of Melton, who'd thus bettered himself from the sheep farm the Gonsons held for centuries, in Wasdale of Cumberland.' Will recalled the old man taking an extraordinary, unprecedented leave of ten days in August, before the summer's guard was paid off; he had said not a word of the purpose until now. 'Yet here I am, so very far from Melton, and the Gonsons so very far from Wasdale.' Gonson looked out across the river, toward a small bark trying to make headway through a tangle of skiffs and barges. 'What are our lives, Will? What are they, that such things happen? They say there are now heretics in the Swiss land who claim that God has determined our lives before we are born, and that we have no free will. Can that be true, do you think?'

'The k-king and the archbishop would say not, master.'

Gonson looked out over the shipping in the Pool.

'Yet I have come from Melton to here. To this. To all of this. And that David went from here to Malta, and thus to...'

He fell silent, and shook his head. 'I must pray, Will. I must confess, and have the opinion of a worthy priest. My mind swims with it all. Swims with it, Will.' He seemed older then; so much older than Will Halliday had ever known him. Then he rallied. 'But first, lad, we have ships to despatch.'

–

In his youth, Thomas Ryman reflected, he could have walked the thirty or so miles from Dunwich to Kenninghall Palace in a day, even if weighed down by a breastplate, helm, and enough weaponry to deter even the most determined of *banditti*. But his feet and limbs now demanded a gentler pace, so he broke his journey by spending the night in a barn outside Hoxne, arriving at Kenninghall early in the following afternoon. The approach had become utterly familiar to him: the road through the wide deer park, leading to the sturdy brick H-shaped residence of the mighty dukes of Norfolk. Perhaps not quite so mighty, since the unbridled promiscuity of the duke's niece, Catherine Howard, had led her husband, the king, to order her pretty, devious head cut from her lily-white shoulders; but the Howards of Norfolk remained one of the most formidable families in the realm, with the current duke being entrusted with command of the royal armies fighting in France.

Ryman stopped, and took in the view. Kenninghall gave him a comfortable existence, and the duke paid him well for remarkably little work. He knew how lucky he had been to secure such a place, following the dissolution of the Dunwich Greyfriars. Little Meg Stannard once asked him if he was not bitter at the ending of the monasteries, and he had made some bland reply, founded upon Ephesians Four, which she had seen through in an instant. In truth, he had been bitter, even angry and wrathful as Ephesians had it. He had even been tempted to go north and draw his sword again in that glorious but hopeless cause, the Pilgrimage of Grace, as young Friar Martin did; and, no doubt, Thomas Ryman's song would have ended with him hanging in chains from a gallows, as did his erstwhile young friend. As it was, a place in the household of a worthy but retiring knight presented itself, tutoring the knight's son, who died suddenly of the sweating sickness in his tenth year. Fortunately, the knight was, in turn, some sort of distant connection of the Duke of Norfolk, and knew that His Grace was seeking a tutor-in-arms, of unimpeachable loyalty to the old faith, for his grandson. *Deo gratias*, then. The young Lord Howard might be a devious little cub, but for the time being, he was biddable, especially as he was in awe of Ryman's tales of ancient wars, some of which were even true. This Scottish campaign would provide another fund of stories to keep the lad entertained for many months to come. But he repeated the vow he made to himself as he knelt in Saint John's church at Dunwich before he set out: Thomas Ryman had fought his last battle. It was time to hang up the sword, live in contentment here at Kenninghall, and earn enough against the day when Lord Howard no longer needed training in the martial disciplines. On that day, God willing, he would purchase a house in Dunwich, tend to his herbs, and watch over the young Stannards until his dying day.

'Master Ryman,' said an unexpected female voice, behind him.

His soldier's instincts were failing him. Once, no-one, least of all a woman, would have got so close to Thomas Ryman without the point of his blade being at their throat.

He turned, blinked in surprise at the sight before him, then remembered his place and bowed low.

'Your Grace,' he said.

'I have been here five weeks, Master Ryman,' said a diminutive, red-haired woman in her mid-twenties, clad in most unladylike fashion in hunting green, and speaking with an elevated haughtiness that betrayed her station. 'You, however, have not. In your absence, my nephew neglects all his studies, not only those for which you are nominally responsible. Most nominally, as far as I can judge.'

She stood several paces ahead of the group of men that had emerged from the copse behind Ryman. He recognised a few of the faces: Bleasdale the duke's falconer, a couple of the grooms, and one of the guards. All were attired in hunting green, and all were armed with bloodied knives.

'Your Grace…'

Ryman knew how to handle all the members of the immediate House of Howard. The duke appreciated plain speaking, and respected Ryman for having fought under his father at Flodden Field. The duke's son and heir, the Earl of Surrey, revelled in incessant flattery, especially of his poetry. Surrey's wife wanted only to hear Ryman and all of Lord Howard's other tutors declaim as frequently as possible that her son was the most intelligent pupil they had ever taught. But although he had previously encountered her only twice, and then only very briefly, Ryman knew that this woman was a very different case indeed. Cousin to two queens, she might have become a queen herself, had history dealt the cards of fate differently.

'And even when you are here, Master Ryman, your influence upon my nephew is, shall we say, questionable? I know my brother Surrey gives you free rein, but I wonder if he would if he knew some of the words the future Duke of Norfolk seems to have learned under your tutelage – or, indeed, some of the fighting methods you seem to have taught a child who should become a flower of chivalry, that would disgrace the meanest guttersnipe punk from the Cheapside sewers?'

Mary Fitzroy, Duchess of Richmond and Somerset, would have had rank enough by virtue of being the only living daughter of the Duke of Norfolk. But her marriage had elevated her to become the closest thing England had to a Princess of Wales, her late husband being Henry Fitzroy, illegitimate son of the king, and the undoubted apple of the old monarch's eye. Ten years before, when Great Harry still had no son and his marriage to the Boleyn whore was failing, it was said that he seriously contemplated legitimising the newly created Duke of Richmond and making him his heir. Then, alas, Richmond died, leaving his duchess a widow at seventeen. But nothing could take away the fact that the proud, angry young woman now standing before Thomas Ryman had been the daughter-in-law of the King of England, and was said still to be looked upon fondly by her sometime good-father. More than fondly, if some of the gossip in the servants' quarters of Kenninghall was to be believed.

'Your Grace, I...' Thomas Ryman began to bluster, as his younger self would have done when confronted by one so superior to himself. But Thomas had lost his deference while fighting and bleeding for worthless generals across the length and breadth of Europe. 'Well, my lady, what you say is perfectly true.'

The duchess raised an eyebrow.

'You are impudent, sirrah!'

She turned to her attendants, who either feigned shock or laughed. Bleasdale, for one, had never liked Ryman, and the feeling was reciprocated.

'Perhaps, Your Grace. I have been called worse. But it seems to me that when your nephew becomes the Duke of Norfolk, he might benefit from knowing a little of how the peasants in his fields speak when in their cups. And no matter how great a personage, there is no guarantee that every opponent you ever face will fight you fairly and honourably.'

The duchess stamped her remarkably small foot.

'*Enough*, man! I will not be spoken back to by the likes of you! I will not have *you*, a creature of your rank, dictate what my nephew should and should not know! I have witnesses, sirrah! My brother shall hear of this! My father, too, by God!'

Ryman bowed with exaggerated formality. He had never seen the erstwhile queens Anne Boleyn and Catherine Howard, but he had often heard both their names mentioned in the same breath as the word 'bitch'; and the same blood flowed in the veins of their cousin, standing before him. He knew from his young charge, and from allusions by the boy's father Surrey, that the duchess interested herself in the young Lord Howard's upbringing, no doubt believing she could make a better job of it than his father, mother and Ryman too. After all, apart from snaring another duke, or even the king himself, as her second husband, one of the few ways in which the duchess could return to the influence she once possessed was by becoming the power behind the future Duke of Norfolk.

Once, after the Marignano campaign, Ryman was in Ferrara, and saw its duchess going in a grand procession to the cathedral. He recalled the name she had borne before her marriage: Lucrezia Borgia. He suspected that the little woman before him fancied herself cast from the same mould, but Thomas Ryman knew milkmaids in Dunwich who had more of the serpentine and allegedly murderous Duchess of Ferrara in them.

Ryman rose from his bow, glanced at Bleasdale, and saw that the falconer was grinning. Oh, he would support the duchess to the very hilt, and add a few embellishments of his own. If Ryman stayed where he was and argued the case a minute longer, he had no doubt that he would be in chains before sundown.

'Then, my lady, I shall quit my position forthwith. If I may have permission only to remove my possessions from the house?'

She waved a hand, as though swatting away a particularly persistent fly, and made to turn away. Then, though, she turned back to him once again, a strange expression on her face.

'No. No, on second thoughts, not. You have been insolent to the House of Howard once too often, Master Ryman. You will remain here at Kenninghall until my father or brother return to decide your fate.'

Both Norfolk and Surrey were on campaign in France; all of England knew that. If this vengeful harpy had her way, Thomas Ryman might be imprisoned at Kenninghall for months. Most certainly, he would miss going on the next expedition with Jack Stannard.

'You have no power of arrest, My Lady,' said Ryman, regretting the words as soon as they were out of his month. 'And you forget the law of *habeas corpus*—'

Her cheeks flushed with rage.

'*Habeas corpus*, sirrah? This is Howard land, I am the daughter of Howard of Norfolk, the sister of Howard of Surrey, and I am the good-daughter of the King of England. *Habeas Corpus* is for the crows, Master Ryman, not for the likes of Howards. And in any case, who talks of arrest here?' She turned, a mock-questioning expression on her face, and Bleasdale grinned sycophantically. 'You are my father's retained man, and he will continue to retain you, aye, and pay you too – and how can a man be under arrest if he is being paid? It is just that I choose to retain you in a somewhat different manner. In a locked room, in fact.'

Twelve

Southwold's rage, its first attempt to obtain vengeance for Martin Raker, awaited a roke, one of the wetland fogs of that coast. On the second Sunday after Easter, a thick grey blanket duly settled over the Suffolk Sandlings, stretching far inland. The men of Southwold emerged after Mass from the great church of Saint Edward, went into alehouses, then returned to their homes and took up weapons. Punts and skiffs ferried them across the Blyth, with some then continuing on into the Dunwich river, where the tide was flooding. The men on shore made their way through fog-shrouded Walberswick, gathering the two dozen men from that town who were bent on avenging Anthony Maddox. Then they went down to the edge of the marsh fringing the high, dark trees of the Dunwich Westwood, and skirted their way southward, keeping the broad river and the Kingsholme beyond it to their left. They could hear the tolling church bells of Dunwich, and smiled at each other. The people of the ancient town would be at mass, or else in their homes, sheltering from such a foul day. The one place where they would not be was at work in the small shipyard by the Old Quay, where a new hull, almost complete, lay upon the stocks.

–

'I win!' cried Meg Stannard. 'I found you! I am the Devil of the Doom, and I win again!'

Her little brother emerged from behind a knee timber in the hold, his face only just visible in the blackness.

'I'm wet,' said Tom. 'I want to go home now.'

'You didn't want to go home when you won, and you were the Devil of the Doom.'

'Want to go home now,' repeated Tom, stubbornly.

'We won't be able to play here much more, you know. Father'll launch her on the next spring tide, and she'll be gone. No more hide and seek. No more playing at Barbarossa and Andrea Doria. And then I'll marry the Prince of Wales and I'll never play with you again, Tom Stannard.'

'Want to go home!'

'Boys,' said Meg, petulantly. 'You're all so boring.'

Even so, she took her younger brother's hand and guided him to the ladder. They climbed to the upper deck, and Meg looked at the scene around her. Spars and shrouds made ghostly shapes, appearing and disappearing by turns, both on the new ship and on the fog-shrouded half-dozen craft alongside the Dain Quay. Not a soul could be seen. There was no sound, other than the lapping of the tide against the timbers of the quayside and the screech of a seabird.

She frowned. Tom was pulling her arm, trying to draw her away, but she stood stock still, listening hard, squinting into the fog.

There were other sounds, she was sure of it. Not marsh birds; too big for them. Not cows that had strayed. Not the distant, muffled bells of Dunwich's lost churches beneath the waves, which she was sure she sometimes heard in the middle of the night. Meg thought she saw ripples on the water, and heard something strange. What could be the cause?

Rowlocks. Oars cutting through water.

She could see the faint outline of a small, low hull, a hull that seemed to be crowded with dark shapes. One of the shapes coughed. And then she knew.

'We need to run, Tom!' she whispered to her brother. 'We need to run like the wind!'

'Is this a new game, Meg?'

'Yes, Tom! A really important game! And we must be really, really, quiet! Come on!'

The two children climbed out onto the scaffolding, then swung themselves down to the ground and started to run toward the town. As they did so, the first of the Southwold men stepped ashore by the Old Quay, the fleeing Stannard children hidden from them by the fog.

'The French!' cried Meg, as she ran down the road from the harbour, past the decayed Customs House. 'The French are landing!'

That, after all, had been the fear and expectation in Dunwich, if not in all England, for many weeks.

A few townspeople, on their way back from church, stared at her curiously, but took no action in response to her dire warning. Tom, with his shorter legs, was lagging well behind her now, but even so, he, too, was doing his best to raise the alarm.

'French!' he bawled. 'Scots! Romans!'

Meg ran around a corner and collided with a woman coming the other way, carrying a basket of herbs.

'Margaret Stannard!' cried her aunt Agatha, gripping her shoulders and shaking her. 'Is this a way to behave yourself on the Lord's day? I'll take you to your father for a thrashing, girl!'

'But aunt, the French are landing! Hundreds of them! By the Old Quay!'

Agatha Stannard looked down at her niece, and took in her serious, urgent expression. Meg, she knew, was not given to lying. Nor was she given to sacrilege and blasphemy upon the Sabbath. Agatha had no offspring of her own, but she had a name as a healer, and had seen every mood and expression that the faces of children could muster. All that being so, Agatha decided, there was only one explanation for the girl's behaviour.

'Come, children,' she said, as Tom hurtled round the corner, breathless. 'Let's to your father.'

–

The single tenor bell of Saint John's tolled, followed by the equivalent bell of Saint Peter's, then that of All Saints. From doors all across the town, men emerged onto the streets, cudgels, gutting-knives and staves gripped firmly in their hands. They moved like wraiths in the fog, all with one purpose, all in one direction. At their head marched John Stannard, sword in hand, Jed Nolloth, and William Girdler, the senior and by far the more valiant of the two bailiffs of Dunwich, a tall, gaunt figure whose frame belied his trade as a butcher. Beside them strode the unlikely figure of William Seaward, the eager young rector of Saint John's, whose love of Christ and His message of peace did not prevent him cradling an ugly-looking club that served otherwise to kill the rats that infested the church.

The men of Dunwich moved in one body down the High Street. They passed Agatha Stannard's house, once her father's, and Jack saw his sister standing, grim-faced, in the doorway, holding tightly to Meg and Tom. Jack nodded to them. The time to decide whether his daughter deserved punishment for taking her brother to play on the ship, or reward for raising the alarm, would come later.

He saw, too, the strange look that passed between his sister and Jed Nolloth. Some little time before, their father told Jack that, unaccountably, the shipwright was paying his court to Agatha. Peter Stannard gave him short shrift, notionally because Nolloth was nearly a quarter-century older than his intended, but chiefly because the old leper still hoped against all hope to find someone of greater rank, and above all of greater income, who would take such a plain and determined woman, very nearly the wrong side of thirty.

Further on, they passed the small tenement which belonged by inheritance to Thomas Ryman. It was locked and shuttered: Jack wished the old warrior was with them, but there had been no word of him since he returned to Kenninghall, and it was unlikely Ryman would be seen again in Dunwich until after the Howard household decamped to London at the end of the summer.

The fog was thinning a little by the time the Dunwich men reached the harbour. Jack could see men, strangers, upon the scaffolding around the new hull, hammering and cutting at the planking. Others were arranging faggots around the keel. Seeing the approach of the defenders, they were hurriedly attempting to light the pyres, but much of the timber was damp from the recent wet weather, and would not catch.

Between the ship and the oncoming army stood a line of invaders, armed with the same kinds of weapons as their opponents from Dunwich.

'They don't look French,' said Seaward.

'And don't sound it,' said Girdler. 'Swear I've seen some of them before. That fat one – he's the miller of Reydon, as God is my judge.'

'French or Southwold,' said John, 'those plague-sores aren't burning Dunwich's ship!'

'My ship,' murmured Nolloth.

The men behind them growled their approval.

'As bailiff,' said Girdler, raising his voice, 'I answer for the keeping of the peace in this town to Sheriff Drury, and above him, to the king himself. Now, boys, it seems clear to me that the breakers of Dunwich's peace are those fellows, there, and our undoubted duty is to drive them from the bounds of our borough! So jammock the fuckers, my lads!'

Cheering erupted at the bailiff's uniquely Suffolk permission to beat their opponents to a pulp, and the men of Dunwich surged forward.

Jack Stannard made for the supposed miller of Reydon, who stood his ground, swearing oaths of defiance. But the fat man was no fighter. He raised his club and swung it at Jack, but had no control over the attack. Jack, for his part, ducked low and slashed his sword across the miller's ample gut. It was not a fatal wound, merely an ugly gash, but the miller howled as though he had been struck a mortal blow, and sank to his knees.

For a keeper of the peace and a man of God respectively, both Girdler and Seaward, to Jack's right, were proving themselves to be remarkably ferocious fighters. Girdler had a hook-bladed bill, and was wielding it as easily as though he were scything corn. A thin youngster was coming at Seaward with a small blade, but the Rector of Saint John's swerved away from the attack before landing his club on the side of the youth's face, shattering the cheekbone. Jed Nolloth, meanwhile, swung his shipwright's adze as though it were a battleaxe, and his opponents from across the Blyth fell away before him.

All around, more and more Dunwich men were coming into the fray, but the confined space meant that their opponents could still hold their own. Jack, though, had no thought of the men directly before him. He wanted to be at the whore-maggots who were trying to fire his ship, and those who were breaking its timbers.

The ship he intended to name *Alice*.

No other man on the strand bore a sword, so the Southwold men preferred to stand at a distance from Jack, blocking his path and stabbing at him with their bills, rather than engaging directly with such a fearsome weapon. Jack thrust, slashed, and parried, but could see no way of breaking the barrier of five billmen who stood between him and his ship. He wished as never before that Ryman was with him, and not at Kenninghall – the old soldier would know what to do.

But the old soldier had taught the young Jack Stannard. He had taught him countless lessons from the old battles, and the ways of the great warriors from Alexander to Bayard.

He had taught him of Hastings.

So Jack Stannard turned and ran. Seaward, a few yards away, stared at him in astonishment. But then Stannard turned back. Three of the billmen had come after him; the other two had sought out other opponents. In any event, the wall of bill-hooks keeping him from his ship was broken, just as William the Bastard had tricked the Saxon shield-wall into breaking on Senlac Hill. Jack charged the first billman, stabbing him in the right arm, parried a thrust from the second, and slashed the third across the face.

He was through, and running for the hull, where three separate fires were finally gaining some purchase, as was another upon the unfinished upper deck. He was aware of an ally at his right shoulder – a glance told him it was Seaward – and sensed there were others behind him. Everywhere upon the shingle adjoining the Old Quay, the men of Southwold and Walberswick were breaking. Those upon the scaffolding, seeing how the fight went, hastily climbed down and retreated into the fog. One, who was too slow, had his hamstring severed by Jack's sword, and yelled as though to wake the dead. The fire-starters, too, abandoned their kindling and joined the retreat.

'Save the ship!' cried Jack. 'Water, now! Fetch pallings from the warehouses!'

With his sword, he began to fence with the nearest fire, knocking burning brands out onto the shingle. Girdler joined him, using his longer bill to good effect. Then more and more Dunwich men appeared, some with buckets filled with water from the river, some with large palling-sheets. They attempted to douse the fires, but even if they succeeded, the damage would be serious: the blaze on the upper deck was harder to reach than those set beneath the hull, and might yet consume the entire ship. Nolloth was on his knees, weeping, and Jack laid a hand upon his shoulder, then went round to the other side of the ship.

The men of Southwold and Walberswick were retreating along the Kingsholme, screaming oaths as they went. The men of Dunwich who were not employed in tackling the fires held their ground around their precious hull, staring silently after the attackers.

One of the retreating invaders was more forward than the others. He still spoiled for a fight, and had to be pulled away by some of his fellows. His feet dug into the shingle as he tried to resist their efforts. He was a very young man, probably not yet twenty. Jack had never seen him before, but the face was somehow familiar, although he was not sure why. It was the last face that disappeared into the swirling fog, the eyes wide with fury, the mouth still yelling at Jack.

'We'll bring you down yet, Stannard! You and your fucking damned Dunwich! I'll have revenge for my father if it takes me until Judgement Day! I curse you. I curse your whole family, I curse your ship, I curse your whole shitting town. Remember my name, Stannard. Remember the name of Stephen Raker!'

Thirteen

St Paul's Cathedral looked splendid in the strong May sunshine. Its tall steeple pointed the way to heaven, while its stout walls and brightly coloured windows, towering far above even the tallest buildings round about, provided reassurance of the eternal presence of God. To tell the truth, though, Will Halliday's thoughts were of a somewhat less spiritual nature as he made his way toward Paul's Cross, in the open space before the west front of the great building. Marion Bartleby, the young lady whose favour he sought, daughter of a prosperous master pewterer of Bassishaw Ward, was much given to frequenting the cathedral, and Will had received certain indications that she would be there today. With all the shipping having finally been despatched from the Thames, William Gonson was in a rare mood of good cheer, and had awarded Will a half day's holiday, which the young clerk intended to employ to its best advantage, even if that meant spending much of it in at least nominal prayer.

A great procession, the climax of Rogationtide, was meant shortly to be entering the cathedral, prior to a service of thanksgiving for the victory in Scotland, while also imploring God's blessing upon the king's ongoing and undoubtedly righteous war with France. Will, who spent most of his waking hours employing earthly means to achieve that same end, would have wanted to take part in this even if he had not had another motive for so doing, and a large crowd had gathered, lining the road all the way down to the Lud Gate and the bridge over the Fleet river beyond. As was the custom on such occasions, wine was being dispensed with seemingly limitless liberality from the many serving stations that had sprung up all over the City. As Will moved through the throng, though, he heard whispers and rumours, not all of them fuelled by the wine. Something different was going to happen today, people were saying. Something new. Something important.

He caught sight of Marion Bartleby, and made his way through to her side. Of course, she had an attendant, but Will had encountered her before: a large old woman who once served as Marion's wetnurse, but who was now, thankfully, entirely deaf. In any case, the oldster looked favourably upon Will, which Marion's father and mother certainly did not; it seemed he reminded her a little of her only lover, who had perished on Flodden Field thirty years before.

Will bowed to both in turn, and smiled.

'Mistress B-B-Bartleby.'

'Master Halliday. Such a surprise.'

She was some years younger than him. Red hair, just protruding from beneath her gable hood, framed a small, pale face, which might have been stern but for her delightful, slightly lop-sided, smile. She wore a dark green gown which concealed most, but not all, of the curves that so interested Will Halliday.

'You have been well, I trust?'

'Most well, thank you, sir. And you have been busy, I trust?'

'Most busy, mistress. The k-k-k-k-king's Navy Royal is a busy affair – well, that is to say...'

Will hoped to heaven that he was not blushing, but rather suspected that he was. A loquacious sort of fellow in spite of his stammer – Jack Stannard certainly thought him so, at any rate – Will was invariably rendered tongue-tied by the young lady before him, even though (or perhaps because) he had only spoken to her on a half-dozen or so occasions, and then but briefly.

He essayed a recovery.

'Most excellent weather for the time of year, m-m-mistress.'

She nodded, her expression still bearing more than a hint of amusement.

'Most excellent indeed, Master Halliday.' She fell silent, and there was an awkward silence. Will knew it was his task to further the conversation, but he could not think of a single topic.

'But hark,' Marion cried excitedly, 'the procession comes!'

The sound of distant singing reached them, but so, too, did the unexpected response to it. People were not bowing and crossing themselves in silent devotion; instead, there was murmuring, frowns, sideways glances, and something else, too. Will, though, the sometime choirboy of Cardinal College, was intent upon the music. Not plainchant, but five-part polyphony – ambitious, whoever had set it – *yet something was not right*.

Realisation came to him by way of Marion Bartleby, who was quietly mouthing the words.

'English,' said Will, unable to believe what he was hearing. 'The l-liturgy is in English.'

'A great day, is it not?' said Marion. 'So very right. So very due.'

For many months, there had been rumours that Archbishop Cranmer wished to change the entire language of faith, not just small elements like the Lord's Prayer, from Latin to English. But the king, who favoured many of the old ways of Rome, except naturally for its bishop, was said to have set his face against it.

Until now.

They could see the procession now, the priests in their copes, albs and chasubles, the choristers in their white gowns, the acolytes swinging great censers of incense. But none, Will included, paid any attention to the spectacle. Instead, everyone in the crowd was concentrating on the words, intelligible for the first time in the whole span of English history. Some faces were red with rage, and not a few turned away in disgust. Will saw one man risk arrest by spitting upon the ground in front of the procession. But others, Marion Bartleby among them, were enraptured.

'My father has many dealings with the court,' said Marion. Her voice was so delicate that Will had difficulty concentrating on her words. 'With the royal purveyors, and so forth. He heard that last year, the king witnessed how the people made nearly no response to the services calling for God's blessing upon the Scottish war. So this year, with a greater war, the king wants folk to take part – to understand what they are praying for. Ah, and listen! This must be the part that the queen has written.'

'The *queen*? C-Catherine Parr?'

'Queen Catherine herself, yes, indeed. The regent of this realm, Master Halliday, while the king goes off to war. Had you not heard? A woman in command of the kingdom.' She smiled, and he was smitten once again. 'That is a thought indeed, is it not?'

Oh, it was a thought. As the processional cross went past and onward, up into the cathedral, followed by the ranks of brightly-garbed clergy and singers, Will lost all sense of Marion Bartleby, standing at his side. His thoughts raged. Some of them were singing the glorious, seductive bass line along with the choir. Others were turning over the enormity of this new innovation, the simplest but most profound of all the changes the king had yet brought to religion: the liturgy *in English*. And yet another part of his mind was wrestling with the notion of a woman ruling the realm. A woman, moreover, who could write the kind of words that were being sung there, in front of the great cathedral.

> *'Bring down the power of the wicked, that they may perish together with their wickedness. Let thy zeal suddenly come upon them: the fiery thunder-bolts and the spirit of the whirlwind be portion of their part.'*

The spirit of the whirlwind did, indeed, seem to be abroad in England that day.

-

Halesworth was far enough from the Suffolk coast for both men to be as certain as it was possible to be that no-one from their respective towns would stumble across them by chance. By the same token, though, it was a prosperous market town, at the junction of major highways, and therefore a place where it was perfectly plausible for both men to have business. The Angel was a large inn, close to the church and the market square, where the bustle of travellers and tradesmen made it possible for the two men to be utterly anonymous.

'They are very generous terms,' said the younger man, dressed more innocuously than was his usual wont.

'Generous,' said the older, who had an air of sadness and regret about him. 'Yes, very generous.'

'And you'd be protected. For the service you'd be rendering us… You'd be the best guarded man in Suffolk, my friend. Not even the old duke over at Westhorpe would be so safe.'

'A reassurance. If I do what you ask, I'll make many enemies. Some of them men I now call my friends. More than friends, too.'

'If these men are truly your friends, then why do you not prosper more? Have you asked yourself that, my friend? Why do they possess land and gold, in a way that you do not?' The younger man was relentless. 'I'll tell you why. They exploit you, and others, to enrich themselves.'

The older man smiled.

'And you do not? No bailiff, no merchant, in your town, does not?'

It was the younger man's turn to smile.

'Men are men, my friend. And I see in you a man who craves greater recognition for his work. Greater reward.'

The older man nodded. He looked away, through the unshuttered, open window of the inn, toward the east. Toward the sea.

'Greater reward indeed,' he said at length, 'but still not great enough.'

'How so?'

'There is one thing more,' said the older man.

The younger man, Stephen Raker of Southwold, listened to the demand, and granted it with a simple nod of his head. Fulfilling this one last term might involve certain difficulties, although probably not insuperable ones; but it would involve no cost, and given the gold he and his family had already committed to this cause, that was only to be welcomed. When all was said and done, it would be a small price to pay for bringing down the Stannards, those cursed and murderous whoremasters, and if God willed it, for obtaining a far greater prize, too.

Delenda est Carthago; and just as Rome had risen in place of the fallen Carthage, so Southwold would rise to take its rightful place. To it, instead of to its rival, would come all the revenues, all the privileges, and, if God and the king smiled upon it, the two seats in Parliament also. Perhaps Southwold could do to its fallen enemy as Rome had done to Carthage, ploughing salt into the soil so nothing would ever grow there again.

Stephen Raker smiled. Ultimately, the price he would have to pay the weak creature before him was well worth paying for the prize that might ensue.

The downfall of Dunwich.

Fourteen

'This Bullen, Father,' said Meg Stannard, standing by Jack's side upon the Dain Quay. 'Is that where the Bullen whore came from?'

Jack turned, and frowned sharply at her. The quay was busy, and many Godfearing, respectable folk were within earshot, including a brace of Cuddon brothers standing just outside the door of their warehouse. Ever jealous of the greater prosperity of the Stannards, the Cuddons, long displaced from the rank of the richest family in Dunwich, would think nothing of turning the words of a child against their rivals.

Jack stooped down and whispered sharply, 'Where did you learn such a word, child? You must never, ever say that word again, or I shall have to belt you.'

'But it's what everyone in the town calls her,' said Meg, stubbornly. 'Anyway, Father, just what is a whore?'

The sea washed noisily over the shingle of the Kingsholme behind them, the breeze whistled, and Jack Stannard imagined it bore the sound of Alice's laughter, unrestrained in Purgatory. To stop himself following suit, he turned toward the charred, badly damaged hull of the *Alice*. By a miracle, the main body of the ship had been saved, but much of it would have to be taken apart and made new. Southwold's attack had set back completion by months; but completed she would be.

Finally certain that he was in control of himself, Jack turned to his daughter again. She was still looking up at him, serious-faced, awaiting a proper answer.

'No, Meg,' he said, 'the late queen was named Anne Boleyn, which most men render as Bullen. Whereas we are setting out the *Osprey*, yonder, for the campaign against Boulogne, which, again, Englishmen render as Bullen.'

'So are there whores in Boulogne, Father?'

Jack turned right and left in desperation. Providentially, rescue came in the form of his cousin Simon Bulbrooke, master of the Stannard ship *Osprey of Dunwich*, who had, indeed, brought her home in time to be the replacement for the shattered *Blessing*, as Jack had prayed he would. Moreover, Jed Nolloth had insisted that he should remain ashore to work on the repairs to the badly damaged hull of the *Alice*, an opinion immediately and enthusiastically accepted by the Stannards. But with Nolloth ashore and Christopher Eagle dead, it meant that there were precious few shipmasters in Dunwich willing enough, or whom the Stannards trusted enough, to go with Jack upon the latest campaign. Indeed, only one man fitted both criteria: and that man was Simon Bulbrooke.

Meg ran over to Bulbrooke, who gathered her up easily in his arms. He was a big man, clad in a favourite but now shrunken doublet that had become too small for him, his face framed by an unkempt, greying bush of a beard. He was nearly twenty years older than Jack, but he had always been as much a good friend as blood kin. Of late, though, there had been something of a distance between him and his cousin. Bulbrooke had moved to Ipswich and tried to set himself up as an independent merchant and shipowner, but as Peter Stannard observed, he lacked the quick wits, application and connections essential to success in those capacities. Consequently, the only outcomes of his venture into independence were that he had returned to Dunwich and become even more indebted to the Stannards. Simon Bulbrooke also had a renowned fondness for the bottle, even more so since he returned from Ipswich, and ashore or afloat, his gait was never entirely steady.

For the moment, though, his disposition was sunny enough; it was too early in the day for him to have taken very much ale.

'Well, Mistress Stannard,' said Simon, smiling at the girl, 'why are you not about a young lady's proper business, learning how to be a good wife and mother?'

Meg pulled a face.

'Eugh! I'd rather sail with you to the wars, Uncle Simon!'

Bulbrooke laughed, and turned to his cousin.

'God in Heaven, Jack, what sort of a creature are you bringing up?'

'I have tried to have masses said for me, that I may know the answer,' said Jack, merrily. 'But, Meg, be off home with you now. Uncle Simon and I have much to attend to.'

Meg pouted as Simon Bulbrooke set her down on the ground.

'Only Tom's at home, with Joan,' she said, 'and he's asleep.'

'Well, then, you may go to see your Aunt Agatha, or your grandfather at Saint James's, as you choose, but only after you've lit a candle for your mother at John's church.'

Meg grinned.

'Of course, Father. As you say, Father.'

With that, she ran off. Jack Stannard and Simon Bulbrooke looked at each other, and as one, the cousins burst into laughter.

'Would that my own daughters had lived to be like your Meg,' said Simon.

'If you had five Megs, Si, you would truly regret those words,' said Jack.

Simon Bulbrooke's wife had borne him no sons, but rather, five daughters, all of whom seemed to be healthy and flourishing, all of whom died before their tenth birthdays, followed swiftly by their broken-hearted mother. The failure of his family, and then, shortly afterwards, the failure of his mercantile dreams, meant that there was always an air of discontent about Bulbrooke, even when he was in relatively good humour.

They turned to inspect the work on the *Osprey*, which was proceeding apace. Many in Dunwich, notably the Cuddons, said it was impossible for the town to provide a ship for the Boulogne campaign, so soon after it had sent one against Scotland. But Jack Stannard was determined to impress his betters by providing a ship for Boulogne from Dunwich, and those betters, in turn, had points to prove of their own. The king wanted England to demonstrate to its rivals that it could fight two wars in such short order, and Lord Lisle, the Lord High Admiral, was a mightily ambitious man, who knew it could only resound to his honour if he brought his ships from the north down in time to join those already assembling in the south. Jack, though, knew the truth of it from Will Halliday's letters, namely that it was William Gonson, not the elegant Lord Admiral, who was making it happen. Thus the largest possible English fleet would sail against France, and against the king's principal target, the city of Boulogne. It would carry a colossal army, which would be commanded by England's mightiest generals. War with Scotland had been a business for earls and lords: war with France was the preserve of dukes, with both Norfolk and Suffolk in command of the army. But not the overall command. That would rest with the man who was to cross with the fleet from Dover.

King Henry the Eighth was going to the wars, for what every man in England knew would be the last time.

–

'...and *that*, granddaughter, is why Dunwich must have a ship in this fleet,' said Peter Stannard, sitting on a stool in the small herb garden of the lazar house. He could no longer tend to the herbs, for his hands were useless, but he claimed that their aromas soothed him. 'The king himself will be present. Imagine it, Meg! Great Harry, in person. That's why your father and I have set Nolloth and his men to work on the *Osprey* every hour that God sends.'

Meg, sitting on the ground at his side, was thoughtful. This was her habitual state, for she thought much. For instance, she thought it unfair that her younger brother would one day inherit all the Stannards had, for he was a tedious little dolt with a runny nose. She thought it puzzling that, in recent weeks, she had several times overheard her father mention the name of a Mistress Barne to Joan Cowper. (At first, she thought he was speaking of a mistress who had a barn, but this seemed not to be the case.) Above all, Meg thought it strange that her aunt Agatha would be so very angry if she knew that her niece was again visiting her grandfather alone. She had heard her father and aunt arguing when they thought she was asleep, and although she could hear only a few of the words, and that only when one or other of them shouted particularly loudly, she knew that her grandfather was the cause of the quarrel. So Meg no longer told her aunt about her visits to the leper hospital.

There was only one way to get to the bottom of the mystery, Meg decided.

'Grandfather,' she said.

'Yes, child?'

'Why does Aunt Agatha hate you? Why does she say I shouldn't visit you alone?'

Meg was good at reading expressions – Joan and her aunt told her so, and that it was a gift she had inherited from her mother – but she usually had no idea of how to read her grandfather's disfigured face. Now, though, she could see emotions, but she could not tell what they were. He was trying to form words, but none would come. There was anger, and for a moment Meg thought he might hit her – her playmates in Dunwich, especially Miriam Day, said that her grandfather was a monster who had killed countless men, including one of his own brothers, but she had never believed such stories.

There was something else, too. Pain? Grief? Were those tears in his eyes?

'You are like her,' murmured Peter Stannard, so quietly that Meg barely heard. 'As she was when she was your age. *Vade retro, Satana.*'

Why was Grandfather calling her Satan, and telling her to get behind him? But he was silent again, his eyes averted from her, and Meg knew better than to voice the countless questions in her mind.

'I'm sorry, grandfather,' she whispered.

'I too, child. The Doom awaits me, you know. It awaits me.'

He fell silent, and they sat, wordless, for some minutes. Meg thought of leaving, but then she thought of something Grandfather had said earlier, and brightened.

'Have you ever seen the king, grandfather?' she asked, with genuine interest.

Peter Stannard looked steadily at her over the remains of his nose. His thoughts still seemed to be far away, perhaps still on the reasons for his daughter's hatred of him. Slowly, though, he began to register what Meg had said.

'What was that, child?'

'Have you ever seen the king?'

'Have I not told you the story? No? Well, then.' Peter Stannard sat a little more upright. 'Yes, child, I saw the king just the once, in the year 'twenty-six, when I took the *Gift of God* up London river, after coming back from the Iceland voyage. The king was jousting in the tournament at Greenwich for the birthday of Catherine, who was his queen then. December, it was, but a mild one, thanks be to God.'

Meg sat up excitedly.

'What was he like, grandfather? What did the king look like?'

'A giant of a man, taller than any in Dunwich. Red hair that looked as though it was aflame in the winter sun. He moved with grace, and power, and looked with such love upon his queen. But love is a fragile thing, child, as you'll find, in your time. Even then, the seed of doubt from Leviticus must have been in his heart. But he was noble, Meg, so very noble – every inch the epitome of a great king.' Peter Stannard shook his head. 'England's last winter of harmony and good content, that was.'

Meg frowned.

'But grandfather, if he is such a great and noble king, why do so many fear and hate him? Why do they whisper over their pots in the Pelican and the Lion?'

Peter Stannard looked around in alarm. There seemed to be no-one within earshot: the other patients were either upon their beds or at prayer, while Franklin was nowhere to be seen. He breathed more easily.

'Dearest Meg,' he said, stooping as low as he dared, and whispering to her. She came closer; she was accustomed to, and could ignore, the smell of decay. 'Some lessons that you learn are more important than others, and this is one of the most important of all. Never, ever speak ill of the king. No matter what thoughts about him breed in your heart, suppress them. Promise me you'll do that, granddaughter, and make sure that your brother does the same, when he's old enow to understand. Ask me any question you will, accuse me of anything you will, *but do not speak ill of the king.*'

She looked at him gravely.

'I promise, grandfather. But why must we do this?'

Peter Stannard sighed. He knew that with his singular granddaughter, even at her tender age, 'because I say so' was as effective as besieging the walls of Rome with feathers.

'First, Meg, for the good of the family, and I trust you know by now that nothing, apart from our duty to God, outweighs the good of our family.' *Hypocrite, Peter Stannard*; he could hear the mockery and disgust of half a hundred dead souls, and several living ones. But his granddaughter merely nodded. 'Second, child, for your own wellbeing. Remember always that the king can do no wrong in the eyes of God. Those things he does which some men think wrong, or to which some object… well, for all we know they are part of God's higher purpose, expressed through the king, His vice-regent upon earth. The ways of kings are not for the likes of us to judge, Margaret Stannard.'

Meg whispered, 'But Miriam Day says the king is evil.'

She saw her grandfather's eyes widen.

'Whatever she says, Meg, and whatever you think, *you* must never say such a thing. Swear to me that you will not.'

'I swear it, grandfather. But grandfather, it isn't only Miriam Day. I hear men's whispers, not just in the alehouses, and not just old Uncle Spatchell – they think all children are invisible, deaf, or stupid, so can say anything before them.' *Out of the mouths of babes*, thought Peter Stannard, whose own true thoughts upon the doings of Harry the Eighth would have filled volumes. 'I hear them say that the king is evil for dissolving the monasteries, for renouncing the Pope, for tampering with the true religion, for putting aside his lawful queen. I hear them speak a word, but I do not know what it means. Tell me, please, grandfather – what is a tyrant?'

Peter Stannard closed his eyes, breathed deeply, and said nothing. Meg was still thinking upon the significance of this when she emerged from the lazar hospital, directly into the path of her aunt Agatha, who had been collecting herbs in the Westwood.

Part Three

This Island Empire

July to September 1544

> *...by divers sundry old authentic histories and chronicles, it is manifestly declared and expressed that this realm of England is an Empire, and so hath been accepted in the world, governed by one Supreme Head and King having the dignity and royal estate of the imperial Crown of the same...*
>
> Statute of Parliament in Restraint of Appeals, 1533

Fifteen

The sun shone upon Dover and the pride of England. The great castle stood foursquare on its mighty cliff, brooding over all. The royal standard flew from the roof of the colossal square keep, for the king himself was there, preparing to embark. The harbour beneath the cliffs was packed with shipping. Several of the king's great ships lay furthest from the shore, by virtue both of their greater draughts and so that they could defend the inshore vessels if the French launched a surprise attack. Jack recognised several of them from the Scottish campaign; by some miracle, but at a cost to his health described in Will Halliday's letters, Master Gonson had managed to bring the ships south, have them repaired and revictualled, and sent back to sea again in ample time for the campaign against Boulogne. Some of the transports had been in the Firth of Forth, too. Yes, it was a miracle – a very English miracle.

Jack Stannard took in the spectacle from the poop of the *Osprey*. This time, he had come into harbour without incident: there was no arresting party waiting to take him off into captivity, no malevolent enemy upon any of the ships in his company.

Simon Bulbrooke joined him on deck.

'Ready below to take on our cargo, Jack.'

'Very good. We'll edge inshore on the next tide, try to get alongside one of the wharves before the morrow.'

'Why so eager? We'll only be carrying cask ale, not soldiers. Won't matter if we don't go over to Calais with the vanward. Look around, Jack. Most of these will be stragglers.'

'True enough, cuz, but I'll not have it said that a Dunwich ship was tardy. A Stannard ship. God willing, Si, we'll sail over with the flagship, under the eyes of the king and the Lord Admiral.'

Bulbrooke said nothing, but the scowl on his face told its own story. A man thwarted in his own ambitions, he no longer understood them in others. For his part, Jack, too, was disappointed that the *Osprey* had not been ordered to carry troops. But unlike the Scottish campaign, this was not the expedition carrying England's main force to the war. That had already crossed, weeks before, and was now divided into two vast armies, the Duke of Norfolk besieging Montreuil, the Duke of Suffolk investing Boulogne. The fleet assembled in Dover harbour was tasked with taking over to Calais troop reinforcements and victuals, the latter intended both for those troops and for the Calais garrison itself. Above all, though, it would carry to France the new commander of the army besieging Boulogne: King Henry the Eighth.

From their position in the southern part of the anchorage, Jack and Simon could hear the distant cheers upon the shore, and the firing of guns. At such a distance, the smoke from the cannon on the castle walls appeared minute, like tiny fragments of gossamer. Then the great ships, hard under the lee of the castle cliff, began to fire too, and cheering broke out from men lining their decks or hanging from their shrouds. More and more bunting broke out from mastheads.

Jack turned to his cousin, smiled, then turned to the eager young lad nearest him.

'Run up the colours, George, and ready larboard guns for the salute!'

Young George Vincent grinned, and went to the task.

Just then, through a gap between the nearer ships of the fleet, Jack saw a flash of oars. A low, gilded craft was cutting through the waves, and from its ensign staff flew a huge green, white and red banner, far too large for the little vessel.

The row-barge had a platform at the stern. Jack could just make out the chair upon it, and the vast figure – obviously vast, even at such a distance – that occupied it. And in that moment, John Stannard knew he had his first sight of that most famous prince, Henry, eighth of the name, by God's grace King of England and Ireland, rightful King of France, Defender of the Faith.

He glanced skyward.

'Behold, beloved,' he whispered to the soul of Alice Stannard, 'your Jack looks upon the king.'

Then the barge passed out of sight, behind the host of hulls, and the moment was gone. On Jack's command, the *Osprey*'s two little fawconets fired, making their tiny contribution to the thunderous chorus that echoed and re-echoed off the towering white cliffs. Merrily, Jack sang the first words of *Pastime with Good Company*, the song written by the king himself, and the rest of the crew joined in enthusiastically, if not as tunefully as their leader. Simon Bulbrooke shook his head and looked away.

–

Thomas Ryman had been detained at Kenninghall for fourteen weeks. At first, he wrote letters: to the sheriff, to the Earl of Surrey, to the Duke of Norfolk. He even wrote more than once to Peter Stannard at the leper hospital in Dunwich. But even as he wrote them, he knew in his heart of hearts that Bleasdale or some other, acting at the Duchess of Richmond's behest, would destroy them as soon as they left his hand. He saw next to no-one, other than the occasional kitchen hand or groom bringing him his food or taking away his slop pail, and they had clearly been instructed not to speak to him. Requests to speak to the duchess, whom he presumed was still in residence and to whom he was now prepared to abase himself in as humiliating a manner as possible, were ignored; and as he knew from both experience and reputation, Mary Fitzroy had both a long memory and an unforgiving nature. But as the days passed, and then the weeks, Ryman found that a strange thing happened. The rage, and the impotence, and the anxiety, all dissipated. Even his concern for how the war progressed subsided. He did not know if Jack Stannard, or his employers the duke and earl, lived or died; and after a while, he stopped asking those who came to feed him. The solitude of his room – and it was his own room where they had decided to hold him, a small cell high up in the service wing – this solitude gradually took him back to the Greyfriars, and to the monastic life he had so relished before he was forcibly torn from it by royal whim. Ryman had his Bible, and returned to contemplation of it. He had Thomas Aquinas, and Augustine, and a few of the other fathers of the Church, and revelled in rediscovering their teachings. Before his confinement, he had been much troubled by thoughts of his increasing age, and an awareness of mortality that had never concerned him in all the years when his life had been in mortal peril in every waking moment, be it from a Frenchman's knife, or from an Italian's crossbow quarrel, or else from camp fevers on the Scottish border. *Timor mortis conturbat me*, as all the poets had it: fear of death disturbs me. But, for Thomas Ryman, no longer, thanks to the unlikely agency of Mary Fitzroy, Duchess of Richmond. Instead, the tolling of the clock in the stables of Kenninghall Palace allowed him to resume the observance of the monastic hours, and although he was alone, he somehow felt the presence of all the Grey Friars who had gone before him, and those with whom he had known good fellowship at Dunwich. They prayed with him, they sang with him. Ryman had no doubt that if Bleasdale, or the duchess, or anyone else, chanced to hear him at his devotions, they would have thought he had gone entirely mad.

Such an opinion of his sanity might have been strengthened if his captors had been privy to his dreams and nightmares. There were the usual ones that had tormented him for twenty years and more: the burning churches and villages, the screams of enemies and innocents alike, the feel of his blade running through flesh or striking bone, the fear, the stench, the delirium of victory. But one dream recurred, more and more often. He was a boy again, on the cliff at Dunwich. Son of one bailiff of Dunwich, intended soon to be apprenticed to the other, his father's friend Adam Stannard, young Jack's grandfather, a brutal, arrogant man who had lost his right arm in the Tewkesbury fight. Ryman saw the ship again, as he really had seen it that day over forty years before. He saw the tattered sails and the shattered bonaventure, just as they had been on the day itself. A ship torn by the recent storm, forced to seek refuge in the nearest safe harbour. He watched it make for the mouth of the Blyth, and ran over to the summit of Cock Hill to watch its progress up to the Dain Quay. It was a dream, of course, so this ship, unlike the real one, could move with no need of wind nor tide, and could make a passage that might have taken many hours in reality last no longer in his mind than several blinks of an eye. He could see halberds, swords, and armour glinting in the sun. These, said his father, were part of the escort of England's Princess Margaret, being sent by sea to Berwick ahead of the overland procession taking her to her marriage with the Scottish king.

The young Thomas Ryman had never seen soldiers before, and thought he looked upon gods. He had never seen one, let alone talked to one, but in that moment, he knew that he would become a soldier, and not an apprentice to the foul Adam Stannard. He looked up to tell his father so, but in that moment, his dream passed from memory into nightmare. His father had turned into a skeleton, and crumbled into dust even as he still held his son's hand. When Thomas turned to look back at the ship, all of the soldiers were turning to skeletons, too, their brilliant armour rusted and streaked with dried blood. Yet still he wanted nothing more than to become one of them.

Even as he had the thought, Thomas Ryman saw the flesh crumble from the bones of his hands, and knew that if he looked into a mirror, he would see only a skull.

–

William Gonson had been studying the paper in his hands for several minutes, his eyes seemingly blank.

'Master?' said Will Halliday, for the third time.

Gonson finally raised his eyes. He stared at Will, but there was no spark of recognition. Then, slowly, he came back from the far distant place where he had been, and waved the letter in front of him as though swatting away a fly.

'A summons to the Tower,' he said. 'By order from Secretary Paget. There is some new problem with the ordnance stores, it seems.'

'You wish me to accompany you?'

'No, Will. Continue with the despatches to Portsmouth and Woolwich. They need to be on the road as soon as possible, and God knows how long I'll be kept waiting at the Tower.'

Gonson stood, donned his overgown, took up the stick which supported him as he walked, nodded to Will, and left. The clerk felt a moment of concern, but it swiftly passed. The Tower was not a long walk, and perhaps the exercise and the air would do the old man some good. In the last few days, he had seemed more content, his mind less inclined to wander, the night terrors diminished. With the Scottish campaign done, and the fleets for France despatched, the work of the office was a little diminished: or at least, it was confined largely to the tedious business of despatching victuals and paying off, matters that could largely be delegated to Gonson's clerks. Unfortunately, such delegation meant that Will had no time to pay his respects to Marion Bartleby. He feared that if he did not advance his cause, her father would soon make a match for her with the insipid son of a vintner, or a clothier, or some such. City liverymen were notoriously clannish, and in his wiser moments, Will Halliday had little doubt that he, as a mere clerk to a man whose primary title was that of a mere storekeeper, stood only the slimmest chance of acceptance by a man who aspired to membership of the Common Council.

No, not the slimmest chance: no chance at all, in truth.

An hour or so later, Will Halliday's colleague returned from an accounting expedition to the victualling agent at Cheapside. Benjamin Gonson, his father's fifth son, was a pale, thin, unassuming fellow, a year or so younger than Will.

Ben nodded to Will, then said, 'Where's father?'

'Gone to the T-T-Tower. Some issue with the ordnance stores.'

The younger Gonson turned in alarm.

'The Tower? You're certain?'

'Aye, B-Ben, that's what he said. Why? What's amiss?'

'Did you not hear, Will? Don't you know what happens today at Tower Hill?'

Will Halliday shivered. He knew, as every man, woman and child in London knew; but he had forgotten.

'He will know too,' said Will slowly. 'He'll know what happens there. What if he's taken it into his head?'

He picked up the paper upon Gonson's table. It was no order from Secretary Paget, no direction to the Tower at all, merely a list of stores to be sent to Woolwich yard.

Ben Gonson needed no words from his colleague; Will Halliday's face told its own story. The two young men turned and ran out into the bright London day, making for Tower Hill.

-

As they got nearer to the forbidding walls of the old fortress, the throng of people grew larger by the yard, eventually blocking the highway entirely. The two young clerks pushed and jostled their way through the crowd, prompting cries of derision. But their own shouts of 'the Navy Royal's business! the king's business!' quelled most protests. They made their way slowly through the mass of people in the shadow of the Tower. As they came closer still to Tower Hill proper, they could hear the intermingled cheers, groans and jeers of those who could actually see the spectacle taking place there.

A scaffold had been erected in the open space to the west of the Tower. Upon it, five men were condemned to suffer the fate assigned to traitors: hanging, drawing and quartering.

'Perhaps he didn't c-come for this,' said Will, hopefully.

'I pray he – no, Will! He's there! There, by God!'

In the very front of the crowd, directly facing the scaffold and the Tower behind it, an old, bearded man knelt on all fours, his head touching the ground. As Will and Ben Gonson struggled to get through to the front rank, the old man raised his eyes to the spectacle in front of him. His face was awash with tears, but still he looked at the sight.

The first of the traitors had already suffered his fate. The four quarters of his body were being taken down from the scaffold, blood smearing the timber, and then flung unceremoniously into the cart that would take them to the destinations specified for them, the head being reserved for the most potent place of all, the south gate of London Bridge. Now the second man had the noose around his neck, and despite themselves, Will and Ben paused, unable to look away from the dreadful scene.

The stool upon which the man stood was kicked away, and a great cheer went up from the crowd as he kicked vainly at the air. His face turned purple, the tongue protruding, and the man's breeches stained as he pissed and beshat himself. The executioner, standing at the top of a ladder next to the dangling man, judged his moment, then leaned forward with his knife and severed the rope. Four attendants rushed forward, seized hold of the traitor, and lifted his twitching body onto a broad table. The executioner took up a large blade, the sort that butchers use to carve carcasses. It was still bloodied from the first victim, although a perfunctory attempt had been made to clean it. The executioner held it up for the crowd to admire, and was greeted by more cheers from his audience. Children squealed and clapped in delight. Then the executioner sliced deeply into the belly of the doomed man, whose strangled throat could muster only a feeble succession of screams. The executioner reached in and pulled out the entrails, raising them for the crowd to see. There was a roar of approbation.

Will Halliday looked at Ben, and saw the horror, saw the memories take hold, saw the tears flow afresh. For a moment, Benjamin Gonson was in the same place as his father, shuddering in pain on the ground a few yards ahead of them. For Ben, too, had seen his proud, gallant, and honourable brother David, the Knight of Saint John of Rhodes and Jerusalem, die by exactly this means.

But Ben was a younger man, and seemed to have made his peace with God over what had happened to Sir David Gonson. Not so with their father.

Ben led the way as they made their final push to the front, and fell to his knees beside the old man. Will knelt down, and rested his hands on William Gonson's shoulders.

'It isn't David,' said Ben Gonson. 'It isn't him, Father. These men were only coiners.'

For long moments, William continued to shake with horror and anguish. Then he looked up at his living son, turned to look tearfully at Will, then looked directly into the dreadful spectacle before him. Finally, he turned to look at Ben once again.

'No, son,' he said, his voice broken and full of sorrow, 'they are all David. All of them.'

Sixteen

The *Osprey* lay at single harbour in the Road of Calais, close under the north-west redoubt of the castle, in the midst of the fleet that had crossed from Dover. The king was gone, along with his escorting regiments, making for Boulogne by way of the coast road. Soon, most of the ships in the harbour would return to England. Most, but not all; and that was the substance of the raging quarrel between the cousins Jack Stannard and Simon Bulbrooke in the master's cabin. Elsewhere in the ship, there was utter silence. The men of the crew stood or sat perfectly still, listening to the argument. Even young George Vincent, on duty in the bows where he was checking that the anchor cable did not snag in such a tightly packed anchorage, could hear almost every word.

'Our time's up, Jack!' shouted Bulbrooke, a man to whom the notion of whispering was alien. 'We were taken up for ten weeks, no more. We were taken up for Dover to Calais and back, nothing further – not for a war voyage, by Christ's holy wounds!'

'The Lord Admiral needs ships to run supplies from here down to Boulogne,' said Jack, as patiently and quietly as he could. 'Then they are needed to lie in the mouth of the river, to stop the French sending in ships or galleys to try and break the siege.'

'Lisle can send the king's own ships,' snapped Bulbrooke. 'Why should we care? Why should we do the fighting for the Navy Royal? Our hire is finished, I say. We should go home, I say.'

'The estuary there is shallow,' said Jack, with as much patience as he could muster. 'The king's ships draw too much water to run close inshore, and into the river itself. Besides, Lisle will pay generously for those ships whose owners volunteer for the service.'

'Will he, now? And will he pay if we're sunk or burned by the French? This hull is my livelihood, Jack. I have nothing else.'

'This hull,' said Jack, levelly, 'is my father's. And if I need remind you of it, cousin, he has granted me power of attorney over all his affairs.'

Bulbrooke frowned.

'Oh, I know full well how you and my uncle organise your business, *cousin*.'

Jack stared at him. There was a depth of rage to Si Bulbrooke – and a depth of emptiness, too – that he had not glimpsed before.

'Come, Si, don't be nifflin nor waspy. Don't dwell only upon the worst that could happen. Boulogne is where the war is, which means it's where the glory is. Where the plunder is. Where the women are.'

For once, Simon Bulbrooke was not to be mollified so easily.

'And even if you're right, Jack Stannard, do you think my luck would bring me any of those delights? Do you, now?'

With that, he turned on his heel, left the cabin, and made for his berth in the fo'c's'le, where, Jack knew for certain, there would be a flagon of strong ale or wine concealed among his possessions. Most likely, several flagons.

–

Will Halliday and Ben Gonson sat in a quiet corner of the Pope's Head in Cornhill, but neither was in much of a mood for drinking. The horror of the scene at Tower Hill was still very much in their minds, although William Gonson had been put to bed under a physician's direction, lulled by the strange, foul-smelling concoction that the man prescribed. As he slowly lapsed into sleep, he kept murmuring the same thing: 'the shame, the shame'.

'Coiners,' said Ben bitterly. 'No greater crime than clipping or debasing coins. Yet that's counted as high treason, and earns them execution on Tower Hill, where those of royal and noble blood have perished before them. Not Saint Thomas-a-Watering, where David died.'

'I don't know the place,' said Will. 'I'm n-naught but a Suffolk foreigner, as you keep telling me.'

Ben Gonson ignored the attempt at levity.

'The southern boundary of the City liberties, the far side of Southwark. There's a bridge over a stream that comes down from the Peckham hills, which forms the boundary of Camberwell. No better than a common sewer, in truth. And that's where my brother suffered that same fate. No, the king didn't want a Knight of Saint John perishing before a great crowd, in case they showed sympathy. In case they made a demonstration, Will. The knights were popular, to the very end, and David's case was a sham. Every man who studied it in any degree at all knew that. One perjured witness – Babington, a renegade knight who'd deserted the order, who always hated David, who'd sworn revenge on him after my brother rightly accused him of cowardice. We heard tell that Babington had already been bought by the Lord Cromwell, before he fell, to act as a spy against his fellow knights. All of Babington's evidence against David was a lie, there was no trial at all, but my brother had to die as an example, out there in the arse end of beyond.'

Will looked round urgently, but the tavern was relatively empty, and none seemed to be listening. He had to shift Ben's talk onto safer ground, although he had no real idea how to do so.

'Well, then. Well. All passing s-sad. T-t-ime, though, to think of the future, surely? How go your affairs with Mistress Hussey, Ben?'

Ben Gonson's pursuit of a wealthy lawyer's daughter seemed as optimistic, and, mayhap, as hopeless, as Will's of Marion Bartleby. But Ben was not to be distracted so easily.

'He didn't need to leave Malta, Will. He could have stayed there, been safe, been alive today, like the other English knights who decided to ignore the king's commands and stay loyal to the Order. Christ's wounds, Will, he might have been Grand Master one day! But no, he came back. He knew the king had passed a law ordering the English knights to renounce their loyalty to the Pope, but still he came back – and then, within weeks, Parliament passed another act, this time dissolving the Order in England. I saw him for the last time not long after that, and told him he should get out of the country, get back to Malta. We all did, all of his sibs, and father, too. Especially Father. He'd been a gentleman usher to the king when he was younger, so he knew him.' Benjamin Gonson, too, finally glanced around, and lowered his voice. 'Father knew what the king could be like. But David just smiled – you should have seen his smile, Will, it was truly a gift from the angels – and said he was an Englishman, he would obey his king, and perhaps he would even go back to Melton and turn farmer. He was the most loyal of Englishmen, but because he had another loyalty, beyond these shores, some would name him traitor, and put him to death.'

There was now a silent, sullen fellow, sat upon a settle in the far corner of the room, and Will wondered if he could overhear Ben's words.

'Ben, we should talk of other things, or we should l-leave.'

'So all of that sits upon Father's soul, but most of all, he feels the shame of Saint Thomas-a-Watering. That's the strange thing, Will. I think he could have lived with it more easily if they'd carved my brother apart on Tower Hill.'

'We should leave, Ben. We are leaving. *Now*.'

–

The *Osprey* was in company with five other English ships, four of London and one of Southampton, making their way under easy sail down the coast. Three of the London ships carried troops, archers but lately despatched from London as reinforcements; the other three, including the *Osprey*, carried barrels of ale for the besieging army at Boulogne. The day was hazy, with strong sun and what seemed to be thunder in the far distance, but Jack was confident they would be able to run into the river of Boulogne long before any storm broke. The great headland that the French called Gris Nez already lay well astern, the fishing village of Saint John, which the French named as Audreselles, visible on the shore to the east, its church tower providing a convenient seamark. The low, swampy land Jack Stannard could see from his larboard rail marked the border between the English Pale and the French kingdom, but soon, if God willed it, the capture of Boulogne, to the south, would surely mean that this entire shore would be part of King Henry's realm. As it had once been a part of the dominions of his ancestors.

He saw Simon Bulbrooke, down in the waist, carrying out running repairs on one of the spare sails. A common sailor's work, far beneath a man who was still, nominally at least, the shipmaster of the *Osprey*; but since the altercation at Calais, Jack's cousin had preferred to keep his own company, and to attend any menial task which gave him an excuse to avoid the stern and his much younger kinsman. Jack thought little of it. Cousin Si had always been prone to moods, and he had no doubt that the darkness which presently afflicted him would lift in a few hours' time, after they arrived at Boulogne. Good wine and a good whore would do wonders for Simon Bulbrooke's spirits. They always did.

'Sails ho!'

The lookout's call was urgent and unexpected. Jack looked away to the south-west, where the lookout's arm was pointing, and realised at once that what he had thought to be thunder was, in truth, the sound of distant battle. Three ships, as far as he could see, running a little north-easterly upon the weak westerly breeze: a course which would bring the battle to the *Osprey* and the other ships from Calais, if it lasted that long.

'A falling out between sea-thieves, most like,' said Simon Bulbrooke, finally deigning to stand alongside his cousin. 'Bretons or Brabanters, I'll wager. Best steer well inshore, away from them.'

Jack made no reply. He was screwing up his eyes, endeavouring to make better sense of the spectacle before him. He could see one small ship, with a larger one seemingly grappled to her. Another ship, about as large again, was standing off. This third craft was equipped with cannon, hence what Jack had first assumed to be thunder. The middle ship seemed to have no more than hand guns. She was a ballinger, by the looks of her, with just a single mast, the signifier of her kind: her assailant was a more modern affair altogether, with two masts. The ballinger looked to be in trouble, listing a little toward the smaller craft to which she was secured. So, the likeliest case, thought Jack, was that the small ship had been running from the ballinger, which had caught her and boarded, but then a more powerful ally of the small ship had come to her aid. As Cousin Si said, not a battle to concern.

A sudden gust unfurled the flag flying from the shattered, leaning mast of the ballinger. It was the cross of Saint George.

'All sail!' cried Jack, as he moved to take the whipstaff.

'No!' Bulbrooke's protest was urgent, and he grasped his cousin's forearm fiercely. 'Still not our fight, John Stannard! Let the ships with the archers go, if they have to – but what do we fight with? Do we dowse them with ale? Don't think of being so damned shanny!'

At first, Jack wondered if his cousin was right: perhaps he was being shanny, impetuous. Only the *Osprey*'s head seemed to be coming around to bear down for the battle, the sails cracking as they were brought round to catch more of the wind. And the *Osprey* had only her two small fawconets, firing one-pound shot, an armament that was likely to unsettle naught but grandmothers and babes in arms. If all the other masters in their little fleet decided upon discretion, then the *Osprey*'s course was suicide. Jack would have no choice but to veer away and apologise to an insufferably vindicated Simon Bulbrooke.

Then, very slowly but in turn, each of the other ships in the little fleet shifted their helms and their sails, and followed the *Osprey* toward the battle.

It should have been a close fight. The larger French ship – for the two enemies of the ballinger could surely only be French – not only mounted at least six cannon and a score or more handguns, but she probably had as many men as the crews of the six oncoming ships together. But she was already furiously engaged with the sinking ballinger, which was resisting all efforts at boarding while still subduing the crew of the smaller French vessel, alongside her. It was an unequal struggle; trying to fight both sides of a ship at once was one of the seaman's many nightmares. As Jack watched, the larger Frenchman secured to the stern of the ballinger, its men swarming over the wales to attack the beleaguered English crew. The Frenchman's position was such that he could still bring most of his cannon to bear on the oncoming English ships, and two of the Londoners, the other two ships carrying ale, veered away. But the Southampton ship, full of hard-bitten Welshmen, made straight for the Frenchman's bows, tacking into the final approach. As she did so, the archers on her deck let loose. Jack watched the cloud of wooden darts rise, then fall, some into the sea, most onto the deck of the Frenchman.

Jack made his decision. He shifted the whipstaff a little to larboard, making for the bows of the ballinger.

'Stand off, for pity's sake!' cried Simon Bulbrooke. 'Go with the *Richard* and the *Grace of God*! Their masters have more sense, John Stannard!'

But the *Osprey* continued on its course. Now the three ships carrying archers were all in positions from which they could assail the larger Frenchman, their masters manoeuvring to avoid the cannon-fire as much as possible while remaining within the bowmen's range. But the Englishmen on the ballinger were still losing the battle on their own vessel. Jack could see the man whom he took to be her captain, a swarthy fellow in what looked to be a finer shirt than the English Channel warranted, swinging swords ferociously in both hands and fighting off several men at once. *Even Ryman would be impressed*, Jack thought. But the enemy's numbers were against the captain and his crew, and his ship was sinking under him.

Still the *Osprey* edged closer and closer to the action. The large French ship opened fire with her chase guns in her starboard bow, but the angle was impossible, the hull of the ballinger obstructing the line of fire. In any case, the French captain had more pressing concerns, notably deterring the three seaborne troops of archers, the heirs of the heroes of Agincourt, all of whom were well within range and shooting at will.

Simon Bulbrooke had vanished; he was the only man of the *Osprey*'s crew not on deck and not armed with some form of weapon. But his cousin's whereabouts, and his faintheartedness, did not matter now. On Jack's command, grappling hooks were thrown, and made fast to the bow of the ballinger. Jack took up his sword, formerly Thomas Ryman's second-best blade, the weapon which the old man had once employed to train Jack relentlessly upon

Dunwich cliff. He made his way into the bows, and led the men of Dunwich over onto the deck of the ballinger.

'God for Harry, Suffolk and Dunwich!' he bellowed. '*Nobiscum deus!*'

A party of Frenchmen detached themselves from the main body of their crew and rushed forward to attack them, screaming '*Le roi et Saint Denis!*' Jack swung his blade brutally, slashing at the men running toward him. He cleaved one skull open, and even before the brain-blood could properly stain his blade, he hacked into the gut of a fat creature and saw the entrails spill out. Jack Stannard had been well trained in swordplay, but this was no place for finery and delicate feints. All around him, *Osprey*'s men were fighting in the Dunwich way, hacking and stabbing ferociously. He saw young George Vincent wielding one of the old gutting-knives from the days of the Iceland fishery, screaming obscenities that would have horrified his virtuous mother in Peter's parish, and smiled. The lad had the makings of a decent fighter.

The Frenchmen rallied. Jack could see their leader, a bearded, one-armed fellow in a buff-jerkin, extolling his men from the ship's waist, directing some of them against the newcomers from the *Osprey* who were fighting to establish themselves in the bows, most against the English captain and his men, trapped toward the stern. The Frenchmen began to band together more tightly, pushing back against the men of the *Osprey*. Stephen Ball, a lad of no more than fifteen on his first voyage, took a pike in the stomach, looked astonished as his death-slime poured onto the deck, and fell forward into it. But two of Jack's men avenged themselves upon his killer, one driving a bill into the man's side and the other sticking a knife through the nostril, pushing up hard into the brain.

The deck of the ballinger lurched. She must have been holed beneath the waterline by cannon fire from the larger Frenchman, and it was obvious to Jack that she would not swim much longer.

A short, dark-skinned fellow came at Jack with an axe, but he ducked away and slashed into the man's throat. Blood spouted over killer and killed, soaking the deck beneath them. Jack wiped it from his mouth with the back of his hand. Suddenly, there was a moment's respite. His enemies were giving him a wide berth, realising he was a formidable fighter, and concentrating on the men with him. Jack looked again at the French officer, still exposed in the ship's waist, directing more and more men toward the stern, against the ballinger's captain.

A captain should not bloody his hands, Thomas Ryman once said. *A captain should stand above the battle, moving his men like chess pieces.*

But Ryman also taught Jack that killing a captain was akin to cutting the head off a human body.

There were too many fighting men between Jack and the Frenchman. Time for a gamble, to stake all upon one throw of the dice. Taking his sword in his left hand, Jack used his right to pull out his bollock-knife from his belt. Praying that the ballinger did not lurch, he pulled back his arm and threw, remembering as he did so the long hours that he, John Day and the other Dunwich boys had spent practising knife-throwing at targets on the Dain Quay.

The Frenchman leaned forward to exhort his men once more. Had he not done so, Jack's blade would have missed, and he would have lived. As it was, the knife struck him full in the forehead, turning him into an obscene parody of a unicorn. The man reached up, gripped the blade, and fell dead to the deck.

The officer's death threw the Frenchmen on the ballinger into confusion. It was evident in short order that it was the last straw for their captain, strutting the quarterdeck of the larger man-of-war but already hard pressed by the three hulls full of archers which assailed him. A trumpet sounded three short, sharp notes: a recall. The Frenchmen fell back, making a fighting retreat back to their own ship, harried all the way by the combined crews of the *Osprey* and the ballinger. Swords and axes hacked desperately through grappling ropes. The ballinger shuddered as the two vessels parted. The Frenchman put over his helm and bore away northward. Whoever was in command of her was clearly aware of the fact that if the English ships were minded to pursue, they would lose time by tacking to do so. Besides, the four Englishmen were merchant hulls, slower than that of a purpose-built man-of-war, and stood no realistic chance of catching it. Perhaps a man-of-war out of Calais or Dover might meet and overpower the Frenchman somewhere over the horizon, Jack thought. If not, the enemy would get clean away.

On the decks of the ballinger and the *Osprey*, men laughed, shouted, slapped each other on the back, and praised God and the Virgin for their lives. Others went below to quench their thirsts with ale.

Jack Stannard turned, and saw the ballinger's captain approaching him. He was older than he had appeared from a distance. Tall and dark, with shining hair that still bore traces of careful grooming, he bore himself with a prideful grace that Jack had seen many times in noblemen, but rarely in ship captains.

'A fine throw, my friend,' said the captain. 'A very fine throw, indeed.'

Strange: the accent was not English, but neither was it that of a Frenchman or a Fleming speaking English.

Jack inclined his head.

'John Stannard of Dunwich, sir,' he said, 'owner with my father of the ship *Osprey*, carrying ale to Boulogne by order of the Lord Admiral.'

The foreigner inclined his head in turn, and smiled broadly.

'An ale ship,' he said, laughingly. 'That I have been saved by such. Time to abandon the sea-business, I think. But yet, I am honoured to make your acquaintance, John Stannard of Dunwich, especially as I think you have saved my life, for which I thank you *con tutto* – ah, with all of my heart. I am in your eternal debt, John Stannard, *amico mio*. For my part, I name myself as Ottavio Valente, sometime of the Republic of Genoa, captain of the ballinger *Holyghost* in the service of your King Henry.' The hull lurched again. 'But not, I fear, for much longer. May I trouble you for passage to Boulogne for myself and my men, Master Stannard?'

Before Jack could answer, God or the Devil intervened. The Frenchman, now running to the northward with all sail set, fired two speculative parting shots from her stern guns. There was a gap between her and the *Osprey*, the other English ships having fallen away to leeward, and the Dunwich ship was no longer masked by the sinking hull of the ballinger. Thus the two iron balls struck the *Osprey*, the impact reverberating through the conjoined *Holyghost* and knocking Jack off balance. The Genoese captain lunged forward to take hold of him, and as Jack recovered, he registered the hurt his ship had sustained. One shot had struck at the bow, shattering part of the beakhead and driving on into the fo'c's'le. He heard screaming from there, but knew at once that it was too shrill to be his cousin Simon. The other shot had struck amidships, taking away part of the starboard rail, a good three feet of the upper deck, and some of the top timbers. The hit must have come above the waterline, but it was still serious damage, and the ship would need substantial repair.

Jack made for the bow of the ballinger, intending to cross back to the *Osprey* to see what the damage was below decks. But just then, Simon Bulbrooke emerged from the fo'c's'le. His forehead and left cheek were a mass of blood, and he limped heavily, a tell-tale dark circle on his left stocking. In his arms he carried the bloodied, shattered body of George Vincent. He stood upon the deck, staring silently and accusingly across at his cousin on the deck of the ballinger. He seemed to be struggling to speak, but no words came. When they did, they were damning.

'See the upshot of your pride, John Stannard!' he cried.

He laid the dead boy on the deck, then burst into uncontrollable tears.

Seventeen

A score or more of English ships, men-of-war and merchantmen alike, lay in the estuary before Boulogne. With some difficulty, Jack had brought the damaged *Osprey* in to join them that afternoon, and his passenger, Ottavio Valente, the Genoese sea captain in English pay, pointed out the principal features of the spectacle before them. Boulogne, upon the north bank of the estuary, was a town of two parts: a sprawling lower town on the flood plain, a much more compact upper town upon the hill above it. The latter evidently contained all the principal buildings – a castle, a great church, and so forth – and was much more strongly defended, with substantial walls, strengthened at regular intervals by round towers. The principal river ran east-west to the south of the town, but a substantial tributary came in from the north, along the western wall of the lower town. Much of the English army was concentrated on the western side of this stream, between it and the sea, although encampments and gun batteries could be seen all around the besieged town, including on the south bank of the main river.

The most remarkable feature of all, though, was an extraordinary conical tower, standing upon the cliff at the mouth of the estuary. Built of many layers, diminishing in size toward its apex, it resembled nothing more than some vast cake, fit for a royal banquet.

Valente noted Jack's incredulity.

'The Tower of Caligula,' he said.

'Caligula? The Roman emperor? Wasn't there something about a horse and a sister?'

Jack had a vague recollection of lessons in the classics at Cardinal College, which he and Will Halliday had looked upon as dull interludes between the exhilarating times spent at rehearsals and services.

'*Si*. The same. Yonder stands his great lighthouse, built when the emperor fancied the notion of conquering your isles of Britain. By then, *certamente*, Caligula was *pazzo*, a madman, as you say – hence the business of his horse, which he made consul. Pour me more ale, *amico mio*, and I will tell you the story of the sister, too. But it was the same here. The old tale, that I learned as a boy in Genoa, has it that he assembled his great invasion army on those beaches, and then made them do nothing more warlike than collect *conchiglie* – what is your English word? Ah, yes, seashells. Yet Caligula's tower still stands. The French call it the *tour de l'Ordre*.'

Whatever it was named, the strange tower was evidently still formidable, and had been transformed by the French into a strongpoint. Surrounding its base was a powerful modern fortification, with ramparts and ravelins. English flags fluttered from dug-in emplacements a few hundred yards from this defence. As the *Osprey* passed beneath the tower and into the estuary, mortars and cannon began firing at the French position. One shot struck the lighthouse itself, and some of the stone that had been there since Caligula's day broke off and fell to earth amid a cloud of dust.

Jack brought the ship to an anchor, and went from station to station, encouraging his men and seeing that the hull was made as fast as it possibly could be. During the final stage of the voyage toward Boulogne, the atmosphere aboard the *Osprey* had been sombre. The bodies of George Vincent and Stephen Ball had been cleaned, wrapped, and laid with reverence in the fo'c's'le, awaiting the arrival of a chaplain from the army camp to say prayers over them. As soon as the ship dropped anchor, Simon Bulbrooke went ashore, giving his cousin not even a backward glance, let alone a request for permission. Jack made no objection. He was not quite sure which conversation with his kinsman he wanted to avoid more: that in which Simon upbraided him once again over his wounds and the death of the two boys, or that in which Jack accused his cousin of palpable cowardice in the sea-fight. In these gloomy circumstances, Jack craved diversion, and thought that his exotic passenger might provide it. Thus he decided to entertain Valente to as good a meal as the *Osprey* could muster. Bixley, who served as cook, was a brother of Widow Green, who kept the Lion tavern on Dunwich's market square, and sometimes helped there in the intervals between voyages. Thus, unlike the great majority of ships that sailed under the English flag, the *Osprey* had a cook who knew at least the rudiments of preparing a meal, and Valente clearly appreciated the fare on offer. With a vengeance, the Genoese devoured the proferred salt beef, stockfish, bread and cheese, washing it down with a brimming cup of ale. He seemed to be profoundly unaffected by the deaths of a dozen or more of his crewmen.

'If I live in your land for a century,' he said, 'I will never understand your liking for this "ale". For any man who suckled on wine as a babe, it is an abomination.'

'For an abomination, you seem to drink it quickly enough, Captain,' said Jack, mildly.

'*Chi ha bisogna s'arrenda*, my friend. Or, as you English say, a beggar cannot be a chooser. But when we take Boulogne, and break open the casks of good wine the French must have in their cellars – then you will see Ottavio Valente drink.'

The Genoese raised his tankard to Jack, took another sip, and grimaced.

'I have a friend,' said Jack, 'an older friend, who has told me much of Italy. He fought there many times, in his youth.'

'Ah, so he would have been a *condotierro*,' said Valente. '*Si*, we knew their kind. Knew them too well. Italy has been a land of endless wars since long before I was born, my friend. The tragedy of a land with too many riches but too little government. No, I am wrong. Too many governments, too many little states, all with their own princes who think themselves almost gods.' Valente chewed thoughtfully on a piece of salt beef, then smiled. 'Think of it this way. Imagine your Suffuck an independent *principato*, and Essex, and – what is the other one? – yes, Norfuck, of course. Say that Essex covets the greater wealth of Suffuck, so allies with Norfuck to attack it. But Suffuck is rich enough to buy soldiers from abroad.'

'Kent?' asked Jack, entering into the spirit, for he wondered how Valente might mispronounce that particular shire. Yet he did so reluctantly; part of his thoughts still mourned for George Vincent and Stephen Ball, lying stiff and cold a few dozen feet forward of where they dined.

'If you will,' said Valente, disappointingly. 'So, Suffuck defeats Essex, and forces it to change sides and join Suffuck against Norfuck. But Norfuck then appeals to a greater power.'

'Yorkshire?'

'*Cavalo! Si*, Yorkshire, then. I have heard of this "Yorkshire". So the Emperor of Yorkshire sends his mighty army to help Norfuck – but now Suffuck appeals to somewhere still greater and richer.'

'London,' said Jack.

'Of course. So you see the way it is. Generation upon generation, our little states fight each other, buy *condottieri* and other mercenaries, change sides, bring in the Emperor or the King of France, and then they in their turn change sides – *merda*, my friend, all of it.'

Valente fell silent, drinking deeply from his mug of ale, while Jack reflected on his words. Italy, to him, sounded not so very different to the Sandlings of Suffolk: perhaps Dunwich was a miniature Venice, Southwold a little Florence, Walberswick a tiny Milan. A strange thought. He would have to ask Ryman about it – if, that is, Thomas Ryman still lived. Perhaps even now, he walked with Stephen Ball and George Vincent and Alice Stannard through the unknowable shadowlands of Purgatory.

To take his mind from the dead and the possibly dead, Jack ventured a fresh remark to Valente.

'Men say that you Genoese are great seamen. Your Columbus, for instance.'

'Ah, the great Cristoforo! *Si*. I knew some of his family, you know. How they strut, these days. But you are right, friend Stannard, so many great seamen. Andrea Doria, our famous admiral, who lives still – I fought under him at Preveza. What a – what is your English term? – yes, fuck-up, that battle was. We might have beaten Barbarossa that day, but for the shithead Venetians. I give you this advice *gratis*, Englishman – never trust a Venetian, never sail with them, and above all, *prego*, never fight with them.'

'I have never met a Venetian. But then, I had never met a Genoese, until I joined in with your battle.'

Valente's eyes widened.

'You call yourself a sailor, yet you have never met Italians before me? Where, then, have you sailed, Master Stannard? From your Dunwich to Dover and back, over and over again?'

'Flanders,' said Jack. 'Hamburg, Emden and the like. Lubeck. Scotland. Once to Norway. To the Iceland fishery, when I was a boy.'

'That,' said Valente as his teeth tore off a piece of stale bread, 'is not seafaring. That is stepping over puddles.' Jack bridled, but said nothing. Valente, though, was warming to his theme. 'You English! You have not sent a single ship into the Middle Sea in centuries! Your only lands across the ocean came to you because of Cabot – a Genoese! I, Ottavio Valente, have voyaged to Constantinople, to Tunis, to Madeira, to Riga!' It was, in essence, the same jibe that Martin Raker had levelled at Jack before William Gonson in the great hall of Framlingham Castle. But Valente had none of Raker's obvious motive against Jack, so his words cut more deeply. 'Pah, John Stannard, you English are not seafarers at all! You stick your toes in the sea, and say to yourselves, "Ah, as long as we can reinforce Calais, and sell our wool in Flanders, what care we for the world beyond?" And now, my friend, if your king takes Boulogne, you will be content. "Here is our mighty empire," you will say, but the world will laugh at you, because while you sit proudly within the walls of Calais and Boulogne, we will be sailing the oceans, finding new lands, mining the gold and silver of the new worlds as the Castilians do!'

Jack tried to form a reply, but could not. Instead, Jack did what countless generations of Englishmen had done when faced with a discomfiting foreigner: he took a swig of ale.

'And yet, Captain Valente, you seem mightily content to fight for us laughable Englishmen, and take our gold,' he said.

Valente shrugged.

'A man has to find his bread where he can. Besides, you English fly the same flag, and venerate the same saint, so it is very nearly like home, except for the rain. What, you did not know that George belongs to Genoa too? The red cross upon white flies from Genoa's ships – you only fly it with our *permesso*, my friend. So it is not such a very difficult thing to fight under the same colours, you see.' Another mouthful of ale. 'And now that the Emperor has made peace with the French, and the Ottomans are quiet, the Middle Sea is a lake at peace. It will not last, of course, but for the time being, thank God for you English, who seem to like nothing better than to pick a quarrel with your – *vicinato*, what is the word? – yes, neighbours.'

Jack started to form a protest, but realised at once that he had no argument to present. After all, within only the last twelve weeks, he had fought and killed both Scots and Frenchmen, England's closest neighbours.

'But you are not alone in making trouble. In the taverns of Calais, I heard much talk of a Frenchman who is said to be doing great things in the Carib ocean. Roberval, or some such name, and one of their Huguenots, one of the devil Luther's kind, so a heretic doomed to eternal hellfire, of course. But if he's bold enough to attack Cartagena de Indias, he's the kind of captain I like. Whereas you, John Stannard... I like you, but a man who has no ambition to sail further than Norway or Iceland? And you English – a people who seek nothing but a tiny *frazione* of the land in France they held a century ago? A kingdom that lives in the past?' Valente shook his head. 'Cast your eyes beyond the *orizzonte*, the horizon, my young friend. There are other seas out there, and great prizes to be had by the bold. Cathay! Russia! Africa! America and the Indies, above all. Much greater prizes than Boulogne, by the blood of Giovanni Battista – ah, John the Baptist, as you say it.'

Jack wanted to respond, to object to the Genoese's version of his situation, but he knew that in all truth, he could not. Simon Bulbrooke, drinking himself into oblivion somewhere ashore, would deny the thrust of Valente's words, but then, Si had always considered a voyage to Hamburg an expedition very nearly to the ends of the earth. And then there was the old leper, his father, still scheming to restore Dunwich's lost greatness from his bed in the hospital of Saint James, but wedded to the false hope that it could happen by turning back the clock, to restoring an old England that, in truth, had gone forever, as Valente said. For years, Jack had felt in his heart that there had to be a different hope, a different fate for Dunwich and himself, but he had never been able to see what that might be.

Perhaps now, thanks to this strange, garrulous foreigner, he could.

'Then will you return to sailing those other seas, Captain Valente?'

The Italian was silent for a moment.

'I will have to account to your Lord Admiral for the loss of the *Holyghost*,' he said. 'He will not be pleased. But she was old – who sails ballingers now? Who builds them? She had great leaks, long before the *Francese* put a dozen shot in her. Still, I think Milord Lisle will be an unhappy man. So he may dismiss me, and even if he judges I might remain in the English service, there will hardly be a new command before next summer. So we will see, John Stannard. We will see what tomorrow brings.'

Eighteen

The *Henry Grace à Dieu*, the largest and most powerful of all the king's ships, was known more readily throughout England as the *Great Harry*. Vast and impressive she may have been, but her sheer size also greatly limited her utility. It took so many men to man her that, in order to send her to sea, nimbler, more useful craft would have to be unmanned. Her great draught limited the number of harbours she could enter, and certainly rendered her useless in the shallow waters and confined estuary off Boulogne. So in that summer of 1544, the *Great Harry* swung, empty and forlorn, at double anchor just off the king's storehouse and dock at Erith, far down the Thames, waiting for the call to come, for her moment of glory finally to arrive.

It was, then, seemingly perverse of William Gonson to insist that he had to make a tour of inspection of her. Ben Gonson and Will Halliday concurred that a visit to Erith dockyard itself was perfectly natural, if apparently superfluous: the other ships were gone from there, and the storehouse was almost empty. But the older Gonson was insistent. He was determined to go alone, too, but Ben and Will had made a pact that one or other of them would always keep him within sight, in case his wits deserted him once again. The two young men tossed a groat to see which of them would stay in London to deal with correspondence, and which would accompany the old man to Erith. Will called heads, and the coin came up with the unmistakeable visage of Harry the Eighth.

Thames watermen would usually never venture as far downriver as Erith. But by special dispensation of the king – or, more precisely, of Secretary Paget – William Gonson could call on the services of one of the smaller royal barges, generally employed to transport members of the king's household to Greenwich Palace. As they were rowed past that edifice, a pleasant, red-brick jumble of buildings on the Kent shore, with its formal gardens, tilt yards and the like immediately adjacent to it, Will Halliday attempted once more to strike up a conversation with his master.

'Still nothing but good news from France, sir, other than the loss of the old *Holyghost*, of course,' he said. 'Do you not concur?'

Gonson seemed to be staring at the ribs of an old hull, protruding from the shore in front of the palace. The tide was still ebbing, aiding their progress downstream. The treasurer of the navy made no response, but his eyes appeared to be welling up.

'Did you know that ship, sir?' ventured Will.

Still no response. Will knew that the old man had once owned a veritable fleet of his own, which traded to distant parts on his own account. From time to time, he had put some of these into the king's service – the *Christopher Gonson*, the *David Gonson*, and so forth. Perhaps the wreck on the foreshore was the remnant of one of those. Will saw the eyes of the liveried oarsmen, glancing at Gonson, then knowingly at each other. The only sounds were those of the oars cutting the water, of the river-birds upon the marshes of the Isle of Dogs, and the distant cries of sailors bringing a small merchant carrack down into Blackwall

Reach. All the while, the treasurer and storekeeper of the Navy Royal stared into space. He became a little more animated as the boat passed Woolwich dockyard, gazing intently at the frames of the hull upon the stocks, even seeming to smile faintly. But in Barking Reach and Halfway Reach, he became sullen again. The boat turned into Erith Reach, the familiar tower of Saint John the Baptist Church coming into view on the Kent shore. Now William Gonson would have to talk. Now he would have to answer a question.

'The storehouse or the ship first, sir?' asked Will.

'*Great Harry*,' said Gonson, almost inaudibly.

The oarsmen brought the boat alongside the great vessel, and a couple of the shipkeepers assisted Gonson in boarding. He stood in the ship's waist, looking around as though he were a captain assessing his new command. Perhaps that remembrance of the time when he had been an active young man-of-war revived Gonson. His eyes widened, and he seemed to see Will Halliday for the first time since they had left the house in London.

'Check the bilges, Will, see that she's not taking on more water. Then the orlop, and the cable tier.'

'All in order there, sir!' said the principal shipkeeper, a small, round, bald man, who evidently considered that some slur had been made against his competence.

'No doubt,' said Gonson, 'but as long as I have breath, I have to account to the king for this ship, as you have to account to me. Go, Will. I'll begin at the great cabin, then the poop.'

Will complied reluctantly. Even by recent standards, there seemed to be a strangeness about Gonson's mood: a kind of emptiness, indeed, which had been present since the execution at Tower Hill. Nevertheless, William

Halliday of Ipswich knew his place, unless the matter related to Mistress Marion Bartleby, in which case he would vault as far above his place as he possibly could. He went below decks, down through the vast, empty hull, devoid of its men and cannon, consequentially riding high in the water. He had just come to the orlop deck, where his senses were assailed by the odour of the bilges, when the senior shipkeeper's cry reached him.

'Master 'alliday! 'Tis Master Gonson, sir! Come quick!'

The hairs on the back of his neck pricked up, and he shivered. He mouthed a prayer to *Maria maris stella*, then turned and ran. He took the ladders two steps at a time, striking his head on beams several times. Out onto the upper deck – a glance toward the fo'c's'le – empty – then astern.

At last, Will Halliday knew what his master intended to do.

William Gonson stood at the very highest point of the poop deck, far up in the aftercastle of the *Great Harry*. It seemed as though he was contemplating the ship before him, perhaps imagining sailing her into battle.

'Master!' cried Will.

He began to run toward the ladder that led up into the aftercastle, followed by one of the younger shipkeepers.

With surprising nimbleness for a man of his age, Gonson climbed up onto the ship's wale, his face turned away from Will's. The young man shouted again, but Gonson ignored him. Instead, he reached his hands toward the heavens, mumbled something that Halliday could not properly hear, and fell forward.

Halliday reached the wale, and saw William Gonson enter the water, far below. He knew the old man could not swim: who could, other than Jack Stannard, who had always been perverse? But Gonson did not thrash about, or fight to stay afloat. He stayed perfectly still, and sank in an instant.

For what seemed like countless millennia in purgatory, but could only have been a few moments, Will Halliday stared down at the place where Gonson had disappeared. When he turned away, he registered the senior shipkeeper's shouts for a boat, and saw that the watermen were already swinging the bow of their craft around, back into the tideway. Will, no seaman, no rower and no swimmer, could do nothing but stand mutely, and wonder how he would report the death of his father to Ben Gonson. Then it would have to be reported to Secretary Paget, who, in turn, would have to report it to the Lord Admiral; and one of them would have to report it to the king.

But Ben most of all. Death stood at the shoulder of every man and woman alive, taking their parents, their children, each other. Yet natural death was, simply, that: natural, a proper part of God's expected order of things. Poor Ben Gonson, though, barely Will Halliday's own age, had now lost two of those closest to him to the most unnatural deaths of all, a brother literally torn apart in a traitor's death and his father drowning as a suicide. And suicide, of course, was both a mortal sin and a human crime, with dire consequences in both the visible and invisible realms.

The shipkeepers pointed toward an object bobbing in the water, and the boat steered toward it. Will Halliday knew it could only be one thing. He began to sob, both for the old man's method of dying, and for the one mumbled word of his that Will thought he had made out, just as Gonson began to fall: 'David'. Although he did not know if it was permissible for a Christian to do so in the case of suicide, Will began to finger his paternoster, and, in his deep, tuneful bass voice, which his stammer never impeded, to sing the prayers for the dead: not the prayers of the new and still unfamiliar, unsettling English liturgy, but the old Latin words, that William Gonson would have known and loved long ago, in Melton Mowbray, far away in the middle of England, so very far from the sea.

> *'Requiem aeternam dona ei, Domine, et lux perpetua luceat ei. Requiescat in pace. Amen. Requiem aeternam dona ei…'*

Nineteen

The English army completely encircled Boulogne. From every quarter, even from across the estuary of the Liane river, King Henry's artillery pounded the lower town, the smoke rolling over the countless flags of Saint George that flew from the English positions. Sometimes, from the deck of the *Osprey*, Jack saw a great cannonball strike a church tower and bring masonry crashing to the ground, or a mortar round plunge through the roof of a tall building. He imagined the scene ashore easily enough: all he had to do was envisage Dunwich under siege in the same way. He could picture the vast mortar balls shattering walls and roofs, or crushing men, women and children as they ran in terror down the streets, desperately seeking safety. There would be no respite when darkness fell, either. Night after night, along every part of the walls of Boulogne, troops of English archers, hackbutters, billmen and pikemen probed at the defences, wearing down the Frenchmen on the walls. Fires broke out in the lower town as fireballs or fire-arrows struck home, the flames illuminating the night sky and lighting up the walls of the upper town and castle, still defiant upon the great hill.

In the harbour, though, all was quiet. Since the sinking of Valente's command, the French had not attempted to run the blockade in either direction. This gave Jack and the returned Simon Bulbrooke time to attend to the repairs of the *Osprey*, although it was clear that the ship would have to be docked or beached properly to make good the damage beneath the waterline. Bulbrooke was sullen, and drinking heavily. He blamed Jack for his head and leg wounds, still swathed in bandages; for the deaths of young Stephen Ball and George Vincent; and for the damage to the ship. But he also knew the Stannards well enough to know that old Peter, the leper, would always support his own son against his sister's child. Jack knew it, too, and avoided his cousin's company as much as he could, difficult as it was in such a small hull. All the while, though, Jack thought on Valente's words. The Genoese was gone. Lisle proved forgiving, and Valente had said he was returning to London to secure his back pay and petition for a new command. At least, that was the story he had spun to Jack. The younger man had a suspicion that Valente sought a very different harbour, and was gone off to sail and plunder with the Huguenot Roberval. But although their encounter had been only fleeting, Jack still thought much on Valente's words. By night, indeed, he found himself dreaming more and more often of distant shores, of blazing sun beating down on golden beaches, of gold itself.

Then, one morning, the great bombardment fell silent. The report came out from the shore to one of the closer ships, and was then shouted from hull to hull.

'A truce!' The cry reached the *Osprey*. 'A truce! A parley!'

A few hours of uncertainty passed. Then, toward evening, Jack saw a small party ride across the bridge into the lower town. A little later, the cross of Saint George broke out upon the gate tower. Cheering broke out throughout the huge encampment, then on the ships in the harbour.

Simon Bulbrooke came up from the hold. He looked around, askance.

'What's to do?'

'They've surrendered, Si! We have Boulogne!'

The older man glanced across the water.

'No,' he said. 'Fleur-de-lis still flying in the upper town, and on the castle, yonder. Lower town only has surrendered, as it always would. Indefensible. Full of the lower sort of people – not the sort worth fighting for. But the upper town… that's a very different case. Very different.'

Bulbrooke was slurring his words, and Jack suspected he was replenishing his tankard frequently below decks.

-

The damaged *Osprey* was out of the water. Following the fall of the lower town, Jack had requested, and been granted, permission to bring the ship upstream, under the shattered outer wall of Boulogne, and run her ashore, so that repairs could be effected more easily. Simon Bulbrooke continued to disappear for hours on end, no doubt into the taverns of the lower town, but Jack still made no attempt to reprimand him. Si had made an almighty effort over the temporary repairs during the more difficult time when the *Osprey* was afloat in the harbour; now that the hull was aground, it was easy for Jack and a work party to repair the hull from the outside, untroubled by constant leaks, every hole, rotten plank, and failure of caulking, easily visible. If Bulbrooke thought that he had earned a long and drunken respite, one in which he could avoid the young cousin whose impetuosity had brought them to this pass, then he was probably right.

The *Osprey* was beached just downstream from the lowest bridge into the lower town, a position which gave Jack an unrivalled view of the activity ashore. A steady stream of traffic crossed the bridge, bringing the English army across from its original siege positions and encampments on the other bank. Troops of soldiers, billmen, archers, hackbutters and other sorts, tramped across into the lower town, singing songs that ranged from the religious to the scatologically profane. Jack joined in with some of them, and earned more than one curious glance across to the possessor of a voice finer than any that the army seemed to possess. A sound much akin to thunder presaged the slow progress of cannon and mortars, their wheeled carriages rumbling as teams of oxen pulled them across the bridge toward their new positions in entrenchments at the base of the hill upon which the upper town stood. Jack could hear, and sometimes even see, houses being pulled down to create better fields of fire for the artillery. From time to time, a high-ranking officer rode over the bridge on horseback, his splendidly uniformed escort at his back. One particularly impressive retinue attended a man whom Jack recognised, for he had seen him, once, when he was on the Blythburgh road. Charles Brandon, Duke of Suffolk, was very old now, even older than the king, his closest friend and erstwhile brother-in-law, but he still carried himself splendidly upon a horse, and was still every inch a mighty warrior. He did not see Jack, and would not have recognised him, but this duke had been a good friend to Dunwich, in part because Peter

Stannard, and Peter's father Adam before him, had once been trusted men of business for His Grace.

Jack thought he would never see a greater personage than the Duke of Suffolk, nor a greater retinue than that which accompanied him into the lower town; but in this, he was mistaken.

The distant sound of trumpets gave Jack his first inkling. Then he saw soldiers running toward the road, jostling with each other for the best view. Cheering went up on all sides – 'God save the king!' 'Vive le Roi!' 'God save your highness!' 'God for Harry and Saint George!'

Jack saw the vanward of men-at-arms march onto the bridge, their spearpoints gleaming in the bright sunlight. The bridge was too narrow for any but the escort; any who attempted to line its sides were brusquely swept out of the way by the armed men. That meant Jack had a nearly uninterrupted view of the spectacle crossing the bridge.

Behind the men-at-arms came a party of demilance cavalry, heralds and trumpeters at the head of them, resplendent in glorious tabards. Then came one man, one single rider, on by far the largest horse Jack Stannard had ever seen – and for a man of Suffolk, renowned for its colossal punches, that was no mean claim. But even such a huge steed was very nearly not sufficient for the man upon its back. With his broad girth and square white beard, he bore a passing resemblance to the Duke of Suffolk: but whereas the duke's bulk still gave the impression of muscle, that was not the case with this man. Although his gambeson and half-armour could probably have accommodated two much smaller men, they were still barely sufficient to encompass the amount of flesh contained within. Great folds of fat fell out over the man's paunch and sides. He wore no leg armour, and from his unique vantage point, Jack was close enough to see why: one leg was bandaged all the way from the ankle to the groin. Even so, yellow patches were seeping through the bandages, and the north-easterly breeze brought the faintest trace of a strange, sweet odour.

The man had to be in agony. Every few moments, he slumped a little, and it seemed as though nothing could prevent this enormous mound of flesh falling from his mount. Jack had a terrible presentiment of the vast figure going over the side of the bridge, into the river; and although Jack could swim, and duty would demand that he dive in to try and save this most special of lives, he did not doubt that the decaying colossus would sink like a stone long before he could reach him. But by what must have been both a tremendous effort of will, and the remembrance of the consummate horseman he must have been in his youth, the man stayed astride his steed. But he dared not take his hand from the reins to acknowledge the cheers of the men who lined his route.

As he came level with the *Osprey*, he turned his head slightly to study the spectacle before him. For just one fleeting moment, his gaze seemed to be directly upon Jack Stannard. From his father's description of that one occasion, twenty years before, when Peter Stannard had seen the King of England, Jack expected to look upon the face of an Adonis, the lofty, red-headed demigod whom Erasmus, Thomas More, and even Pope Leo, had extolled. Instead, the face of Henry the Eighth was a frightful mask of decay. The eyes were no more than slits, insignificant between the unnaturally puffed-up cheeks and the high, sweating forehead. From certain angles, even Jack's father looked healthier. But even in shock at the sight before him, Jack still knew his duty, and bowed deeply to his sovereign.

There was no acknowledgement of any sort. Indeed, it was impossible to tell whether the king had even registered his presence, such was the flow of sweat into the already narrowed eyes.

Great Harry rode on, into the Lower Town, and was gone from sight.

Jack straightened, and despite the summer heat, he shivered. Even his father, the leper of Dunwich, seemed set fair to live longer than the mountain of flesh which had just ridden over the bridge, barely yards away from him. But only the appallingly frail body of King Henry stood between England and the accession of a seven-year-old boy, not very much older than his own Tom.

Ecclesiastes Ten, verse sixteen: both Seaward at Saint John's and Overfield at All Saints had preached upon it often enough.

Woe unto thee, oh land where a child is king.

–

The capture of the lower town meant that Jack, Bulbrooke and almost all of the crew of the *Osprey* could attend mass, having been unable to do so since Calais. The church they chose for the purpose had been badly damaged in the bombardment, with its west window shattered and a large hole, presumably from a mortar ball, high up in the north wall, but it was still useable. Of course, its French priest had fled, but a few particularly devout, if nervous, members of his regular congregation joined the fringes of the throng of English soldiers and sailors, queueing to take the Holy Sacrament from a bumptious young chaplain of the army. Simon Bulbrooke still kept his distance from Jack, but the very fact that he had chosen to attend mass as part of the company of the *Osprey* suggested at least a slight thawing of his hostility. He was relatively sober, too, but it was an early service, and there was no guarantee that this condition would endure beyond noon-tide.

Jack swallowed the wafer, crossed himself, and was getting back to his feet, when he first heard the commotion outside the church: the sounds of women screaming, of glass breaking, of drunken men laughing and jeering.

The congregation spilled out of the church to see what was amiss. Jack realised his cousin was at his side, and that Simon was shaking his head.

'Fuckwits,' he said. 'Bringing dishonour on England.'

Some of the soldiers from the congregation evidently thought differently, and were already running to join their drunken fellows on the rampage. Men were breaking into shops and houses, stealing whatever they could carry. Just across the road, three soldiers were kicking a Frenchman who had fallen to the ground. A little further along, a woman, of no more than Jack's age, had her arms pinned back by two drunken soldiers, while a third clawed at the front of her dress.

A girl child of eight or nine years, presumably this woman's daughter, was kicking at the legs of the third man.

Jack felt his muscles tighten, sensed his hair bristling.

'Not your battle, John Stannard,' said Simon Bulbrooke, echoing the words he had spoken at sea.

Jack barely heard him.

'The girl,' he said, his voice hoarse. 'She puts me in mind mightily of my Meg.'

He made to run forward, but his arm was gripped by a powerful, unrelenting hand.

'No, Jack,' said Bulbrooke urgently. 'No. She looks nothing like your Meg. Nothing like at all.'

Jack Stannard turned, his face a mask of fury. But his cousin's expression was not what he had expected to see: not the face of the drunken coward, the craven determined to avoid a fight at all costs, that he now knew Simon Bulbrooke to be.

'Si?'

'No, cuz. She looks nothing like your Meg. But she reminds me of my youngest. She puts me greatly in mind of my Cicely.'

Jack gave a nod, then shouted, 'Men of Dunwich! To us!'

The cousins, with the men of the *Osprey* at their backs, charged the soldiers. Jack took hold of the one in front of the woman, swung him round, and struck him hard on the jaw. The man fell back, feeling for the injury, looking in astonishment and fury at the man who had hit him. Meanwhile, Simon punched the man on the woman's left in his stomach, while two of the *Osprey*'s men pulled away the man on her right. A gaggle of half-a-dozen friends of the would-be rapists ran to their aid, but there were more than enough men of Dunwich to give them a warm greeting; and unlike their assailants, the crewmen of the *Osprey* were sober.

Jack's target regained his wits, roared, and ran forward, drawing a knife from his belt as he did so. But the attack was clumsy, driven by rage rather than strategy. Jack sidestepped to his left, grabbed hold of the extended knife arm, and pulled it hard toward him. The man's drunken momentum snapped his arm like a dry twig on

Dunwich heath. The fellow screamed, dropped the knife, and grabbed at the broken right arm with his left.

'Fuck you,' he gasped between sobs.

The other looters were already turning in flight, Simon Bulbrooke waving his fist and screaming obscenities after them as they ran. The man with the broken arm looked around, spat blood onto the road, and staggered after his friends.

Jack turned to the woman. The little girl was clinging to her skirts, tears streaming down her small face, looking up uncertainly at her saviours.

'*Merci, monsieur,*' said the woman. '*Vierge Marie, merci, merci.*'

'Not all Englishmen are alike, mistress,' said Jack, even though he knew she would not be able to understand him.

Her face was not unattractive, he thought. With a little attention to her appearance, she might even make something of a beauty. Jack was aware, then, of how long it had been since he was with a woman. Perhaps he could escort her to wherever her home might be.

Simon Bulbrooke came over.

'We'd best away, cuz. If their officers take their word over ours.'

Jack nodded, the aching in his loins dissipating. The sounds of damage and shouting from all quarters of the lower town suggested that the looting was endemic and ongoing, and if officers were doing anything at all, they would surely be struggling to regain control. More likely was the prospect of the men they had faced returning with an even larger crowd of their friends, and if they had time to collect their weapons from their billets, the men of Dunwich would be in dire straits indeed. Either way, it was time for a retreat to the harbour, where they would simply be one anonymous ship's company among many, and under the indisputable authority of the Lord High Admiral, not of those allegedly now responsible for law and order within Boulogne. It was no time for Jack Stannard to make a chivalrous offer to a French woman he did not know, in the almost certainly forlorn hope of a less than chivalrous sequel.

'Aye, true, let's away,' said Jack. 'And Si – thank you.'

The older man nodded. The two cousins bowed to the woman they had saved, then, as one, both of them laid their hands on the head of the young girl, as if in benediction.

Twenty

Simon Bullbrooke was entirely right about the progress of the siege. The rapid capture of the lower town lulled the English army into a complacent belief that the fall of the rest would be accomplished easily and swiftly, but nothing was further from the truth. All sallies against the walls of the upper town proved fruitless, and those same walls continued stubbornly to resist the limited bombardment of the few mortars that could be brought to bear against them. Countless parleys, where the king's representatives sought to persuade the French commanders that no relief was coming and that further defiance was hopeless, ended in failure. The white fleur-de-lis standards still flew proudly from the walls of Boulogne, mocking King Henry in his vast palace of a tent on the plain outside the lower town, and on most nights, the French sent out raiding parties to strike directly at their besiegers, killing any Englishmen foolish enough or unfortunate enough to be in their path.

For Jack, Simon Bullbrooke and the repaired, refloated *Osprey*, there was nought but the tedious routine of patrolling the river mouth, always taking their bearings on the astonishing edifice of Caligula's Tower. But nothing remotely hostile attempted to come in or out of the harbour. There were supply ships from Calais or Portsmouth, the occasional royal man-of-war putting in from cruising in the Channel, and that was all. Simon Bullbrooke was much less sullen than before, but even so, he still spent most of his time ashore.

On a fine July morning, the *Osprey* was alongside the wharf of the lower town as two heavily laden ships came alongside the empty berth astern of her. Dozens of men, most of them small and dark-haired, disembarked, many carrying pickaxes or shovels, all talking rapidly to each other in unfamiliar tongues.

'Welsh and Cornish,' said Bullbrooke, standing alongside Jack at the stern of the *Osprey*. 'Sailed to those parts, picked up a few words. Obvious what they're about.'

Jack nodded. Yes, it was obvious. The great, steep-sided hill upon which the upper town stood made it nearly invulnerable to artillery fire, but it also made it ideal ground for mining; and in that art, the Welsh and Cornish had few equals. From the wharf, and later from their berth in the harbour, they could clearly see the small parties of miners, picks and shovels over their shoulders, moving up the slopes, to the point where they were just beyond the limit of the range of the French archers and hackbutters. True, the English artillery, with the exception of the mortars, could not be elevated sufficiently to fire upward against the walls; but by the same token, the French cannon could not be depressed far enough to fire against the besiegers. So, apart from the occasional shot from one of the few mortars that the French in the upper town seemed to possess, the miners from the west could work with impunity, digging their tunnels into the hillside, edging closer and closer to the foundations of the great walls. At times, by both night and day, the French sent out sallies to try and disrupt the works and destroy the tunnels; and word carried down to the harbour of countermines, and vicious hand-to-hand battles far below ground. But the English had more than enough troops available to defend the mines and beat back any attack, and after some days, the French stopped making the effort, although they still mounted occasional nocturnal raids into the easier target of the lower town. That meant they accepted there could now be only one outcome, the sole remaining question being how long it would take their commanders to feel that their honour had been satisfied.

–

To Jack's surprise, Simon proposed one evening that his cousin join him for wine and good fellowship in a tavern ashore, quite close to the bridge into the lower town. It proved a poor choice of date, for after long weeks of sun, the heavens chose that day to open. Heavy rain hammered down on the roofs of Boulogne, forming large puddles on the rock-hard streets and drenching the decks of the ships in the harbour. But Si Bulbrooke was determined, and the two cousins made their way to a small, low building from which hung the sign of the cross keys.

As soon as they entered, it was clear that Simon was well known in the establishment. The host, an old, stoutly-built Frenchman, even greeted him with a little of his own tongue: 'Ah, *mon ami*, the best of the *godons*! A jug of claret again, *monsieur*? Two jugs? *Mais oui!*'

Jack knew little French, but *godon* was familiar. It was the Frenchmen's half-friendly, half-hostile nickname for the English, derived from their neighbours' supposed propensity for swearing. Over the years, 'God damn' had become corrupted into *godon*, which, Jack reckoned, was considerably milder than the habitual English characterisation of the French as 'frogs'.

The tavern had one large room, like so many of its equivalents in England. Fortunately, it seemed to be favoured by sailors, rather than soldiers; Jack was concerned that they might encounter the looting party again, but the Duke of Suffolk had apparently executed a dozen men as an example, and the wilder elements among the army seemed cowed, for the moment at least. Others may have been deterred by the suddenly inclement weather. As it was, Jack recognised a few familiar faces from other ships in the harbour. Indeed, it was almost like drinking in one of the inns of Dunwich, but then, sailors' drinking dens were the same, wherever they were. He thought of Ottavio Valente, and wondered if the same held true of sailors' taverns in Genoa, or on the far shores of the Levant, or in the Americas. One day, perhaps, John Stannard of Dunwich might find out.

Simon Bullbrooke was swiftly into his cups. Jack could hold his drink – few men of Dunwich could not – but he could not hope to keep up with his cousin, who took two cups of wine to his one, as he always had.

'I owe you an apology, Jack Stannard,' he said, slurring on the surname. 'Seems you were right and I had it arselins, cuz. I know the amount we've made in extra tonnage hire, all these days we've been here, for no risk. None at all. Your father will be a happy man. As happy as he ever is. *Deo gratias* indeed.'

'We still have to get back safe to England, Si.'

'Pah. An easy sail, Jack, nought but an easy sail. No, you were right, I was wrong. I've been wrong about so much, cuz.'

Jack sighed inwardly. He had encountered his cousin in this mood many times, and wondered how many hours of pathetic self-pity lay between him and his bed.

'All now water under the bridge, surely, Si? Come, let's toast continuing good success to the voyage of the *Osprey*, and to victory in the siege.'

Bulbrooke shook his head in the ponderous manner of the very drunk.

'No. No, I must needs confess to you, Jack. I have confessed to a priest. I have received absolution. But I must confess *to you*, cousin. I have wronged you. I nearly wronged you greatly, and your father, too – so very greatly, Jack.'

Jack Stannard said nothing. Simon would either tell him in his own time, or he would fall into a drunken slumber. In any event, the amount of middling French wine that he had consumed made it likely Simon Bulbrooke's confession would be a thing of little consequence, perhaps no more than yet another apology for quarrelling with his cousin over the voyage of the *Osprey*.

'I was nearly seduced by the devil, Jack. The devil tempted me, as he tempted Jesus in the desert.'

'You compare yourself to the Christ now, cuz?'

Simon narrowed his eyes, as though trying to examine Jack Stannard for any sign of insolence. Then he sat back on his stool, so far that he overbalanced and very nearly fell off.

'I must confess to you, I say. I nearly betrayed you, y'see. Nearly betrayed Dunwich.' He belched, then looked up as though seeing his cousin for the first time, then looked for the door, then belched again. 'But first, young Jack, I must piss before I burst. And bezzle your wine, lad, you're as abstemious as a nun in Lent.'

He got to his feet, found an uncertain balance, and weaved his way to the door. Jack took a sip of his wine, and smiled. It was good that he and Si were on terms again: his cousin was a good man, at bottom, and the family had to.

Jack heard distant shouting and screams, along with the hooves of many galloping horses, the sound getting nearer by the moment.

He ran to the door of the tavern, but he already knew what he would see beyond it. Fifty or sixty horsemen galloped past, the beasts' hooves splashing through the puddles, swords slashing and spears thrusting right and left. Far from preparing to surrender, as every man on the English side had expected them to do, the French were getting bolder with their night-time raids, bursting out of one or other of the posterns of the upper town, riding hard through the streets, or else attacking the trenches where the mines began. Their aim was simple and obvious: cause fear among the English, bring hope to those French in the lower town who privately detested their new masters, wear down their enemy, attempt to make more time for the Dauphin's army, which was said confidently to be on the march, to come to the relief of Boulogne.

'Si!'

Jack watched in horror as his cousin emerged from the alley across the road, where he had presumably gone to piss. One of the last horsemen in the French raiding party swung his sword, and Simon Bulbrooke sank to his knees, a large dark gash opening from his shoulder to his belly.

Jack ran to him, but it was obvious that nothing could be done for his cousin. Rainwater poured down his face and chest, where it mingled with the free-flowing blood.

'Must confess—'

'No, cuz. No need to make any sort of peace with me. Make it with God, now.'

But Simon Bulbrooke was already dead.

-

The world did not stop to mourn. Jack's cousin was one of a dozen Englishmen who fell victim to French swords that night, and although half the raiding party had been cut down, nothing was more certain than that the enemy would send out more, night after night. Still there was no sign of the upper town falling, nor yet of the Dauphin's great army coming to its aid. Mortars kept up their bombardment, the miners continued to do their work, and the *Osprey* and her consorts in the harbour continued to patrol, or else just lay at anchor, awaiting orders.

It was during one such lull that Jack decided he had better go through Simon's sea chest. Better to occupy himself thus, he reckoned, than to think further upon the seemingly senseless manner of his kinsman's dying, or to dwell upon his grief for the good man that Simon Bulbrooke had once been. No: the opening of the sea chest, and the sifting of its contents, was the last service that Jack could perform. True, there was no wife or children to receive any personal effects, but it may be that his cousin had papers or other materials that pertained to the business affairs of the Stannards, and Jack presumed that he and his father had to be the dead man's only heirs.

Two of the crewmen carried the chest from the fo'c's'le to Jack's cabin, and placed it upon the small oak table. It was a battered affair, much like Jack's own, and contained very similar things: the familiar, expected possessions of a seafarer, such as spare shirts and breeches, Si's best doublet, several combs, thimbles, dice, and his favourite pewter tankard, from which he would never quaff ale again. There were, as expected, bills of lading, inventories, letters from factors and from Jack himself, and similar items of business, all of which Jack assembled into one package, to be deposited in due course in the Stannard's counting office in Dunwich. There were weapons, too: three large, well-polished knives and a handgun, any one of which might have saved Si's life had he carried them on the night of his death. And, very nearly at the last, there was a locket of gold, upon a chain. Jack opened it, and saw five locks of hair, the last relics and keepsakes of Simon Bulbrooke's five daughters.

There was also a bag of coins. This was heavy, the coins within being of unexpectedly substantial denominations. It was more money than Jack's cousin could have made in several months of trading for the Stannards – and this was presumably what remained after Simon's apparently indiscriminate spending in the taverns of Boulogne. There was also a letter with the bag; or rather, some sort of arrangement, or contract. It specified the delivery of the sum within the bag to Simon Bulbrooke, but did not indicate what services, if any, these monies were intended to pay for. It suggested that the bag was a downpayment, the balance to come in due course. There was a signature and a wax seal, and Jack puzzled over both. The seal was familiar, but he could not place it.

Then he deciphered the signature, and the provenance of the seal came back to him. It was the seal of Southwold, a mark that could only be affixed legitimately by high officials of that town. As indeed it had been: for the signature was that of one of the two bailiffs of Dunwich's arch-rival.

It was the signature of Stephen Raker.

-

It took three more days. On the very afternoon of Jack Stannard's discovery, a great rumbling, more violent than any thunderstorm ever to strike Dunwich, presaged the fall of a section of the wall around the upper town, which collapsed in a vast cloud of dust. The miners had achieved their goal, and by evening, a succession of English attacks was hammering at the new breach in the French defences. Still the town held out, but it could now only be a matter of time, especially as there was still no sign of the Dauphin's great army. There were fresh parleys, with heralds riding hither and thither under flags of truce. It took a little while for the news to reach the harbour, but when it did, it was unequivocal. After sixty days of siege, the governor of the city, the lord of Vervins, had sent three emissaries to offer King Henry the surrender of Boulogne, this to be accomplished on the following day.

So it was that, on a warm September morning, Jack Stannard watched from the deck of the *Osprey* as the fleur-de-lis banner flying from the gates of Boulogne came down, and the royal standard of England ran up the staff in its place. Great Harry was in his city: his new city. Jack knew where he was bound, and what he would be doing there. He and the Duke of Suffolk would be making for the great church of Notre Dame, there to give thanks to God and to hear *Te Deum* sung. The choristers of the Chapel Royal had been brought over especially, in anticipation of victory, and Jack remembered how, as boys at the short-lived Cardinal College, he and Will Halliday wished for nothing more than to join that august body, the finest singers in all England. Would they be singing the settings by Fayrfax or Sheppard? Or had Taverner produced a new setting for the occasion? But Taverner was an old man now, and he knew from Will that there was supposed to be a brilliant new composer at the Chapel Royal, one Tallis by name.

Jack Stannard sighed. He could almost sense Alice reproving him, as she often had when she knew his thoughts were turning that way, or if he was struggling to sing a half-remembered faburden line of Cornysh's *Gaude Virgo*. That world was lost to him, and had been for nearly fifteen years, as his wife had known better than he. But a part of him, one small, stubborn part, still wished that he was there, in the choir stalls of Notre Dame, singing glory to God before the King of England.

As it was, he had paid for a requiem mass to be sung for Simon Bulbrooke in the battered church in the lower town where they had last taken communion together. Jack and the crew of the *Osprey* formed the entire congregation, and although Jack could only regret that his cousin had been buried in Boulogne, rather than upon Dunwich cliff, he would, at least, rest in what was now English soil. Whatever dealings Si may have had with Stephen Raker – and, God knew, that must have been what he had been attempting to confess, the night he was killed, when he had talked of nearly betraying the Stannards and Dunwich – they would now be judged by a higher authority, that which dictated the passage from Purgatory. When all was said and done, Simon Bulbrooke was still blood kin, and he deserved the respectful burial Jack gave him, the locket containing the hairs of his daughters lying upon his chest as he was laid to rest.

That done, Jack Stannard turned his thoughts toward readying the *Osprey* for sea. The king and Lord Admiral Lisle wanted many of the men who had been most active in the siege carried back home, to be replaced by fresh men coming out from Portsmouth and Dover, the men who would form the backbone of the new English garrison of Boulogne. So, for Jack and his crew, there would be one final voyage in the king's service, then a return to Dunwich and winter ashore. After that, in the spring, there would be another campaign, this time aboard the new *Alice*, if Jed Nolloth had her ready in time. Nothing was surer than that the war would continue. The colossal pride of King Francis would demand that he took back his lost town, and the equally colossal pride of King Henry would demand that he retain it at all costs.

No, hard as the campaigns of 1544 had been, they seemed set fair to be a children's game alongside the Armageddon that 1545 threatened to bring.

Twenty-One

The side chapel in the south transept of Saint Dunstan in the East, just west of the Tower of London, was illuminated only by a very few tapers, the air stale from the August heat, flies buzzing all around. The coffin of William Gonson lay, plain and unadorned, upon a trestle in the middle of the vaulted space. All the other mourners had left: Gonson's widow still confused, distraught and inconsolable; his three daughters tearful and hostile, taking their lead from the formidable eldest sister, Thomasina, Lady Tyrell, who treated every man in the building like an infant; the two sons that Will Halliday had not formerly known, Christopher and Anthony, both stern-faced and seemingly still intent, several weeks later, on blaming Will and their younger brother Benjamin, the two men who worked most closely with their father, for somehow not preventing his death. Both still clad in their mourning cloaks of black, the hoods over their heads, Will and Ben were the only living souls left in the entire church so late at night.

Benjamin Gonson stood at the foot of the coffin, staring down at the lid.

'You know the fate of suicides as well as I,' he said. 'Sir Philip Babington has consigned my father to eternal hellfire, just as surely as he did my brother. A suicide cannot rest in such a place as this, and he cannot enter the kingdom of Heaven. Not ever. I swear it, Will – if I ever find that man Babington, I'll be avenged upon him. The fate David suffered will be as nothing.' Tears welled in Ben Gonson's eyes. 'But that'll come too late for the bones in that box, for we know where they must lie.'

Will nodded. It had been the bitter, unspoken, unspeakable truth in the chapel when the entire family was assembled there: the cause of much of the rage that consumed the other members of the Gonson family. Suicides could not be buried according to the rites of the Church, in consecrated ground. Instead, they were buried at crossroads with stakes through their hearts, a warning to all who might seek to deny God's divine law. As if they did not know it well enough, Palsgrave, the priest of Saint Dunstan's, reminded them as he stretched the Church's injunctions to their limit by saying brief prayers over the body.

One Corinthians Three, verses sixteen and seventeen.

> *'Know ye not that ye are the temple of God, and the Spirit of God dwelleth in you? If any man defile the temple of God, him shall Gdod destroy; for the temple of God is holy, which ye are.'*

William Gonson had destroyed the godly temple that was his body, so the teaching of the Church was unequivocal. He could expect only hellfire for all eternity, and no decent burial for his mortal remains. It had taken weeks of persuasion for Palsgrave to allow even this small concession, that the embalmed body which had previously rested within Gonson's own house could now lie here, in respect.

Will Halliday put his hand on Ben Gonson's shoulder.

'We'll find a way, Ben. There has to be a way to have him b-buried here, in Saint Dunstan's.'

The other's cheeks were wet with tears.

'You heard the coroner's verdict, Will. Not a shadow of a doubt. Great God, you gave the most powerful evidence of all – but even if you hadn't, there were, what, a score of other witnesses among the shipkeepers, and the men on the shore? The verdict's indisputable, man. No priest in England will bury him on consecrated ground. Not even his own brother, my uncle Bartholomew, even if we could somehow get the body half way across the country.'

Will Halliday knew the case was unanswerable. Marion Bartleby had told him of an uncle of hers who had taken his own life, and was buried at a crossroads in Hertfordshire. The foxes dug him up and devoured him within a week.

'Surely, though, P-Palsgrave might?' said Will, knowing he was not really convincing himself. 'He knows and respects your family – Gonsons have worshipped here for, what, forty years? He knows how much your father gave to the church in alms. It was obvious when he was here with us, Ben. He g-g-grieves for you all. He would help you, if he could.'

'And risk being charged before a church court? Perhaps defrocked? Yes, he's a good man, and he respected my father. But it would be asking him to place his mortal livelihood and immortal soul in danger, Will. What's more, he's a man with a considerable reputation, once tutor to the king's sister, she that was the Queen of France. Would he risk all that, do you think, just to bury the corpse of a suicide?'

'He will have a price,' said Will, thoughtfully. 'All men do.'

Ben Gonson pulled back his hood, and shook his head.

'I doubt it. But then... Palsgrave likes living well – we've dined with him, and you won't find gristle in his meat or mouse droppings in his ale. This is a rich parish, though, Will, so he'll make a good income from tithes. Which means any price he might demand is one that the Gonsons can't pay. My father's affairs are in chaos. He left many debts... so many debts...'

'There's talk of you t-taking his place. Treasurer of the Navy Royal, Ben – surely you could draw off some funds?'

Gonson smiled, but it was a bitter, humourless smile.

'I've not seen my twentieth birthday, Will. The king, Lord Lisle, all the rest of them, will never make me treasurer. And I've seen enough of what it did to my father to know that it's too great a task for one man. The Navy Royal's grown so much since my father first began. Bigger and bigger, year after year, as he always said. They all know that, they all see it. Lisle will change things, appoint four or five men to do the work of the one, and I doubt if I'll be one of those new men. Certainly not treasurer.'

Will placed his hand on his friend's shoulder.

'Then I'll get money. Enough to convince Palsgrave to set his scruples aside, and give your father a Christian b-burial, here, in this church.'

In spite of his grief, Ben Gonson smiled.

'You, Will? You're a mere clerk, no better than I, as you keep saying of your prospects with Mistress Bartleby. Where in the name of all the saints will you find such a sum of money?'

Will Halliday only nodded, for an idea was forming in his mind. He was thinking of a conversation with an old school friend, some six months before, in a tavern in Suffolk, beneath the walls of Framlingham Castle. He recalled a promise made. And with that memory in his mind, he resolved to write a letter: a letter to an ancient and decayed man, in an ancient and decayed borough.

When the Gonson family next came together in Saint Dunstan in the East, again gowned and hooded, one dusk-time a little over a fortnight later, there was no bitter recrimination toward Ben and Will Halliday. As John Palsgrave, the eminent rector of the church, uttered the words of Christian committal over the coffin of William Gonson, the dead man's children, even the formerly icy Lady Tyrell, looked toward Will in particular with gratitude, respect, and not a little puzzlement. But then, they had not been privy to the conversation, in the church vestry some days earlier, between Will and Palsgrave; a conversation at first strained and something of an embarrassment to both, then rendered very easy indeed when the rector of Saint Dunstan's weighed in his hand the bag of coins that had come from Dunwich that very morning. John Palsgrave might once have been tutor to the Queen of France, but, as he said, she had been dead for eleven years and her king for thirty, and ancient titles of honour pay no bills. John Palsgrave might have written the best book about the French language ever produced on either side of the Channel, but, as he said, it made him no money, the English generally being as interested in learning French as they were in being sober. Above all, Ben Gonson had been right about one essential truth. John Palsgrave liked living well, and was evidently aggrieved that the tithe income from Saint Dunstan's had been in precipitate decline for some years, thanks to the loss of all those tradesmen who had depended upon custom from the abbey of Saint Mary Graces, just the other side of the Tower. And Will Halliday, too, had been right. John Palsgrave had his price.

The keeping of parish registers was a new innovation, brought in by the Lord Cromwell only a few years before as one of his many schemes to make the Kingdom of England a beacon of efficiency and modernity, in marked contrast to the Church of Rome from which it had just broken. As Cromwell had intended, once an entry was made upon a register, it was legal proof: an unchallengeable record, laid down for the scrutiny of all future generations. Thus no-one would ever be able to challenge the bald statement, written proud in Palsgrave's own hand, that William Gonson, sometime treasurer and storekeeper of the king's Navy Royal, was given due Christian burial in his own parish church of Saint Dunstan in the East on 20 August 1544, and therefore could not possibly have been that most despised and rejected of all sinners, a foul suicide.

-

Jack Stannard took his bearings on each familiar seamark in turn, his heart leaping as Dunwich got ever nearer. The same spirit prevailed among his crew: the smiles grew broader with each sighting and each change of course. Even the seagulls circling the ship seemed to be happier, cawing more lustily with every mile the ship progressed. From the North Foreland, Jack steered north by east, as his father had taught him to do, running between Longsand and the Kentish Knock before turning north-west into the Sledway, his course set directly for the great square tower of Bawdsey church. Then north by a little easterly, laying over for the night at single anchor in Hollesley Bay before crossing it in the morning, always keeping his bearing on the ancient but still mighty polygonal keep of Orford Castle. The fair south-westerly breeze carried the *Osprey* easily past the spit of Orford, then Aldeburgh, until Jack caught his first sight of the best beloved seamark of all.

'Home safe, my love,' he said to Alice, lying for eternity beneath the tower of All Saints, unmissable there on Dunwich cliff. '*Deo gratias, deo gratias, deo gratias.*'

The *Osprey* hove to and lay off the Minsmere shore, awaiting the turning of the tide. Then Jack took her into the mouth of the Blyth with the very first of the flood, hoping to tack as far as he could up the Dunwich river before he was forced to tow and warp. He wished, if he could, to avoid any unpleasantness with Southwold, half-a-dozen of whose ships lay ashore or at anchor on the north bank of the Blyth. He thought he glimpsed the malign shape of Stephen Raker on one of them, but the figure disappeared from view almost at once. On, into the Horse Reach, where even the oft-resented sight of the boat carrying Lyman, the customs searcher, was, for once, very welcome. The familiar and much-loved buildings of the town were now clearly visible ahead: there the warehouses of the Stannards, the Cuddons and the rest on the quays, there the houses with the thin wisps of smoke rising from their chimneys, there the Maison Dieu, there Saint John's, there the tower of All Saints, next to the ruins of the Greyfriars. The sight of the latter put Jack in mind of Thomas Ryman. Where was the old man? Had he reappeared in Dunwich while the *Osprey* was at Boulogne? Had he gone back to the Scottish war? Was he dead?

Whether he was or not, the living were very much present. Jack could see people up on Hen Hill, others nearer still on the Kingsholme itself, all of them waving, some shouting. Two of them were much smaller than those all around them, and both were jumping up and down. Running awkwardly and breathlessly after them was the unmistakeable shape of Joan Cowper, accompanied by a very large dog.

Jack grinned, and waved at his son and daughter.

Truly, it was good to be home.

Part Four

The Lost City

October to December 1544

Ye venerable walls, with ivy crown'd,
The sad remains of ancient Gothic state,
Whose scatter'd honours strew the hallow'd ground;
The spoils of time and unrelenting fate.
Thy pomp, thy pow'r, O Dunwich, now's no more;
Lost is thy splendor, sunk in endless night,
Fair trade and commerce have forsook thy shore,
And all thy pristine glory's vanish'd quite.
Thy pleasant hills, thy vales, thy rich domains,
The sea's devouring surge hath wash'd away;
Disclos'd the graves, and gave their last remains
To the remorseless waves, the fated prey.

Henry Dell, Verses Written at Dunwich, in Suffolk
(1762)

Twenty-Two

Thomas Ryman had now been detained at Kenninghall for five long months. The letter writing had stopped many weeks before; but his adherence to a version of the monastic hours had not, and the nightmare of the ship of the dead no longer came to him so often. True, he still dreamed of, or perhaps remembered, the sound of the bells of all the lost churches of Dunwich, still ringing out from beneath the waves. That was the heritage of every man, woman and child of the town born since the days of its greatness: to hear, or, as some had it, to imagine, the tolling of the ancient, sunken bells. That aside, Thomas Ryman was, as much as he could be, content, although his thoughts often strayed to the distant war, to how Jack Stannard might be faring, to whether or not he even lived. Thomas offered up more prayers than any layman would have time to do, and as he did so, a thought often struck him, and amused him. In a sense, and thanks to the bitter animosity of the Duchess of Richmond, he had become the last monk in England.

One day, as autumn was coming on, Ryman heard the unmistakeable sounds of a large retinue leaving the palace; and then, a week or so later, the nearly identical sounds of a similar force arriving. The former could only be the duchess, he concluded, but what was the latter? Maybe Her Grace had returned from a brief visit to a neighbour, perhaps the Duchess of Suffolk at Westhorpe. Or maybe Norfolk or Surrey had returned – but if that was so, why would they be back from campaign so early? Yet still no-one spoke a word to him, and after a few days, Ryman entirely forgot about the undoubted facts that he could hear, and smell, a far larger complement of domestic staff than the palace usually possessed.

The explanation came on a damp, foggy October morning. The door opened, but it was not one of the usual silent, anonymous junior retainers. It was Bleasdale.

'Great hall,' he said. 'My Lord's command.'

The falconer's expression provided ample proof of his disapproval of that command.

'Which lord?' said Ryman.

Surely that form of address could only mean Surrey: Bleasdale, like Ryman himself, would have referred to the Duke of Norfolk as His Grace. But Bleasdale simply turned on his heel and left Ryman alone. It was only after he had changed into a clean shirt that Ryman registered the startling truth which should have been immediately obvious to him. The falconer had left the door open. There were no guards in sight. Ryman knew the palace intimately, and could easily have turned the other way, gone down to the stables, taken a horse, and ridden away. Bleasdale knew that full well. Which could mean only one thing: Thomas Ryman was a free man once again.

He made his way out of the service wing and crossed the courtyard to the great hall. There was no sign of the mighty retinue lodging in the palace, but then, there was no sign of the duke's men either. But Ryman could hear distant cheering and jeering, out in the park, and had witnessed enough great lords' retinues descending upon the palace to know what it meant. Some damned fool had challenged the other establishment to a game of football; there would be blood and broken limbs a-plenty before the day's end.

The great hall of Kenninghall Palace was a high, well lit room, large windows casting what little light the day afforded onto suits of armour, tapestries, and paintings of the Howards. Ryman strode into the room fully expecting to see Surrey, with his unmistakeable forked red beard, darting eyes, and weak mouth. Instead, he saw only two young boys. One, tall for his age, thin, red-haired and dressed only in a plain white shirt and black breeches, was in a shaded corner, examining a suit of Milanese armour. Ryman could only assume he was a friend, or perhaps the new whipping boy, of the child who stood in the centre of the hall, eyeing him confidently. Dark haired, much shorter than the other but far more richly dressed in an elaborate gown of satin, the young Thomas, Lord Howard, heir and hope of the great ducal line, broke into a broad grin as he saw Ryman approach. He started forward, as though to run into the old man's arms, but then remembered who he was, and stopped himself.

'My Lord,' said Ryman, bowing.

'Master Ryman,' said the child confidently, with not a little lordly pomposity. 'You have your freedom. My aunt left, you see, to go back to court, to plot against the queen. I think she wants to put aside the Lady Catherine and marry the king herself.'

The tall red-haired lad sniggered, but did not turn away from the armour. Ryman suppressed a smile himself. If even this young boy knew exactly what the Duchess of Richmond's intent was, then Queen Catherine Parr could undoubtedly sleep safe in her bed.

'But that left me the head of the household, you see, Master Ryman. And I knew a great wrong had been done to you. A very great wrong. All these months – but I could do nothing about it while my aunt was here, no matter what I said to her. And she wouldn't let me see you, and left orders so Bleasdale and the others stopped me going to you after she left. So I schemed to find another way to secure your freedom.'

A born conspirator.

But it was one thing to be a conspirator if one was a duke, or the immediate heir to a duke. It was quite another to be so as a seven-year-old child.

'You'll be thrashed by your father, My Lord,' said Ryman. 'Perhaps by your grandfather, too, when they both return from the war.'

'No, Master Ryman, I doubt that I shall. Although I implored him to do it, you see, it's not I that I that has freed you, but my good friend Ned, here.' The lad grinned. 'Such an easy business, in the end, to convince my aunt I would be lonely when she left, and that she should arrange for another lonely boy to come here for a few weeks, for friendship's sake.'

The carrot-topped child turned away from the armour at last, and smiled confidently. Ryman could finally examine the little face: the familiar set of the jaw, the unmistakeable similarity of the eyes, the hands on hips, arms akimbo. Then he knew.

How his old comrades-in-arms would have laughed if they had seen him like this, freed solely at the behest of a brace of seven-year-old boys.

No.

When all was said and done, Bleasdale and all the rest of the Duke of Norfolk's servants would not have deferred so readily to the young Lord Howard, no matter what his future might hold. So Ryman's liberty had been achieved very much at the behest of the other; and even at such a tender age, that behest could not be denied.

Thomas Ryman bowed.

'Your Highness,' he said.

Edward, Prince of Wales, acknowledged the act of reverence with due gravity, the gravity that came naturally to one born to be king.

'Your freedom comes with one condition, Master Ryman,' said Great Harry's son, his voice already full of the arrogance of royalty. 'Tom Howard, here, says you were at Flodden.' Then the mask slipped, and an eager, overly tall, excited seven-year-old stood before Ryman. 'Tell me of Flodden Field, Master Ryman. Oh, tell me, I beg you. Nay, I command you!'

So Ryman did.

-

'A sovereign of twenty shillings,' said Venison, licking his lips as if he were tasting the coin in question, 'and a half sovereign of ten. The new coins ordered by the king.'

'For a man who'll never touch a single one of 'em,' said Joan Cowper, towering above the recumbent blind beggar in the corner of the market square, 'you seem to know much about the king's new coinage, Venison.'

'I've no eyes, Goody Cowper, true enough. But it don't mean I don't hear, and folk say all sorts in my hearing. Their eyes are always cast far above me, so they don't have to see me and my kind.'

It was market day, and the square was busy with the cries from traders' stalls. There were fewer now than Joan could ever remember, no more than a half-dozen, so there was plenty of room for the flock of sheep being driven into town from their pastures upon the heath. Although the number of stalls had declined, there was no equal diminution in the number of gulls, who still circled the square in their dozens, cawing venomously as they waited for a momentarily unguarded piece of meat, or for a careless rodent to scuttle into the open. Beyond, the waves of an early autumnal high tide could be heard, breaking loudly upon the base of Dunwich cliff.

'So a gold royal is now twelve shillings, and an angel eight?' said Meg, standing alongside Joan and keeping half an eye on Tiberius, who was growling tentatively at a supremely confident ginger cat.

'Aye, child. And a new silver coin, the testorne, worth twelve pence.'

'Changes,' said Joan, taking care to lower her voice, 'always changes. The churches, and now all this of the coinage.'

'Prices, too,' said Venison, 'now fixed by law. Beef to cost no more than five and eight a pound until Christmas, best lamb two shillings. That's the word carried in by a tinker from Ipswich, not this hour past. But as you rightly say, Mistress Cowper, I'll never touch those, neither.'

'I heard of the prices,' said Meg, excitedly. 'Miriam Day's brother John writes to tell her all that happens in London, even though *she* can't read, and has to have everything read to her by her other brother. But there, she says, all kinds of other things have had their prices fixed, too. Swan five shillings, she says. Old peacock twenty pennies, sparrows threepence a dozen. I've never tasted any of them.'

'Sparrow is my banquet, Mistress Meg,' said Venison, sadly.

'Here's a half groat for thee, Venison,' said Joan. 'Go see if Goodwife Vicary has slops to spare at the Pelican.'

The beggar could not have seen the slops if he had waited until Doomsday. Meg registered the slip at once, but Joan was oblivious.

'God be with you, mistresses,' said Venison, 'and with you especially, Margaret Stannard. I still pray for Saint Alice's intercession for your mother's soul.'

As they walked back toward the Stannard house, Meg looked up at Joan.

'Was Venison always a beggar?' she asked.

'No man was always a beggar, child. Once, he would have run and played and laughed, as you do.'

'But what was he as a grown man?'

'Well now, some say he was a Dominican, but that can't be right, because they all got pensions when the king did away with the monasteries. He wasn't in the Blackfriars here, for certain. Mayhap he was a lay brother, though – that could explain it. But others say he was clerk to a lawyer in Norwich, and lost his sight poring over papers by candlelight. Either way, he talks quite respectable-like, for a beggar.'

'Miriam Day says it is a shame on England that there are beggars, and a shame on Dunwich that it does not treat Venison better.'

'She does, does she? That little madam makes too much use of her mouth, and only uses it to spew forth her brother's treasonous words. So tell me this, Meg Stannard – if a household of Dunwich, or mayhap the Maison Dieu, took in Venison, and fed him and provided for him, what d'you think would happen? Word would get out, and every beggar in England would make his way here to inflict himself upon our charity. That's what would happen, you mark my words.'

Meg thought on this. She sensed there had to be some flaw in Joan's argument, but she could not quite grasp it. Instead, she whistled for Tiberius. The large dog abandoned his half-hearted confrontation with the ginger cat, and ambled to her side, wagging his tail. Meg patted him, then turned to Joan Cowper once again.

'Why has the king put a limit on prices, Joan?'

The servant laughed.

'Lord, what a question from one of your years! What a question from a woman of any years!'

Meg already knew – had, in fact, known for almost as long as she could remember – that when Joan Cowper answered one of her questions with a laugh, and such words as the ones she had just uttered, it meant she did not know the answer. When she did know it, or thought she knew it, she answered at great length, and with seeming authority, as she had in the case of Venison. Meg resolved to ask her father, or, failing him, her grandfather. In the meantime, she cast the new coinage over and over in her mind, adding so many sovereigns to so many angels, subtracting so many royals and testornes, and then totalling them back up again.

'Joan,' she said, as they neared the house, 'can I go to the quays?'

'The quays, child? You spend half your life on the quays. But aye, I must needs attend to your brother. Just make certain that dog doesn't get amongst the fish catches. Be back by the noon-bell, though, so I can teach you more of the cooking of pigeon.'

Meg detested pigeon, but said nothing. Instead, she and Tiberius ran down Maison Dieu lane, then under the lee of Cock Hill. Father was away, negotiating with some Danish factors at Lowestoft, so she skipped past the Cuddon warehouse, breathed in the delicious smells of freshly-sawn timber, brine and caulking tar, and made for the skeleton of the *Alice*, rising again upon its slipway. Meg was proud that her mother would have a ship named after her; and if she could not have her mother alive again, to hug and kiss and love, then a ship in her name was the next best thing upon earth. So Meg was impatient to see the hull afloat, to see it fitted out, and to see it sail away, to carry her mother's name across the seas.

Nolloth was there, as he always was, seeing to the fitting of the first of the new top timbers. He nodded to Meg, who, as was her wont, immediately scurried down into the hull, looking for new hiding places. For his part, Tiberius sniffed around the quay, a place of endless fascination thanks to the spillages from each and every cargo being laden or unladen. It was an old adage that there were no thin dogs, cats or gulls in Dunwich.

When Meg emerged from below, she had a question formed in her mind, but hesitated to ask it.

'Master Nolloth,' she said at length.

'Busy, child,' said the shipwright, frowning at her.

'Yes, Master Nolloth. Sorry. It's just – no, it's no matter.'

She cast her eyes sadly to the deck. This, she had learned, was a sure way to melt the resolve of most grown men, and Jed Nolloth was no exception to that.

'Say whatever you have to say, child, then leave me in peace to do my work, I beg you!'

'Yes, Master Nolloth. Well, I knew the ship before the Southwold men attacked it – before you had to rebuild it. And you're building it differently now. You've shifted some of the futtocks, and the knees – and you've altered the keel, and changed the shape of the stern.'

Nolloth gawped at her.

'That a child, and a girl-child at that, should tell me my business!' he cried. 'Damn, how much more can the world be turned upside down?'

'No, Master Nolloth, not that – but *why*?'

Nolloth sighed. Since the rebuilding began after the attack, he had heard the same question from this child's father; heard it, indeed, more than once. And he knew Meg Stannard well enough to know that she would only be satisfied with a version of the answer he had given her parent.

'There are new ideas out of the shipyards in Flanders,' he said. 'From Antwerp and Flushing. Good ideas. I told your father, and your grandfather too, that they could have one of the first ships in England to take account of these ideas. They concurred with me. They're always men who want the best for Dunwich.'

Meg nodded. In the distance, she could hear the bell of Saint Peter's begin to chime noon, followed a little later by John's, then finally All Saints, high upon the cliff. She thought no more of Jed Nolloth's words as she skipped home, Tiberius trotting obediently at her heels. Instead, she tried to imagine the number of sovereigns and half-sovereigns it would cost her family to finish this ship, the *Alice*, and send her to the next summer's war.

Twenty-Three

Autumn was coming on apace, the first gales having come early and shaken the bulk of the leaves from the trees. Even so, the folk of Dunwich were well content. The storms were not yet bad enough to disrupt the sea trades or the fisheries, nor to carry away yet more of the cliff. The harvest had been bountiful, and as yet, there were no further changes in religion to comprehend, despite all the unsettling rumours of the liturgy perhaps changing to English. The king, it was said, was showing no signs of casting off this latest Queen Catherine and seeking a seventh wife; on the contrary, she had apparently wrought the minor miracle of reconciling him to his two daughters, Mary and Elizabeth, the offspring of wives whose very existence it had once been treason to proclaim. Southwold and Walberswick had made no further attempt on the hull of the *Alice*, rising once again upon the stocks, and for once, they were making few difficulties over harbour dues for ships entering or leaving the Dunwich river. Of Stephen Raker, there was no word. Meanwhile, letters from London and Flanders said that the dauphin's mighty French army had finally appeared before the walls of Boulogne, but had failed utterly to retake the town. So the armies were readying their winter quarters, and the great ships were being brought into harbour and paid off.

Jack Stannard was in his family's warehouse on the Old Quay, checking the inventories of the latest cargoes brought over from Flanders, when Meg ran in, red-faced and breathless.

'Father! Father!'

'Steady, girl! Slowly, now, slowly. What's afoot?'

'A message, Father. A message has come to the house. Joan sent me to fetch you back.'

'Did she say what it was?'

'Only that it concerns Master Ryman, Father.'

The name was sufficient to make Jack, in his turn, run across the quay, up into the town by way of the Guilding Gate, and to his front door, with Meg some way behind him, rattling off questions that he barely heard.

Joan Cowper was waiting at the door.

'What's this of Ryman, Joan?'

'A scrap of a lad came to the door,' she said. 'Never seen him before. Said he had a message for you from Master Ryman, to meet him at the priory in Blythburgh this day, at dusk-tide. To come alone. A matter of great importance, the boy said.'

'That was all?'

'Aye, all. Don't like the smell of it, Master Jack. Why can't Master Ryman come here? Why Blythburgh?'

Joan gave voice to Jack's own thoughts. There had been no word of, or from, Thomas Ryman in months, and now it seemed as though his return was shrouded in as much mystery as his disappearance. It did not feel right.

And yet…

Where had Ryman been, and what had he been doing all this time? Could he have unearthed some great and secret matter which, for whatever reason, meant that he could not enter Dunwich? Had he, perhaps, discovered the truth of Simon Bulbrooke's dealings with Stephen Raker?

The message might be a trap. But what if it was genuine? Jack missed Ryman – his steady advice, his stout sword arm. And it was the sort of thing the old man had done before, when he had a matter of confidence to divulge. No, Jack could not ignore the summons. Saying his farewells to the children, he went to the stables of the Pelican in its Piety and hired a horse for two days. The road to Blythburgh took him down Saint James Street, past the leper hospital, and he called briefly on his father to let him know what he was about. Peter Stannard was even more sceptical than Joan had been, and implored his son to take some men along with him. Jack dismissed his concerns. If the message truly was from Ryman, he argued, then he must have good reason to insist that Jack should come alone. And if it was a trap, Blythburgh was a busy place, if decayed from its ancient glories, and well disposed toward Dunwich; there were bound to be worthy men aplenty in the White Hart or the other taverns and alehouses of the place to come to his aid. The old leper was unconvinced – *a goose chase, boy* – but Jack dismissed his concerns, told him to light a candle for his safety in the hospital chapel, and rode on, out onto the ancient highway known as King John's Road. The track, deeply rutted by cartwheels, ran through the thick forest of Westwood, then out onto Dunwich Heath, where the dense purple gorse was slowly losing its summer glory.

The first that Jack saw of his destination was the tower of Blythburgh's great church, one of the most prominent landmarks in the entire area. Similar to All Saints at Dunwich, but much larger, it towered over the marshes and the little town that stood at its foot. Jack arrived just after four, nearly two hours ahead of the time specified by Ryman, so he stabled his horse at the White Hart and went into the inn for some bread and ale. There was no sign of his old mentor; he had not expected there to be. But there was also no sign of anyone suspicious. The customers seemed to be the usual mixture of bargemen, carters, ploughmen and travellers, and none seemed to take any special interest in Jack Stannard. A couple of fellows of his acquaintance nodded their acknowledgments. It all boded well.

As the clock in the church tower struck six, Jack made his way through the lanes to the priory. This had been a house of the Augustinians, and well respected in the area for its good works and charity, but like all the rest, it had been swept away by royal order. The buildings still stood, although some of the outer walls had been robbed for stone for houses in the town, while the lead had been stripped from the roofs to refurbish the Duke of Suffolk's palace at Westhorpe. The new owner had not yet converted it into a house, or whatever else he intended for it, and in the meantime, the buildings were open to the elements, a playground for bats and children.

Jack walked carefully through the gloom of the church, stepping over the great stones that had fallen from the walls. Then out into the cloister garth, overgrown with grass and weeds, treading carefully between the overgrown graves of long-dead monks. Jack shivered. He chided himself, for it was a cold evening, perhaps set for the first frost of the season. Even so, he felt a sudden pang of doubt over his decision to come alone. Instinctively, he felt for the hilt of the knife in his belt, although he knew full well it was there.

He called out:

'Master Ryman!'

No answer.

'Thomas Ryman!'

There was a movement across the way, in the cloister proper. It was too dark to see whether it was Ryman, or the shade of a long-dead monk, or someone else entirely. Jack peered into the gloom, trying to make out the figure who was moving into the open.

It was not Thomas Ryman. It was Stephen Raker.

Jack's immediate reaction was not surprise, nor fear. It was that same strange sense of half-recognition he had felt when he first clapped eyes on his young enemy, that day upon the Kingsholme after Southwold's attack on the hull of the *Alice*.

A half dozen other fellows emerged from the cloisters, entirely surrounding Jack. All, no doubt, were Southwold men, or else Walberswick. All were strongly built, all had hostile expressions, and all were armed. All were enemies of Jack Stannard and Dunwich. Jack sensed at once the enormity of the mistake he had made, and the likely imminence of his death.

'John Stannard,' said Raker, smiling in an almost friendly manner. His voice was educated, and carried little trace of Suffolk; Jack recalled his father saying once that the Raker boy had been sent to the cathedral school in Norwich. 'My uncles said you'd never swallow my little tale. But I've grown impatient, you see, and said to him that nothing ventured was nothing gained. All the ways I've put in train to bring you and Dunwich low, to raise Southwold to its rightful place… so much time, so much money, so many little acorns planted. But at bottom, the simplest will be the quickest and the best, especially as you've been so obliging as to play into my hands. So say your last prayers, John Stannard. You're bound for Purgatory before the last of the light dies.'

Despite the hatred and threat in his words, there was a song-like quality to Raker's speech. Perhaps he, too, had sung in a choir-stall.

No time for such an idle thought.

Jack drew his knife from his belt and crouched into a fighting posture. It would be a hopeless fight, one against seven, but if he could take Raker with him, then he would not die in vain.

Raker drew out his own blade, and advanced.

'My lads, here, could rush you,' he said, almost pleasantly. 'We could have you dead in an instant, all our blades in you at once, like a stuck pig. But I'd rather it was slow, Stannard, as my father's hanging was slow. Like my mother's death but lately, still grieving for him, was slow. And I'd rather it was by my hand. My hand alone. An eye for an eye – a Stannard life for a Raker life.'

Raker's men moved forward slowly, so slowly, relentlessly closing the circle around Jack. He stepped forward suddenly and stabbed at one, catching him in the arm, but that only left Jack's flank and back exposed. The men rushed in, grabbing his arms, forcing the blade out of his hand, and gripping him firmly. There were growls of triumph and hatred.

Raker walked forward and stood before Jack, toying with his blade. Then he raised it, and pressed the tip under Jack's chin.

'I shall slice you, John Stannard,' he whispered. 'Piece by piece. As a boy, I loved nothing better than watching the butchers slicing the cuts from the carcasses, so I know the business, you see. And you know what? I'll send your parts back to your father, the old leper in Dunwich, one at a time. And then, one day, I'll do the same to your son and your daughter.'

Jack attempted to cry out in the hope that someone, anyone, was within earshot, but one of the men holding him clasped a hand across his mouth. Raker pressed the tip of the knife closer to his flesh, making a nick and drawing blood.

'I hope my father laughs when he sees you join him in Purgatory, John Stannard. I hope he laughs long and hard, and then longer and harder still when he ascends to Heaven and watches you descend into the fiery pit.'

Raker moved even closer. He whispered in Jack's ear, too quiet even for the men holding the prisoner to hear.

'And I hope my mother's soul will finally be at ease, *my dear brother*.' Jack's eyes widened in disbelief. 'You didn't know? The old leper never told you? She confessed to me, upon her deathbed, not a week past – the hurt, the shame, she had borne for all of my life. So ask him about it, the leper, when he joins you in Hell.'

Stephen Raker stepped away, looking at Jack with a strange expression of triumph and hatred united. Jack could say nothing, and not only because of the hand over his mouth. He knew in his heart that Raker's shocking revelation could only be the truth; for he now knew why the fellow's face had seemed so familiar, when he first saw him on the Kingsholme, during the attack on the *Alice*, and then again a few minutes earlier.

Stephen Raker bore more than a passing resemblance to Jack Stannard's long-dead elder brother, Adam.

Raker spoke loudly for the benefit of his men.

'Time for Southwold and my father to be avenged, boys. Time to make the first cut, I think. The first of very many. What do you think, lads? His cock first, or else a finger or two?'

Raker moved his blade down toward Jack's groin, very slowly, but inexorably. Laughs and growls came from the Southwold men. A couple of them cried obscenities.

'This was a house of God,' said a new voice from the shadows, suddenly, shockingly, but very calmly. 'A holy place. To some, it still is. And you'll kill no man here today, Raker.'

Thomas Ryman stepped out of the darkness of the cloister, his sword in his hand.

'Ryman,' said Raker. 'Which circle of hell spewed you forth?'

'Behold, a Southwold man who can read Dante. A Southwold man who can read anything at all. The Lord be praised indeed. Now drop your blade, boy, and release my young friend, there.'

The man of Raker's who was closest to Ryman rushed at him, reckoning that his youth and speed would get him past an old man's feeble reflexes. The speed with which Ryman's sword came up, and then thrust deep into the fellow's chest, disabused him in an instant.

Ryman calmly withdrew his blade from the dying body, not even bothering to glance at it as it fell to the ground, then made a beckoning gesture with his left hand. Half a dozen men emerged into the cloister garth. Jack recognised all of them. They were Dunwich men: two were distant kin of the Stannards. All were armed with a variety of blades and cudgels.

'I'll kill him before you can touch me, Ryman!'

'True. Oh, very true indeed, Master Raker. So you could. But you've already got one man dead, another with a wound in his blade arm, so the odds are heavily against you. And I have this sword, a better weapon than any other in this place, just as I know how to use a blade like this better than any man here, as I don't doubt your uncles told you long ago. So trust me in this, Stephen Raker – holy ground or not, I'll happily use it to spill your guts out of your worthless body. So release Master Stannard, there, and be thankful I'm letting you escape with your miserable lives. Until another day, at any rate.'

Jack was close enough to Raker to see the fury and indecision in the man's face – *his brother's face*, if Stephen Raker's impossible, terrible words were true. The tip of the knife was still pressing against Jack's flesh. But then, almost imperceptibly at first, Raker reduced the pressure. Finally, he withdrew the blade altogether, nodded to his confederate to release his grip on Jack, and with evident bad grace, beckoned to his men to follow him out of the priory ruins.

The Dunwich men came up to Jack, grinning and slapping him on the back. Ryman, though, remained apart, merely nodding at his sometime pupil.

'Too trusting, Master John Stannard. How often did I teach you that?'

There was no anger in Thomas Ryman's voice, only quiet disappointment.

Jack could barely think. Stephen Raker. *His brother.* How on God's earth could that be so? But he could not tell Ryman. Not here, not now. With an effort, he made himself answer his old teacher's question.

'I wanted the message to be from you. I made myself believe it had to be from you. But how did you know I was here?'

'I must have come into Dunwich by Middlegate almost as you were leaving by Saint James Street. Your daughter and Goodwife Cowper told me of the false message, then I called upon your father, whose note of hand was enough to supply men and horses. I could have brought a small army of Dunwich men willing to come and save you, but I knew speed was all.'

Jack silently nodded his thanks.

'But where have you been all these months? We thought you dead, Thomas Ryman.'

The old man sighed.

'That, my friend, is a long story.'

And that night, as the men of Dunwich slept in the empty rooms of the sometime prior's residence, Thomas Ryman told it: of how the capricious whims of a slip of a woman, and then of a mere boy, had imprisoned and then freed him. In turn, Jack Stannard told him of the Boulogne campaign, of his sightings of the king, and of Raker's apparent attempt to suborn Simon Bullbrooke.

'Raker is a vengeful young man,' said Ryman. 'Determined, too. He'll have other schemes in hand, we can be sure of that.'

'Aye, he admitted as much to me when he had me in his power. God willing, though, we'll put paid to all of them, especially now you've returned. You'll come back to Dunwich, and sail with me next summer?'

Ryman shrugged. In the dim light of a single candle, he looked far older than he was, the single flame picking out every line, every scar, every ancient dagger-nick on his face.

'I can hardly go back to Kenninghall – at least, not until I have a chance to lay my case before the duke or the earl. So yes, Jack, for now I'll return to Dunwich, and go on campaign again. I'd hoped my campaigning days were behind me at last, but *Investigabiles sunt viae Domini*.' The old man chuckled, convinced that if his life, and especially the last few months of it, proved anything, it was that God did, indeed, move in mysterious ways. 'For one thing, your father wants me to watch over you, to ensure you get safely to the altar and your new bride.'

'Ah. He told you, then.'

'You don't have the tone or appearance of a man in the throes of passion, John Stannard.'

'That, Master Ryman, is also a long story. A very long one.'

But even as he smiled, Jack knew that he had matters to discuss with his father, and that of his proposed wedlock with Mistress Jennet Barne was the very least of them.

Twenty-Four

The leper of Dunwich sat before a blazing fire within the infirmary of Saint James, reading a tightly bound book that his son knew to be a volume of the works of Cicero. He did not turn as Jack entered the room.

'Ryman saved you, then, boy,' said Peter Stannard. Apart from a slight hardening of the rasp in his voice, it was impossible to detect whether he felt anything at all at his son's escape. 'God's providence, that he should come back when he did.'

'And God's providence that Stephen Raker should tell me he is my brother.'

The leper looked up from his page of Cicero, gazed into the flames for a moment, then closed the book and placed it on a stool.

'I heard she'd died,' he said. 'I paid for prayers to be said for her at John's. So she told him, then, at the last. Never thought she would. She never told Martin, for certain, although I think he had some inkling, some suspicions over all these years. But he thought he had cause enough agin me as it was. The number of times I'd thwarted him in one or other of his schemes... And there was the matter of your mother, of course.'

'It's true, then? And yet you never saw fit to tell me?'

Peter Stannard bristled, as he had done in times past just before erupting into yet another tirade against Jack. *Never answer back, boy. Never question your father, boy. Ephesians Six, boy.* But now the shoulders merely slumped into a feeble shrug.

'What good would it have done to tell you, boy? Would you have gone over to Southwold, cried "hail, brother, well met!", and carved a roast ox with him? What would he have done, do you think, other than try to put a blade in your guts so much sooner than he has? Do you think he would happily acknowledge you as your brother, boy, when all his fortune, all his rank within that town – Christ's nails, bailiff at twenty! – all of that depends upon his being the lawful son of Martin Raker?' Peter Stannard shook his head. 'All best forgotten. I thought Sindony Raker believed so, too, but they say Martin's death unhinged her, made her starve herself to death. And at the end, she told the lad. Women and secrets, boy, women and secrets.'

'How?'

'How did I come to father him? Apart from in the obvious sense? You really want to know?'

'Do you not owe it to me?'

Something that might have been a sigh escaped from Peter Stannard's mouth.

'I owed it to you to keep this knowledge from you, boy. There's enow bad blood between Dunwich and Southwold, between Stannard and Raker, without stirring a little hemlock into it. What purpose would it serve, for you to know?'

Jack stared at the old leper, and sensed how little he really knew this man, his father. Over the years, he had feared him, envied him, hated him, but never truly known him. Would he, too, in time become like Peter Stannard: closed and bitter, secretive and sickly? He prayed not. But he knew that, in one sense, he was already very, very like his father.

The younger Stannard, too, knew how to drive a hard bargain.

'What purpose? The purpose of my marrying Jennet Barne, Father. You want that. I want this. A simple trade.'

Peter Stannard turned a little, to look at his son more fully. He nodded and smiled, although it was barely possible to tell that his broken lips had moved.

'Your grandfather told me, when he was starting to fail, that there comes a day in every man's life when the roles of father and son are reversed. And behold, the babe who spewed all over me when first I held him in my arms now becomes my master.' The leper beckoned for his son to sit, and Jack perched on the stool, placing the copy of Cicero in his lap. 'August of the year 'twenty-four, Jack. We'd had twenty barks in the Iceland fishery that year, Southwold and Walberswick another twelve. What a summer that was! Such catches, it seemed as though the fishermen apostles themselves were driving the fish into our nets!' Jack was startled at this glimpse of the father he had known so rarely in his childhood: a man who could, perhaps as often as twice or thrice a year, laugh and be happy. 'So we returned well content, until we struck one summer storm after another. Martin Raker's ship fell by the wayside first, forced to take shelter and repair in Orkney with two or three others. We of Dunwich were nearly home, though, almost off the Ness of Lowestoft, when another storm blew up.' The old man closed his eyes, and Jack sensed that he was there again, young and whole, recalling every moment. 'The *Virgin's Falcon*, old Sanders' ship, ran aboard us, shattered our larboard quarter and the rudder. I managed to run us onto the beach between Kessingland

and Covehithe. We salvaged as much as we could, then made our way down the Reydon road into Southwold. I should have known better, of course, should have taken the longabout way through Blythburgh…'

'Why didn't you?'

'Asked myself that very question many times these last twenty years, boy. The urge to be home, to my own hearth, to your mother? I can't recall, now. Anyhow, rumour had flown before us – rumour that Raker and most of their ships were lost, but that the men of Dunwich and most of their ships were saved. Didn't take much ale for that to become a tale that we'd made it so, wrecking their ships on purpose so we could profit more from the catch. So when we came into Southwold, they were waiting for us, drunk and armed. Scores of them, all in a frenzy. Four of our men were killed, my brother George among them.'

'I remember him a little.'

'A good lad, the one closest in age to me. Betrothed, he was, set fair to be wed that summer. Killed by my impatience, as surely as if I'd stuck a dagger in his heart.' The old leper made a sound that might have been a cold laugh. 'I know they whisper through the town that I murdered my brother Arthur, that had no wits. But he loved watching the gulls, and came to believe he could soar with them, so one day, he tried to fly from Dunwich cliff. There's an irony, boy. They say I killed my brother, and they are right, but none of them know they mean *the wrong brother*.'

Peter Stannard's eyes and thoughts seemed to be wandering further toward his dead siblings and away from his living sons, Jack Stannard and Stephen Raker.

'So what became of you, Father?' asked Jack, gently.

'Mm? Oh, I was cudgelled, had some ribs broken, but got into an alley and hid. Didn't know George was dead – if I had, then maybe what happened next never would have. Sindony Raker found me there. We knew each other of old – she was of Blythburgh, like your mother, and they'd been friends when they were young. That's how I knew them both, y'see, how Martin Raker knew them both. Now, boy, Martin already hated me for stealing Anne from him, as he saw it, and for ten score of other things too, but Sindony never did. I think she'd taken a shine to me, before I married your mother, and that night, as she washed me, and tended to my bruises... I never meant it, boy, although I doubt you believe me. Your sister wouldn't, for sure. But I'll swear to it on the holy book or any relic of your choosing. I never forced her, may Saint Felix strike me down if I did.'

No bolt came down from the patron saint of Dunwich. Jack studied the ruin of his father's face intently, but there was no trace of dissembling. He had a host of questions, but felt he could not interrupt. He looked up at the simple wooden cross upon the wall of the lazar house, and sensed that he was akin to a priest, hearing the confession of the sinner before him. Priests did not interrupt. Priests listened, and so would Jack Stannard.

'It took Martin Raker a month to bring his ship home,' his father continued, 'and when Stephen was born, the following spring, I knew he had to be mine. When I saw Sindony at Blythburgh Fair that summer, she told me outright, and that she'd convinced Martin the babe was born early. I even felt sympathy for him, then, for no man knows the truth of what women say, when they talk of their number of weeks, and their bleedings, and all the rest. Sympathy, too, because I'd had the only two women he'd ever loved in the world.' The old leper sighed. 'The only moment of sympathy I've ever felt for any from Southwold, especially any called Raker. But there, John Stannard, that is my tale done. Stephen Raker spoke true. He is your brother, and I don't doubt that's why he seems to have so much guile, when his supposed father had none at all.' Peter Stannard's face was grimmer than ever. 'And that, boy, is why you should be on your guard, for Stannards fear only two men, the king and another Stannard. So there's my side of the bargain, which I've told before only in the confessional in John's church, to old Feryhe when he was priest there.'

'He gave you absolution?'

'Token penances, for we both knew I was already far beyond any absolution he could give me, or that any pilgrimage could bestow. No, he told me very much what I expect you're thinking – I know it's what your sister would think, for certain, if she knew of this. He said I had committed yet another mortal and irredeemable sin to bring the wrath of the Doom down upon me, to consign me to eternity in hellfire. So, what say you?'

Jack Stannard was silent. Then he spoke, very quietly and slowly.

'I think perhaps you've been right these many years, Father. I am not my brother.'

The leper of Dunwich nodded.

'Aye, well, when it comes to it, I wasn't mine, either – none of the six I knew, nor the others I reckon your grandfather sired half way across Suffolk.'

Simon Bulbrooke, son of one of the seven brothers' two sisters – the other having become a nun after being disappointed in love – once told Jack that those of his uncles whom he had known, apart from the simpleton

Arthur, were roaring men, quick to draw blades and lift skirts, and that Peter Stannard had been the quiet one of the family, often beaten raw by his older siblings and their brutal one-armed father. That had been the case until the day dawned when Peter was the last brother living, and suddenly became the sum of all the others. If Si's shade was present there, at that moment, in the Saint James lazar, Jack believed it would contradict Peter Stannard, and tell him that he, of all men, truly had been his brothers.

Jack's father shuffled upon his stool, making himself more comfortable.

'And now, boy, enough of ancient history. Not that Stephen Raker will think it so – he'll return to plague us, by some means or other. You'll needs be watchful, Jack. But in the meantime, let us talk of your side of the trade. Let us talk of Mistress Jennet Barne.'

Twenty-Five

On the crisp, fine morning of *O Rex Gentium*, three nights before Christmas Day, John Stannard and Jennet Barne walked out upon Dunwich Cliff, by way of Duck Street and the Middle Gate. For decency, Agatha and Meg accompanied them, but remained at a discreet distance behind. Her aunt pointed out this or that plant to the girl, commenting on the healing qualities of one, or the dangerous nature of another. All this was much to Meg's frustration. In ordinary times, she loved learning from her aunt, although the questions she asked Meg about her visits to her grandfather were sometimes strangely worded and a little annoying. But now she wished nothing more than to be allowed to leave Agatha Stannard's side and run ahead, to listen to what her father and this woman were talking about. Jennet Barne was tall for Suffolk, and sturdy, too, as though she had already borne many children; which, Meg knew, she had not. Her kirtle of cambric was modest enough, as was the gown over it. Short, straight black hair, creeping out from under her coif, framed a plain, round face. It would be an instantly forgettable face, the face of an oft-rejected spinster already passing her prime – a spinster like, say, Agatha Stannard – were it not for the brilliant smile from a mouth still, somehow, full of all its teeth, and they gleaming white. It was the teeth that most unsettled Meg. Such completeness, and above all such whiteness, was surely unnatural. Perhaps Jennet Barne was a witch, as sorcery was surely the only explanation for such perfect teeth in one so very old as to be nearly twenty-five.

A few yards ahead, the witch was serious in tone.

'My grandfather died many years before I was born,' she said. 'He was naught but a husbandman of Westleton, I believe. The Barnes have prospered mightily since his day.'

'I knew mine,' said Jack. 'At least, I have some memory of being picked up by an aged one-armed man who stank of herring. He'd been a soldier in the wars between York and Lancaster – married three times, and sired my father when he was near fifty. Stannards are lastenest, by and large, long lived unless the hand of God intervenes, as with my poor brother, or unless they go to London and are taken by the plague, like my cousin Hal.'

They came to the edge of the cliff, to the south of the town, nearly in the shadow of the great windmill that had stood on the cliff for longer than any living soul could remember. Even here, though, a good way from any house, they were still within the Palesdyke. The ancient defence had guarded Dunwich for a thousand years, or so it was said, and the extent of the land it enclosed gave proof of the town's former greatness. Now, it was little more than an overgrown ditch with an earthen bank on its inner side, the ramparts having fallen long ago. A little way inland, grass and ivy grew among the ruins of both the Blackfriars and the Temple of Our Lady, the old Hospitaller house, with its little round vaulted church that Meg loved. The monastery gardens, where countless generations of monks had grown vegetables and herbs, were overrun with weeds and brambles. A half-dozen men were at work on the roof of the Blackfriars church, stripping it of its lead. Out at sea, to the south-east, a fleet of Tyne colliers was beating down toward Hollesley Bay, bound for London to satisfy the great city's voracious need for coals to fuel its midwinter fires. The wind was south-westerly, so at the base of the cliff, with the tide ebbing, it was strangely quiet, the waters lapping gently upon the beach.

Jack pointed out to sea, toward a point further north than the fleet, and Meg, just out of earshot alongside her aunt, knew what he would be saying to this Mistress Barne. It was the tale a father had often told his daughter.

'My father knew his grandfather, too, another John Stannard. He could remember days agone, when the shore was as far out as what the men of those times called Beacon Hill. It was a headland even higher than the cliff upon which we stand, Mistress, or so men said. It was where fires were lit to warn of invasion, as when King Edward came back to take the crown from King Henry.' Jennet Barne nodded, although her attention seemed to be elsewhere. 'There was a South Gate through the Palesdyke in those days, and another church, Saint Nicholas, which my grandfather saw go over the cliff—'

'Yes, most interesting, Master Stannard. Most interesting indeed, of course, and you must tell me more of all this when we are wed. But I think you and I must talk, must we not, of the letters exchanged between your father and my cousin? We must agree upon the arrangement proposed. Of the dowry, for one. And we must talk of a date, I think.'

'Ah,' said Jack. 'A date.'

Meg noticed the change between her father and Mistress Barne. She felt her heart race. Perhaps Father was finally set to reject this woman, this witch who was being foisted on him. She had used all her wiles on Grandfather during her recent visits to Saint James, but he either laughed or glowered, and ignored her in either event. The old leper, who otherwise gave her everything that she wanted and more besides, much to Aunt Agatha's inexplicable annoyance, had failed her in this, the most important thing of all. Perhaps, though, Father had finally seen through the witch. Perhaps, Meg hoped, he had finally noticed the teeth. Perhaps he would at last seek a bride worthy of him. Goodman Ryman had told her of how the Duchess of Norfolk was estranged from her husband. True, she was very old, but that meant Father would soon be a rich widower, and could then marry for love again.

But no. Jack stepped forward and kissed Mistress Barne lightly upon the cheek, thereby earning a look of utter reproof from both his daughter and his sister. Although Agatha Stannard had said nothing to her brother, nor, of course, to her niece, the latter could already read the faces of adults with an accuracy that verged on the unsettling. Thus Meg knew that upon this matter of Mistress Jennet Barne, she and her Aunt Agatha were as one.

Rather than concentrating on the unwelcome spectacle before her, Meg Stannard looked out to sea instead, to where Beacon Hill had once stood, and recalled the tales handed down from her grandfather's grandfather, the tales that she loved so much. This Stannard ancestor of hers could recount the stories handed down from the generations long before even his time, of the days agone when there was another Dunwich within the Palesdyke: a greater Dunwich, a Dunwich of even more churches, a Dunwich that some said had been a city to rival London, a

Dunwich lost forever. A Dunwich with a harbour packed from side to side with its own ships, which could send more hulls off to the old kings' wars than even London itself. A Dunwich whose greatness thrilled Meg, just as she knew it thrilled her father when he told her of it. A Dunwich humbled in one night by a mighty storm which threw up so much shingle that the old harbour, the best harbour on the entire east coast of England, was sealed forever. Ever since then, every third or fourth winter had carried away a little more: a few feet from the cliff there, a half-acre of the marsh there, but never enough of the vast shingle bank, the Kingsholme, that blocked the port's direct access to the ocean. But the sea would not defeat Dunwich, both her father and grandfather always said. As long as a Stannard breathed in the town, they said, the inexorable sea would have an opponent. And Meg knew that, whatever name she eventually took upon marriage, she would be a Stannard until her dying day.

Yards away, other concerns were paramount.

'The spring is impossible,' said John Stannard to Jennet Barne. 'The new ship needs at least one trial voyage before the summer's campaign, and I have a mind to take her over to Flanders, if I can secure a decent cargo. My father has another scheme afoot in Flanders, too – but that is not an affair with which I need trouble you, Mistress.'

'And the summer, I take it, will be the campaign itself?'

'No doubt, if we receive a summons to send a ship. Ryman says there'll be no peace with the French before then, and certainly none with the Scots.'

'Ah, this Thomas Ryman. I long to meet him. A friar who was a soldier and has become a soldier again. A man who had the confidence of a duke. An intriguing fellow indeed.'

'He says he will come to the great Christmas Mass at Saint John's. God willing, Mistress, you will meet him then.'

'Mayhap not, Master Stannard. The Barnes are of Westleton still, in name at any rate, and I'll take mass only there when in these parts. The Reverend Berte's view of divine service is also more to my taste than that of any of the Dunwich churches. More reformed. More London. Less devotion to the old ways – Doom paintings, the Lord's Prayer still in Latin, all such Popish superstitions. In the fullness of time, I hope we can be married at Westleton, once you have ceased your voyaging and campaigning. In the autumn, perhaps, if your father and my cousin can come to acceptable terms?'

'In the autumn, perhaps, lady. Or the spring after that.'

-

'I do not like Mistress Barne, Father,' said Meg Stannard, when the two had returned to their house and were seated before the fire, Meg upon her little stool, Jack upon the family's ancient settle, facing the vast Flemish tapestry of the fall of Troy. This had been Peter Stannard's pride and joy, even though it was bought second-hand and had to be cut to fit a wall that was much too small for it; but it was the only tapestry of its size in Dunwich. Across the way from it, Tiberius snored loudly upon the hearth, occasionally emitting a prolonged and noxious fart.

'It is not your place to like or dislike her, daughter.'

'Do you like her, Father?'

John Stannard stared at his daughter. Many a father would beat a child for such insolence, but although Jack did not hesitate to discipline young Tom, he always felt guilt at punishing Meg, no matter how terrible her misdemeanour. He knew why: she looked so much like Alice, and sometimes, just as now, she spoke with a wisdom far beyond her nine years. A wisdom very much akin to Alice's, and words very much like those his wife would have spoken, in the very way she would have spoken them. Jack had other words in his mind, too: the words that Jennet Barne had spoken against the forms of faith that were the cornerstone of belief for every man, woman and child named Stannard. The prospect of spending what might be, God willing, the remaining forty, or even fifty, years of his life, with one who detested what she called 'Popish superstitions', weighed heavily on his mind.

'It is not your concern, Margaret Stannard,' he said, half-heartedly. 'If it's God's will that I marry her, you will show her all the respect due to a mother.'

'Of course, Father,' said Meg gravely. 'All the respect due to a mother. But do you like her?'

Twenty-Six

The storm began in the morning of Christmas Eve, and by dusk, it was in full spate. A sudden blizzard from the east brought fresh snow to Dunwich, whipping up colossal seas that drove against the foot of the cliff. The guards appointed to the new ship, still upon the stocks, huddled around their brazier as they watched huge waves crash over the Kingsholme. Yet still the parishioners of Saint John's responded to the summoning bell, and struggled against the driving snow to make their way toward the church for Midnight Mass. Some families were even merry, and sang *Adam Lay yBounden* defiantly, into the very teeth of the storm.

'Fitting, in its way,' shouted Thomas Ryman, as he and the Stannard family stepped out from their front door into the street and braced themselves against the force of the storm. 'Fitting that God should thus mark the passing of John's church.'

'Or His displeasure with this kingdom,' said Jack.

'A sour sentiment from you at the coming of Christmas Day, Jack Stannard!' said Ryman.

'Why should God be displeased with the kingdom, Father?' asked Meg, who was holding Jack's left hand, her brother on his right, and shouting her very loudest to be heard above the howling wind.

'Nothing, child,' said her father, looking around to check that no-one else could have heard his unguarded remark. Agatha Stannard raised her eyes to the heavens. 'Come, let's hasten to the church, this is no sort of weather for Christian folk to be abroad in.'

They hurried down into the market square. Saint John's stood on the eastern side, towering above the Guildhall, inns, shops, and the ancient market cross. The land, full of houses and streets, had once sloped gently away from it, down toward the sea, but that land was there no longer. Instead, the east end of John's church now stood at the very edge of the cliff. No more burials took place in its churchyard, no more endowments supplemented its coffers. Over the years, countless timber and stone defences had been thrown up against the foot of the cliff, paid for by selling off the church plate, but they were all swept away by the sea. The church was doomed, and after this final celebration of the mass, it would be stripped of its contents, close its doors forever, and wait for the unforgiving sea to carry it away. But not before Jack Stannard, Thomas Ryman and the Reverend Seaward had undertaken one last task.

-

Saint John's was a large building, laid out like a small cathedral with side aisles, transepts, and a tower above the crossing; some said it had indeed been a cathedral, a thousand years before, when Dunwich was the seat of a line of bishops that commenced with Saint Felix, but others like John Day scoffed at this. The congregation within its high walls was larger than it had been for many a year, with parishioners of Saint Peter's and All Saints joining the usual flock. Men sported their best doublets, women their finest gowns. All of them, and the children too, were looking left, and right, and upward, trying to commit to memory every inch of the ancient church. The wall paintings and the Rood screen had not been cleaned or refreshed for years, but they were still a glorious blaze of colour. Men, women and children picked out, and pointed at, their favourite characters, perhaps John the Baptist, Mary Magdalene, the war-like Archangel Michael, or Saint Nicholas, patron of seafarers. Meg's favourite was a Saint Christopher who, to her mind, seemed the very image of Jed Nolloth. Candles stood in every corner of the nave and chancel, illuminating the ancient images on the walls and venerating the dozens of saints' statues in the niches. There were fewer lights now, since the changes enacted by the late Lord Cromwell. Under him, the king was pushed toward the new thinking, and the likes of relics and pilgrimages had all vanished. Even sacred, splendid, Walsingham, whither Jack and Alice Stannard had processed barefoot to mark their marriage, was fallen, its image of the Virgin thrown onto a fire; and with it, the heartfelt devotions of centuries and of thousands. The veneration of Thomas Becket, Saint and Martyr, was also prohibited. The shrine to him within Saint John's church had gone down, the space where it once stood still pointedly empty. But then Lord Cromwell, too, had gone down, justly brought to the block by his manifold vanities and ambition. Dunwich, like all of England, rejoiced at the fall of the malevolent serpent.

The Stannard party made their way through the throng, toward their accustomed position near the front of the congregation. Jack nodded to Grindal and Clampe, the be-chained and overdressed bailiffs, and others of his acquaintance, principally his fellow Guildsmen, of whom there were many. The Stannards pointedly ignored the Cuddons, standing across the nave, long their rivals to be the greatest merchants of Dunwich.

The church was a cacophony of noise, the bells ringing the last of their summons, the worshippers talking loudly, the wind howling ever more violently and shaking the ancient stained glass in the windows, the waves roaring as they broke against the cliff.

Then all except wind and wave fell silent.

William Seaward came out of the vestry, accompanied by his acolytes, and went to his position behind the Rood. He was attired in a splendid cope that seemed to be made of very gold, over an alb and chasuble that seemed hardly less grand. Meg gasped; she had never seen a costume so utterly glorious.

The young priest made the sign of the cross, and uttered the first of the familiar words of the Christmas Mass.

'*Dominus dixit ad me: Filius meus es tu, ego hodie genui te.*'

The Lord hath said to me: Thou art my son, this day have I begotten thee.

The mass proceeded after its eternal fashion, the bells ringing, the censers swinging. The words thrilled Meg, but not as much as the numbers. There were the twelve apostles upon the Rood screen, three Alleluias after the Gradual, two Green Men high up, six acolytes, twenty-two angels flanking the roof beams, thirteen horns upon the head of the Devil of the Doom. Both of her parents, and her brother, had long found it unaccountable that she should look down the columns of figures in the Stannard ledgers and smile at the sight of old friends, rather than recoiling from a burden that no man, and certainly no woman, ever undertook voluntarily.

The acolytes rang their bells again. Seaward faced the altar and elevated the host as the congregation behind him crossed themselves, many fingering their rosaries in their other hands as they did so.

Then the new sound began. At first Meg thought it might be some tiles coming off the roof in the wind. But her father and Thomas Ryman looked at each other. All around the packed nave and side aisles, others were doing the same. Some were already turning, and starting to run toward the west end. In no more than a moment, the sound grew into what sounded to Meg like the galloping of a thousand horses. She reached down and took her terrified brother's hand. Very young as they were, they were children of Dunwich, which meant they had known and feared this sound since they were in the womb.

A moment after the galloping came something that sounded like a great tearing. Dozens, men and women alike, screamed. The ground shook. Dust fell from the beams supporting the roof. Then one beam came away, fell into the chancel, and pinned one of the young acolytes, the blood spouting from his mouth like a fountain as he was crushed to death. Four or five of the brightly coloured wooden angels fell as the beams supporting them split. The Reverend Seaward turned, his face a mask of utter terror. The floor broke apart a little way behind the Rood, no more than three or four yards in front of where the Stannards stood. The walls of the chancel broke and crashed in a cloud of dust. The east window shattered, and the roof above the chancel fell. As the entire east end of the church fell into the raging sea, miraculously not taking the Stannards with it, Meg caught one last glimpse of William Seaward's face, his mouth screaming silently as he fell to his death.

Jack and Agatha pulled Meg and Tom away from the new cliff edge. There was panic behind them, every member of the congregation trying to save themselves, a murderous crush pushing toward the west door. Meg saw Miriam Day, but Miriam's eyes merely stared blankly back at her, the little body crushed to death beneath trampling feet. *God's judgement upon Miriam for calling the king evil?* thought Meg, as she sought her own salvation.

Above, by some miracle, the Doom remained in place, at the very end of the ruin that remained of Saint John's church, above the shattered remnants of the Rood screen. The wind blew hard against it, seeming to make the devil's great black winds flap. But the devil of the Doom survived, looking down toward the carnage by the west door.

With the east end gone and the body of the church open to the elements, the full force of the blizzard struck the people within.

'Roof's holding!' cried Ryman into the gale, as snow began to cake his shoulders and hair.

'Sister, save the children!' shouted Jack, struggling to make himself heard above the wind.

'How, brother?' cried Agatha. 'There's no way through the west door!'

The Stannards' rightful place at the front of the congregation in the nave now put them at the very back of those trying to flee the building.

'With me!' shouted Ryman.

He ran into the south aisle, where the pillars gave a little shelter, and picked up a fallen statue of Saint Jerome. It was heavy, but as nothing to the loads Ryman had lifted on countless campaigns. He looked into the carved face of the saint.

'Forgive me,' he said. '*In nomine patris, et filii, et spiritus sancti, Amen.*'

Upon the 'amen', he hurled the saint into the nearest window. The glass shattered, its gaudy fragments falling out onto the cliff. Ryman took hold of one of the stools provided for the infirm, placed it beneath the window, and beckoned to Agatha Stannard. Jack pushed his sister forward. Lifting her skirts, she climbed onto the stool, then took hold of the window frame, and hauled herself up. She cried as she cut her hand on broken glass, but then used her missal to clear as many jagged remnants of the window as she could. That done, she leaped down onto the ground outside.

Jack lifted young Tom high in his arms, stepped up onto the stool, and handed him to Agatha. Ryman, in turn, took hold of Meg and passed her up to her father, who lifted her into the window. Before Agatha could take hold of her, she jumped to the ground, broken glass cracking beneath her feet as she landed. A shard cut her leg, and she screamed. She looked up, and saw folk running in terror through the market square. The Red Lion alehouse, that had stood next to John's church for years, was gone over the cliff too, as was the house of Shelley, the Comptroller of Customs, on the other side of it. Then Agatha was upon her, tearing another length of cloth from her skirt to make a bandage for Meg's leg, akin to the one she had fashioned on her own hand.

Within the church, at every window, men were emulating Ryman's bold act. Stools and saints alike smashed into the ancient stained glass. The crush by the west door eased as more and more parishioners escaped by way of the windows. And still the Doom of Dunwich did not fall; still the devil's wings stretched out to envelop the people below.

-

Saint Stephen's day dawned bright and clear, the blizzard having blown itself out in the course of the previous day and night. Despite the frawn, as Dunwich folk called the bitter cold, people trudged through the thick snow to stand at the edge of the new cliff, staring down upon the piles of stone and timber on the beach, forty feet below. Others inspected the ruins of John's church, or of the buildings beyond it. Some burrowed in the snow, seeking pieces of stained glass as keepsakes. Old Tom Melton, the cordwainer, was on his knees, weeping for his wife Margery, buried in the churchyard barely five years before. Most of her bones were gone in the night, fallen into the sea and swept away, but some of her ribs, still encased in shreds of her flesh and winding-sheet, protruded from the new cliff, nearly, but not quite, within Tom's reach. So consumed were the folk of Dunwich with the latest disaster which had befallen them that many walked past the slumped form of Venison the beggar without a downward glance, not realising that he had frozen to death during the blizzard.

Jack Stannard and Thomas Ryman stood within the shattered nave of John's church, now open to the elements at the crossing. Everything precious or sacred which survived the catastrophe had been taken away by the erstwhile deacons and churchwardens first thing in the morning. The only thing that remained within the empty shell was the Doom.

'Seaward was a good man,' said Ryman. 'A little too eager, maybe, but a fellow of sound faith.'

'They're singing masses for him at both Peter's and All Saints,' said Jack. 'I'll go to Peter's later, after I've spoken with Nolloth about launching the new ship on the next spring.'

'And I. Mayhap Peter's is our parish now, Jack. Only two churches left in Dunwich, by Christ's holy blood. That I should have lived to see it.'

Jack Stannard nodded slowly, as though in a dream. His eyes were fixed upon the Doom.

'That it survived yesterday,' he said.

'Proof of God's will – Seaward would have been the first to tell us that. Archbishop Cranmer, whom the saints preserve, can ordain all he likes that Dooms be taken down and destroyed. But I tell you this, God has surely ordained that the Doom of Dunwich should survive.'

Just then, Meg limped into the ruined nave. All eyes turned to her. Her father went over, knelt down, and placed his hands upon his shoulders.

'Child,' he said tenderly, 'you should be at home, resting your leg. And this is a mighty dangerous place for one of your years to be.'

'Nonsense, Father,' she said, firmly, 'it was only a scratch. And Joan and Aunt Agatha fuss so, even though Aunt has so many other patients today. But they wouldn't stop me going to Leonard's Alley to see Miriam Day laid out in her shroud. And it was but a short step from there to here. I had to say farewell to the Doom, Father.'

Ryman and three Stannard kinsmen, one on Jack's mother's side and two on his father's, were already erecting ladders against the pillars on either side of the nave, immediately adjacent to the Doom.

A thought struck John Stannard in that moment. He stood, took Meg by the hand, and led her closer to the terrible painting.

'Farewell to it, Meg? What farewell?'

'But you're taking it down, aren't you?'

Ryman was climbing the northerly ladder, Stannard's kinsman Ned Fletcher the other.

'Taking it down, aye, daughter. But not because some biggety royal commissioner has come to Dunwich to order it destroyed. The Doom had to come down anyway – we'd have been taking it down today even if there'd been no storm, and the east end was still there, and Reverend Seaward was still alive. He approved it months ago, when the archdeacon, Grindal, and the rest of us, decided that John's church couldn't be saved, and we'd have to abandon it to its fate. Good, honest Will Seaward would have been here with us today, up one of those ladders, helping to take it down.'

Ryman was securing a rope around the northern end of the Doom, then set to work to loosen it.

'Then what will happen to the Doom, Father? Won't the king's men come to destroy it anyway?'

'We'll hide it, Meg. One day, pray God may it be soon, the king's eyes will be opened to the truth once more, the new heresies will be sent packing, England will return to the Universal Church, and all men will be content once again.' From the top of his ladder, Ryman shouted an enthusiastic 'amen'.

'And then, perchance, we'll bring out the Doom from its hiding place, and raise it in glory once again. Perhaps in Saint Peter's, perhaps in All Saints. Or perhaps in some fine new church we'll build, that glorious day when Dunwich is great again. How would that be, daughter? Would you like to see that?'

Meg clapped her hands, although she noticed Ryman was shaking his head.

'Nothing more, Father!'

'But until then, the Doom will need to be hidden, and it'll need a guardian.'

'Where will you hide it? And who will be its guardian? Will it be Master Ryman, there?'

Ryman smiled down at her, and waved.

'Well, Meg, if you wanted to hide a tree, where would you put it?'

The girl screwed up her face in concentration. An answer came to her at once, but it was so simple, so silly – and yet…

'In a forest, Father?'

'Good girl. Yes. A forest.'

With Ryman and Stannard's cousin George Beeching holding the ropes secure above the Doom, the men on the ground began to haul. Slowly, gently, the great devil began to descend toward earth.

'So, then,' said Stannard, 'where would you hide the Doom, Meg?'

She looked into the eyes of the devil. She had never seen them so close, had never realised how very red they were. And yet, the veins of the wood were clearly visible behind the paint. The devil, and the whole Doom, was naught but paint upon timber, just like any boat in Dunwich river.

Any boat in Dunwich river.

'I would hide it in the harbour, Father. Where better to hide timber than in a shipyard?'

Jack Stannard kissed his daughter. The shade of Alice was especially alive in her today, he thought.

'Your mother would be proud of you,' he said. 'But you're wrong about one thing, Margaret Stannard.'

'Father?'

'Master Ryman, there, can't be the guardian. He and I are for the war again when the spring comes, and once the war is done, who knows where he'll find himself? And I can't be the guardian, because when peace comes, I'll be voyaging, so that we can live a good life and Dunwich can prosper. Besides, it may be that our prayers go unanswered, and the king won't turn back to the good old way, and it may be many years before England is restored to true religion. So the guardian needs to be someone young, one who'll carry the memory down the years, who'll be ready to raise high the Doom when the right time comes.'

'Father?'

'It can't be Tom, because when he's old enough, he'll be voyaging with me. So it can only be you, dear Meg. You will be the guardian of the Doom.'

Part Five

Mary Rose

July 1545

Here lies a member of the Ship's Company of the Mary Rose.
The King's ship Mary Rose was lost in the Solent on the 19th July 1545 and was recovered on the 11th October 1982.
May they rest in peace.

Gravestone in Portsmouth Cathedral

Twenty-Seven

'She is a pig, Master Nolloth! You have built us a crank pig! A crab-sided thing!'

Jack Stannard jabbed his finger at the shipwright. The deck upon which they stood, the sterncastle of the *Alice* of Dunwich, was heeling noticeably to starboard, despite the breeze east of Dungeness being only light. The bow wallowed through the gentlest of waves.

'Guns bugger the trim,' said Nolloth, angrily, nodding toward the four demi-culverins upon the deck. 'Make a hull gripe. A score of other faults. Told you that a hundred times. But no, you had to have those guns. Should have waited for fawcons or port pieces out of the Tower, but no. Demi-culverins, on a hull this size. Too fucking heavy for the deck. Told you that, Master Stannard. Told your father.'

''Tis more than the guns, Nolloth!' cried Jack.

The helmsman, George Chever, and a few of the men within earshot, glanced around, or turned their heads slightly. Thomas Ryman, standing by the stern rail, watched the confrontation, but did not intervene. This, after all, was a matter for seamen. It was the fourth or fifth such quarrel since the *Alice* sailed from Dunwich, bound for the king's fleet at its appointed muster anchorage in Portsmouth. Ryman learned from some of the men that there had been other open arguments between young Jack and the old shipwright during the proving voyage to Sluys, where the *Alice* embarked the guns that the Stannards had purchased from a Flemish gunfounder; just as they had purchased the services of the hard, bitter Flemish gunners who mingled uneasily with the Suffolk crew. The ship did not sail well from the very start, or so Jack Stannard said, and despite all Nolloth's attempts to adjust her ballast, and the stepping of her masts, and the shape of her beakhead, or whatever else it was that shipwrights did, she was even worse during this, her second voyage. They had been forced to put into Maldon to stop a leak, then into Dover to shift ballast yet again. The *Alice* fell away to leeward, as the seamen put it, and stubbornly refused to steer anything resembling a straight course. In a nutshell, she was slow and cumbersome, when she was intended to be fast and fleet.

With the *Blessing* and the *Osprey*, Jack said, none of it would have mattered. Simple transport duty did not require speed, nor even a particularly good trim. But this was a very different ship, intended for a very different sort of campaign. The king's summons to the ports of the realm demanded only true men-of-war, ships that mounted heavy ordnance and could fight other ships. The only such vessel that Dunwich, or, indeed, any of the ports around the estuary of the Blyth, could send to sea in the summer of the year of grace, 1545, was the new *Alice*, and it was God's will that of all the ships Jed Nolloth had ever built, this should be the first failure. Jack Stannard wondered upon the fact that this was the first ship launched at Dunwich since Saint John's had perished and the Doom was taken down and hidden, but Ryman told him such thoughts were fanciful. If the Doom really was as potent as old folk said it was, then its disappearance would surely be marked by a catastrophe rather greater than a sluggardly ship.

Nolloth went below decks, and Stannard crossed to where Ryman stood.

'Never known him so pullicking', said the younger man. 'Contrary and sullen since the proving voyage, he's been.'

'Accepting that your child is flawed beyond redemption is a hard thing for a man to accept, Jack.'

'Your meaning?'

'Jed Nolloth, yonder, never married, did he?' Jack kept his peace about Nolloth's failed courtship of his sister. 'The ships he builds are his children, Jack. You're blessed with your Tom and Meg. Blessed indeed. But what if you'd had five daughters, and your sixth child, the long hoped for son, proved to be a simpleton?'

Jack thought of Si Bulbrooke, who had indeed been blessed with five daughters, and was now as dead as all of them. Then he looked away, toward the distant church towers of Lydd and New Romney, so prominent above the shingle of Dungeness and the lowland of Romney Marsh behind it. As always, Thomas Ryman had the right of it. And Jed Nolloth was a proud man.

The old shipwright emerged from below.

'Something you need to see, Master Stannard,' he said, seemingly more emollient than before.

He and Jack went down into the hold. The *Alice* was still a new ship, so the bowels of the hull had not yet acquired the legion of competing stenches that characterised every vessel on the seas. The ship's stores were piled high against the bulkheads: sacks of bread, barrels of salt, white herring, biscuit, cheese, beef, tar, pitch, and all the rest. But John Stannard knew at once why Nolloth had brought him below decks. He wore no shoes aboard ship, even in the depth of winter, and, even though it was very dark, he could feel the dampness on the soles of his feet.

Nolloth lifted his lantern, and placed his other hand on the side of a large barrel, low down. Jack stepped forward and did the same. A trickle of liquid ran over his hand. He knew it at once from the smell, but licked his hand all the same, and tasted Valkenburg's familiar Dunwich beer.

'How much left?' asked Jack.

'Two days at most.'

'We might make Portsmouth, then.'

'Or we might not, if the wind turns, or if the French fleet's in the way.'

Nolloth was right; of course, he was right. And Jack knew better than the shipwright that even if the beer did hold out until they got into Portsmouth, there was no guarantee that they would be able to replenish it immediately. The royal ships would have first call, and the fishermen of a Dymchurch peterboat, with whom they'd spoken early that morning, said it was certain that the king himself had gone down to Portsmouth to encourage his crews and watch the battle to come. If that was so, the royal household would have gone with him, and the Portsmouth victuallers would be overwhelmed.

'Your advice, then?' said Jack.

'Put in to Hastings. Lose less time than going into harbour at Rye or Winchelsea. Just anchor offshore, send in a boat, buy fresh barrels. I know a victualler there, from when I sailed in the Channel trades.'

Jack Stannard stared at the leaking barrels, deep in thought. He and his father had used barrels from Birkes the cooper for countless years, and none had ever leaked this badly before. But that was a concern for another day.

The *Alice* was already late, very late indeed, for the muster of the king's Navy Royal at Portsmouth. Any credit Jack had accrued with Lord Admiral Lisle was running out with each grain of sand at each turn of the glass. But that, too, was a concern for another day. The ship needed beer, and she needed it almost at once. True, there was water aplenty, but no sane mariner – no sane Englishman – would drink water, with all the sicknesses that it carried. No beer would mean no crew, and that in the shortest of orders.

'Very well, Master Nolloth, set our head toward Hastings.'

–

The longboat had been away too long. It was early in the evening, and Nolloth had gone into Hastings beach not long after the noonday bell. Now, at last, the boat could be seen pulling off from the shore, beneath the cliff on which stood a ruined castle erected by the Norman conqueror. But it contained no barrels. Worse, it contained no Nolloth.

The boat's crew secured to the side of the *Alice* and came back aboard. Chever, the boat captain, presented himself before Jack, shaking his head.

'Master Nolloth be gone.'

'*Gone?*'

'Went ashore, saying he was going to find the victualler he knew. Half hour passed by the church clock, then another. So I goes up into the town. None of the victuallers have seen him. But one old beggar, he hears our voices, says he was once of Stowmarket. For a farthing, he tells me that he'd seen and heard two other Suffolk men meet there, in the market square, just an hour before. And when I describes Nolloth to him, he says one of the two was the very spit. Says they walked out of town together on the road toward Winchelsea and Rye.'

Chever looked down at his feet, and Jack Stannard knew there was something else.

'Well, man?'

'This beggar. Says he'd been in Rye only on Tuesday. Says there was a Suffolk ship in the harbour, which he thought strange, as our hulls venture this way only chance-time. So he goes down and gets talking to some of the crew, hoping for alms for a fellow countryman.' Chever took a breath. 'And he learns it's a ship of Southwold, and its master is called Stephen Raker.'

Twenty-Eight

The French were coming.

King Francis, outraged by the loss of his city of Boulogne to the English, was intent upon revenge. So, too, were his allies the Scots, still incensed at the burning of Edinburgh. A double invasion, then, the Scots attacking across the border, while the French came against the south coast of England in all their Gallic might and splendour.

The Most Christian King did not stint in his ambition, nor in his preparations. In the mouth of the Seine, France amassed a great fleet of over two hundred ships, carrying an army of over thirty thousand men. In command overall was the Admiral of France, Claude, Marshal d'Annebault. None, other than King Francis and he, knew his orders, nor his precise destination. In alehouses, though, men whispered that no greater force had been massed against England since the fatal year of 1066.

For his part, King Henry assembled his men along the shores of Hampshire and Sussex. He ordered his own fleet to assemble at Portsmouth, under the command of the Lord Admiral of England, John Dudley, Viscount Lisle, and went down in person to observe proceedings.

Thus England waited for the storm to break.

–

As he lay on the truckle bed in the shipmaster's captain, Jack Stannard could find no sleep. Nor could he find thoughts of the French, although he knew full well that they should have been his only focus. He fingered his paternoster, mumbled '*Ave Maria, maris stella, gratia plena*,' time after time, and thought of Jed Nolloth. Of a man that he and his father alike had, many a time, trusted with their lives. Of a man that had been like a father to the young Jack Stannard; the father he wished for, but could never have. Of a man who had betrayed him and Dunwich in the foulest manner.

You're not to blame yourself, said a thought that he took to be the voice of his Alice, whispering to him from Purgatory, as the sunken church bells of Dunwich seemed to toll in his imagination.

The unbalanced hull pitched sharply, even though the sea was light, the breeze gentle. It was the depth of the night, and a single candle, half spent, burned in the lantern swinging from the beam. Jack's eyes were fixed on it, but his ears seemed to hear the voice of the dead.

He turned onto his side, thinking he should tell Alice that if he did not blame himself, who could he blame? But none can talk to the dead, other than by the intercession of the saints.

A well laid plot, said the half-memory of Alice, using the exact words that Thomas Ryman had spoken as the ship *Alice* weighed anchor off Hastings.

A well laid plot indeed. Stephen Raker and his uncles must have begun working toward it within days of the news of their kinsman's death reaching Southwold. First, they must have tried to suborn Simon Bulbrooke, thinking that his debts, known the length and breadth of Suffolk, would compel him to betray his own town and his own kin. Such were Jack's suspicions at Boulogne, after discovering the money and the letter in Bulbrooke's sea-chest. But he had wronged his cousin: whatever his faults, whatever the scale of his discontent at the Stannards, he had remained true to his dying day. That must have been what he wished to confess to Jack on the night he was killed. So the Rakers and the other men of Southwold must then have cast around for another potential target, another member of the Stannards' close circle whose allegiance they could buy. That must have been when they remembered, or were reminded by one of their brethren across the Blyth, that Nolloth was originally a man of Walberswick, whose service had been bought long ago by Peter Stannard. By some means – gold, a better house, a wife, perhaps all of them, God knew what – the Rakers must have bought it back again, their task eased by whatever secret anger Nolloth felt at the old leper's contemptuous rejection of his offer for Agatha Stannard's hand. In that sense, Stephen Raker's attempt upon Jack's life in the ruins of Blythburgh Priory had been at once an aberration and an opportunity, presented by a dying woman's confession. Stephen Raker, whom he could still not think of as his brother, had lost patience with such long, slow stratagems, as he had said to Jack at Blythburgh: but that did not mean he would abandon his last, best revenge of all. Whatever the outcome at Blythburgh, Stephen Raker and Southwold would still triumph in the fullness of time, when the ship Dunwich sent to the war, the ship built by a man who had sold his soul, proved an utter failure.

No, the *Alice* was not a simpleton, the runt of Nolloth's litter. She was his masterpiece. Although her keel was laid long before the Scottish campaign, Nolloth would have had ample opportunity to adjust the design here, to modify her lines there. To ensure that the *Alice* was, indeed, a pig of a ship.

Now Jack thought on it, as he tossed and turned upon his bed in the dark small hours of the morning, he recalled Meg prattling on about how Nolloth was altering the keel, and the futtocks, and God knew what else. He had dismissed it out of hand: what could a child, and a girl at that, possibly know of such things?

A well laid plot, said the creaking of the lantern as it swung from the beam, the drowned bells of Dunwich tolling far beyond it.

Well laid beyond measure. To have Nolloth himself dare to bring the ship so far, thus ensuring that Jack Stannard had no experienced steersman to take her onward, into a certain war. To arrange in advance, as he and Raker must have done, that Nolloth would damage the beer casks, allowing him to put forward the perfectly plausible suggestion of going into Hastings to replenish. If Nolloth really did know these havens from his days at sea, he could have told the Rakers to have one of their ships awaiting him at Rye, to the east. Stannard would be unlikely to try and beat back against the wind, especially because doing so would make him even later to the war-muster at Portsmouth.

Ave Maria, maris stella, gratia plena…

Why go to the trouble and expense of sending a Southwold ship to Sussex, when Nolloth could simply have returned overland to his new home?

Hue and cry, the shade of Alice seemed to murmur.

Jack Stannard shuffled on the bed, as though he were trying to fend off the thought. He was the sea-merchant of a ship taken up for the Navy Royal, by virtue of the king's commission. That made Nolloth a deserter, and Stannard could have insisted the Sheriff of Sussex call out a hue and cry. But the Sheriff of Sussex was at Lewes. If Nolloth made his way north on foot, the *posse comitatus* might, perhaps, take him before he reached the border; Sussex was a large shire, or so Stannard had learned as a child. But Jack could never have got word to Lewes, and the *posse* could never have set out, before the Raker ship sailed from Rye, no matter how contrary the state of wind or tide – and both can only have been favourable, by his judgement of the conditions a little further west. All of which assumed the sheriff did not simply dismiss such a request out of hand. After all, Sussex was the front line against the imminent French invasion, and undoubtedly had more urgent concerns.

A reckoning, whispered Alice, or the wind, or Saint Michael, or whatever half-dream had lodged in his head.

Oh, there would be a reckoning, once the war was done. In the winter, mayhap; if not, then perhaps in the following year. Or the year after that. However long it took, Jed Nolloth would pay for his betrayal. Southwold may take him into his bosom, may think to protect him in its midst, but Dunwich would be avenged. Stephen Raker, Jack's unlooked-for brother and Nolloth's Lucifer, would pay, too, as his nominal father had done. But none of this vengeance would imperil Jack's immortal soul. He would not know, and would not seek to know, what was intended for his enemies. There would be no blood on his hands. When it came to vengeance, one thing was as sure as the ebbing and flowing of the tide. Peter Stannard, with nought else to do in the lazar house of Saint James but contemplate God's judgement upon him, beg forgiveness for his manifold sins, and devise intricate revenges upon his enemies, would think of some way to accomplish it all, no matter how long it took, for time was now of no consequence to the old leper. Nor was money, within reason. He already had another such case in hand, the consequence of a request from Jack's old schoolfriend Will Halliday; this, though, was not on Will's own behalf, but on that of another, well known to him. Peter Stannard had no worries for the fate of his own soul, for as he told his son – his acknowledged son – often enough, he had been damned long, long ago.

Aye, Nolloth and Raker – and Peter Stannard's other target, too – had better pay for masses aplenty, for they had one foot in Purgatory, the other already burning in hellfire.

At long last, as the lantern continued to swing to and fro, John Stannard's thoughts turned to the prospect ahead. To the French, massing across the Channel and due at any hour.

–

A splendid, flaming dawn was just breaking, but no man aboard the *Alice* stood at the stern rail, watching the golden beams striking out from beyond the distant shore of France. Jack and Thomas Ryman stood upon the fo'c's'le, looking away toward the west. A great mass reared up from the sea, several miles ahead, off the larboard bow.

'The Isle of Wight,' said Ryman. 'I was there once, before the campaign of 'twenty-two. Miserable place. The women stink like rotten mackerel.'

The mainland lay off the starboard bow, the fires still burning in the beacons along the shore. Nolloth had, at least, left behind his portolan charts, and from them,

Jack Stannard could take bearings on what he took to be Pagham church and Selsey.

As the sand ran through the glass, the day brightened, and it was possible to see shapes upon the water, before Wight and between the isle and the mainland.

'A mightier fleet than we had in Scotland,' said Jack. 'We've not missed the muster after all, God be praised.'

'Wait, Jack,' said Ryman, his voice tentative as he screwed up his eyes to peer into the far distance. 'I know the Spithead. Sailed out of it, and back into it, with the king's army, over twenty years past. Something's amiss here. Very amiss.'

Still more sand passed through the glass. The distance between the *Alice* and the fleet off the Wight closed.

'*Jesu Maria*,' said Jack Stannard, at last.

'Amen,' said Ryman.

With only a few exceptions, the ships ahead were stern on to the *Alice*. That might have been expected of the English fleet if it were at single anchor, and the tide was running out of the Solent. But the tide was flooding; and in any case, any English fleet should have had its bows to the south-east, facing the enemy.

Now it was possible to see flags, too, although they were limp in the negligible breeze. There were white crosses upon burgundy, white crosses upon green, and many, many banners with white emblems upon blue. More and more blue, from more and more masts. Not a sign anywhere of the red cross upon white, the banner of Saint George.

The fleet was French.

The invasion of England had begun.

Twenty-Nine

'Madness,' said Ryman. 'Aye, futility. And to what purpose, Jack? One ship more or less will make no difference to Lord Lisle. Not against such a host as lies yonder.'

'We were ordered to join the fleet,' said Jack Stannard, sullenly.

The two men stood upon the sterncastle of the *Alice*, almost dead in the water a very little south and east of Selsey, the breeze having died away to nearly nothing.

'Listen, Master John Stannard – in war, nothing happens more often than orders being overtaken by events. Not wounds, not slayings, not battles. God's teeth, how often have I witnessed proof of that, and the consequences? Nothing can be more certain than that the French being here renders your orders ancient history, not worth the paper they're written on. Besides, Jack, as you know better than I, without Nolloth, you have no steersman able to carry out your intentions. Certainly none who's sailed these waters before.'

Simon Bulbrooke would have said the same to him, just as he had said it at Calais and off Boulogne. *Not our battle.* Thomas Ryman was more eloquent, and more right, than cousin Si had ever been, but Jack, of course, could never say so.

'You're wrong in that, Master Ryman. Aye, mayhap I've not sailed these waters before, but I've taken a helm and set courses countless times. I can sail this ship past the French, directly into Portsmouth.'

I can do this. I will do this.

The years-old memory of the young Jack Stannard, at the helm of the *Blessing* off Dunwich shore, returned unbidden.

'Christ's holy nails, boy,' protested Ryman, 'and do you think the French will just allow you to do that?'

Jack Stannard turned away, leaned heavily on the starboard rail, and looked out toward distant Portsmouth, the high tower of its church visible even so far away. He could not tell Ryman what else was in his mind, of the dark, competing thoughts that lurked there. Bringing the *Alice* to the fleet would redeem the reputation with Lord Lisle that the scheming of Nolloth and the Rakers threatened to destroy. True, the *Alice* might be late to the muster, delayed beyond measure by her purposefully crippled and tardy hull, but bringing her into harbour, in the very teeth of the great French fleet, would surely forgive all.

But, God willing, not only Lisle would be watching. If the king was at Portsmouth, then he, too, would see John Stannard triumphantly steer the *Alice* into harbour. If the king was sufficiently impressed, who knew what rewards would accrue to Dunwich and the name of Stannard?

Jack turned, and looked out over the waist of the ship. Men were milling about. The Suffolk men and the Flemish gunners eyed each other suspiciously, but from time to time, members of both parties turned and looked across to him. They knew, as did he, that any course of action he embarked upon would have to be agreed by them. They were not fools or bedlam-men, and they would hardly agree to an attempt to outsail the entire French fleet. Besides, they all knew the evident truth that the *Alice* could barely outsail the most ancient Lubeck hulk.

Jack Stannard smiled, and offered up prayers of thanks to *Maria maris stella*, to Saint Nicholas, and to his dear Alice.

Ryman saw the smile, saw Jack walk forward and call for the crew's attention, and shook his head throughout the young man's speech to the men. It was insane. No: it was insane beyond all measure, more insane than anything he had ever heard or seen in war. But if all his years of soldiering had taught Thomas Ryman one thing, it was that the most insane schemes were often the most brilliantly successful.

Either that, or they brought their instigators to terrible, bloody, and utterly deserved, ends.

-

The ship that edged its way under the lee of Selsey Bill during the late afternoon was undoubtedly a man-of-war, finely painted, and with castles fore and aft. But the ship that rounded the headland the following morning with all sails set, trying to catch every whisper of breeze coming off the land, was a very different beast. Very nearly flush decked, its hull dark and dirty, it was every inch a poor trading vessel, low in the water, making heavy going even of the lightest of seas. It turned west, struggled to make any headway at all, but finally managed to complete a clumsy tack, stayed, and got onto a beam reach, then began to pick up the flood tide. The ship headed for the shore, then began sailing west along it, painfully slowly, as close inshore as it dared. Lookouts on the French fleet, if they took any notice of the ship at all, would observe its clumsiness, its awkward trim, and decide that this poor, lumbering hull, struggling toward Portsmouth or Southampton, was of no interest to them.

That, at least, was Jack Stannard's prayer.

The castles had come down during the night, while the *Alice* lay at single anchor off Pagham. God knew what the poor villagers made of it – the night had little moon, and the many lanterns, lighting the work of bringing down the redundant castles or repainting the sides of the ship, must have given the *Alice* the semblance of Satan's own state barge, summoned up from the fiery river. Add to that the cacophony of sawing, hammering and swearing in strange Suffolk tongues, and the good folk of Sussex must have been cowering under their beds.

Now the *Alice* was coasting westward. The breeze remained negligible and intermittent, and despite all courses and topsails having bonnets to them, the ship's progress painfully slow. Every eye was on the terrible sight to the south-west of them: the easternmost ships of the huge French fleet, lying in the anchorage that Jack's portolans named as Saint Helen's Bay.

'By the lead, three!'

The leadsman's cry from the bow was reassuring. But then, the *Alice* was crossing the mouth of Chichester harbour, and there was bound to be a decent channel up to the ports at the head of it. As to what lay ahead, though, Jack was in utter ignorance. This was where Nolloth would have come into his own. He knew these waters, knew where the shoals were, knew how the tides ran. But none of the other crew of the *Alice* had ever ventured so far west: all of Dunwich's voyages were northward or eastward, and, if southward, no further than London. Jack Stannard could remember his father once telling him that this seaway, this Solent, had a strange pattern of double tides. The *Alice* was being carried forward on a strong flood, but how long it might last was an utter mystery. Her young shipmaster could rely only upon prayer and the soundings from his leadsman.

'By the lead, three and a half!'

There was other activity in the Solent now. Ryman, standing in the bows, could already see many ships lying opposite to, and west of, the French, clustered around the mouth of Portsmouth harbour and off the shore beyond that. Now, though, more and more ships were emerging into the waterway, including several very large ones. They had no sails aloft, so their emergence from the harbour could be due only to towing. Once beyond the harbour mouth, sails fell from their yards. But they did not fill, and the great ships did not move forward. The very slight breeze that the *Alice* was managing to catch would be lost to the fleet ahead, thanks to the lee of Wight; while even a landman like Thomas Ryman knew that the flood tide propelling Jack Stannard's ship forward would work against King Harry's Navy Royal, trapping it in the immediate approaches to the harbour. But then, no man of Dunwich was truly a landman, for every child of that town, above any town in England, drank in the ways and perils of the tide with their mother's milk.

'Master, yonder!'

The lookout's call from the crow's nest atop the mainmast was shrill.

'Larboard, abeam!'

Ryman in the bows, and Jack at the stern, moved as one to the larboard rail, and saw at once the object of the lookout's attention and alarm.

The French were deploying a squadron of two dozen or so craft from the northern vanward of their fleet. They were a magnificent sight: long, low vessels with brightly painted hulls, sharply raking bows, and ensigns and pennants of burgundy, adorned with white crosses. They had lateen rig, but no sails were set. They did not need to be. The vessels moved heedless of wind and tide, edging further out into the middle of the Solent. The French galleys were advancing to challenge King Henry's fleet; but one of them was not. One of them, a small but still obviously powerful vessel at the rear of the galley squadron, had detached from its fellows, and was steering its own course toward the north-east.

Toward the *Alice*.

-

Ryman watched the galley until he was certain that it was bound for them, and only them. Then he crossed the waist of the ship, making for the stern and Jack Stannard. He knew that all men's eyes were on him. Several were crossing themselves, others turning and bowing toward the carved statue of the Virgin that stood atop the belfry. But they all knew he was a warrior, and had been a man of God. If any man could save them from the French, they would be thinking, it was Thomas Ryman.

He stood before Stannard, and saw that the young man's face was white. Jack was a good lad, and might make a good warrior one day – if he survived this one. Thomas Ryman intended to ensure that he did.

He put on the broadest, falsest grin he could muster.

'Be of good cheer, Master Stannard!'

'Good cheer? We can't resist a galley, Master Ryman, and in this light a breeze, we can't outrun her.'

'Be of good cheer, I say, and listen to my words, Jack. You're the man of the sea, and I'll take your word for it that we can't outrun her. But I'm the man of war, and you take my word for it that we can resist her. Let me tell you how, Jack Stannard.'

Thirty

The galley was a splendid sight. Although she was by no means at full speed, she had enough momentum to create a breeze of her own, allowing her flags and swallow-tail pennants to spill out splendidly. She was bow on, and Jack Stannard could only admire the fineness of her lines. They could hear the drumbeat now, and the banks of oars on either side cut the water in time with it. The range closed with each grain of sand that ran through the glass, and Stannard prayed to *Maria stella maris* that Ryman was right. If the old man was wrong, then Jack would shortly be joining his Alice in Purgatory, or else rotting away his remaining years as a slave upon an oar in just such a galley.

He could see the Frenchman's gun, too. It was a single great cannon, mounted in the bows, and its mouth seemed to be pointing directly at him. The galley had to be within its range, and the moment of truth was at hand.

But he could now see the faces of individual Frenchmen, too, and they were the faces of men with lazy smiles. A few were slapping each other on the back, but in doing so, they demonstrated that they were not carrying weapons. They were anticipating making the easiest of prizes out of this wallowing, ungainly English merchantman.

Still the great gun in the bows did not fire.

Jack looked down into the waist of the *Alice*, and saw Ryman standing alongside Capelle, the captain of the Flemish gunners, a tiny, wiry fellow with no teeth. He and Ryman had taken to each other at once; thanks to his years as a solider, the erstwhile friar could speak a smattering of most of the languages of Europe, and he and Capelle swiftly established that they could have been only a few yards from each other at one point during the great Battle of Pavia.

Ryman looked back at Jack, and nodded. But it was still nominally Jack Stannard's ship, and, as her nominal captain, he gave the necessary command.

'Now!'

The gun crews on the larboard side whipped back the pallings covering the two demi-culverins. The guns, already primed and loaded, were run out. Jack turned, and saw the smiles on the faces of the Frenchmen turn to looks of dire alarm. A bell was rung furiously aboard the galley. Men ran to the great gun. But it was already far too late.

'Give fire!' cried Ryman.

Capelle repeated the command almost simultaneously in Flemish, and the two guns fired, almost precisely together. Jack Stannard had seen and heard sea-ordnance fired many times, most recently in the Forth, but he had never been aboard a ship doing the firing. The impact of the recoil almost knocked him from his feet. The noise was deafening, worse than the loudest thunderstorm he had ever known at Dunwich, and the stench from the powder smoke stung his eyes and nostrils. The entire hull shook violently, and large cracks appeared in the deck. In that, at least, Nolloth had been right: partly through his malignant design, partly through the Stannards' ambition for too powerful an armament, the hull of the *Alice* could not bear the firing of such heavy ordnance.

For what seemed like entire minutes, the dense cloud of acrid smoke lay thick upon the ship. Neither Jack nor any other man of the *Alice* could see anything, not even the person standing closest to them.

Just after the guns fired, there were sounds of timber shattering across the water, then the screams and wails of dying men. Jack still expected the galley to come on, to fire her great gun or simply ram the *Alice*, as the *Galley Subtile* had rammed the Scotsman in the Forth, thereby giving the lie to Ryman's confident assertions. But as the smoke finally cleared, the sight before him confirmed that the old man had been right. The balls of both guns had struck the bow of the galley, shattering timbers and bringing down the jackstaff. Two bloodied and mangled bodies, obviously dead, were slumped over the larboard rail, and several more dead and wounded lay inboard, some being tended to. Best of all, men were trying desperately to repair the carriage of the great gun, which leaned at an angle. The galley was turning to starboard. Along the larboard rail, archers and hackbutters were belatedly appearing, and loosing shots at the *Alice*. But the range was too great, and splashes in the water told where their efforts fell short.

Jack shook the hand of Capelle, then stood before Thomas Ryman and smiled.

'You were right, old man!'

'God be praised for that, and praise Him for the old truths of my former trade, which Master Capelle here knows as well as I do. In war, Jack, always think as a warrior thinks. And a warrior would never waste precious shot from his best weapon on what he takes to be a feeble, ugly craft, barely able to keep the sea. But your turn now, Master Stannard. The galley captain will be in a rage, and will want revenge. So get us safe into Portsmouth before he can come against us again.'

-

The galley took an eternity to make its turn, first east, then south, then north-west again. As it did so, Jack Stannard prayed for the wind to get up. A fresh easterly, in the name of God, to carry the *Alice* home into Portsmouth harbour. But the sails stayed nearly limp.

Ahead, the English fleet was finally drawn up in battle order. Its own galleys were to the fore, exchanging cursory shots with their French counterparts. But the English had no more than a half-dozen such craft, together with a dozen or so smaller rowbarges, and would be overwhelmed if they ventured too close to the French. Behind the galleys, two huge flagships were to the fore of the main fleet itself. Jack Stannard recognised the great ship that was further away, closer to Wight. He had seen it once, lying off Erith, during one of his father's voyages into the Thames river. Peter Stannard had taken great delight in telling him its name, and its famous history, and the features of its design. The *Great Harry*, it was, England's mightiest carrack, named for the king himself: more properly, the *Henry Grace à Dieu*. Dunwich caulkers, including a cousin of John's mother, had gone to Woolwich to work on her when she was built. Thanks to Will Halliday's letters, Jack also knew of the part the great ship had played in the demise of William Gonson, although neither young man could fathom what might drive a man to do away with himself in such a perverse manner. Now, though, the *Great Harry* was in full commission. She flew vast ensigns bearing the Saint George Cross, an impossibly long swallow-tail pennant in the same colours hanging limply from its main-topmast head. The ship flew the royal standard at the jack, and as the king himself could not be on board, that could only mean the presence of the Lord High Admiral, Viscount Lisle.

The nearer flagship, nearly as large and flying the colours of a vice-admiral, John Stannard did not know. But the king could not be aboard her, either, for there was no doubting where Henry, eighth of that great and famous name, was at that moment. Although it was still two or three miles distant, Jack could make out a squat stone fort, standing on the very beach just before Portsmouth. From its ramparts flew a vast royal standard, far larger than that on the *Great Harry*. Around the fort was arrayed a huge army, the sun glinting upon the helms, armour and weapons of those defending the King of England himself.

'He's through his turn,' said Ryman, pointing astern.

Jack swung round, and saw the galley head on once again, coming directly for the *Alice*. The drumbeat, though still very distant, was more urgent now, the oars cutting the water with vehemence. And the French were not going to make the mistake of underestimating Jack's ship a second time. A large crew stood around the great gun in the bow, which had evidently been righted. There would be one shot, to shatter the ship and demoralise her crew, then the galley would close for boarding. There were no empty hands on her deck now: pikes, halberds and swords were being held aloft, the French roaring as they closed on their prey.

One chance. One chance only.

'Two points a starboard!' yelled Jack to Chever, the helmsman, who immediately put over the whipstaff.

Ryman looked curiously at Jack Stannard.

'We'll not make the fleet,' said Jack, 'nor Portsmouth itself. But that channel, yonder – the portolans say it leads into a wide harbour called Langstone. If we can get in there—'

The galley fired.

The blast seemed a hundred times greater than that from the guns aboard the *Alice*. Jack Stannard heard the ball whistle through the air, and prepared himself for Saint Peter, and his longed-for reunion with his Alice. Instead, there was a terrible impact forward. Planks and top timbers seemed to leap into the air, taking on a life of their own. The top half of Bateman, a foretopman from Blythburgh, fell to the remnants of the deck, twitching and bleeding, his shocked eyes seemingly still staring at Jack, but of Bateman's bottom half there was no sign. Capelle was struck in the left breast by a huge oaken shard, which drove right through his body, the force carrying the master gunner over the starboard rail. All along the deck of the *Alice*, men screamed or fell to their knees in supplication.

The *Alice* would never make the safety of Langstone harbour. The galley was closing rapidly, the eagerness and bloodlust all too visible on the faces of the Frenchmen in the bow.

Thomas Ryman drew his sword, and kissed its blade: better to meet death at the hands of a dozen seasoned French soldiers than lying in his own piss ten years hence in a bed in Dunwich, he reckoned. For his part, Jack Stannard drew out his own blade. It seemed wrong that he should die here, so far from Dunwich, so far from Alice or Meg or Tom. But if God so willed it…

There was a strange sound, like the roaring of a monster from the deep. In the blinking of an eye, the headway came off the galley. Its bow reared up for a moment, then fell back. Oars crossed, clashed, and snapped. The drumbeat ceased. The serried ranks of French warriors dispersed in confusion.

Aboard the *Alice*, in contrast, cheering broke out as her men realised what had happened.

'*Te deum laudamus*,' murmured Ryman. '*Te*—'

'Not yet,' said Jack, who moved swiftly to take the whipstaff himself.

The helm felt wrong. Even for such an unresponsive slug as the *Alice*, something was—

The hull shuddered and slowed, as though it were a child trying to close a door against a gale. Jack beckoned over Chever and three other men, and together, they tried to work the whipstaff both ways. But the ship did not respond.

'Jack?' said Ryman.

'Both fast,' said Jack. 'A bar not marked on Nolloth's portolans – not that any of them are. The Frenchman grounded first, that's all. All galleys have a great draught, and hers would be far greater than ours.'

'We'll come off, though?'

'They may,' said Jack, his voice tense with urgency, 'if they're on the edge of the bank and reverse their oars. But the flood must have been running a good six hours at least, and must be nearly at the turn. If there's a double tide, there may only be a brief ebb, but we've no certainty the next flood will rise higher and float us off. And we won't have the time to wait.'

He pointed toward the galley, where men were already hauling in the two longboats towed behind their hull. Ryman made a swift, imaginary headcount based on the size of the boats, envisioned that many dozen Frenchmen were rowing for the *Alice*, and knew the truth of Jack Stannard's speech.

'Haul in the boats!' cried Jack. 'We'll throw the guns overboard – God willing, it'll be possible to salvage them.' That, at least, would be what he would tell his father, whose greatly prized, and very considerable, investment the demi-culverins had been. Rather, it would be what he would tell his father if he survived the day. 'Then we'll burn the ship and make for the shore in the longboat. Will you take the skiff, Master Ryman, and report what's occurred here to the admiral in that flagship, yonder?'

Ryman smiled.

'Report how a ship of Dunwich valiantly fought off a French galley, you mean, Master Stannard?'

'Aye, Master Ryman. Something very like.'

'Then I shall, and gladly. God be with you, John Stannard.'

The old man extended his hand, and Jack took it.

'And with you, Master Ryman.'

'I'll see you in a Portsmouth alehouse in a day or two, Jack, and we can raise our tankards to the king's great victory over the French, to our part in it, and to the glory and honour that will accrue to Dunwich.'

'Amen to that, old man.'

Ryman looked across toward the great flagship, a brilliantly adorned and beflagged carrack.

'Time to revisit an old friend, then,' he said, cheerily. 'I was last on her deck in 'twenty-two, when we invaded France. She's the old *Mary Rose*, God bless her.'

Thirty-One

Two men of the *Alice* rowed Thomas Ryman toward the flagship. The water was still calm, but a few more ripples were now crossing its surface, and Ryman could feel the tentative beginnings of a firmer breeze on his face. He sat looking astern, toward the flames beginning to rise from the stranded ship. The crowded, heavily armed crews of the French longboats from the galley abandoned all thought of seizing the burning hull, turned away and began a pursuit of Jack Stannard's longboat instead, firing off the occasional hackbutt. But the men of Dunwich had too great a head start, and the Frenchmen soon turned and began to row back toward their own vessel. Ryman saw the *Alice*'s boat ground on the beach of the island, and offered up a prayer of thanks for the safety of young Jack and his men. That done, he turned and looked toward the glorious spectacle rising from the water before him.

The *Mary Rose* was an old ship, but she still made a brave sight. A four masted carrack, standing tall, she carried castles fore and aft. Her wales were painted brightly in red and gold. She bristled with guns, over a dozen of them protruding from ports along the larboard side which Ryman's skiff was approaching. Smaller swivel guns were mounted every few feet along the ship's rails. Flags of Saint George, royal standards, the personal banners of her admiral, and streaming green and white pennants, the same show that adorned the entire fleet, gave an appearance of a floating carnival. Men swarmed upon her deck. Soldiers manned the sides, the blades of their swords, bills and halberds catching the sun. The *Mary Rose* was nothing less than a vast floating fortress, mounting ordnance which outdid even the greatest artillery trains Ryman had ever seen ashore, and carrying a small army to sea to repel England's enemies.

However, Ryman's reception at the larboard port left much to be desired.

'An' what in the name of Jesu be ye?' said a stout, barefooted, dark skinned fellow with a rasping voice.

'Thomas Ryman,' he said, 'sometime tutor-in-arms to the grandson of His Grace the Duke of Norfolk. Sometime sergeant under His Grace the Duke of Suffolk.'

'Bless me, but ye've got a full surfeit of dukes and sometimes, haven't ye, Goodman Thomas Rhymer? An' yer business?'

'To report to your admiral. And I answer to Master Ryman. Or Sergeant Ryman.'

A small dog sniffed warily at Ryman's heels, perhaps wondering if his shoes contained concealed rats, then wandered away, seemingly satisfied.

'And report what, sirrah? How a dirty merchant's hulk got itself stranded and had to be burned? Sir George don't need a report on that. Saw it with his own eyes, and laughed himself hoarse. We all did.'

Ryman endeavoured to maintain the patience and calmness that had been inculcated into him in his earliest days in the Greyfriars.

'That ship was the *Alice* of Dunwich, man-of-war under the king's commission, trying to run the gauntlet of the French fleet to join the navy royal here assembled.'

'Dunwich? That right? Some of it still above water, then?'

'Aye, Dunwich.' The patience of the friary was wearing thin. 'A borough of Parliament, that enjoys the favour of the Duke of Suffolk. The ship's master, a good, loyal man who enjoys the favour of Lord Admiral Lisle. D'you want to answer to either of them, sirrah?'

The stout man's distaste for Ryman struggled against the suspicion that perhaps, just perhaps, this strange old man really could call down the wrath of the mighty names he deployed like regiments. With bad grace, the man turned and beckoned to Ryman to follow him.

Despite the gunports being open, the principal gun deck of the *Mary Rose* was a low, dark and stinking space. Ryman had nearly forgotten what an apparent hellish chaos such places could be: ropes, netting, breech blocks, a thousand other kinds of tackle, men of the off-duty watch crammed into whatever space remained between and behind the great guns of bronze or iron, and the huge timber knees and beams that supported the deck above. Some men looked at him curiously, but most ignored him, and continued with games of dice, sewing their garments, or trying to snatch a few moments' precious sleep on their jealously guarded few square feet of deck. The accents of a hundred men or more talking at the same time made the deck a Babel, but Ryman, who had fought with men from all parts of the British Isles and far beyond them, recognised the voices of Londoners, men of Devon, Kentish men, Yorkshiremen, and Welshmen. Whatever their origin, they all seemed impossibly young, Jack Stannard's age and even younger.

Your last campaign for certain, Thomas, he thought. *Time to leave war to the young men.*

Just then, whistles blew, and somewhere high above them, trumpets sounded, drums began to beat, and the ship's bell clanged repeatedly, as all hands were summoned to their quarters. Men thrust aside their games, and donned their jerkins and woollen caps. There was a flurry of shouts and activity as mess tables and sea-chests were packed away, and clutter cleared from around the great guns. Boys began to arrive from below with armfuls of small stone shot and bags of powder.

'What's afoot?' said Ryman.

'That much of a lubber, are ye?' said the stout man. 'Can ye not feel and hear the hull straining, man? Wind's getting up, at last. Getting up just enough, at any rate. We're going to teach them fucking frogs a lesson, that's what's afoot.'

They emerged onto the upper deck, into a great crush of men. Sailors were running to the shrouds, swinging themselves outboard, and climbing up to the yards, their movements dictated by the shrill piping of officers' whistles. Soldiers were securing their breastplates and helmets, then checking their weapons. The unfamiliar shouts of the seamen mingled with the all too familiar cries and commands of longbowmen, pikemen, billmen, and hackbutters. Gun crews were preparing to run out the cannon, while others attended to the swivel guns. Everywhere, Ryman saw smiles and heard cheerful cries. Every man on the deck knew that the calm which favoured the French galleys was gone, and it was now time for England's great ships to do their work.

A shout went up – 'Remember Agincourt, lads!'

The scores of men within earshot cheered lustily, and Thomas Ryman felt a surge of pride. This would indeed be the new Agincourt, an Agincourt at sea, and he would be a part of it. He felt as though he were thirty years younger.

He glanced upward. Large nets, intended to hinder boarders, stretched across the entire deck. Above the nets, the canvas courses and topsails were filling with the ever-freshening breeze.

Ryman looked out to sea through gaps in the blinds, the protective fencing erected on the rails. The *Great Harry* already had all sail set, and was beginning to edge her way to larboard, easterly into the heart of the Solent. Behind came four score of sturdy English men-of-war, the Saint George Crosses flying ever bolder in the breeze as it strengthened by the minute. Out to the east, well ahead of the *Mary Rose*, the French galleys were advancing steadily, the enemy sailing ships behind them finally getting under way.

Ryman was taken up and onto the sterncastle. As was the modern fashion, the *Mary Rose* had her fore- and sterncastles built integrally into the hull, and the ship's commander, the vice-admiral of His Majesty's fleet defending England against invasion, stood by the starboard rail, close to the highest part of the sterncastle, above the level of the final net. He was attended by a small retinue of young men clad in gleaming new breastplates, virgin swords dangling at their sides. Ryman knew their kind.

The stout man went forward and whispered to one of the youths, who frowned at Ryman, then turned and spoke quietly to the tall man of forty years or thereabouts who stood at the centre of the group. The tall man wore no armour; in his simple buff-jerkin, he might have been taken for a plain seaman, but for the immaculate grooming of his brown beard and the splendid gold whistle which he wore upon a chain around his neck.

Sir George Carew beckoned for Ryman to approach.

'A Sergeant Ryman, you say. Known to the Dukes of Norfolk and Suffolk, you say. And the ship ablaze yonder, you say, a man-of-war from Dunwich. Would that be the strength of it, Master Ryman?'

Carew's accent was clearly that of Devon, tempered a little by years of courtly discourse.

'It would, Sir George, begging your excellency's most humble pardon. Despite a heinous and treasonable conspiracy by the shipwright, also her master's mate, and a gaggle of malcontents from the towns of Southwold and Walberswick, Master John Stannard of Dunwich brought the ship *Alice* to the muster, as commanded by My Lord Admiral. He and his crew bravely fought off an attack by a French galley, and would have brought the ship safe into harbour, were it not for an uncharted sandbank.'

Carew sniffed, and looked steadily at Ryman.

'I assure you, Sergeant, that the bank in question is most certainly marked upon *our* charts. The knowing men amongst my sea-officers, the ones who know the Solent like the backs of their hands, could not believe their eyes when they saw a ship taking such a course – and, indeed, taking it in such a manner! "What sort of ship is that," they said, "that labours in such a fashion, and upon such a course? Is it a true ship at all, or some ugly sea-elephant?"'

The young men around the admiral laughed loudly, as though it were the funniest jest they had ever heard.

'Sir George, as I say, the ship's sailing was caused by a plot of Southwold.'

Carew's face creased into a ferocious frown.

'*What*, man? You say one English town conspires against another, as if they were at war with each other, rather than with the French, yonder? Sergeant, I was born and raised in Devon. So I know too well of the rivalry that one place can have for another – of Plymouth for Exeter, or Totnes for Dartmouth. But none of them – I say, *none of them* – would aim deliberately to render useless a ship intended for the king's service. We are all Englishmen in Devon, and know our duty. Yet you say matters are managed differently in Suffolk?'

'Sir George—'

The admiral raised an impatient hand.

'Enough, Sergeant Ryman! This ship is England! We, here, are all England! We are sailing to crush the French, so we have more pressing matters to concern us!' Yet Carew seemed still to be studying the old man's face, noting the scars, observing the way he held himself, judging his claimed connection with England's two greatest dukes, and reached a decision. 'But if you are as experienced a soldier as you claim to be, you might prove to be of use to the king. Aye, mayhap you can yet redeem the name of this Master Stennett of yours. Several companies have lost captains, sergeants and corporals to the bloody flux and the sweating sickness while we lay at Portsmouth. Go down into the waist with my commission, Sergeant Ryman. Prepare to draw your sword for England once again.'

Thirty-Two

On the beach of Hayling Island, Jack Stannard and the exhausted crew of the *Alice* slumped upon the sand, drinking ale and eating the bread and cheese that local villagers had brought them, once they were certain those who had come ashore were not French. Offshore, the *Alice* was burned almost to the waterline, while the French galley remained firmly upon the sandbank, despite the best efforts of the men in her longboats to tow her off.

Jack knew Ryman would be doing his best on his behalf aboard the *Mary Rose*, but a bold, glorious scheme to do even better was already in his mind. The harbour mouth between Hayling and the island upon which Portsmouth stood was narrow, there were boats further down the beach, and once on the other side, it would be an easy walk to the fort where the royal standard flew. What might Dunwich and the Stannards reap, if Jack could go before the king himself! And if the king was in a jubilant mood following the inevitable victory of his fleet, then who knew what he might order? The hanging, drawing and quartering of Jed Nolloth and Stephen Raker, perhaps. The destruction of Southwold, or at least, the withdrawal of all its pretended privileges. Even the deployment of the royal ordnance to blow apart the Kingsholme, reopen Dunwich's ancient harbour, and restore the town to its rightful greatness. Jack Stannard's ambitions now looked in a different direction, too. He still thought much upon the words of the Genoese Ottavio Valente, and had begun to dream of voyaging further afield than any Stannard – any man of Dunwich – had ever done. Who knew what riches might lie that way? There was talk of a Southampton skipper, one Reneger, who, in the spring, had taken a great treasure ship belonging to the Emperor, the first time an Englishman had ever done such a thing. If Jack Stannard could stand before the king, and have royal bounty bestowed upon him, might not such commands follow, and might not the rewards be boundless?

Please God, such an outcome might even impress his bride-to-be, Jennet Barne, who otherwise seemed to be impressed by precious little.

With such happy thoughts in his mind, Jack sat contentedly upon the sand, ate a piece of bread, washed it down with a mouthful of ale, and settled down to watch the mighty scene unfolding before him. The Navy Royal of England was putting on sail and advancing against the French, the *Mary Rose* to the fore. He could imagine Ryman's joy at being in the forefront of a battle once again. Nor was it a mere skirmish, nor even a Flodden, nor a Pavia. This would be the battle to save England from invasion, fought directly in front of her great and mighty King Harry.

There would be glory in abundance this day.

-

'Bowse hoa!' cried the master gunner of the *Mary Rose*.

The cry was repeated by every gun captain on the upper deck, and muffled echoes of the same order came up from below.

The gun crews hauled on their tackle, and ran out the bronze and iron guns of the great carrack. Their shouts re-echoed around the entire hull.

From off the starboard bow, the foremost three or four of the French galleys fired. Standing at his new station in the ship's waist, Ryman saw one shot tear through the *Mary Rose*'s main course, while the others fell short. The great ship was turning rapidly to starboard, bringing her entire larboard battery to bear against the French. Each of the galleys, like the one that had attacked the *Alice*, had just one great gun, mounted forward. But the *Mary Rose* mounted over thirty on this one side alone, from little hail shot pieces to vast demi-cannon firing thirty-two-pound shot; and now, the master gunner gave his command.

'Give fire!'

All along the deck, linstocks were put to touchholes, there was a brief glimpse of flame and smoke, and then the great guns erupted.

Ryman had once been close to the siege train of the Emperor Charles when it opened fire, but even that was not as terrible as this. The ship seemed to be driven across the water, while the blast of the guns seemed to rend the very heavens. Thick smoke made the air reek of hellfire itself. Gun captains bellowed their orders. Some men screamed obscenities or prayers: 'God for Harry! God for England! God for Saint George! Fuck the frogs!' A chaplain, standing next to the ship's wooden Virgin, intoned almost inaudible prayers. All the while, the ship continued its turn to starboard, the sails straining in the breeze, the timbers groaning. There was a sudden gust of squally wind, and some of the men on deck cheered. If the wind continued to strengthen, the English fleet would have a tremendous advantage over the French, who had nothing, nothing at all, of the same scale as the *Mary Rose* and the *Great Harry*.

But something was not right.

Ryman had to stagger to keep his footing, shifting more of his weight onto his right side.

He could see some of the seamen starting to look at each other, puzzlement swiftly giving way to concern. Men began to whisper. There was a great rending sound, like a vast tapestry being torn apart by warring gods. Ryman looked up, and saw that the mastheads were at a greater angle than seemed natural. The deck was beginning to tilt further and further to starboard. A pikeman overbalanced, and fell against his fellows. Unsecured barrels and cordage began to slide toward the ship's side. Most of all, there were strange and terrible creaks from the hull, as though it was being pulled in every direction at once.

The first scream came. It was from somewhere high up, near the stern, perhaps from one of the young men in the admiral's retinue. A young man who had a clear view of the scene unfolding before him.

An old man stood close to Ryman: impossibly old, among all the young men of the ship's company. Who he was, what office he filled on the ship, and where he had come from, he could not say. Ryman thought his face was familiar, but he knew that was impossible.

'No man thought to order the ports closed on the lower gundeck,' said the old man, very quietly. 'Not our mighty admiral, not any of them. Ports cut too close to the waterline in any case. So perishes England's pride.'

A press of afeared longbowmen surged around them, and the old man was carried away into the throng of ever more agitated souls.

But thanks to him, Thomas Ryman now knew for certain what he already suspected.

The ship was no longer heeling to starboard as a natural part of its turn.

The *Mary Rose* was sinking.

-

Jack Stannard got to his feet. He could say nothing, think nothing, feel nothing. He could not pray. He could see only the great ship begin to settle onto its starboard side, the overset hull sinking lower and lower in the water. He could see men escaping from the doomed vessel. Some swung themselves down the ropes that towed the ship's boats behind her. Others simply jumped from the gunports, or from the topmasts. Some clung on to forestays or backstays for as long as they could before they, too, went into the water. A few bobbed back to the surface, and could be seen striking out to swim for the boats. Most did not bob back at all. And those who did get away from the hull, to live or die in the sea, were few. Far too few.

At last, an unbidden memory of Alice came to his mind, calming him and enabling him to pray. He prayed aloud, in plainchant, for Thomas Ryman. The old man could not swim, but somehow, he would survive. He had to survive. He always survived. How could God intend for him to survive Flodden, and Pavia, and the end of the Dunwich Greyfriars, only for him to drown like a rat in England's own waters?

There would be no glorious report to the king now, and no rewards. Harry the Great, and Lord Lisle too, would not care what John Stannard and a ship of Dunwich had done this day. All of them would care about one thing only, and remember one thing only.

Still the *Mary Rose* sank deeper and deeper into the Solent.

-

All was hell.

The water was up to the starboard rail, the tip of the mainyard very nearly touching the sea. Everywhere, men were trying to climb up, to cut through the nets, to somehow get free of the ship. It did not matter if they could swim or not; just get away from the dying hull, then worry about the sea afterwards. That was Ryman's thought as he hauled himself up onto the rail and began to hack at the netting with his sword. Behind him, he could hear screams from below decks, where the great majority of the ship's crew was trapped. Men were punching and gouging and stabbing and killing to get up the companionways, to somehow reach the upper decks and a chance of life. Some within his sight were weeping, some praying, some wailing. Soldiers were stripping off armour, hoping that they would stand a better chance of floating clear. But no-one would swim, and no-one would float, unless they could get through the nets.

Ryman held a strand of the net with his left hand, and tried to saw through it with the sword in his right. He prayed for strength. He thought of the Greyfriars, of all the prayers he had uttered there, hoping they would count in his favour now, and offset all the mortal sins he had committed in his youth. He lost his footing on the rail as the hull slipped away from under him, but still he clung on, his face barely above water, framed within a square of the netting. Still he sawed. But his sword was made for cutting and stabbing, not for sawing. Polished to perfection, it was a beautiful blade for killing, but a most terrible one for living.

The water was lapping into his mouth, nose, eyes and ears. His old dream came to mind, the dream of the ship of the dead, full of skeleton soldiers. Then Ryman thought he heard the voice of his Beth, his Beth Stannard, whom he had loved and lost in Dunwich so many years before. So very many years, long before she took the veil, longer before she perished trying to defend a statue of the Virgin at Campsey Priory.

Ryman looked one last time at his sword's blade, saw it was less than half way through the strand of netting, and felt a sharp pull on the net as the doomed ship suddenly lurched further beneath the waves.

'Farewell, my angel,' he murmured. '*Deo gratias*.'

At the end, a curious thing happened. As he fought for what would be his last breath, the erstwhile friar thought he could hear the ringing of distant church bells.

Then the waters closed over him for the final time, and Thomas Ryman went to his Calvary.

Epilogue

March 1547

Spring came early to Dunwich, and a warm sun shone upon the marriage of Jack Stannard and Jennet Barne. The sea lapped benignly upon the beach and the Kingsholme. Another buttress had gone over the cliff from the ruin of Saint John's, and yet more of the buildings on the east side of the market square had been abandoned; but as the bride wished, the wedding was held at Westleton, a mile or more inland, where such concerns, and the eternal sea itself, all appeared far away.

It seemed an auspicious time. King Henry was eight weeks dead, and King Edward, sixth of that name, now sat upon the throne, set fair to reign for fifty years or more. The new sovereign was close to Meg Stannard's age, and the rule of the realm was in the hands of Edward's uncle, the former Lord Hertford, now the newly elevated Duke of Somerset. In some senses, though, it seemed as though Great Harry still reigned from beyond the grave. Above all, his wars continued. Despite the sinking of the *Mary Rose*, the French had not been able to invade, failing even to conquer the Isle of Wight, while the Cross of Saint George still flew from the ramparts of Boulogne. Nothing, though, was more certain than that the new King of France, news of whose accession had reached Dunwich only on the previous day, would redouble the efforts to recapture it. Meanwhile, the Scots continued perversely to refuse to do what England wanted, namely, to marry their little queen to King Edward. Although there was an uneasy truce, Meg's great-uncle Spatchell was proclaiming loudly in his corner of the Pelican in its Piety that come the summer, Scots and Englishmen would be shedding each others' blood once again.

Jack Stannard was confident that if and when the summons came to set out the Navy Royal once again, Dunwich ships would be called upon. This confidence stemmed in part from his ongoing correspondence with Will Halliday, now principal clerk to the newly-established Council of Marine Causes, the body that had taken on all the functions previously undertaken by one man, the late William Gonson. The members of the Council complained of their workloads, and never ceased to express their wonderment at how all the affairs of the Navy Royal had been carried on for so very long by just one man. Benjamin Gonson, first holder of the newly created office of Surveyor of the Navy, took much satisfaction from such remarks.

It was a time of signs and wonders, which, as the ancients had it, often attend the passing of kings. It was said, for instance, that King Henry's corpse, resting overnight at Syon in its journey to Windsor for interment, had burst open, the vile fluids from within dripping onto the chapel floor. Letters from the east claimed that the Grand Duke of Muscovy, one Ivan, had the gall and presumption to declare himself Caesar of a new empire, which he christened 'Russia'. Then there were strange reports from Devon, to the effect that a respectable gentleman of those parts, who lived very privately, had perished by a strange accident, torn apart by a pack of wolves, or other wild beasts, that somehow found a way through the bolted doors and shuttered windows of his house. Some said that this gentleman had once been a Knight of the Order of Saint John of Rhodes and Jerusalem, and that his name was Sir Philip Babington.

A wedding, of course, was no occasion for the recounting of such horrors. Nor was it a time to utter too loudly the names of living ghosts, although many mentions of them were whispered in corners, especially when more drink began to flow. Peter Stannard, the last leper of Dunwich, did not attend the service, telling Meg that his appearance would frighten children and dampen the festivities. But she had overheard her father and his new bride talking, and knew that Jennet Barne had insisted the old man should not be invited. In this, she had an unexpected ally in Aunt Agatha, whose willingness to talk of her hatred of her father to Meg seemed to increase with every new month of her niece's age. Of course, no invitation went out to Jack Stannard's one-time friend and mentor, Jed Nolloth. He was said to have been set up in a fine house in the very middle of Southwold, to have been given a plot of land for a new shipyard, and to have been married to a wife thirty years his junior, some sort of distant kin to the Rakers. But his new neighbours shunned him; even Southwold men detested a turncoat, it seemed. His yard failed for lack of orders, and he had to find any work he could as a jobbing carpenter. Meanwhile, his young wife proved to be both a shrew and a notorious whore.

Meg was now of an age where she knew precisely what this meant.

The wedding was a well-attended affair, the guests relishing a little relief after a harsh winter and the manifold uncertainties surrounding the death of the old king. The bride was given away by her cousin, George Barne: a very rising man in the City of London, already an alderman (Meg Stannard had no idea what such an 'olderman' might be, as all men, to her, were older), full of ideas for opening up all sorts of new trades for England, perhaps even to this new, vast emptiness called Russia. He expounded upon this theme at great length to any who were unfortunate enough to find themselves within his earshot; Jack Stannard was one of the few who listened to him intently. There were Stannard kinsfolk of variously remote canonical degrees, even some from as far afield as Norwich, but precious few guests whom Meg counted as friends, with the exception of Joan Cowper. Tom was there, of course, as the son and heir of the groom, and had been dressed in a ridiculous-looking tabard which made him itch. To Meg's annoyance, Tiberius was forbidden from attending the occasion: she had relished the prospect of the hound depositing a great, stinking turd in front of the altar at the very moment of the exchange of vows. She spent much of the ceremony urging Tom to do so instead, but her brother proved irritatingly reluctant to comply.

Will Halliday had been invited to the wedding, both because otherwise, and especially with Thomas Ryman dead and gone, Jack Stannard would have precious few friends in Westleton church, and because, as Jack said, without Will's strong bass line allied to his own tenor, the singing at the service was likely to be lamentable. But Will had sent his apologies, for he had marital plans of his own on the same day. Ben Gonson's elevation, and the apparent indispensability of both young men to Lord

Admiral Lisle, one of the most important figures in the new government, had softened the once implacable heart of Marion Bartleby's father, especially when a significant contract to supply pewter plates to the ships of the Navy Royal came his way. Ben Gonson himself had experienced the same sudden change of sentiment from Mistress Ursula Hussey's father, and had already been wed to his lady for some months. Jack Stannard promised to raise a glass in the direction of Saint Michael Bassishaw in the heart of London, just as Will Halliday promised to raise one toward Saint Peter's at Westleton.

As it was, Meg Stannard played her part splendidly. At her father's insistence, she had carried sprigs of rosemary before the bride, all the way to the altar, hearing as she went several approving whispers about her poise. But she felt sick when she heard her father pledge his trothplight, and felt so again as she watched the newly married couple raise Venetian glasses of hippocras to toast each other. For she saw, as she was convinced her father did not, the way in which Mistress Barne – Goodwife Stannard, rather – looked at him out of the corner of her eye, and the set of her mouth as she did so. And even before the marriage, Meg had already taken more strappings from this new stepmother than she ever had from her real mother, or even from her father.

Despite all that, Meg would call Jennet Barne 'mother', if that was what Father wanted; but whenever she could, she would do so with her fingers crossed behind her back. She would lower her eyes and bend her knee dutifully, as a good stepdaughter should. But as she lay upon the bed that was already almost too small for her, waiting for the sound of the waves breaking on the Kingsholme to lull her to sleep, Meg Stannard made her plans, and then, when she was asleep, those plans turned into dreams. One day, she, not some little runt of a Queen of Scots, would marry King Edward, of whose height, red hair, good looks and intelligence she had been amply informed by Thomas Ryman some months before his death. In the fullness of time, she, as queen, would restore her husband to the true faith, lay a brass *in memento mori* to Master Ryman in Saint Peter's church, then immediately order the burning of Jennet Barne as a witch, her incontrovertible evidence being the teeth. Then she would hang everyone in Southwold, especially all those named Raker, and level the vile place to the earth, planting the ground with salt, as the Romans had done to Carthage. (She was, as yet, undecided on whether a similar fate would befall Walberswick.) That done, she, as its guardian, would order the great Doom brought out from its hiding place in the Stannard warehouse on the Dain Quay, and see it raised high into a place of honour once again. With the divine force of the Doom as her ally, she, Margaret, Queen of England, would finally restore Dunwich to its former greatness.

Nothing, she thought, could be simpler.

Historical Note

While the Stannard family is fictitious, many of the events, contexts and characters in this story are not.

I based the accounts of the attack on Edinburgh and the battle in the Solent closely on the historical record, with two exceptions. Firstly, the Scottish warships *Unicorn* and *Salamander* were actually captured in dock at Leith; at least, there is no surviving record of them attempting to put to sea, so the battle that I have conjured up off Cramond and Inchcolm islands is entirely fictitious. Secondly, there was, of course, no fight between any English ship, be it of Dunwich or anywhere else, with a single French galley immediately before the battle of the Solent in 1545 (although Dunwich ships were certainly present in both the 1544 and 1545 campaigns). As far as the sandbank where both the *Alice* and the galley come to grief is concerned, I had in mind the East Winner, off the west end of Hayling Island. However, the sandbanks in the Solent shift position so often that I feel fairly sure no-one can upbraid me for placing one in the wrong location nearly 500 years ago! Otherwise, the English invasion of Scotland in 1544, and the attempted French invasion of England in 1545, happened essentially as I have related them: as, of course, did the sinking of the *Mary Rose*, although there still remains debate about exactly what caused the disaster to happen. (The notion that the *Mary*

Rose sank on her maiden voyage, rather than when she was a very old ship, is a surprisingly enduring piece of 'fake news'.) Naturally, I revisited the ship, and the wonderful museum which now surrounds it, as part of the research for this story, and can highly recommend it for anyone who wants to learn more about the naval warfare of the mid-sixteenth century.

The Boulogne campaign of 1544 was the last time when King Henry VIII went to war in person. Annoyed by Francis I's support for the Scots, and ambitious to regain at least some of the land lost to England at the end of the Hundred Years War, Henry made peace with the Emperor Charles V and launched a two-pronged invasion of France, the Duke of Norfolk leading one force to besiege Montreuil, the Duke of Suffolk leading the other to attack Boulogne. Henry himself then went to France to take charge of the latter siege.

'Caligula's Tower', or the *Tour d'Ordre*, was a real place, which survived until, in a curious echo of the fate of Dunwich, the cliff on which it stood collapsed in 1644. I have invented the various specific operations in which Jack Stannard was involved, and compressed some of the events and context of the siege, but the essentials of the assault – the rapid conquest of the lower town, the undermining and eventual surrender of the upper – took place largely as I have described them. There are relatively few detailed sources for the siege: probably the most detailed is Antoine Morin's verse history of the event, *Chroniques du siège de Boulogne en 1544*. Unsurprisingly, the French soon counter-attacked and very nearly retook the town on a number of occasions; it was finally returned to them in 1550, leaving the Pale of Calais as the only English possession on continental Europe for a further eight years. Ottavio Valente is an invented character, but a number of Genoese mariners served the English Crown in the sixteenth century, following in the footsteps of John Cabot, or, to be strictly correct, Giovanni Caboto; indeed, the grizzled old salt who points the way to the ocean to an enthralled Devon lad in Millais' famous painting *The Boyhood of Raleigh* is meant to be a Genoese. The fact that Genoa adopted the cross of Saint George as its emblem long before England led the mayor of the city, in 2018, to propose writing to Queen Elizabeth II with a demand for 247 years' worth of arrears of tribute payments.

Writing naval historical fiction set in the sixteenth century is problematic on several levels. We often have little evidence of how things were done; many treatises relating to how ships were sailed and fought date only from the seventeenth century, and although one can sometimes extrapolate that *X* is surely likely to have been done in the same way eighty or a hundred years earlier, it is dangerous to make that assumption in all cases. Above all, the way in which naval warfare was carried out was very different, and the very word 'navy' itself had a distinctly different meaning, in the period covered in this book to that described in my series of novels set in the late seventeenth century, 'the Journals of Matthew Quinton'. Firstly, seaborne ordnance was still a relatively recent and somewhat unreliable innovation, ships carried few heavy guns in comparison with the later period, and tactics therefore relied heavily upon boarding. Secondly, what might be described as England's maritime fighting force consisted of a combination of the ships personally owned by the monarch – in a strict semantic sense, the true 'Navy Royal' – and those owned by towns or individual shipowners, taken up for clearly defined periods (generally as short as possible, to save the Crown money) and for specific purposes, such as, in this story, the invasion of Scotland, or the siege of Boulogne. But this essentially medieval, and essentially temporary, fighting force was already evolving and expanding into something very different, a fact borne out by the story of the second family at the heart of this book, the Gonsons, who, unlike the Stannards of Dunwich, were real historical figures.

William Gonson, originally of Melton Mowbray, held the various offices that I have attributed to him, including that of vice-admiral of Norfolk and Suffolk (the first 'vice-admiral of the coast' ever appointed). He was largely responsible for day-to-day naval administration for the majority of Henry VIII's reign, a burden that increased substantially during the 1530s and 1540s as the king faced increasing threats from abroad, culminating in fighting wars against Scotland and France simultaneously. Gonson's final years were also lived under the shadow of the execution of one of his sons, David, a Knight of the Order of Saint John, for treason. David, who commanded warships of the Order in the Mediterranean in the 1530s, returned to England in 1540, but was arrested on trumped-up charges brought by his fellow knight, Sir Philip Babington, who had deserted the Order a little earlier and who seems to have been acting as a paid agent of Henry VIII's government, tasked with denouncing his erstwhile comrades. A number of quarrels between Gonson and Babington are recorded in the Order's records, including one in which Gonson slapped Babington with the flat of his dagger hilt. The treason proceedings against David Gonson were brought under the dubious new procedure of attainder, and he was hanged, drawn and quartered at Saint

Thomas-a-Watering, on the boundary between Camberwell and Newington, on 12 July 1541. The Sovereign Military Order of Saint John of Jerusalem, otherwise known today as the Knights of Malta, regards him as one of its martyrs, and commemorates him on the anniversary of his execution; he was made Blessed by Pope Pius XI in 1929.

William Gonson certainly committed suicide some time in the summer of 1544, although I have invented the circumstances. Such a death would normally have resulted in the body being buried with a stake through the heart at a local crossroads, but – whether as a consequence of bribery, or some other form of influence – the affair seems to have been discreetly covered up, as he was, indeed, buried in the parish church of Saint Dunstan-in-the-East, London. (John Palsgrave was the rector, and had the distinguished early career I have attributed to him, but he must have been at least complicit in the decision to give Gonson Christian burial within the precincts of his church.) Posthumous proof of the fact that the navy had grown far beyond the point where it could effectively be run by one man is provided by the rapid formation of a Council of Marine Causes, later rechristened 'the Navy Board', to replace Gonson. One of its earliest members, who then served the naval administration for over thirty years, was Benjamin Gonson, William's fifth son, initially as the first-ever Surveyor of the Navy, and then, a year after the conclusion of this story and at the age of just twenty-three, its treasurer also. Ben Gonson married Ursula Hussey in the summer of 1546, and their daughter Katherine married the legendary Elizabethan 'sea dog', Sir John Hawkins (who will loom large in the second book of this trilogy).

Mary Fitzroy, née Howard, Duchess of Richmond, is also a real historical figure, and Henry VIII undoubtedly did toy with the idea of resolving the potential succession crisis created by his first two wives' failure to give him a male heir by legitimising her husband, the king's son by Elizabeth Blount. Richmond died in 1536, aged seventeen, before the plan could bear fruit, and the birth in the following year of Edward, Prince of Wales, finally gave Henry the legitimate male heir he craved. There is no evidence that Edward visited Kenninghall Palace when he was seven years old, or at any other time, and indeed, even from a very early age, his religious views were the polar opposite of those held by almost all members of the House of Howard. (The one exception, oddly, was Duchess Mary: she seems to have been a genuine and committed convert to Protestantism.) However, the prince was almost exactly the same age as Thomas Howard, the future fourth Duke of Norfolk, so it would have been entirely possible for them to have been acquainted, if not playmates. Thomas Howard became a leading Catholic conspirator against Queen Elizabeth I, and was even touted as a potential husband for Mary, Queen of Scots, to strengthen her claim to Elizabeth's throne. Memorably played by Christopher Eccleston in Shekhar Kapur's film *Elizabeth*, Thomas was ultimately convicted of treason and executed in 1572, thus carrying on a family tradition: his father, the Earl of Surrey, had gone to the block in 1546, and the third Duke of Norfolk avoided the same fate only because King Henry VIII died on the day he was meant to be executed. At Surrey's trial, his own sister, the Duchess of Richmond, testified against him, her evidence revealing what one writer has called her 'vindictive and bitter' personality. On the other hand,

Surrey had once suggested that his sister should seduce the king, her father-in-law, and become his mistress, so Mary's actions might have been a form of payback for a fraternal suggestion she found utterly outrageous. Despite this remarkable family rift, Surrey has a grand tomb in the parish church of Framlingham, Suffolk, just across the way from that of the Duke – and, yes, the Duchess – of Richmond.

Kenninghall, a few miles east of Thetford in Norfolk, was the principal seat of the Howard dynasty in the sixteenth century. Most of the H-shaped palace was demolished in 1650, but the former service wing, where Thomas Ryman was imprisoned in my story, survives as a farmhouse.

-

The religious situation in England in 1544–5 was deeply uncertain, with both conservative and reforming parties seeking to influence the old and increasingly sickly monarch. Despite the break with Rome and the dissolution of the monasteries, much of the liturgy was still essentially Catholic, and was still in Latin. A number of ancient and much-loved practices, alluded to in the text, had been abolished, especially when Thomas Cromwell was Henry VIII's chief minister, but many others still survived. Exhaustive detail on all of these topics can be found in Eamon Duffy's magisterial *The Stripping of the Altars*, and, specifically for the situation in Dunwich and its surrounding area, Judith Middleton-Stewart's *Inward Purity and Outward Splendour: Death and Remembrance in the Deanery of Dunwich, Suffolk, 1370–1547*. If the evidence of wills and other documents is insufficient, the matter is surely put beyond doubt by the number of rosaries, or paternosters, and the nature of other religious artefacts, recovered from the wreck of the *Mary Rose*. At the time during which this story is set, then, the years 1544 and 1545, England was still essentially a Catholic country, despite its king's break with the Roman church.

Even so, although many still clung to the old ways, many others favoured the new teachings coming from the Continent. One of them was John Day, who does, indeed, seem to have come from Dunwich; he commissioned the earliest known history of the town. By the mid-1540s, he was established as a printer and publisher in London, and radical Protestant works poured from his presses. After Elizabeth's accession, he both sealed his place in history and made his own fortune by publishing Foxe's *Book of Martyrs*, the runaway bestseller of the age. Composers of church music had to take account of these changing fashions: Thomas Tallis, for example, famously wrote in Latin or English as required, and managed to accommodate all the religious changes from before Henry VIII's break with Rome to Elizabeth I's moderate Protestant settlement. For my references to this musical epoch, and to Jack Stannard's thwarted choral ambitions, I leaned heavily on Andrew Gant's *O Sing Unto the Lord: A History of English Church Music*; the song *Benedicite*, sung by Jack in the prologue, was composed by Robert Fayrfax (1464–1521). As for the Rogationtide processional service at Saint Paul's on 23 May 1544, almost certainly the first occasion when the liturgy was sung in English, and Queen Catherine Parr's astonishingly forthright and belligerent prayer, *See Lord and Behold*, set to music by Tallis, was performed, I was fortunate enough to attend the concert by Alamire at Saint John's, Smith Square, London, on 14 April 2017, the first modern performance of the piece following its identification by Dr David Skinner of Cambridge University.

–

The story of Dunwich, 'England's Atlantis', is not really as well-known as it should be. Indeed, it's possible that some will know the name only from H P Lovecraft's famous and seminal tale of the supernatural, *The Dunwich Horror*; this took only the placename from the village in Suffolk (and that probably unwittingly), otherwise setting the story in rural Massachusetts, but it has spawned two films and countless references in popular culture. As for the real Dunwich, almost certainly once the seat of the Bishops of East Anglia, as late as the thirteenth century it possessed the same geographical extent as London, was listed as one of the ten most important towns in England, and was regarded as the best harbour on the east coast. But a series of catastrophic storms, notably in 1286, 1287, 1328, 1347 and 1362, effectively blocked its harbour and swept away large areas of the town, which eventually declined to merely the tiny hamlet that remains today. The story of this 'lost city', and its endless battle against the sea, was well told in Rowland Parker's famous book *Men of Dunwich*, first published in 1978, which was an important source for this story; so, too, were Nicholas Comfort's *The Lost City of Dunwich*, Thomas Gardner's *An Historical Account of Dunwich* (first published in 1754), and many archaeological reports on the digs and surveys, including those underwater, carried out at Dunwich over many years. Thanks to these sources, many of the character names in this story are taken from real people who lived there at the right time. Indeed, some of them held the actual offices I have attributed to them. For example, William Girdler and William

Clampe really were the bailiffs of Dunwich in 1544–45, while Joseph Overfield and William Seaward were, indeed, parish priests of All Saints and Saint John's respectively. However, I have taken something of a liberty with the history of the real Barne family. Although they were the principal landowners in Dunwich by the eighteenth and nineteenth centuries (indeed, their mausoleum occupies the principal surviving remnant of the Saint James leper hospital where Peter Stannard was a patient), there is no evidence that they were originally from the area, or had any connections there in the sixteenth century. The roots of the George Barne mentioned in this story seem to have lain in London and perhaps in Somerset; but it suited my narrative for the family to be natives of Dunwich's hinterland.

At the beginning of the sixteenth century, the town of Dunwich experienced something of a limited revival, thanks to the success of its Iceland fishery. However, this proved short-lived; as Chapter Nine relates, the dissolution of the monasteries dramatically reduced the demand for fish, and the town's decline resumed. Greyfriars, the monastery to which Thomas Ryman once belonged, is now the last substantial relic of old Dunwich, with its gates, refectory and enclosing wall still standing upon Dunwich cliff. (For purposes of narrative convenience, I brought forward the date of its dissolution from 1538 to October 1537; the abrupt termination of a monastery's life in the midst of a service is a true story, albeit not from Dunwich but from Evesham Abbey, where the evensong service was abruptly terminated 'at this verse, *deposuit potentes*, and [the royal agent] would not suffer them to make an end'.) However, some remains of the Maison Dieu hospital supposedly still exist beneath the beach café and adjacent public conveniences – the lane behind them is the road John Stannard would have taken to visit his father – while the sunken lane that was once Midgate Street can still be walked as far as its abrupt end at the cliff edge. All Saints, the last of what were once seven churches, lost its final rector in 1755, although burials continued in its churchyard for some time afterwards. The last grave of all, that of Jacob Forster (who died in 1796, aged thirty-eight) is still *in situ*, roughly in the place where John Stannard meets Thomas Ryman in Chapter One, although it is now precariously close to the cliff edge. The ruins of All Saints fell into the sea between 1904 and 1922; the last buttress was moved further inland and re-erected in the churchyard of the nineteenth century Saint James's Church, which also contains the ruins of the leper hospital where Peter Stannard was a patient. The historical record suggests that the last leper died, or otherwise left there, in about 1536, so I took a slight liberty by bestowing the title on Peter in 1544. Similarly, Saint John's church was certainly abandoned at some point in the mid-1540s, but there is no record that its chancel fell into the sea during a Christmas Day mass. On the other hand, to use the classic novelist's defence, there's no record that it didn't, either. There is also no record of a great Doom painting in Saint John's or any other Dunwich church, although they must have had such things at some point; I got my inspiration for the Doom of Dunwich from the astonishing Doom which can still be seen at Wenhaston Church, a few miles inland.

Dunwich's struggles with its rivals Southwold and Walberswick are well documented, although whether Southwold was ever a kind of Tudor cross between Dodge City and Sodom is open to debate. In any event, its more current, and thoroughly well-deserved, reputation is as one of England's most genteel seaside resorts, where the inhabitants only become vaguely alarmed by such calamities as the arrival of the wrong kind of coffee shop or bookshop. The struggles between these three coastal communities will be revisited in the second and third stories of this trilogy. So, too, will the lives of Jack Stannard, his son Tom, his daughter Meg, and the subsequent generation of the Stannard family. However, these books will continue resolutely not to focus on the lives of two of the monarchs under whom they would have lived: nor, indeed, on the wives of the one, and the alleged lovers and actual rivals of the other. To those who are disappointed by this, I would respectfully suggest that in England and Wales, at least, there are more than enough books, films, plays, TV series, documentaries, advertisements, blogs, social media quarrels, cod 're-enactments' at heritage attractions, overpriced banqueting 'experiences', and History syllabuses for children of pretty much every age from five to eighteen, to make good my undoubted and shocking deficiencies in this regard.

Acknowledgements

In writing this book, I've inevitably incurred a number of debts of gratitude. First and foremost, thanks to my agent, Peter Buckman, and to Michael Bhaskar at my publishers, Canelo, for their faith in the idea. Secondly, thanks to all those in Dunwich and its environs who helped make this story a reality. Jane Hamilton, Tim Holt-Wilson, and above all John Cary of Dunwich Museum, provided me with information and ready access to the museum's wonderful collection of material; a visit to it is highly recommended, especially to view the splendid model of Dunwich in its heyday. Also in Suffolk, I owe a special thank you to Fran Abrams, and another to the staff of the Ship Inn at Dunwich; my fictional sixteenth-century tavern, the Pelican in its Piety, would have been on pretty much exactly the same site. Thanks also to Sarah Wright, Head of History at my old workplace, Bedford Modern School, for invaluable information on aspects of the reign of Henry VIII. I taught Tudor history there for many years, and the questions and comments of several generations of former A-level students – not quite all of them, thankfully, pertaining to the sex life of King Henry VIII – have found their way, consciously or subconsciously, into the way in which I have written this book.

While many of the characters in this story are fictitious, some, notably the Gonson family, are not. Novelists – and, indeed, historians – sometimes write about people in the past from a detached perspective, assuming, albeit perhaps subconsciously, that it doesn't particularly matter what one writes about those who lived so very long ago; or, as the old publishing cliché puts it, it's impossible to libel the dead. In all of my books, I've tried to show respect to the memories of real historical characters, even those whom the judgement of History has labelled, fairly or unfairly, as 'the bad guys'. But in writing this book, I've been more aware than usual that some of those I've written about have descendants alive today, who still care about their ancestors' reputations. In particular, I came across one website relating to the burial of William Gonson at Saint Dunstan in the East, London, which included this simple but telling comment: 'God speed, 14x great-grandfather'. I hope that if any descendants of the Gonsons, or else of those who lived, loved and died in Dunwich during the sixteenth century, read this book, they'll feel that I've treated what is, after all, a part of their personal stories, with appropriate sensitivity and dignity.

Finally, thanks as always to my partner Wendy for her shrewd criticism, constructive ideas, and decisive input. Apologies for the fact that the writing of this story explains why I didn't empty the dishwasher as often as I should have; the roses and chocolates are in the post.

Possibly the dishes, too.

J D Davies
Bedfordshire
February 2019